# With Our Dying Breath
A.R. Kavli

This is a work of fiction. Similarities to real people, places, or events are entirely coincidental. And if the events described in this book do transpire, accept my sincerest apologies. I didn't know!

# Chapter 1

LIEUTENANT COLONEL Pierce Oswald often wondered what would finally kill him. Especially at times like this, reading the names of dead friends as they scrolled across the holo-projection in the lobby of Xichang's Sol Defense Fleet Command Center. They had all died fighting the Proximans, but there were many ways to die in space. And he'd seen them all.

Sudden vaporization from a direct hit seemed best. No pain. No desperate attempts to save yourself. No terminal disappointment at the realization that rescuers aren't coming. The official listing for many casualties was battle-induced environmental failure, which is to say death by asphyxiation, hypothermia, or extreme heat stroke.

Oswald would prefer to die long after the war had ended, surrounded by family and old comrades. He didn't expect that, though. If he was killing Proximans when he got flamed, it would be a worthy death.

But he couldn't kill them while he was dirt-side.

The projector flickered after each sixth or seventh name change. Apparently no one in this command center thought it worthwhile to make sure the names of the honored dead didn't flicker like an old lightbulb. It wouldn't take three minutes to reboot the projector and clear the trouble.

Of course, the frames holding the smiling 3-D portraits of the chain-of-command were immaculately dusted. Oswald waved a hand at Secretary Tasha Minkov's picture. Her PR blurb flashed to life in the air with no interference or delay. It was as crisp as the lines on her suit. He waved it away.

Even lieutenant colonels had to wait on their superiors, and he'd been examining the displays for nearly an hour. His legs and back were sore from the weeks of physical therapy astronauts required upon return to a gravity well. He wanted to sit down, but his limbs were apt to get painfully stiff if he did.

The corporal manning the duty console had streaks of white in his short-cropped hair and jowls that jiggled each time he looked up at Oswald to offer an embarrassed apology for his wait. The man had either been busted down in rank or Sol Defense Fleet had raised the maximum enlistment age again. Given the corporal's ribbons, being busted down was more likely.

Either way, the corporal couldn't be bothered to fix the KIA display in his lobby or open a trouble report to someone who could. Not someone Oswald would approve for assignment on his ship.

Oswald didn't mind waiting though. If there's one thing space travel teaches, it's patience. The boredom helped cool his temper about being here instead of back in the battlespace. It wouldn't do to meet the general while angry. He hadn't seen her since the funeral. It was already likely to be an uncomfortable meeting.

Historical information projections materialized around each display. The antebellum histories cheered him, reminding him of a time before the war. In those years, before the Global Space Service became the Sol Defense Fleet, space had been about exploration.

The SDF allowed each command center an amount of local flavor, and most gladly decorated well beyond the standard, bland, inoffensive conformity. Oswald traced a finger along the edge of a small, gold-trimmed shrine. A forest of tiny, flickering, holographic candles appeared over it. Above those floated two golden spacecraft with glowing engine plumes, each commemorating fatal accidents at Xichang.

In 1996 an unmanned orbital rocket crashed into a nearby village, and in 2098 a Mars resupply mission failed during liftoff, killing all aboard along with several ground crew. For a launch facility that was almost two hundred years old, Oswald considered that a superb record. Space had always been a bloody affair for humanity.

Next to the shrine was a titanium plate listing the vessels lost since the start of the war. Or two wars, or three wars depending on the politics of the historian. The list of lost spacecraft had grown long during the course of the fighting. Oswald knew from the last fleet-status report that this list was outdated. The names of the destroyed spacecraft he'd served on acted as a *memento mori*, a reminder he too would someday die. Many of those who'd gone before him had been much more worthy officers.

He reverently touched the engraved names of the CTR-13 *Sao Paulo*, CBR-54 *Miami*, NBR-61 *Sol Hammer*, and the unnamed satellite, CSS-8. Satellites might not have names, but their dead crews did.

The corporal coughed. "I'm very sorry, sir."

"Not your fault. Majors wait on lieutenant colonels and lieutenant colonels wait on generals. We don't just wait, we hurry up and wait."

The corporal gave a perfunctory laugh before smoothing his uniform and turning back to his task of looking busy. That was his part of the game. Oswald saw the mix of respect and resentment in the corporal's gaze when it paused on Oswald's mosaic of honors earned over two decades of battle. The ribbons were arranged to resemble an orbital ecliptic around Earth. Above them was a gold Combat Comet, and above that boldly flew a gold Rocket of Valor.

For some reason, the fleet had issued a new uniform to the space crews during his last deployment. Oswald was sure some brave CEO or Secretary of Logistics had waged war to push the contract, but he had to admit he liked the royal blue coat and slacks trimmed with stylized gold flames.

The colors were supposed to represent Earth and Sol according to the *SDF Basic Orbital Operations Manual*, commonly known as "the BOOM book." Oswald didn't know about all that, but the cut of the new uniforms was an improvement. And the SDF uniform always looked better than the moribund funeral suits of national militaries.

It also helped mask some of the ravages middle-age and extended microgravity had inflicted on his physique.

The click of his dress shoes echoed in the lobby as Oswald meandered between the historical displays until stopping in front of the Sol Defense Fleet emblem that dominated the far wall.

It was a flat, oval piece of granite two meters across. Carved into the rock was a gold-ringed Earth with 3-D reliefs of the terrain. The Sol Defense Fleet motto was engraved in the gold ring around the carving.

*A People United. A Species United. A World United.*

It was, as Pierce Oswald's sage father was wont to say, unmitigated horseshit.

They were good words for political campaigns and recruitment brochures. They had worked on a younger Pierce Oswald, and part of him still believed those words. Or at least still wanted to believe them.

Jump tunnel tech changed everything. The lure of the stars was enough to make men and women from around the world forget their differences as they lived the dream of stellar exploration. But it wasn't enough to unify those they left behind.

It took the destruction of NASA's Proxima Centauri research station, which stood at the top of the spacecraft casualty list as NACRS-1, to give Sol Defense Fleet the steel it needed to come together in the fires of war.

Alien lasers had burned away the dreams of those who'd left Earth for a life among the stars. It had been Oswald's dream before the war.

"Attention!" called the corporal. He and Oswald snapped to attention.

"As you were," said General Anahita Khadem as she strode across the lobby to Oswald. She returned his salute. "Sorry to have kept you, Oswald. Things are afoot."

"Why am I here?" asked Oswald.

Her bright smile shone in contrast to her dark Persian features. "I haven't seen you in two years and that's all you have to say?" She walked back towards the elevator.

"I saw you at the funeral."

"You didn't say much."

"I didn't think you'd really want me to say much," Oswald said. "But it has been a while with me off fighting the war and all."

"Yes, well, we've all been fighting the war."

"Some more than others." Oswald hiked his thumb back towards the lobby. "That guy can't even fight to make sure the KIA projector works."

Anahita shook her head but said nothing. The elevator panel displayed Mission Control Center Complex and the doors slid open. She led him down plain, unoffending halls designed by military health-and-welfare experts to reduce commander stress. Oswald was dubious about the whole idea.

The door to Anahita's office scanned her and slid open when she approached. She paused inside to keep it open for Oswald.

"He's been fighting with building maintenance for two months to get it fixed."

Oswald brushed past Anahita and waited for her to take her seat before sitting himself. "Just have him reboot it and clear the dynamic holo-matrix."

"He doesn't have access to the server room and they won't give it to him."

"Why don't you make them?"

"I have more important things to worry about."

Oswald nodded. "Of course, General." Honoring those who had died in space wasn't high on the list of the MCC staff, apparently.

"And before you get all bent, Pierce, you have more important things to worry about, too. You have to pick your battles. Drink?" Anahita thumbed a console and a wooden column rose from her desk to unfurl into a small wet bar.

"Not all of us have the privilege of picking our battles." Oswald glanced at the selection in the bar. Fine scotch and brandy still gently swirled in their bottles, their color inviting. In the middle was an elegant bottle of Delamain, trimmed in decorative bronze nudes. Anahita had never been a heavy drinker but in all things that she deemed worthy to invest in, she was a connoisseur. They had shared from that bottle over the years. The honey liquid inside called to him, promising a taste of the good old days.

"No, thanks. Why am I here?"

Anahita sniffed loudly. "Obviously, because I have orders for you. And you're going to hate them."

"Orders are orders. But you pulled me from my squadron, so I just can't wait to hear them."

"You're going to have to. At least until the mission briefing. You'll get your flight package there. But the short of it is that I'm pulling you to command one of the Earth Guard squadrons."

Oswald could feel the heat crawling up his neck and over his face. "To hell with that! I'm needed in the fight. I need to get back to Barnard's Star."

"Welcome to the war of politics. I'll tell you more later if time permits." Anahita leaned forward and pointed at his Rocket of Valor, the highest honor available in the SDF. "But, basically, you have the RoV. Having an RoV awardee commanding Earth's defense will make people happy. Having an RoV awardee killed in the battlespace makes people sad."

"This is bullshit."

"So?"

Oswald traced his index finger in small circles on the table as he considered his words. "Look, you can modify those orders. Sherman's a good commander, but she needs my help. Don't waste what we've won there for some PR crap. Don't waste the lives we spent there."

Anahita furrowed her brow. "I'm sorry, but... I'm the one that requested you here, Pierce." Anahita sank back into her chair and ran her fingers through her black hair to clasp it into a silver hair clip she'd taken from the desk. The arch of her back caused her breasts to jut forward. A whiff of jasmine drifted across the table to Oswald. He tried hard to not breathe it in deeply.

Oswald wasn't used to seeing women in uniform with long hair. All crew members in space were expected to wear regulation cropped hair. Long hair was a liability in a combat vacc-suit and in zero-g operations. And the short curly hairs that came free during a patrol were hard enough on the filters. While Oswald found the regulation buzz-cut sexy on most women, it had spawned countless crass jokes about the difference—or lack thereof—between men and women of the SDF.

"Don't you want to be with your family? If you're in Sol, you'll have more Earth time. So will your crew. The orders are for you and your ship."

Of course he wanted to stay with his family. But his family was extended across the stars. His wife, his daughters, and the men and women he flew with. They were all his family, too.

He tapped the small, blue-tinted holo-cube on Anahita's desk. She raised an eyebrow but said nothing. A picture of her village flickered into focus above the desk, centered on a gathering of a dozen handsome Iranians. Oswald found a ten-year-old Anahita in the crowd; he always could find her in those pictures. A mosque, its sparkling minarets and gold-embossed framework, loomed over them, beautiful and menacing at once.

Anahita's great-grandfather towered over the children. He'd been an influential imam during the Muslim Reformation wars and had been a driving force in building the mosque. He'd died a martyr or a traitor, depending on who told the tale. Her staunch atheism would have thrown him into apoplexy.

The picture was replaced with another, this one inside the mosque. Then a picture of the imam's wake. Anahita next appeared in her Sol Defense Fleet graduation robes.

Oswald grinned despite himself at an image of him and Anahita laughing on a beach in Florida, their uniforms folded up on nearby rocks. It cheered him. It made him feel old. A much newer image appeared of a young woman in a flight suit. The cadet patches were so new and crisp Oswald could almost smell the academy. She had Anahita's beaming smile... and his eyes.

Anahita jabbed the holo-cube with a finger and the image blinked away. Narrowing her eyes at him, she slid the cube to the edge of the desk and let it clatter into a drawer which she then slammed shut.

Oswald looked away and found himself staring at the row of bottles.

"Changed your mind?" Anahita flashed a sardonic smile and reached for the Delamain. The bottle was halfway out.

"Whiskey."

Anahita let the bottle fall back into place. "If you say." She slid two glasses from a hidden cabinet in the bar and poured two fingers of Star Fire Premium into each. After setting a glass in front of Oswald, she stowed the bottle and folded the bar back into her desk.

The whiskey swayed in the shot glass as Oswald rolled it between his hands. He lifted it to his lips and took a sip. Pride pushed him to throw it back and slam the glass on the table. But he feared making a spluttering fool of himself. He was no lightweight when it came to drinking, but they didn't get much of the good stuff up there. Spitting it all over her desk in a coughing fit wouldn't help convince her to change his orders.

Anahita tilted her head back and drained her glass in a single, slow pull. Oswald refused to look at her. When she set the empty glass down, she interlaced her fingers and waited. He took another sip, ignoring her impatient gaze. He'd already waited an hour on her and whoever was next in her virtual assistant's appointment file could go to hell. "Sometimes there are things even more important than family."

"Obviously."

Oswald glared at her. "You should have told me."

"You shouldn't have accessed her DNA record without authorization. That's a punishable offense, Lieutenant Colonel."

"You should talk, General. I'm attached to Barnard's Star Command. You have no reason to pull my logs."

"You *were* attached to BARSTARCOM. Now you're with SOLCOM." Anahita's jaw jutted forward. "And, there was a reason

I didn't want you to know. And it isn't about you. I was never angry with you and I never blamed you."

"I deserved to know, dammit."

"Would you have married Misty if you'd known?"

Oswald looked away. "I would have asked you."

"Exactly. Do you question your decision to order *Bonwei* into the fight?"

"Yes. Maybe."

Anahita raised her brow. "Look at me."

Oswald reluctantly turned to face her, running his finger along the rim of his glass. "No."

"Ululani died doing her duty to save Earth. Like many others. You couldn't have kept her safe even if you wanted to." She cut off his objection with a chopping motion of her hand. "That's not a jab. People die. There's no such thing as safe. You of all people should know that. You need to let it go. I have."

"For all your tactical genius, you've never been a good liar. You're not even fooling yourself with that bullshit." He finished the whiskey with a quick gulp and slid the glass across the desk to Anahita. "I take that back. You have become a good liar."

Anahita collected his glass and stacked it in hers, setting them aside to be cleaned later. Her lack of reaction disappointed Oswald. He'd wanted to hurt her and thought he had. But she wasn't going to give him the satisfaction. She usually didn't. He'd have to keep trying.

"Look, Pierce. I never got the chance to thank you for recovering her body. Few remains make it back. I appreciate it. Really." She blew out a long breath. "Did you talk to her about it?"

"No. I meant to. I set up secure comms, but I never could." Oswald shook his head, chagrin spreading across his face. "I even pulled a surprise inspection on *Bonwei* just so I could talk to her face-to-face. Ended up chickening out like a first-year cadet. I kept making plans to and then... poof. Too late."

"It wasn't your fault. It was a brilliant ambush. Not even you can control jump scatter. *Bonwei* simply jumped in the wrong place at the wrong time. You gave the orders you needed to win." Anahita pushed the chair from the table and stood, putting her hands on her hips and pushing them forward to pop her back. "Let's go. It's time for the mission briefing."

"Did she know?"

"Let's go, Pierce."

"Did she know about me?"

Anahita turned to face him from the doorway and motioned for Oswald to go through. Her jaw was set in the way it always was when she was done talking. If it were merely clenched, he might have had a chance when she cooled down later. He walked into the hallway and waited until she pointed in the right direction and fell in beside him.

"I know how you feel about us interfering MCC commanders, but I'll give you the short tour on our way to the briefing."

"Still trying to live out your Captain Yasmina of Star Command fantasies? I bet you've even got some fuzzy dice hanging over your monitor." Oswald saw her cold glance from the corner of his eye and smirked. "MCCs have their place. But Captain Yasmina would never be caught dead hiding in one."

He glanced over and caught a glimpse of her face falling, but only for a second. Taking shots at her childhood hero was childish, but he didn't care. It felt good to hit the mark. But only for a second.

Anahita tapped the gold rocket on Oswald's chest. "Not as impressive as that. You're a shit-hot-rocket-jock now. How many people did you hide behind to get it?"

Oswald wasn't sure if he'd covered the pause in his step. Hopefully she wouldn't look over and see his nostrils flaring before he got them under control. No one spoke ill of an RoV. She had more ribbons than he did by half an orbit, but they were political favors or admin tokens. There were no special service medals, no Space Combat Comet. She'd killed her fair share of Proximan invaders from her Mission Control Center. But because she hadn't been in harm's way, she wasn't eligible for the comet.

As it should be. If you don't ride the rocket, you don't get the comet.

"I might trade it for a nice office like yours and the guarantee of not getting shot at. I'd rather have your stars than this comet."

"No, you wouldn't." She motioned at a hologram depicting a *Fenris*-class starship. "You could never give that life up. These stars on my uniform only mean I get a very little more money with a disproportionate increase in stress."

"Those mean they value your life more than mine. Otherwise they wouldn't keep sending me to get vacc'd by aliens."

A quartet of enlisted administration specialists came into the hall, immediately snapping to attention and saluting. Their faces were masks of professional disinterest. Oswald returned the salute. He could still feel his nostrils twitching and imagined the enlisted men were laughing behind his back. The urge to look over his shoulder almost overcame him. He was acting like a cadet.

Why the hell hadn't she told him about Ululani? What the hell had he done to deserve that? Whatever the reason, he'd be damned if he would let her nursemaid him by shutting him and his crew away in Sol, forcing him to abandon his squadron in Barnard's Star. At the first chance, he'd jump back there. Even if he had to commandeer a supply ship.

They came around the corner and two SDF soldiers snapped to attention behind their security bubbles. Between them was a pair of thick elevator doors, the letters "MCC" formed in thick shining plates designed to resemble stencils.

"What we lack in excitement, we make up in political bullshit," Anahita said.

She placed her thumb on the biometric pad next to the doors and leaned forward until the retina scanner blinked green. She motioned for Oswald to do the same and, once he had, the doors slid open.

"Time for your tour of my MCC," she said as the doors slid shut. "But I fear you'll be disappointed."

"Oh?"

"No fuzzy dice."

# Chapter 2

OSWALD COULD FEEL THE elevator's drop in the pit of his stomach. It was nothing compared to a starship in maneuvers, but he hadn't expected it and his muscles ached. He hadn't gotten his gravity legs back. He'd kept from reaching out to grab a handrail, but Anahita's smirk told him she'd noticed.

"Must be nice to have so much protection," Oswald said. "So much rock to hide behind."

"Just in case the Proximans do start dropping rocks or nukes on us. This is the brains of Sol's defense, after all. Well, one of them."

"They tried hiding MCCs in rocks when I was in Alpha Centauri and Tau Ceti." Oswald shrugged and leaned against the elevator wall. He hoped it looked casual instead of as if he needed support. "After they sniffed out and destroyed the third one in AC, command decided not to bother. They wisely left it to the squadron commanders. Of course, our squadron commanders had the good manners to not treat other crews like passengers on remote control."

"And despite no MCC, you still took out that station in Barnard's Star." Anahita clasped her hands behind her back and rocked on her heels. "That was very lucky. I've seen how you do orbital calculations."

Banter was an age-old military tradition. Navy vs. Marines. Army vs. Aerospace forces. Divisions and even sections within those divisions fought and teased. Trash talk was as common between people in different parts of the same team as it was between people on opposite teams. Administration vs. Maintenance vs. Operations. Squadron vs. Squadron. Ship vs. Ship.

Wing vs. Mission Control Center.

Oswald had seen it turn into fisticuffs between crews on liberty. Shit-posting each other in forums, trading insults in chat rooms, and the occasional uploaded cyber-virus were more common given the distances involved and the technical nature of the fleet. The hierarchy of who were considered the outsiders was fascinating, like one suit of cards ganging up on another in the same deck to take a trick. If aerospace got into a mix up with some sailors, any nearby marines were likely to jump in and help their shipmates. Then fight those same sailors later that night over what stream to watch in the lounge.

It looked like machismo bullshit to outsiders, and sometimes to Oswald too. But when all the teeth had been replaced, and all the stitches sewn, it could raise the morale of the men and women involved. Even the losers of those scuffles—though few admitted defeat—had stuck together. It was only healthy competition if leadership knew when to let it slide and when to draw the line.

But this was beyond friendly rivalry for Oswald. It was too personal. He wanted to piss her off. To hurt her. To shatter that infuriating mask. As they descended into the bowels of Xichang, as if into a prison, he thought of what Anahita had done to him. The anger rose hot on his neck. This was not his world, not his Sol Defense Fleet. Oswald was entering the realm of people who sat in safety with the audacity to assume he didn't know how to fight.

"When we were supporting Tau Ceti, the Proximans didn't even have to attack. They just booby-trapped the obvious places similar to where we'd set up MCCs in other systems." Oswald spread his hands and made a raspy explosion sound. "Took out the delivery vessel and the MCC module with the staff still on it."

She stopped rocking on her heels and faced Oswald. "Every platform has its limitations. Even *Roland*. MCCs are vulnerable in toe-hold systems. We know that now." Anahita leaned in close, her warm breath on his neck as she spoke.

A wave of red lust washed over Oswald. He wanted to grab her and press her against the wall and cover her mouth with his. As they had done decades ago. He saw it play out in his mind, the vigor of their youth fueling their passions born of long familiarity and maturity. Fire throbbed in his crotch in time with his pulse. He fought back the erection with a flood of thoughts about the duty rotations, supply schedules, and crew evaluations awaiting his approval.

"And don't feed me any bullshit about *real* flight crews. The MCC staff you so flippantly describe dying, died in combat. Space. Combat. And they are just as dead as..." Anahita choked on the words with a loud glottal stop from the back of her throat. She turned to face the elevator doors. "As dead as your friends."

Oswald knew what she'd wanted to say, what she'd said to herself.

*Just as dead as Ululani.*

Ululani, the daughter he'd never known about before Barnard's Star. Ululani, the combat systems engineer he'd sent to die on the *Bonwei*. The girl who may or may not have known it was her father that had condemned her. But Oswald had known when he'd given the order. He'd known and would do it again under the same circumstances. Oswald's lust evaporated as quickly as it had come.

The atmosphere in the elevator was stifling and silent for the rest of the descent as if they were trapped in a shipboard compartment with a failed environmental control system. Imagining a faulty ECS reminded Oswald of *Roland* and how much he needed to be back with his squadron. Taking swipes at his new superior probably wasn't the best way to make that happen.

The deceleration of the elevator pressed up through Oswald's feet. A panel slid away to reveal another biometric scanner. Anahita motioned Oswald towards it and the elevator doors slid open after verifying they were the same people who'd entered from the surface. Two more soldiers snapped to attention. A short hallway beyond them led to a platform that overlooked an array of large transparent cubes.

Anahita leaned on the railing and spread her arms. "Welcome to my MCC farm. Welcome to battle central."

The cubes held five to ten gesticulating mission operators swiping hands through an endless kaleidoscope of hovering displays. Oswald could make out ship status pages, orbital tracks, and live video feeds. A large holo-screen dominated the front of each cubicle, its controller standing on a raised central platform. Some calmer cubes held only two or three operators whose screens showed deep-sky renderings and navigational tracking. A few cubicles were opaque, gray, and lifeless.

Oswald noticed that he couldn't see all the way through the active MCCs, only into them. He motioned towards the nearest cube with his chin. "One-way transparency?"

Anahita nodded and lead Oswald towards a door on the opposite side of the platform. "Keeps crews from distracting each other."

Oswald rankled at her pretentious use of "crew," as if a group of what were essentially gamers was like a real crew. Like *Roland*'s crew that could be deployed into harm's way. A real crew that gasped together as their dying breaths were ripped from their lungs.

He lifted his chin towards another cube. "And the solid ones are unmanned?"

"That or they're monitoring super secret missions. Even I'm not immune to 'need to know' protocols."

"So that's where all the kids go to get it on."

Anahita snorted. "Maybe that too. But mostly if a crew's on duty, they're open to observation. We never know who might be watching."

"A regular panopticon, eh? Big Brother is real."

"Says the man who can dope his entire crew into oblivion. And anyway, Big Brother's been watching long before our grandparents were born. But the few people here important enough to matter don't have time to skulk around peeking in on my crews."

"I've always found," he said, glancing left and right, "that people with nothing better to do are the most dangerous."

"Papa said idle hands belong to Iblis. Here we are." Anahita led Oswald to a door stenciled 5-11. "Just some heads-up, Pierce. This is big-time. Straight from the top."

"If you're leading it, it must be. Of course, you're pretty much at the top so it's not much of a walk. I've been reading what I can about your missions." Oswald grimaced. "Seems they give you all the suicide runs."

She sighed. "I get the hard missions done. They don't give me patrols anymore. Just suicide runs, as you call them. Though I prefer to think that they're only suicide runs if someone else does them. I hope you know I try to keep my ships alive. I never throw away an asset."

"Asset?"

"It's the lingo, Pierce. Get over it. You know what I mean."

"I'm afraid I do, General."

Anahita's face grew cold. All emotion had drained away except for the fusion-torch glare in her eyes.

"How dare you." Anahita bit the words as they seethed out between her clenched teeth.

"*Bonwei* was never just an asset to me. No crew is. But I don't blame you, Ana. I'm sure it's hard to see that from such a comfy chair."

"You shit!" Her finger jabbed Oswald's chest like a blood-crazed woodpecker.

He ignored the pain and leaned forward to stand his ground against her finger until she stopped. Anahita took a deep breath, looking ready to scream again.

Door 5-11 slid open.

A sandy-haired admin sergeant strode through the door and almost walked into Anahita and Oswald. He pulled up short and blinked in surprise before saluting.

"General Khadem. Sorry, I didn't see you there. I was sent to get you."

The sergeant hadn't moved far enough away from the door for it to close. A row of faces sitting around a table inside stared out at them. Anahita shot Oswald a final glare before smiling and returning the sergeant's salute.

"Carry on," she said, walking through the door without a word or nod to Oswald.

Direct hit with secondary detonation. Oswald saluted and walked into the room after her. The angrier Anahita was, the more tired she was of dealing with him, the better the chance he had of getting out of damned SOLCOM. As long as he didn't go too far, which he might have already done. He needed to convince them that he and *Roland* were needed back in Barnard's Star.

And Anahita deserved a good slap across the face, literal and figurative. He'd had a daughter, and she'd never told him. Anahita had known they were in the same squadron, and even then hadn't bothered. He would get back into the war and make her pay at the same time.

The foolishness of it was not lost on Oswald. It was the dream post for a flight commander with a family. No heart-stopping jumps to distant stars. Regular leave Earthside and lots of support from fleet units when the Proximans attacked. Plenty of opportunities for face time with VIPs who'd be falling over themselves to get caught talking to a Rocket of Valor recipient. There'd be lots of pictures of him shaking hands with the elite of Earth.

He was going to sabotage those orders to get back in the fight and help his hard-pressed squadron. Every day here was a day they were a starship short. When they'd established a permanent station in the Barnard's Star system, they could all come home for a well-deserved rest. Then they could all see their families.

It was something he wouldn't tell his wife. She wouldn't understand, despite being married to the SDF for twenty years. Misty would see it as loyalty to his comrades over his loyalty to her. It wasn't that at all. They were all his family. The one's fighting in the black just needed him more at the moment. His absence from home was hard on Misty and his daughters, he knew. It left them lonely. His absence from the squadron left his fleet brothers and sisters dead.

It was a motley assembly of uniforms and suits that watched Oswald and Anahita take their seats. The table was stained oak and large enough for each of the twenty-three people sitting around it to have their own station with elbow room. Each seat had a workstation set into the wood and trimmed with red velvet. Drinks and snack bowls were fitted into recesses along the sides of the stations, and the nubs of small holo-projectors protruded from the table surface at each seat.

"Thank you for your patience," Anahita said. "Lt. Colonel Oswald has just been transferred to SOLCOM and I needed to give him a quick briefing before bringing him down."

Oswald nodded and looked at the remaining open stations, raising an eyebrow at Anahita. She looked down to her own station without pointing out where he should sit.

"Please have a seat here, sir," whispered the sergeant from over Oswald's shoulder.

Oswald turned and saw the sergeant setting a standard SDF secure box at a nearby station. He then pulled the chair out for Oswald. "Would you care for a drink, Lt. Colonel?"

The cups around the table looked to contain only water, various flavors of tea, or coffee. He almost asked for whiskey, but decided he'd had enough today. Too much, probably. Getting tipsy wouldn't help. "Coffee, please. Strong and black."

The sergeant made his way to a small side table where he poured a cup of steaming coffee and set it next to Oswald. Then he sat at his own table and pressed a selector on his console. A faint hum filled the room, then faded away as the audio-nullification field formed around the man. He continued to scan the table like a waiter watching customers, but the sergeant couldn't hear a sound.

Oswald recognized Prime Minister Tzun before Anahita introduced him. The man had no truly distinguishing features, being an average-looking, middle-aged Asian man. But he was a popular, if authoritarian, world leader, and his face was on anything he could get it on. Anahita's warning had been forthright at least. This was big.

"Prime Minister Tzun, this is Lt. Colonel Pierce Oswald, flight commander of *Roland*."

"It is my honor, Mr. Oswald. I make a point of studying the events surrounding every Rocket of Valor recommendation before signing them." Tzun sipped from a cup of coffee.

"Thank you, Prime Minister. I couldn't have done it without my crew. We're trained and ready to take the fight out to the Proxies. *Roland* has one of the highest kill counts in the fleet." Oswald ignored Anahita's amused smile.

"I prefer to call them the Ay-Yon, as they call themselves," the prime minister said. "When I brokered the last cease-fire, they were very offended to be known as Proximans."

*Failed* cease-fire, Oswald wanted to add. But since Tzun was the only one here that outranked Anahita, pissing off Tzun wouldn't be smart. "Of course, Prime Minister," said Oswald. "I'm just in from Barnard's Star, and the fighting's still hot. *Roland* helped the squadron take down a Proximan command ship."

"Yes, I was sorry to hear about your squadron. Losing them was a serious blow." Tzun bowed. "I have faith we will take Barnard's Star back soon."

It felt like someone had slapped him in the face and punched him in the gut at the same time. His breath was gone. Oswald fought to keep the placid smile on his face. Some at the table looked away from him. Including Anahita. "Sorry?"

Prime Minister Tzun raised his brow at Anahita.

She cleared her throat. "I was not able to fill him in on everything, Prime Minister. I was going to after the meeting. I was hoping it wouldn't come up."

The prime minister accepted her explanation with an emotionless nod. "Well, we knew the push was coming. At least the General pulled you out in time. Be thankful for that."

Oswald felt like vomiting. He lifted the cup to cover the snarl pulling his lips apart. The strong aroma of the coffee clenched the knot growing in his stomach. Everyone else around the table had known already. Their faces told him as much. She'd spent her time giving him shit instead of telling him. Fuck her. Instead he looked to Lt. Colonel Paul Gryphon, flight commander of *Charger*. "Anyone make it back?"

"Sorry, mate," Gryphon said in his Australian accent. "Not even the support ships made it."

Sherman. Torchman. Chen. Vasquez. All the flight commanders and their crews in BARSTARCOM gone. Because he hadn't been there. Because *she* had pulled him out.

Would Anahita have pulled *Bonwei* out too, or at least Ululani, if they hadn't already been lost?

He hoped so.

And he hoped not.

Was she right not to have told him?

As a cadet, Anahita often spoke of fighting aliens and pirates like her childhood heroine, Star-Captain Yasmina Pouran. The Iranian sci-fi show had been running since the early 2100s, its life extended by a cult fan base and advanced CGI that made sure Yasmina never aged from viewing generation to viewing generation. Anahita always dismissed her fondness of Yasmina's adventures as childhood fancy. But Oswald knew better. Anahita's eyes filled with the hope that someday she'd be able to shoot some pirate in the face or fire torpedoes from her bridge. It amused Oswald that entertainment entities clung to outdated naval terminology. Starships were not boats in space.

Oswald hated the war. Was tired of it. He'd joined to explore, to open up new star systems. His dream was to fly around and see what awesome sights the universe had to show him. Even if he was only a janitor. The war denied him that dream while realizing Anahita's. She had her aliens to blast while space exploration for its own sake was a thing of the past. Exploration had been reduced to military scouting missions, the interest in any given system never extending past its tactical considerations. When Oswald's inherent grasp of orbital combat came to light during exams—exams he hadn't wanted to take—they threw him into the fray.

Now he wanted to kill the damn Proxies again. Every last one.

"Do you need a moment, Mr. Oswald?" Prime Minister Tzun asked.

Oswald's head was throbbing. He wanted nothing more than to find a bathroom and scrub his face in hot water. Or punch something. That would work too. He did need a moment, a damned long moment. Instead he said, "No, sir. Thank you. We can start."

Tzun nodded and motioned towards Anahita.

"This is ultra-lock security classification. Nothing said in here is to be shared with your crews until you have entered orbital operation." Anahita swiped a hand over her console and each of the tiny holo-projectors around the table twinkled to life. The words *Operation Prometheus Star* appeared above them.

"Operation Prometheus Star is Sol Defense Fleet's initiative to discover the Proximan home world. While we have had successes in destroying some of their forward bases," she said, glancing at Oswald, "in Barnard's Star and Alpha Centauri, the enemy ability to jump into and threaten our home world has left us on the defensive."

As if no one understood the point, a 3-D map of the local star population replaced the operation title, and red lines extended from several stars to Sol. Oswald had fought in at least seven of those systems, either as flight commander or crew. The arrows disappeared and the display zoomed in until a star labelled Delta Pavonis filled the space over the table. The field of view centered on Delta Pavonis V and zoomed in again until the planet hung in full display.

"And this is where we plan on getting what we need to figure out how to track where a jump point terminates. Delta Pavonis Five."

The assembled officers exchanged glances. Most of the civilians had no reaction; Oswald guessed they didn't immediately grasp the significance of being able to determine a jump tunnel's far end.

Oswald realized he'd been rubbing his eyes when he stopped to stare at Anahita. "That would change everything. But what's there?"

Anahita met Oswald's gaze. "General Will Zaphrim will explain." She motioned to the man sitting next to her.

Vivid burn scars covered the man's bald head, face, and neck, continuing beneath his uniform collar in glossy streaks. He wore white gloves, the material not thick enough to hide the disfiguration beneath. Above his full orbit of ribbons were a golden RoV, Combat Comet, and a Survivor's Star. The latter, colloquially known as the Lucky Star, was given to those who'd survived the destruction of their spacecraft due to hostile action.

"It's been a while, Pierce." Cheeks stiffened by the burn scars slurred his speech and gave the man's smile a look of waxy insincerity. But the smile shone in his eyes.

Oswald stared at his old friend and instructor who'd ridden his ass all the way through the academy. Then became his best friend when they served together on *Longwell*. Now general's stars and a special forces tab adorned his shoulders.

"Sorry, Will. I... didn't recognize you."

"Understandable. But I'm still prettier than you." His smile fell away. "I'm sorry to hear about your squadron. Don't worry, we'll be taking the fight to the Proxies soon enough."

Oswald fought the urge to rail against Anahita's decision that ensured he wasn't going to be taking the fight anywhere. But whining wasn't the right weapon at this point. And his squadron, his dead squadron, deserved better of him. He nodded.

General Zaphrim exchanged glances with Anahita. "I will again remind everyone here that this is ultra-lock classification. To answer your question, Oswald, there are ruins from an alien civilization there. In those ruins are a series of what we're calling jump extension beacons. Operation Prometheus Star will recover those beacons."

"Alien beacons? Like human Proximan aliens?" asked Gryphon.

"No," said Zaphrim. "The ruins have no relation to Proximans or any other human civilization. Dating estimates put them at at least twenty thousand years. Estimates being the key word. Maybe longer."

A murmur rolled around the table as the revelation sank in.

"And how long has fleet command known about these mysterious alien ruins?" Oswald was rubbing his eyes again.

"About ten years," said Zaphrim.

Oswald glared at Anahita. "So we've known about a non-human alien species for ten years, and the SDF decided to keep it a secret? All that time?"

"We've had a war on, Lt. Colonel," she answered. Anahita lifted her cup of chai and blew the steam away, the rich scent of it mingling with the other drinks on the table.

"Delta Pavonis is listed as nearly twenty light-years away. Have we ever made such a long jump?" asked Gryphon. "I thought our jumps didn't go that far."

A muscular man with a Slavic accent answered from the other side of the table. "Theoretically a jump tunnel can be established at any distance for a microsecond—just enough to transition. Distance is irrelevant. The issue is of calculations and being able to gather relevant navigation data to adjust the plot. The distance, as far as we know, is only limited by the accuracy of that data. If you have the data though, the calculations can be run by the Q-puters as easily as any other jump."

"Theoretically?" asked Gryphon, a sardonic smile twisting his lips. He picked up his secure box and shook it; the flight package shuffled inside. "So we're running forward on a theory? I mean, I understand we act on tactical theories about where the bad guys might be, but a theory that we can—"

"We've been to Delta Pavonis twice already, Gryphon," interrupted General Zaphrim. "Please listen to Dr. Dworaczyk."

"The jump extension beacons," Dr. Dworaczyk continued, "give us real-time location data from Delta Pavonis, not a twenty-year-old extrapolation. We discovered their signal quite on accident researching jump pulse communications. It's as if the beacons are transmitting through a permanently open jump point." The man shrugged his meaty shoulders. "But there is no detectable jump point, merely the signal. Our navigation data for Delta Pavonis is more accurate than any other we have. It's actually the safest jump we can currently make. Like a lighthouse for interstellar navigation."

"And we're going to go steal the candles from that lighthouse? Don't we have enough alien problems?" Oswald asked.

"Except for some automated defenses, the planet is abandoned and replies to no communication attempts," said Zaphrim.

Oswald's throat was dry with hidden rage. He took a sip of his coffee and a deep breath. "Are these automated defenses the reason we don't have the beacons already?"

Zaphrim stared at Oswald a moment before speaking. "The first mission was to survey the specific locations of the beacons planetside. They encountered no resistance. The second was a recovery attempt. Automated defenses destroyed the recovery teams and the transport. We have limited information on the enemy capabilities. Only the fragments of logs we recovered from the navsat."

"Sounds like communication to me," said Oswald.

"We are running out of time," said Anahita. "And not just because of increased Proximan attacks. The fleet is falling apart. The US and China are pushing back against budget increases because the African Republics refuse to pay what they already owe. The South American Federation agreed, but only if they get another launch facility and construction subsidies. *Roland* already costs more than ten years of GDP of some member nations. And SDF intel reports that at least three Earth corporations have been trying to contact the Proximans for independent trade agreements."

"Maybe we'll get what we deserve," said Oswald. "No one ever wants to pay the piper."

"You secure that shit right now, Pierce," said Zaphrim. The man's scars muted the anger on his face, but Oswald knew those eyes.

It pained Oswald to see his friend scarred and stiff. Will Zaprhim had been one of the most energetic men Oswald knew. And a skilled athlete. Where Oswald had been happy enough to pass his physical tests with average scores, Zaphrim was never satisfied with less than top ratings. Being paralyzed and stuck on Earth had to be hard for him. Oswald nodded. "Yes, sir. Sorry."

"Perhaps we should let the Ay-Yon drop a few bombs from orbit," said Prime Minister Tzun. "Maybe convince Washington or Beijing it's in their best interest to support us. They might be more willing to listen to me."

If any of the military members had said it, especially Gryphon, Oswald would have chalked it up to standard military-gallows humor. But Tzun, political manipulator of millions and billions, was so casual as he spoke Oswald couldn't decide if the man was joking or calculating out loud. Tzun's face was inscrutable when he wanted it to be.

Zaphrim nodded. "Maybe. Look, the SDF is being pushed in every system. Barnard's Star was only the first to fall. If we don't figure out where we can effectively push back, we're done. And we have to get back in the fight before humanity fails the fleet, or the fleet fails humanity.

"The high-altitude pass on this mission is we send a squadron to Delta Pavonis Five, drop a team of Rangers to the surface to recover what your flight package calls the UXA—Unidentified Xenomorphic Artifact. Then jump home." Zaphrim pointed a stiff hand at the doctor. "Then we can hopefully use the thing to track the Proximans back to their home world. Make them pull back some of their forces. Give us some breathing room."

Gryphon thumped a forefinger on the table. "And we nuke the bastards."

There it was, what Oswald knew most of the flight commanders and generals were thinking too. But being the first to suggest the nuclear option was taboo. Gryphon ate taboos for breakfast and washed them down with the tears of the easily offended. Oswald loved that about the man. Scruples were finicky. Someone could shoot ten thousand enemies in the face in a ground war, and that was terrible but acceptable. Using nuclear weapons planetside to kill those same ten thousand—or even one person—was unthinkable, monstrous. Unless it really needed to be done.

"That's extreme," said Prime Minister Tzun. "Genocide isn't the only option."

"With all due respect, Prime Minister," Gryphon answered, "that's arsetalk. You just suggested letting the Proxie bastards bomb us from orbit as a political action. If peace was an option, they'd have stopped attacking a decade ago. They're out to knock us all off. The only way to stop that is to kill them first."

"Even if they are victorious," Tzun said, "that doesn't mean they'll kill us all. And even if some of their generals make those threats, they're like us. There are factions."

"How many of us would they have to kill for it to be acceptable, Prime Minister?" Oswald asked.

Tzun shrugged. "Maybe all of us. I'm merely saying I don't think it has to come to that."

"Let's not get ahead of ourselves," Anahita said. "Hopefully we can reach some sort of permanent armistice before it comes to mutual annihilation. But first we have to give them a reason to sue for peace."

Gryphon glanced at Oswald and shook his head.

"On that note," said General Zaphrim, "commanders, please open your flight packages."

Oswald picked up the secure box from his station and held its optical scanner to his eye. It flashed green and the box slid open. Inside was a standard-sized dossier with an SDF flight package. A data chip made to fit standard fleet tablets also slid out. He pushed that aside, preferring the tactile feel of the data sheets.

It detailed vehicle configuration, allotted delta-v, navigation points, outlined an objectives timeline, weapons load-out, and other details the planners deemed pertinent.

The flight package for *Roland* was more like a castration. He was to stay in Sol and coordinate the escort of the ships being sent on the real mission. Anahita refused to meet his eyes. Was she punishing him or trying to keep him safe? As if the latter was even possible. She'd said as much herself not long ago. Either way, Oswald wasn't going to float around Earth with his thumb up his thruster. That was a job for political brats and they could keep it.

General Zaphrim popped a mint into his mouth from the bowl at his station. Once he'd chewed it, he started rubbing the corner of his lip. It looked like a person trying to scratch an itchy bandage without hurting the injury beneath. "Let's dig into—"

"Why isn't *Roland* taking the lead on this, General?" Oswald didn't specify which general he was asking. He'd leave it to whichever one felt like answering.

"Excuse me?" Zaphrim asked.

"This isn't about notches on your belt, Lt. Colonel Oswald," said Anahita. She was trying to play it cool, but he could see the burn in her eyes.

"I agree," said Oswald. "This isn't about ribbons. This is about everything you just finished telling us. About how bad things are." The man they'd put in charge of the mission was a capable flight commander, but lacked the fire in the belly to pull it off. Oswald preferred not to denigrate other officers in public, but would if he had to. "*Roland* has the experience and is one of the toughest ships in the fleet. And it's already capable of a tail-first landing if needed."

"If it comes to landing *Roland*," Zaphrim said, "the mission's probably already fucked. If the Rangers and their specially designed landers and rovers can't get it done, I doubt your crew will do better. Now back to the—"

"It's all about contingencies, General." Oswald didn't want to push his old friend too far in front of the onlookers. But he had to get his foot in the door before everything was set in administrative stone. If it wasn't too late already. "My starship—"

"You mean *my* starships, *my* flight commanders," Anahita said, tapping her chest with each, "my." "And *my* assets will do as they're ordered. Once Sol Defense Fleet puts you in command of planning missions, *Lieutenant* Colonel," she continued, stressing "lieutenant" to make it clear she wasn't even addressing a full colonel, "then you can decide who goes where and when. Clear?"

Oswald glared back at Anahita for an instant, then glanced at General Zaphrim. There was a warning glint in the man's eyes. Oswald looked down at his flight package. "Yes, General Khadem."

# Chapter 3

AFTER THE CIVILIANS and political entourages left, it was like a room full of smoke being cleared away. Anahita was finally able to draw a deep breath. The sting in her bleary eyes faded as the air system recycled the overwhelming mix of colognes and perfumes. She rubbed her temples to help massage away the throb brought on by the asinine discussions.

Yes, there were such things as stupid questions.

But Pierce Oswald was still carrying on, digging into every comment she made to uncover any fallacy, real or imagined, in front of the staff. At least he hadn't done it while the civvies were there.

"We'll have a twelve percent saving in delta-v if we don't send *Alahambra* to Delta Pavonis," he said.

He'd spent much of the last hour regaling her and General Zaphrim with numbers explaining why none of the assigned starships were the best for the mission. Not so much explaining as data-hurling. He would throw dumps of information out there like grenades, leaving it to everyone else to extrapolate his points.

It was wearing her out, and she was having trouble focusing. And the chai she'd been sipping all morning was about to burst her bladder.

"Thank you, Oswald," she said, not bothering to mask her irritation. "When we return from our break, perhaps you can give us some numbers concerning *your* assignment instead of everyone else's."

She stood and the rest of the table stood as well. Anahita felt the pressure in her bladder shift, giving her momentary relief. As she was about to rush off down the hall, she noticed a small text message from Will Zaphrim blinking on her display.

*We need to talk.*

Anahita dismissed the other officers with a wave of her hand. She sighed and looked at Will. "I've really got to piss."

She'd had Zaphrim as an instructor in the academy too, but she'd turned down her orders for space duty years ago to properly raise her unplanned daughter. Will had become a good friend in the year since his injuries and loss of flight status. They worked well together planning missions, but she would never be as close to Will as Pierce was. They'd flown together for years.

And now Pierce's wingman was coming in to save him. Will's face was often unreadable to her, but she knew what was coming next. She'd given up her dreams of being a Star-Captain Yasmina for the sake of Ululani. She'd kept the secret for the sake of Pierce's career. Right or wrong, she'd done it for him. And he'd shit on her for it.

"It must be nice to still feel your bladder." He looked up at her from his mobile chair during the uncomfortable silence. Then he let out a bark of laughter. "I'm kidding. Kidding, Anahita."

She stared back with level eyes.

"Hard room."

"I have to piss."

Will held up his tablet and slid his hand across the screen with an exaggerated flourish. He turned it so she could read it, then handed it to her when she squinted. A message from Prime Minister Tzun filled the display.

*Is Oswald right? Should he be leading the mission? What do you think?*

She dropped the tablet on the table. Oswald's little display had put questions in Tzun's mind. No doubt what Oswald had intended. He didn't need help from his wingman, apparently. "Damn it," she muttered.

"Careful with that." Will scooped up the tablet with stiff hands and gave it a cursory inspection.

"Well?"

"Well, what?"

Anahita snorted and shook her head. "What do you think?"

"I think *Roland* is the best candidate."

"I knew it."

"That *Roland* is the best candidate? Good. No debate needed then."

"No," she said. "That you'd stick up for Pierce."

Will stuck a gloved finger into the cup next to his terminal for another mint. The deep-burn damage on his neck prevented him from moving his head; he had to move his whole upper torso to look around. Will leaned his body over to look inside the cup and clucked his tongue. "All gone."

His stiff movements, unmoving face, and white gloves reminded Anahita of stick puppets from her childhood. She hated those freakish toys and their judgmental parables disguised as fun play-time stories. In Happy Land where your daughter didn't get incinerated fifty-six trillion kilometers away.

"We have more." Anahita turned to summon the sergeant, but the steward's table was abandoned. He'd left for break with the rest.

"This isn't about us being buddies, Anahita. It's about Pierce Oswald being one of the best combat flight commanders we have and *Roland* being one of the toughest starships we have. Nunez is a good commander, but Pierce is right. Nunez is better suited to an orbital defense role.

"Especially since the MCC controls all the defense operations in Sol, anyway." Will wriggled his fingers to mime typing without looking away from her. "I mean literally. Your people remotely pilot the vast majority of Sol system engagements. Or at least issue very specific orders down to the millimeter per second of delta-v."

"You think that's wrong? You think I'm pulling one of our best commanders, what, for the fun of it?"

"I think it was a good call to pull him from Barnard's Star..."

"We should have pulled the whole squadron."

Will raised a placating hand. "Agreed. But that wasn't our call. What I'm getting at is that it was a good call to pull him, because I'm not sure even he could have been much help if he'd been there. It was a huge enemy task force. I'm wondering why you pulled him at all. He still had six months on station."

Anahita looked around in disbelief. "Why? You just answered that yourself. To keep one of our ace commanders from being killed for no reason."

"And he's such a good commander that you're parking him in orbit?"

"In case you haven't noticed, the Proximan incursion rates into Sol have doubled in the last two months."

"And *you* have been doing an admirable job driving them back. You. The drone fleet does the majority of the fighting here in Sol."

Anger boiled inside her, clenching her gut, which reminded her of the pressure in her bladder. Anahita thumped the table with her knuckles as she spoke. "Just what are you saying, Will? I feel like I'm being accused of something."

"I think you are trying to protect him."

"Why would I do that?" She crossed her arms and looked away. "We were close once. But that was decades ago."

"Are you really going to make me say it, Ana?"

Anahita stared back, not trusting herself to control the wail building up in her chest. She knew he knew. She knew what he was going to say was right. And she didn't care.

Will let out a sigh. "We know Pierce is Ululani's father and your bereavement is affecting how you deal with him. Not really my area, but the guys in PSYOPS are saying you're suffering through a case of complex grieving. The concern is that you might not be thinking clearly when it comes to him. Especially when he's not making it easy for you." He offered an apologetic shrug. "At least that's what they say."

"How did you know? About Pierce being the father."

Will offered a sad smile. "You know we watch our own as much as we watch the enemy. PSYOPS flagged Pierce's logs after a standard review, but I suspect someone over there already knew."

All the air left her in a loud breath. Anahita's shoulders sagged and her knees buckled. She made the tactical decision to fall into her chair instead of on the floor. The fire, the rage, the fear, had all drained out of her and the tears were on the verge of washing it all away. But she'd be damned if she'd let anyone else see that. She'd cry later.

"Now what?" she whispered.

"That's up to you. I don't have the desire or the authority to order you to do anything. And Tzun, whatever else he might be, is wise enough to recognize when he isn't the best one to make the call." Will picked up his tablet and inclined it towards Anahita. "That's why he's asking instead of ordering. I think we're both hoping you'll make the right call... again."

Anahita allowed herself to double over with her face in her hands for three breaths. Then she sat upright, nodding but not looking at Will. "Fine. Have it your way." She could hear the flight commanders' murmurs from the hall. "I guess we should let them in and tell them."

"I don't think either commander will be disappointed," said Will. "And I still need more mints."

The doors opened and the flight commanders filed in. Anahita watched Pierce take his seat, pointedly not looking at her. His face was now the professional, the consummate stoic warrior. Anahita gave a half grin. It was what he'd always done. Protest and object until he knew he'd lost the argument, then accept it and move on. Her eyes lingered on him.

"Dammit," she muttered.

"What?" asked Will.

"I still have to piss. Thanks a lot."

Will turned to face her and leaned forward. "I don't mean to presume, but you are a general. You can really take a break whenever you like."

"I won't give him the satisfaction."

"If you say so." Will motioned for the sergeant, who strode over and filled the general's cup with coffee, and bowl with unwrapped butter mints. The mints clinked against the ceramic as they tumbled in.

"After some direction from the higher-ups," Anahita started, "there's been a mission reassignment. Oswald, please exchange flight packages with Nunez. Hopefully, the two of you have been paying close enough attention that we won't have to start over."

Oswald and Nunez glanced up at her, then at each other before complying. Nunez's face was a mix of barely suppressed relief and embarrassment.

"This decision doesn't, and won't reflect poorly on your records." Anahita pointed to the ceiling. "Someone up there changed our minds for us. It happens. Our job is to accept those changes—even if we don't like them—and carry on with the mission."

Oswald shuffled the papers in his flight package, refusing to meet her gaze.

"I'll have the reworked delta-v and provisioning mass numbers sent to you ASAP," she continued. "The munition load-outs and equipment will also change significantly."

At least he had the good grace not to smile.

"If everyone will open to the deployment tab, we'll talk about mission start. SOLCOM will be on full alert, with starships on station in each of the coordinates the Proximans might jump in that will give them an opportunity to attack before our squadron can get free of the gravity threshold." Anahita looked over her tablet at Nunez. "Those position assignments will fall on you. The list of ships within the delta-v constraints are listed in your package. I'll review them before we issue burn orders.

"The MCC crews will operate drones and remotes. We'll be using high-thrust tugs to get everyone out of orbit as fast as we can." Anahita looked at Oswald, hoping she didn't appear apologetic. "My MCC crew will coordinate the Delta Pavonis squadron."

Oswald only looked back at her. That pleased her. He'd gotten his way. He could just sit there with his mouth shut for a while and follow some orders.

A map of Earth swirled into existence over the table with a web of blinking yellow tracks showing the escape orbits of Oswald's squadron and the drone fleet. At the jump threshold were three red spheres labelled *Effective Proximan Interdiction Zone*.

"Expecting a fight out of the well, then?" asked Gryphon, a smile on his face that looked both grim and amiable at once. Like a friendly great white shark.

"Always," answered Anahita. "They have too many snoopers in the inner system. I'm guessing they have at least two in orbit around Earth now. We can only hope they don't know what we're about and, as far as we can tell, the Proximans have no presence in Delta Pavonis.

"All survivors of your squadron will immediately jump. You will not perform rescue missions and you will not delay to provide supporting fire. For this mission, *Roland*, *Charger*, and *Triumph* are armored personnel carriers. Each of you will be carrying a platoon of SDF Rangers. They are tasked with recovering the UXA and you are tasked with getting them to Delta Pavonis Five. General Zaphrim with Special Ops will cover the destination objectives." Anahita motioned to Will.

She sniffed the spicy chai wafting up from her cup. Her bladder was still screaming, but she craved the warmth of the cup and soothing heat of the tea. It was not a mission she had high hopes of anyone surviving, let alone of it succeeding. But her money was on Pierce if anyone could pull it off. And if not, he'd at least be able to see that alien world he'd always dreamed of.

Zaphrim tried manipulating the chart above the table, but the tablet screen only registered part of his motions through his gloves. The display centered on the star, jerked away to show nothing, then zoomed into a fuzzy rendering of some undecipherable planetoid or asteroid.

Cursing under his breath, Zaphrim tried tugging at one white glove, but he couldn't get enough of a grip with his other hand. The sergeant saw the general's distress and strode around the table to help. Zaphrim tried to push him away, but the sergeant was too involved helping to notice.

Anahita's eyes bulged as the rescue effort turned into a tug-of-war with Zaphrim's glove. Everyone else around the table was staring too. Oswald's mouth was open and his hand reaching, as if unsure offering more help would actually be helpful.

"Dammit, Sergeant!" Zaphrim finally snapped, giving the man a grandmotherly slap on the wrist.

Not even the mask of scars could hide Zaphrim's embarrassment. If he still had his strength, she suspected the sergeant might already be on the floor.

"Sergeant!" Anahita yelled, along with a chorus of other officers around the table.

The sergeant staggered back as if struck and looked around at all the staring officers. Anahita almost laughed. She could see the scarlet blush working its way up from beneath the man's collar like a storm front on a map.

"Sorry... sorry, sir. I was just trying..." the sergeant stammered.

"Get the hell out of here!" Zaphrim said.

The sergeant snapped to attention and saluted before striding from the room.

Zaphrim threw his tablet on the table. He looked at Anahita and motioned at the wildly spinning holo-display above them. "Can you take care of that goddamned thing for me, please?"

Anahita, eyes still wide, slid her fingers over the display controls until it centered on the star, and zoomed out to include the orbital tracks of the system's planets.

Zaphrim motioned for her to stop with his hand. "Thank you. Delta Pavonis has no Earth-like planets. The astrography teams verified five planets, no gas giants, and possibly two undiscovered planets in the outer solar system as shown by orbital perturbations.

"The planet of interest, if you could zoom in on Five, please, General Khadem, is slightly larger than Mars with a gravity of 3.9 meters per second squared. There is no atmosphere. The terrain is rocky and shows no sign of indigenous life. Four large settlements are scattered across the surface, leading some of the science guys to think that the builders were not from Delta Pavonis Five."

Anahita zoomed the display to show one of the alien cities. It was a landscape of brittle-looking spires and sand-filled doorways of proportions that made it hard for her mind to grasp. The digital recreation was completely still, just as the video of the airless world had been.

"These buildings," Oswald said, "look like they were built in atmo, though. See the sand piled up as if blown there? And all the leading edges of the outer building look like they've been eroded. Those upper antennae look like they have patches of patina or verdigris, maybe."

"Good eye, Pierce," said Zaphrim. "The eggheads in exogeology agree, though they can't pin down exactly what mechanism caused it without more samples."

"So if those were built while there was an atmosphere," Gryphon asked, shaking his finger at the image, "how old are these ruins? Atmospheres don't blow away overnight. Well, not without a nova or something."

Zaphrim popped a mint into his mouth and leaned back, hands in his lap. "Twenty thousand years is the minimum estimate. It's what we tell the civvies. But some theories put the ruins closer to one hundred thousand years or older. Let that roll around in your head for a few days."

"And automated systems are still online?" Oswald asked.

"Unfortunately, yes," said Zaphrim. "That's why we're sending Rangers. Only three of the sites have detectable beacons. One platoon per ship, one platoon per site."

Anahita shifted in her chair as a wave of discomfort rose from her bladder. Will leaned over and motioned towards the exit with a hand beneath the table. When she didn't respond, he rolled his eyes and continued.

"The Rangers have been training on this one for over a year. The Martian training grounds are just about perfect, but the damned Proxies ambushed one of the Ranger transports; all hands lost. So command decided to train them on Luna instead."

Gryphon flipped through his data sheets. "What kind of defenses are we talking about? I don't see any specifics mentioned. Kinetic weapons? Directed energy? Death rays?"

"We don't know exactly," Zaphrim admitted. "We have a few recovered biomechanical samples from the first expedition, but they weren't attacked. The second expedition was wiped out. We did get log fragments the flight commander transmitted to our outer system comm-sat. But no details. Only that they were engaging some automated defense platforms. So we know they can attack orbital targets."

Anahita recognized Oswald's smile. It was the one he always wore when he'd decided he couldn't keep his mouth shut about something he found asinine. It impressed her; he used to only be able to hold off for a few minutes.

She considered his gaunt face. When they were young, it made him look trim and fit, which he was then. Now it made him look haunted. Or maybe it was those eyes. They had been the gray of mist rolling down a mountain. Now they gleamed like steel, distant and unyielding.

How much they'd both changed. How sure they'd been Earth would win the war. It was a testament to the experts of PR in the recruiting department. And their own youthful arrogance.

"So we're going in," Oswald said, "against the automated defenses of a race that built robots that still survive from a time before humanity even knew fire? That have already destroyed an SDF landing force? And try to steal three artifacts from under their noses?"

"The place is long dead, Pierce. Only their bots are left." Anahita regretted saying it the moment his incredulous steely eyes turned to her.

"We've only been twice," he said. "How can you even pretend to know that?"

Anahita shook her head. "Are you saying you want to switch back with Nunez?"

"No," Oswald said. "I'm asking if someone has thought this mission through."

"Many someones have," Zaphrim said. "And that's why we're issuing orbital assault munition this time."

"Just in case we need to nuke these mysterious, priceless, alien ruins and all the knowledge they may hold?" Oswald looked from Zaphrim to Anahita, then rubbed his eyes with a thumb and forefinger. "I have to admit, this is never how my dreams of finding mysterious, priceless, alien ruins ever played out."

"Right on, mate," said Gryphon. "Mine always had lovely green ladies in them."

A few of the officers chuckled. When the two generals didn't join in, the chuckles turned into coughing and throat-clearing.

"I thought we were done with the melodrama, Pierce." Zaphrim's voice was filled with disappointed resignation. "Because Delta Pavonis Five has no atmosphere, this ORBAM package will consist of high-powered orbital lasers and hypervelocity projectiles... conventional and nuclear.

"You'll be jumping in far enough away from the planet that you'll have time to make your own tactical analysis and set up meetings between the flight crews and the Ranger platoon officers. Each of the sites is nearly identical save for their coordinates. You'll have to work out orbital insertions and drop sites yourselves. I think it will be the first time we've actually performed an orbital assault."

The meeting lasted for another hour as they discussed delta-v, intercept vectors, squadron deployments, and the logistics behind it all. Anahita was just about to give in to the pressure in her bladder when General Zaphrim spoke up.

"I think that's enough planning for today. We have another full week before mission start. If we dither too long, the Proximans are bound to know we're up to something." Zaphrim tried to pop a mint into his mouth but it bounced off his cheek and fell under the table. No one laughed except Zaphrim.

"Fleet kept this whole Delta Pavonis thing secret for a long time. Any other secrets we should know about?" Oswald asked. He stared at Anahita. "Keeping secrets can get people killed."

"Nothing we didn't want to tell you," said Anahita. She took a deliberate sip of chai, eyes narrowed at Oswald. The cup *clinked* against its matching saucer as she set it down. The officers around the table stood when she rose. "Dismissed. You will be notified of the next meeting time; probably the same time tomorrow."

She fought the urge to fidget from foot to foot, the shifting of her bladder renewing the pain. The officers filed out. Some stopped to chat, blocking the doorway.

It was a phenomenon that baffled and annoyed Anahita. Despite there being a large room in here and a hallway past the door, there were always people that insisted on stopping in the damned doorway. She'd seen it her entire life, in the mosques as a child, in the theaters, in the social complexes. And some oblivious Cro-Magnon had probably blocked the mouth of his tribe's cave too. If only someone had bashed these entrance blockers out of the gene pool back in the beginning.

"Will you go to the damn head already?" Zaphrim asked. "You're making me antsy."

Without looking at him, Anahita strode to the door. "Make a hole, people." The officers moved aside. She shoved through with her chin raised, and trying to look as though she had urgent business and wasn't to be disturbed. Which was true.

She allowed a breath of relief—the restroom was right around the corner. Two other female officers turned down the hall, not looking as desperate as she felt. Anahita followed, her heels clicking on the polished floor.

"Look, I'm sorry," Oswald said, stepping out of the men's room and stopping in front of her.

Anahita clenched her teeth. "You'll probably regret your choice of assignments, Pierce."

"So it is a suicide mission, then?" Oswald asked, half-grinning. "The fate of mankind is in my hands and all that?"

She shrugged. "It's not a mission I approved. I tried to stop it but was outvoted. Maybe I'm wrong, but I don't give it good odds. I wish you'd reconsider."

"No regrets from me. Ever."

"Bullshit."

Oswald snorted. "Alright. I have more than a few. But not this. No way. A chance to explore alien ruins? And then to use what's there to end the war? It's like the quest for a magic sword to kill the dragon."

"So romantic. You realize you're more likely to have to blow them up than explore them, right?"

"Maybe romantic. But if I'm there, I know I will do everything to avoid collateral damage. Especially if it ends the war. I'd do anything to see that."

"Even surrender?"

"Almost anything," Oswald said.

"What if you had to blow up the ruins to end the war?"

He blew out a loud breath. "I don't know. I do know I'm tired, Anahita. I want it to be over. Barnard's Star... well, I tend to agree with Gryphon. It might come to one side destroying the other completely before it ends." Oswald leaned in close, lowering his voice. "I don't know if I could commit genocide. I probably should know, should be willing. But if this helps us figure out another way, I'm in. I don't want to have to face that choice."

"Well, let's hope it won't become anything so drastic, Pierce. Excuse me." Anahita walked around him and stumbled into someone else. She balled her hands into fists. "Sergeant."

"My apologies, General. About General Zaphrim." The sergeant ran his fingers through his hair, cut to maximum regulation-permitted length. "I was only trying to help him."

"Yes, well, that scene was very... unfortunate. And awkward. We'll just forget it. Or ignore it. But if you feel the need to apologize, talk to General Zaphrim, not me." Anahita raised her hand as the sergeant started to speak again. "Sergeant, please get out of my way or you will be the cause of another unfortunate and awkward scene."

"Better?" Will asked as Anahita walked back into the conference room.

It was quiet and the air recyclers had already replaced the stuffy aroma of bodies with the slightly medicinal aroma of sterilized subterranean air. Anahita walked to her chair and collapsed into it with a loud sigh before answering. "Much better."

"If you can't take a piss when you want, what's the point of earning your stars?" Will laughed and shrugged. "I'm glad you're much better."

He held up his tablet and turned the screen so Anahita could read the message there. Another one from Tzun.

She read the message three times before looking up at Will, unable to read his expression. "No, no, wait. You just typed that in there, didn't you? Ha-ha funny joke time. Right?"

"Nope."

"What the hell is he thinking?"

Will turned his torso towards her. "The mysterious tides of politics are sometimes beyond the ken of mortal man."

She rubbed her forehead. After the shit Pierce had put her through today, she felt more like giving him a throat punch than a promotion. Anahita didn't believe in Allah, but she sometimes believed in Iblis.

# Chapter 4

OSWALD FOUGHT THE URGE to spit, hoping to rid his mouth of the sour metallic taste in the air. Sol was a murky smudge in the yellow clouds of pollution that hung like a pestilence over Xichang space port and most of China. The crews of NBR-57 *Roland*, NBR-101 *Charger*, and NER-32 *Triumph* stood in formation on the cracked tarmac, small flight bags slung across their backs. The air index warning level was high enough that they should have been wearing filter masks, but decorum—and the command staff—demanded otherwise.

Silence came over the formations when General Anahita Khadem took the podium and began shuffling through the notes on her tablet with curt swipes of her finger. She set the tablet down and smiled. "Today before me," she said, her words blaring from speakers set atop nearby poles, "I see Earth's heroes, assembled to meet the enemy..."

Everything important would be kept from the crews for now. Her speech would be one of niceties and morale boosting, generating pride and prejudice in the troops. It would fall to the flight commanders to tell them what mattered. There were ancient aliens. We're losing the war. If this mission fails, Earth will soon fall. Sorry, everyone, it's a numbers game. But thanks for all your hard work.

Oswald wondered how much was still being kept from him and the other flight commanders. Anahita had sent the rest of them two days ago to initiate movement into their assigned defensive positions. Defensive positions wouldn't win the war though.

Nor would peace talks, despite what Prime Minister Tzun may say. They'd tried that twice, and both times been stabbed in the back.

Oswald's job was to kill Proxies. As many as he could. All of them if necessary. They had attacked. They had broken the treaties. And he didn't care about their mysterious origins or even if they were true *homo sapiens*. He only cared about stopping them.

It would be fascinating to search the ruins on Delta Pavonis V for clues though. Maybe their creators had something to do with transplanting humanity. Maybe there were more humans scattered among the stars.

And if they attacked Earth, he'd have to kill them too.

"Ay-Yon, my ass," Oswald muttered.

Major Hashi McFarran, *Roland*'s auxiliary flight commander, shot him a quizzical glance. Oswald grinned and shook his head.

"There are times when men and women are called on to work great deeds. When they are called on to bare their swords at the encroaching darkness. When they are called on to make great sacrifices for the sake of their family and their people. These are those times..." Anahita continued.

She'd been right—he hated these orders down to his double-helix. Delta Pavonis V might be a place he could have been exploring already if not for the damned Proxies.

Ten years wasted! And only two SDF missions mounted... that Will had admitted to, anyway. How much could they have learned in that time? Maybe nothing, maybe everything. Maybe an invitation to join the aliens who'd created such marvels as the jump beacons. Sending signals instantaneously through space like that would change everything. What else could they discover once they'd solved that mystery? They were questions with no answers since the collective assholes and idiots in charge had squandered so much time. People who couldn't think past the war or their own pockets.

There was an actual alien colony in Delta Pavonis. No hoaxes, no fuzzy pictures of extraterrestrial faces. Men had been there—and been killed by those real alien defenses for their trespassing.

And he was being ordered to do it this time. His first experience with verified aliens was a smash-and-grab robbery. Like children stealing candy from a store and running before the store owners could stop them. Oswald was being ordered to do the one thing he most dreamed of in the way that most horrified him; like finding Mrs. Right and raping her.

"Sir," someone whispered from the ranks behind him. "Lt. Colonel Oswald!"

Oswald snapped from his thoughts and tried to pull the logs of the last few minutes from his mind to see what he'd missed while daydreaming.

Anahita cleared her throat politely into the mic. "Lieutenant Colonel Pierce Oswald, post."

Heat rose on Oswald's face. He snapped to attention with an echoing click of his heels and marched towards the platform. Behind Anahita, three shuttles sat on their launch rails, lowered and ready to take the assembled crews into orbit and away from their homes and families. Hissing jets of steam escaped from pressure valves as launch crews made their final preparations.

Oswald climbed the steps and exchanged crisp salutes with Anahita. They both turned back to face the formation.

"It is my privilege to promote Lieutenant Colonel Pierce Oswald to full Colonel."

Oswald broke his finely tuned military bearing to stare at Anahita. A murmur of laughter rolled through the formation and he remembered himself, snapping his eyes forward again. He could feel the smile playing across his lips.

"Just so everyone knows, we sprung this surprise on him so you wouldn't have to listen to another speech," Anahita said. Another rumble of laughter came from the astronauts below. "His service to the Sol Defense Fleet both in the battle space and in the halls of our institutions has been exceptional. Most people here know of Colonel Oswald's record against the Proximans; few can match his tactical acumen and leadership.

"He is a Rocket of Valor recipient and has been commanding squadrons across the stars. If you're unfamiliar with his spectacular victories in Barnard's Star, you should look them up and study them.

"Normally for such a life event, we inform recipients ahead of time and give them a chance to share their own thoughts. And this will happen on his return. For now, the chain of command wished to give Colonel Oswald this award for his bravery and drive to take the fight to the enemy. Mr. Oswald even turned down a chance to head up a Sol defense squadron because he understood the importance of the upcoming mission."

Another murmur rolled through the crew of *Roland*, but it wasn't laughter.

Oswald fought the urge to shoot Anahita a dirty look. He'd already looked like a cadet by staring at her once. That slip of hers—if it was a slip—was something he'd have to answer for later. Not everyone on *Roland* was as eager to kill Proximans or explore distant worlds. He had a tough crew though; they'd come around.

Oswald suspected the timing of his promotion. He'd earned his RoV over a year ago and the SDF could have promoted him at any time. There had to be some angle Anahita was working. She'd probably try to wrangle him into a mountain of admin duties when he got back to trap him in Sol. Anahita Khadem didn't like losing and this promotion was part of some plan to settle up with him. Oswald was a man of tactics; she was a woman of strategy.

Anahita handed him a thin metal plate with the certificate of promotion, signed by Prime Minister Tzun, set with a pair of holographic colonel bars, and shook his hand. "Congratulations, Colonel."

Applause erupted from the formations below. A few catcalled or hooted loudly. Oswald marched back to his place in front of *Roland*'s crew. As he turned, Gryphon caught his eye. The Australian curled his thumb and forefinger into a tight circle resembling a sphincter and kissed it three times. Oswald answered by scratching the side of his nose with a raised middle finger.

History had proven that promotions didn't increase one's ability and were only occasionally predicated on it. If the Earth was doomed, his promotion wouldn't mean shit except that he'd get an extra level of torture when the Proxies moved in.

Major Baker, flight commander of *Triumph*, flashed Oswald a quick thumbs-up. The Nigerian was so dark and so thin that he almost disappeared when the sun went down. Oswald had heard the man wanted to be an infantryman, but his excellent scores and stature assured his assignment in the fleet.

Anahita's smile panned over all the crews below her like a slow-scan radar dish. "Now I will leave you to your flight commanders, your crew fellows, and to whatever goodwill your God or fortune will grant." She looked at Oswald and saluted.

The three flight commanders returned the salute and did an about-face. The formations stood just far enough apart to prevent cross talk as the flight commanders began their own speeches.

"*Roland*." Oswald took in his crew. Their jaws were set and their eyes hard. They'd all been given leave and a fresh psych eval once on Earth. Beneath the resolute expressions of his veterans, he could sense their fatigue. Some of those steely eyes had bags beneath them and he knew it wasn't all from enjoying their last night on Earth before a deployment.

The campaign in Barnard's Star had been long and dangerous; under normal circumstances they'd have been given at least six months of recovery. Of course, they'd have died with the rest of BARSTARCOM if standard procedures had been followed. Many of his crew felt the loss of the Barnard's Star squadron as much as he did.

"*Roland*, I'm not being dramatic when I tell you we've never been on a mission like this before. And those of you who've served with me for any amount of time know we've been in the shit. What we accomplish on this mission could end the war."

He glanced around the faces before him. The mix of hope and cynicism he saw gave Oswald the impression of looking into a mirror.

"*Roland* has always been the brightest star in the SDF, and this will be our chance to shine brighter still. Our squadron will be going somewhere no one in this crew has ever been. Even salty old Wu." He paused to let the laugh roll through the formation. They needed it.

"As usual, briefings start after departure. Know now though, that this flight package is of the highest clearance level and details will be given on a strict need-to-know basis. That's always the case, of course, but this time, it really is.

"I'm hoping everyone noticed the SDF Ranger platoons formed up behind each crew. That alone should tell you how different this mission is. These Rangers have been training and waiting for a chance to do something besides garrison duty. They're coming with us."

Oswald turned to face McFarran. "Aux, make the crew ready for orbital transfer. *Ad astra*."

"Yes, Colonel," said McFarran, enunciating "colonel" in French, each "L" pronounced in its place.

Oswald left his aux to finish up. On the far side of the tarmac stood a transparent dome, covering a small but lush park. Four people were visible inside, watching him approach.

Two sets of doors formed the entrance to the dome, functioning as a not-quite-sealed airlock to keep the polluted air from spoiling the park. The overwhelming aroma of pine and soil wafted over Oswald as he pulled open the inner door. It washed away the metallic taste from the outside air that had been building up in his mouth.

The ground crew at Xichang knew how to landscape. Red mulch surrounded the verdant greens of the pines and other conifers Oswald couldn't identify. White and purple flowers grew along the edges of smooth stone paths shaped to look like running water.

It was a perk of being flight commander to board the last shuttle. Oswald knew it would take at least five shuttles to get all three crews and their Ranger detachments to orbit. He had time.

There was Misty, her long blond hair a shock in the green of the park. She was wearing the same curve-clinging floral dress she always wore when he was leaving. It was a testament to how fit she had stayed in their twenty years of marriage. He wasn't certain it was the exact same dress, but he left such womanly mysteries to her. She was beautiful.

Misty walked forward and laced her fingers between his. "Hey there, astronaut." Her tone was one of resignation. She lifted the back of Oswald's hand to her cheek and held it there. "Congratulations, Colonel. It's about time. Do I get a new house now?"

His two daughters walked up from behind Misty.

"Congrats, Colonel Daddy!" Mary said, hugging him. "That's so awesome. I'm so proud of you."

"About time you got your act together," said Mara, a grin peeking through her usual disaffected scowl.

Oswald grinned and leaned, kissing each of his precious girls. They were really young ladies now, Mary getting ready to ship off to secondary school and Mara with only another year in primary. He insisted they make it to his liftoffs whenever able; his position in the SDF had mostly been accepted as valid absence excuses by the schools.

"Congratulations, sir," said Brent, holding his hand out to shake Oswald's. He was Mary's long-time boyfriend.

"Thanks, Brent." Oswald took the proffered hand and gave it an excessively hard squeeze. He glanced at Misty and raised a brow. While his position as an officer provided leverage, the fleet didn't pay for transportation. That came out of his pocket. He was hoping Brent had paid his own way.

Misty squeezed his hand and giggled. "Don't be so shallow. SDF paid for the tickets. Maybe because of your promotion."

Oswald smiled. Anahita's largesse was making him nervous. "In that case, it's good to see you, Brent."

Misty slapped him on the shoulder.

"Nobody can take a joke these days," Oswald said. "Always good to see you."

Misty smoothed out Oswald's shirt. "We heard your speech, honey. Is it all really that big?"

Oswald gave a sheepish grin and nodded. "You heard that, huh?"

Mara reached over to a nearby bench and pressed a button on a small speaker. Snippets of conversation and laughter mixed with the scraping of boots on the tarmac and the whine of the launch-pad machinery. She pressed it again and the silence of the domed park returned.

"It was hard to hear just you," Misty said, "but we got most of it."

Oswald held up his hands. "You got me. I know that you know better, but if anyone happened to record anything that was said, please delete it." He stared at Mara.

"What?" Mara said, trying to look vaguely offended, but only looking guilty to Oswald as she typed away on her comm unit. Despite years in space, he knew Mara.

"Anyway, yeah. It's huge. Like out-of-a-dream huge. I want to tell you, tell everyone..."

"But you can't," Misty finished for him.

She gave him that sly, sidelong glance that always left Oswald wondering if he was in for a treat or for trouble. His wife could be as bad as Anahita.

"We're all familiar with operational security," Misty said. "But the SDF isn't the only one who can keep secrets. Big mission, big promotion. Ready for some more big news?"

Oswald looked at his family. Mara was still typing on her comm. Mary was looking up at him, biting her lip. Brent was studying the rich green grass with sudden intensity.

"Not really," he said. "But lay it on me."

Misty turned him to face Brent.

"Uh, Pierce, I mean, sir..." Brent went red-faced and beads of sweat hung on his brow. "Mr. Oswald, I'd like, well, that is... we would..." He coughed and turned to Misty, then Mary.

"Spit it out," said Mary through clenched teeth. She was as red as Brent. "You chickened out the whole time he was home on leave. This is your last chance."

"We'd like to get married," Brent blurted.

Oswald stared at Mary and Brent, his smile frozen. Throbbing pain worked its way upwards from his neck. He saw the anxious look on Mary's face; she wanted his blessings. Oswald could still see the little girl in those eyes. Wetness blurred his vision. He smiled and reached to rub her cheek. "Well, congratulations back at you then."

"Oh, Daddy!" Mary jumped up and down, and wrapped her arms around Oswald.

"I hope you'll wait until I get back. I definitely need to give you away at the ceremony."

Mary glanced at Misty, then at Brent. "Well, we were thinking about not having a ceremony. Just a quick civil union."

"What?" Misty stood rigid and frowned. "You never mentioned that. There will be a wedding. This is a mission, not a deep patrol. We can work out the details while your father is gone."

"We don't want to cause a bunch of hassle for everyone. And that's all so expensive," Mary said. "And we want to get on with the next part of our lives."

"Why the rush?" asked Misty. "Your father looks absolutely dashing in his dress uniform."

"No rush, Mrs. Oswald," stammered Brent. "We just, ah…"

Mara's face lit up in a look of spiteful glee; she pointed her finger at Brent, then at her sister. "You're pregnant!" Mara turned to her mother. "I bet she's pregnant! That's the rush."

"Don't be ridiculous," Misty said, scowling at Mara. "Of course she isn't. Are you, Mary?" Misty put a hand to her mouth when she saw Mary's hateful glare at her sister. Brent looked as though he couldn't decide if he should run or puke. Oswald sympathized.

"I knew it!" cried Mara, her finger pointing at Mary again.

"Get that goddamn finger out of my face!"

"Stop it now!" Misty hissed.

Oswald trudged to the nearby park bench and fell into it. Misty rushed to sit next to him, her heels clacking on the stone path.

She grabbed his hand and rubbed it. "Are you OK?"

Mary started sobbing into her hands. "I'm so sorry, Daddy."

Mara stared at her father, her smirk gone.

Oswald looked up at the red-faced Brent. The boy moved to put his arm around Mary and she hid her face on his chest. He looked at Oswald and anger flashed across his features.

That was good. Brent usually held Oswald as something between a ninja and a superhero, despite the attempts to explain he was only a mathematician in fancy pajamas. But Brent should be angry. He wanted to be part of the family and was growing it already. Two good things in Oswald's book. Yet Mara was up to her old bullshit and Misty was already making demands. But that was in part her being blindsided by the news.

And here was Oswald collapsing like an old man who'd been in the sun too long. It was all too much. Now there was a baby to save from the Proxies. Another little Mary to hold in his hands and burble to. He wondered if the baby would have a chin as pudgy as Mary's had been. She would coo and laugh when he tickled it, and he could do that all day.

He could do it until his next deployment.

Oswald pushed himself to his feet over Misty's objections. Brent looked down as Oswald approached. The boy deserved better, and so did his child. Brent tried to pull back as Oswald embraced him.

"That's a lot of big things today," Oswald said. He kept his arm over his soon-to-be son-in-law's shoulder and motioned Mary over.

She wrapped him in a bear hug. She tried to speak but buried her face in his chest instead. Misty and Mara glared at each other, and he was grateful he wouldn't be in Sol for a while.

"I can understand if you want to get the union taken care of." Oswald squeezed Mary and Brent. "And I know I can be old-fashioned, but there's no shame."

"That shame left the station months ago," Mara said.

Oswald glowered at her until she held her hands up and looked away.

"I want to be there. I want to give my girl away. And I don't care if there's a baby there already or not. But your mom's right. This should be a straightforward mission, not a deployment." Oswald stepped away from Mary and Brent so he could look at them both. "It's up to you guys, but I'd love to be there. Plus, I do look awesome in my dress uniform."

"OK, Daddy," Mary said. She wiped tears from her eyes and looked at Brent. Brent nodded, wiping his own tear away.

Oswald wrapped Mary in a hug and tugged on her hair like he used to when she wore pigtails. The act summoned images of her at six, squinting up at him through the thick glasses she had to wear until old enough for surgical correction. It reminded him of why he had to leave. He was fighting for them. He would kill every damned Proxie if it would save his girls—all his girls.

But he hadn't been able to save one of them. There were no memories of Ululani, only possibilities. She was his daughter who was, but never had been.

"I love you, Colonel Daddy," said Mary, sniffling. The hair tug had become the traditional signal of their final farewell.

"Love you too, baby." He squeezed her tight and rubbed her belly. "Love you too in there." Oswald reached out and pulled Brent into a bear hug. "Don't worry, I won't play with your hair or rub your belly. Welcome aboard, son. You guys be strong. I know you'll do well."

Mary grabbed Brent's hand and pulled him away to stand by a copse of miniature spruce trees.

Mara stepped over and proffered a handful of hair. Oswald could see the wetness in her eyes and his heart ached. She was so strong, so wrapped up in not being him. Yet Mara was here for him. He tugged the hair gently and wrapped her in his arms. She hadn't needed optical correction, but she'd refused to be put down, pushing her forehead against his whenever she was in his arms. It was an early omen of their tempestuous relationship.

"Why you always gotta be starting some shit?" he whispered.

Mara laughed until she sobbed and buried her face in his shoulder. "Just how I fly, Dad."

"Don't I know it," said Oswald, followed by an exaggerated sigh. "Love you."

Mara mumbled something into his shoulder and slowly pulled free to sit on a bench away from everyone else.

Oswald found Misty sitting facing the shuttle pad. He sat next to his wife and pulled her onto his lap. "I'm getting too old for this."

"You've been saying that for twenty years."

"And it's always been true."

They sat staring through the dome at the dance of the loading shuttles. Once the last of the crew had filed through the hatches, ground control lifted the shuttles vertically on their rails. A tremor shook the ground beneath their feet as the boosters ignited. An electric hum filled the air as the magnetic launch system powered up to help catapult the first shuttle out of sight.

Soon all three shuttles were nothing but tiny flares at the top of columns of smoke and fire that reached across the sky. Three more shuttles were pulled from a huge hangar nearby and towed to the launch rails.

It would be time to go soon.

Oswald let out a long breath. "Big day."

Misty laid her head on his shoulder. "I'll say."

"Baby surprised you too?"

"That girl needs a good slapping."

"Which one?"

"Both, honestly. No wedding, indeed."

Oswald chuckled. "Too late now. Should have slapped them more when they were younger. But I'll leave any future slapping to you. I want to leave on good terms in case I get blown up." He grimaced as soon as the last words slipped out.

"Shut up."

"Yeah, sorry." He slid his hand up and down Misty's leg, getting higher each time until she slapped it away.

"No public displays of affection," she said. "Not even for full colonels."

Three new lines of crewmen formed and shuffled to the boarding ladders, looking like waddling blue penguins. When the lines grew short, Misty got up off his lap and held out her hand. "Time to go."

Oswald grabbed it and stood. Misty smoothed and brushed his flight suit before handing him his flight pack.

"These things seem to get smaller every year," she said over his shoulder.

Oswald slapped his belly. "Because this keeps getting bigger."

The SDF respected no rank when it came to mass limitations and delta-v calculations. Flight commanders' bags, and bellies, were held to the same standard as the crew. Personal effects were important to morale on deployment, but if it didn't fit in the bag, or was above mass restrictions, it wasn't going. Falling outside of body mass regs was a sure way to get pulled from astronaut status. Oswald had flown with people who failed on purpose when they couldn't take any more. The Sol Defense Fleet did not reward them for their efforts; malingering during wartime was a possible capital offense.

"Just makes it easier to pack." He pulled her tight and pressed his lips against hers. The smell of flowers filled the air. "I love you."

She rubbed his cheek. "I love you, too. Come back to me, hero. And, Pierce..."

He put a finger to her lips. "Yes, I noticed your hair. It looks great."

Oswald spun and strode from the dome towards the tarmac. The heat and smell of spent rocket fuel assaulted him. He stopped to cough and take a final look at his family. They looked back at him, foreheads and hands pressed against the inside of the dome.

He walked to his shuttle without turning back.

Oswald stepped onto the boarding scale and the steward logged the kilos on his tablet. He snapped Oswald a sharp salute and motioned him up the steps.

Someone tapped Oswald on the shoulder and he turned.

"General," said Oswald.

"Colonel," said Anahita. She handed him a small bag. "Back on the scale. Once you have the new mass logged, steward, please board and give us a moment."

"Yes, ma'am," said the steward, snapping a salute, then climbing into the shuttle. A loud hiss of steam muted all other sounds for a few seconds.

Oswald shook the bag and heard a sloshing from within. He held it close to his nose and sniffed. Even through the acrid pollution and charred tarmac, he recognized the whiff of spirits.

"Delamain?"

"Take it, Pierce. Please. You'll need it."

He fought the urge to push it back at her, but just stared at it.

"What's wrong?"

"Mary's getting married. And she's pregnant."

Anahita looked up at him with sombre eyes. "That's wonderful, Pierce. All the more reason for you to come back. If you weren't in such a rush, we could have a toast."

Guilt washed over him. Anahita's daughter would never be married. Anahita would probably never be a grandma. He looked away. "Thanks, Ana. Look, I'm sorry for Ululani. And for how I acted."

Her smile turned icy. "Earth needs you to pull this off at all costs, Pierce. Come back at the helm, come back in a bag, or don't come back at all."

He nodded and turned to climb the boarding ladder. Once he was at the top he stepped into the shuttle and leaned out. "Can you give Misty and the kids a tour of the MCC? Maybe give them some VIP treatment until the jump? Charge it against my promotion bonus."

"Your bonus isn't that much, but I think I can arrange it. As long as Misty doesn't try scratching my eyes out."

"That was a long time ago," Oswald said as he slammed the hatch shut behind him.

# Chapter 5

THE CABIN SHUDDERED as Earth's atmosphere roared by outside. Oswald gripped his straps with white knuckles, hoping the cognac in his pack wouldn't pop open or somehow get spoiled from the shaking.

Then it was still and quiet as the shuttle entered low Earth orbit, or LEO. A moment later, observation portals opened on either side of the passenger cabin. A sliver of blue filled what was just a few minutes ago the top of the portal. Two soft pops sent the shuttle into a roll, and the blue shine of the Earth filled the cabin by degrees. Oswald hated atmospheric transition; the violence left his joints sore and the noise of it left his ears ringing. But it seemed an appropriate passage between worlds. Between color and darkness. Between air and vacuum. Between life and death.

There would be death before Oswald's squadron reached the jump point. He could feel it.

Space had beauty after its own icy fashion, but not so humanity could experience it firsthand. That beauty had to be filtered through monitors or portals or scopes. Even a sunrise or starry night on Earth was seen through a living atmosphere. None of the spectacular wonders of deep space could match Terra in her azure glory.

Oswald listened to the chatter of the crew behind him, the usual braggadocio of leave exploits and lamentations about being stuffed back in the tin can. There was an endless list of memos, orders, and command messages to review, but he didn't feel like reviewing them. He just wanted to get on *Roland* and get underway.

Then he'd get to tell his crew they were in for a fight right off the dock.

The pictures General Zaphrim had provided of the alien ruins were amazing. They were exactly what Oswald always imagined. He'd spent hours poring over them in the days since the first briefing. It was one reason he had an endless list of things to do now. But the pictures that supposedly showed the UXA, the beacon, were blurry smudges recessed into what looked like biomechanical chapels.

It would be at least two hours until the shuttle docked with *Roland*. His mind was filled with contingencies, and his heart raced as he considered the attack Anahita expected. It was hours away, but it would be big if she was right. The worry was exhausting, but he couldn't help it.

Oswald shut off his tablet and tucked it into his seat's secure pocket. Leaning against the inner layer of the portal, he promptly fell asleep. The announcement over the speakers jerked Oswald awake.

"And just because she's so much prettier on the outside than the inside," the pilot announced, "let's take a quick peek at *Roland*."

Another quick pop of a thruster echoed through the shuttle and the starscape outside Oswald's portal drifted until his ship and its small docking station came into view. The pilot would probably get a reprimand from orbital flight control, but Oswald was thankful.

*Roland* was long and sleek; predatory. Her age was not only apparent in the patched outer frame but in the stylish lines and construction that harkened back to a time when starships were designed to grace recruitment videos. Somewhere in a footlocker he still had an old SDF pamphlet with a ship on the cover that looked almost as cool as *Roland*. Despite being stylish, the girl was tough. She'd survived three battles in her career that her crew had not. The hull showed the scars of combat and micrometeorite strikes, but it was sound.

As the shuttle drifted closer, Oswald could make out the armored hatches that covered the laser arrays, missile bays, and the point defense grid. A long red shark with a hungry cartoon grin wound its way down the side of the ship's silvery skin.

Four wide fins extended from the rear of the frame around the main thruster of the LOX-Augmented Nuclear Thermal Rocket; aka LANTRn. The fins contained *Roland*'s heat exchangers and allowed tail-first planetary landings. The rocket boosters added for the mission, that would get her back into orbit if things got that desperate, gave *Roland* a pregnant look Oswald didn't like. Three landing pods hung from the hull like ugly lampreys.

The high-thrust tug was a framework attached over *Roland*'s nose with four chemical thrusters at the end of long booms, canted so the expelled reaction mass wouldn't hit the fins. It would get the ship through the inner Van Allen belt quickly. Coupled with *Roland*'s magnetic shield, the speed would protect the crew from the belt's radiation. And hopefully give them enough velocity to make it to the jump threshold before the Proximans sent *Roland* falling back down to Earth in a cascade of fiery streaks for all to see.

The impact of the docking maneuver echoed through the shuttle. The airlock hissed for several minutes until a green ring around the hatch activated, confirming a positive seal with the external dock around *Roland*. The crew unbuckled and retrieved their flight bags with slow, easy movements. Even veteran crews had to acclimate to free fall each time they came back up from Earthside.

Oswald collected his bag, glad it was dry and didn't smell of booze, and exited after the rest of his crew. As he approached the boarding tube, he thumbed the comm next to the airlock.

"Thanks for the view, pilot. If they give you any grief, just tell them I ordered you to."

"Good hunting, Colonel," the pilot said.

The boarding tube ran straight from the shuttle, through the tiny docking ring, and to the ship. The duty officer saluted as Oswald entered *Roland*'s airlock.

"Flight Commander is on board," the duty officer said into his headpiece. Then he turned to Oswald. "Colonel, all hands are accounted for."

"Very well. Inform the aux that I'll be at my station after I unpack." He patted the tiny bag under his arm and grinned. "Shouldn't be long."

"Flight Commander is aboard," announced McFarran over the ship's internal speakers and crew tablets.

Oswald floated to the central shaft and pulled himself coneward to the berthing compartment. A cluster of engineers was floating and chatting at the hatch, blocking his way.

One of the younger technicians saw Oswald. "Make a hole for the FC."

Oswald drifted towards the beehive, a collection of interlocking, hexagonal sleeping tubes, with thick zippered curtains at each end. There was barely enough room for a person to change clothes in zero-g with practice, or view a holo or tablet; most people changed outside their tubes.

Not even the flight commander had his own quarters on a starship. Even his stateroom was too small for a rack. He slid his pack into the small locker built beneath the pillow cushion. The Delamain sloshed in its bottle and Oswald felt a pang of guilt; the crew wasn't allowed alcohol. He included. The guilt didn't last long; he knew others had sneaked some on too.

The sleep tubes of the beehive were perpendicular to the direction of thrust from *Roland*'s LANTRn. Sleep was difficult in zero-g, even with the tubes' built-in subsonic somnolence generators. The pseudo-gravity of thrust afforded the human body a more restful sleep. Unfortunately, the LANTRn was only lit for any length of time during departures, arrivals, or combat; circumstances when the crew needed to be at their duty stations.

Oswald changed into his loose-fitting, one-piece flight suit. He then replaced his shoes with tackysocks, thick socks with grip-enhancing soles that helped movement in microgravity. Their odor-wicking and cushioning properties also reduced injury from accidental face kicks and the not-insignificant problem of foot odor.

When finished, Oswald pushed further conewards to the hatch of the primary flight control pod. All normally manned compartments, including the beehive, were inside the ship's metal-shielded core. He stopped himself by grabbing the handle of the hatch and pulled in headfirst.

"Flight Commander present," someone announced.

There was no tradition in the fleet to go to attention in zero-g; it was an awkward and pointless gesture.

Oswald strapped into his acceleration couch and activated the SDOS, Software Defined Operating Station, on the smart terminal. *Roland*'s status screen and the duty roster automatically populated the display as per Oswald's preferences. He then inspected which screens each duty station had loaded, making sure all scheduled flight positions were manned.

A quick review of the navigation plot showed MCC's flight profile was loaded. All departments except one reported ready, but that didn't always mean they were. Some department heads reported prematurely so as not look like slackers, and sometimes maintenance issues cropped up and the status report didn't get updated.

It was Tactical that didn't show ready. No surprise there.

Oswald slipped on his headset and connected to the ship's intercom. "*Roland*, I want all departments ready for main burn within the hour." With a swipe of a hand across his terminal, all the other department-ready indicators went from green to red. Time to go see what the tactical officer was up to this time.

Oswald slipped into the tactical flight pod. A junior lieutenant was about to announce the flight commander, but Oswald waved him off and floated just inside the hatch, listening.

"Of course not, Josh," said Lt. Major Roman Karpov into the HAM radio mic. The man's sandy-brown hair floated like a crown around his head at the regulation maximum five centimeters, maybe a bit longer. He was beaming as he spoke. "SDF edited out some of the real juicy shit. Loose lips sink ships and all that.

"Go ahead, YMC32R." Karpov inclined his head as he listened to someone speak in the headset. "I don't think SDFCC cares much about profanity, but if you can get them to arrest me, I'd be much obliged." He looked at Oswald and popped a salute. "Though I don't think my skipper would be happy. I'm his good luck charm."

Oswald pulled along the wall so he could see the display on Karpov's terminal. Everything showed green.

"Well, Juliana, I have a pretty tight schedule between book tours and saving Earth and all that," Karpov said, winking at Oswald. A moment later a chirp came from Karpov's pocket. He pulled out his personal comm, eyed a picture on the screen, and raised his brows. "Perhaps I can make some time—if this is actually you. Looks like this ragchew is over; flight commander's giving me the stink-eye.

"Oh, hey YMC32R. Yeah, that's probably frowned on too. You can add that to your complaint. Be sure to clench real hard when you blow it out your ass." Karpov laughed into the mic. "ATC6FF signing off." He was still laughing as he hung the mic on its hook.

Oswald frowned. The junior officers were still looking at their terminals, but had grown silent. "Why are you talking on an open channel?"

"I know my COMSEC, Colonel. I'm not giving anything away. I never tell them where I'm at."

"They have to know you're up here to even set up their rigs for the signal."

Karpov shook his head. "I know better than that. It's a tight-beam laser-net through SDF command. These aren't direct RF exchanges. They're being passed through HQ."

"That can still be traced and tracked." Oswald pointed to the personal comm floating near Karpov's head. "Especially that. Are you trying to get another Lucky Star? You realize command estimates at least two Proxie micro-sats are in orbit?"

Karpov's face clouded over. He rubbed the golden star patch with two silver diamonds on his left breast. "Just following orders, sir."

"Not mine."

"Nope." Karpov grinned and shrugged. "The public eats this shit up. Talk to Colonel Skevenov at command. She's the one that sets up these PR gigs."

"Can't hurt the book sales."

"Not a bit, FC."

"No more. And in the future, you clear these little chats with me when we're on mission. Regardless of what HQ says."

"Sure thing, sir."

Oswald motioned to Karpov's screen with a toe. "Why didn't you update your department's ready status?"

"You just clear them out anyway and make us start over." Karpov opened up the tactical-status form and hit send. "Should show green now."

Oswald's nostrils flared. It was a tell he hadn't learned to control even after all these years. He knew when he did it, could see the motion in his peripheral vision, could feel the tension in his face. Roman Karpov's celebrity as being the only living person to receive three Lucky Stars, awarded to survivors of destroyed starships, made him a fleet poster boy. More than a few in the upper chain of command favored the man and that afforded him a level of protection that even his flight commander had to consider.

But more than that, Karpov was a hell of a tactical officer. It was hard for Oswald to hear Karpov's sharp, almost dismissive tone. But he'd worked with the tactical officer long enough to know that it was simply his manner. Karpov didn't mean to sound disrespectful; he was just unapologetically blunt and occasionally inappropriately jocular. And because of that, the man probably wasn't destined to rise above Lt. Major, despite being favored. If Karpov's board showed green, Oswald knew it was green. The trick to dealing with the man was trying not to take things personally.

"Very well, Lt. Major." Oswald reached down and reset the status display. All the green boxes were now red. "But a little double-checking never hurt anyone."

"Roger that, FC." Karpov smiled up at Oswald. Their eyes locked for a second before Oswald left the compartment and drifted into the main passage.

The sounds of crew chatter, actuating hatches, and the impact of tools filled *Roland*'s passages and compartments. Oswald shared their eagerness and apprehension; he hoped it wasn't as plain on his face as it was on theirs. The flight commander wasn't supposed to sweat.

He grabbed a nearby conduit and pulled tailward. The fire-retardant coating was smooth from the countless hands that grasped it tour after tour for support as they moved around the ship.

"Make a hole," a young Hispanic lieutenant yelled as Oswald approached a vacuum bulkhead. The three-person maintenance crew blocking the path pulled their test sets aside.

Two more levels down, Oswald caught himself at the cargo compartment that had been converted to berthing for the Ranger detachment. He tried to peek in unnoticed, but as soon as his head was halfway visible one of the Rangers called, "Attention!"

Before Oswald could stop them, the Rangers were all standing rigid, fingers or toes unobtrusively hooked around whatever protrusion was available. Apparently, the Rangers still made the effort to stand at attention in zero-g. They were not all aligned in the same direction, looking like a snapshot of a handful of toy soldiers tossed in the air. Oswald scanned the squad for Colonel Wright. He couldn't see the colonel among the gray uniforms. The highest-ranking soldier he found was Major Luskin, a ruddy-faced young man with a galaxy of freckles spattered across his bald pate.

"Major Luskin," Oswald said. "Aren't you supposed to be leading the squad on *Triumph*? Where's Colonel Wright?" He almost gave the order to release the troops from attention, but Oswald was sensing the start of a major screw-up.

"Yes, sir," Luskin said. "Well, I'm supposed to be here now." The man's head flushed. "Colonel Wright changed our assignments right before boarding the shuttle. He found the description of the soldier berths on *Triumph* more amenable."

SDF engineers had attached something between acceleration couches and sleeping nets to the walls of this compartment. New polysteel-carbon plating covered the tailward surface to provide the troops extra radiation shielding from the nuclear thruster. It wouldn't be suitable for long-term occupation, but that wasn't the plan. They'd either all die, or they'd be to Delta Pavonis and back in a few months.

"The colonel realizes *Roland* is the command ship?" Oswald asked, still keeping the soldiers in their ridiculous stance of attention. This was why astronauts didn't do it.

"Yes, Colonel."

"Could you perhaps shed some light on why you and Colonel Wright didn't deign to mention this little detail to the squadron commander, namely me?"

Luskin stared straight ahead. The major's position left him looking as if he were closely inspecting the ear canal of the upside-down corporal directly in front of him.

"Colonel Wright decided the change in the order of battle was immaterial since each Ranger squad has the exact same load-out, Flight Commander Oswald."

Heat raced up Oswald's neck. He hoped it wasn't a case of a senior colonel acting out just because he could. "Does Colonel Wright have the expectation that I'm going to alter orbital movements so he can jump from ship to ship on his whimsy?"

"The only expectation Colonel Wright has expressed is that this platoon performs its missions, Flight Commander Oswald."

It was a good answer. The major spoke with military bearing and just a hint of genuine contrition. "Very well, Major. I need you and Colonel Wright to come to the understanding that I'm the commander of this squadron and this mission. You will log every duty rotation, medical change, equipment maintenance work, and list the mass and timestamp of every turd your squad dumps into my starship."

Luskin's jaw clenched when one of the Rangers in the back snorted trying to stifle a laugh. "Yes, Colonel."

"We'll be setting up an operations net for departure. Be on it. If you have any needs, contact the duty officer. Please enjoy your stay on *Roland*." Oswald pulled himself back into the main passage. Two electricians floated over an open test panel in the bulkhead, having obviously stopped to listen to Oswald dress down the ground pounders. They nodded somberly at him.

He waved them back to work. "Stop stargazing, *Roland*. Especially in front of the guests."

The technicians grinned and turned back to their work as Oswald made his way back to the flight control pod. He spent the next hour guessing what Anahita would do with his crew. Most battles in space happened in planetary systems, and SOLCOM had measurements of gravitational forces, debris, magnetic fields, RF sources, and every other known navigational concern mapped to the micron. They continually scanned and updated the information for every planet, asteroid, Lagrange point, and jump threshold in Sol.

That level of detail was only available with a system-wide array of sensors Oswald had never enjoyed. No SDF commander outside of Sol had the infrastructure to support that kind of sensor net. Anahita had it. But Oswald still hated someone else telling his ship what to do. At least not on the tactical level. He trusted her skill without question, though. Earth orbit was her house and she knew her business.

She would have made an excellent flight commander. They'd tried to get the same assignment out of the academy. Oswald could still remember how stunned he was when she told him she was transferring from orbital operations to telemetry and guidance. Part of him still hated her for abandoning him, especially since she had been the one so excited to jump into the war. Anahita had left him alone for no apparent reason and without explanation. Now he knew. She hadn't explained it, but there had been a good reason.

Ululani.

He still struggled with being introduced to and then losing the daughter he'd never known, would never know. The woman he'd loved so long ago had given up her dreams for her daughter. And had tried to protect him then too. If he'd known, he would have followed her. And Anahita knew it. He loved her all over again for what she'd given him. And he hated her all the more for what she'd hidden away. He'd have traded a beautiful daughter for this war any day. But then his own daughters would never have been. No thick glasses. No pigtails to tug. It was too much. He had more important things to do than chase his tail over what-ifs.

Communications and Data, abbreviated C'nD and pronounced as "Cindy," blinked green on his display.

He keyed his headset. "Think it's about time, Aux?"

"Yes, I do, Lt. Colonel." McFarran's chuckle was as heavily accented French as his words. "Pardon me, Colonel."

"Please establish operations net one, Aux."

"Yes, Colonel."

McFarran's voice came over the ship's internal speakers and comms channels. "All department heads connect to operations net channel alpha."

He repeated the message two more times. Oswald heard five connection tones before the aux had finished his announcement. People were ready to go.

All ship, department, and crew indicators were still green.

"Colonel, operations net number one-alpha, NBR-57 *Roland*, has been established. Time has been noted and logged."

"Very good, Aux," Oswald said. "The MCC hasn't called for maneuvers yet, but it should be any time. All departments declare status. Life support?"

"Go."

"Engineering?"

"Go."

"Tactical?"

"Go for flight."

"Comms and Data?"

"Cindy, Go."

"Astrogation?"

"Good to go."

"Rangers?"

"Roger that, Colonel."

"Flight?"

"We are go, sir!"

"Command?"

"Command is go, Colonel."

"Flight Commander shows good for burn," Oswald said. "MCC, this is *Roland*. We are ready for orbital operations. Please relay status, MCC."

After a pause, Anahita answered, "*Roland*, this is MCC. All telemetry is up and up. We are on standby. *Triumph* is having difficulty with the Rangers' payload. Apparently someone decided to move stuff around without consulting the load engineer. They're re-balancing. I've logged *Roland* as departure-ready."

It sounded as if it was a good thing Colonel Wright was Major Baker's problem. Oswald wondered if Wright's superior rank over Baker was the real reason behind his decision to move to *Triumph*. If it was, Wright was going to be disappointed; Baker didn't put up with foolishness on his ship from anyone. Oswald appreciated that about the man.

But ultimately, no matter where Wright was causing trouble, he was Oswald's problem. He considered calling out Luskin over the net to drive home the point that this was why the ground pounders, the gropos, were not to play with the ship. But he decided against it. It wasn't the major's fault his CO was a dumbass. What military person hadn't had an inferior-superior experience at least once in their career? There were probably some on *Roland* that felt the same way about Oswald.

*Roland* was on standby for two more hours. They were approaching the limit of their departure window.

"Hey, Luskin," Karpov said. "Your boss must have done a real screw job over there. You apes keep your hands away from all the shiny buttons, hear?"

"That's enough, Lt. Major," McFarran said. "This is an official—"

"I know," Karpov said, his voice dismissive. "I just—"

Oswald muted everyone else's mic. "Lt. Major Karpov, you will not interrupt the Auxiliary Flight Commander again. Understood?"

"Yes, sir."

"You will also keep in mind that Major Luskin is a major. You will address him as befits his rank and will show him courtesy that *I* deem appropriate. Also understood?"

"Got it, FC."

A frowning face emote popped up in Oswald's text message screen from Karpov. He ignored it and released everyone's mic.

*Triumph* radioed ready for burn.

"About damned time," Karpov said.

Oswald pulled up the vector plot. The plan was for his squadron to make burns as if they were getting into the Hohmann transfer orbit to Titan. Three unmanned cargo freighters had been sent ahead in the same transfer orbit to make it look like they were a standard in-system convoy and *Roland*'s squadron their escort. It might fool someone. He was doubtful, but it depended on how smart the Proximan observers were. "No plan survives contact with the enemy," was as true an adage as ever, even before it was coined.

"Command, Astro," Lt. Major Breen said over the net.

"Go, Astro," Oswald said.

"Sir, I've been running this jump tunnel plot—"

"Lt. Major!" McFarran said. "You were to have that jump plotted hours ago."

"Yes, sir," Breen stammered. "We're good. We've run the checksum with the MCC several times. It's just that this one isn't in *Roland*'s jump history. I've run it forward and back to account for celestial drift even. The coordinates aren't even in the latest fleet jump-nav update. What gives, FC?"

Oswald flashed a grim smile. "It's a mystery, Breen. One of those need-to-know mysteries. I will say there's a reason it's not in any of the databases, that you'll find out why, and that you'll be amazed when we get there."

"So you weren't kidding," Breen said.

"Not in the least."

Ten minutes later the ship status displays flashed yellow to indicate the MCC was issuing remote commands to *Roland*.

"MCC to *Roland*," Anahita said over the net. "Make ready for departure burn in one minute. Still no sign of enemy presence."

"Roger that, MCC," Oswald said. "Aux, log the T3 report for mission start."

"Time, Terrain, and Trajectory report logged, Colonel."

"Flight, Engineering. LANTRn is lit."

Oswald felt the push and saw the gimbaled acceleration stations in the flight pod rotate as one to put the crew on their backs in relation to the direction of thrust. It was more than the *Roland*'s usual 0.5 gravities at combat burn. According to the navigation display, the tug was bringing them up to 1.5 g and he could feel it pressing on his chest.

The thrust cut out several minutes later. They were now at the upper limit of low Earth orbit. *Roland*'s radiation shield coils powered up to wrap the starship in a powerful magnetic field. They'd be passing through the dangerous radiation of the inner Van Allen belt immediately above them.

"Hazard condition. Hazard condition. By duty section, all hands report to duty stations and armor up," Oswald said. The magnetic field and *Roland*'s own internal shielding were highly effective, but there was no reason to take chances. Especially with expected enemy contact.

He and half of the crew with him in the flight compartment reached behind their acceleration couches and withdrew the sections of their vacc-armor.

They were not the soft suits used for EVA, nor were they the powered armor of modern infantry. Starship vacc-armor was heavy and thick, designed to protect the crew during the hazards of combat and space. A suit wouldn't stop a direct hit from a starship's weaponry, but it could protect from secondary shrapnel, thermal flashes, and catastrophic atmospheric evacuation. Oswald could attest to that.

He slid into the legs, then clamped the torso and arms, and finally latched the helmet. Colonel stars had been painted on the suit's thick shoulder pads and the stencil of his name retouched.

Once he'd strapped into his couch, the other half of the crew did the same. Utter silence came with the donning of the helmet. Oswald took a moment to enjoy the peace until someone imparted information to the net.

"Now we sit back like monkeys in a missile," Karpov said.

"Roger that, Tactical," Oswald said.

The second orbital burn kicked them into the Van Allen belt, setting off external radiation alarms. The lack of personal dosimeter alarm warnings indicated the shielding was doing its job. But Oswald was glad to leave the inner belt behind. Radiation baths creeped him out.

The MCC triggered two more half-orbit burns that pushed the squadron out past geosynchronous orbit. The tugs detached from the ships and used their remaining fuel for a retrograde burn back down to a lower recovery altitude.

The jump threshold was only two hours away. Oswald's squadron was now in the protection envelope of three orbital defense platforms. Hopefully, the Proximans hadn't noticed the extra shipments of ordnance recently sent to them.

"If they're coming, it should be any time now, Colonel," McFarran said.

Oswald nodded, a pointless gesture in his helmet. He was watching the composite tactical feed from the Mission Control Center on his helmet's visor when three pulses flashed from positions around Earth.

"Flight, Cindy. Three jump comms pulses!"

"Defense condition one!" McFarran called over the net. "Defense condition one!"

"Initiated," Karpov answered immediately.

Oswald opened *Roland's* tactical status screen and watched the main laser turrets deploy and blink green, the words "Online" appearing next to them. The missiles each showed linked and ready for targeting input.

Two seconds later the MCC issued the same order.

Oswald smiled. Two seconds didn't really matter in a battle that was still an hour away, but it felt good to beat the MCC to the punch. It reaffirmed to him that it was the fighting crew that responded first and best. Even if only by two seconds.

Incoming jump signature icons filled the screen directly in *Roland's* path.

"Right where we expected, Colonel," McFarran said. "Someday we'll be able to enter a system with that accuracy."

"Someday." Oswald zoomed the tactical display over the area of incoming jump indicators. The display updated, paused, and updated with the final number.

"We're fucked," Karpov said.

It read: *New Incoming Jump Tunnels: 23*

The mission had just failed. There'd never been a jump-capable squadron that large ever reported, SDF or Proximan. It meant they were desperate to stop Oswald or that they could now afford to assemble such strike forces whenever they needed.

It was no good for *Roland* either way.

Fucked indeed.

# Chapter 6

OSWALD FLOATED ON THE edge of what he'd come to think of as his tactical fugue state. Voices were vague murmurings until important keywords caught his attention. His fingers danced across display screens, taking in everything and nothing. Vectors and delta-v expenditures coalesced, solved, and then shifted into command decisions, like clouds on a windy day. Those who didn't know how Oswald processed the ballet of war assumed he hadn't heard if he didn't immediately reply in the rapid-fire parlance of military battle-tongue. Those who knew better, waited.

"Command, Tactical. *Roland* pegs our new friends as Proximan Type-12 fast assault starships. MCC concurs."

"Roger that, Tactical," Oswald said. "They'll try to rush us before we jump, and they dropped in far enough away to give themselves time to recover."

"I'm always impressed with the accuracy of their jump insertions, Colonel."

"We'll get there someday, Aux."

"Command, Tactical," Karpov said.

"Go, Tactical."

"Twenty-three? That means we're about to have hundreds of missiles and billions of pieces of shrapnel up here. Not sure all the MCCs on Earth can track that."

Oswald could hear the nerves in Karpov's voice. It wasn't often the tactical officer's tone held anything besides sarcasm or pointed indifference. However else Oswald felt about Karpov, the man was

*Roland*'s bellwether. If the man who had survived three destroyed ships got concerned, everyone got concerned.

It was too early to give up; the numbers hadn't resolved.

But twenty-three?

There might not even be twenty-three starships in SOLCOM. There were only nine, including the other two escort squadrons, in the area to protect *Roland*. They'd need to rely on the orbital defenses. Statistics weren't Oswald's specialty, but the odds didn't seem all that great.

"This orbit's going to be messy for the foreseeable future." Oswald tried a casual laugh that he hoped didn't sound forced. "But the wheels are in motion. I suspect as soon as target vector envelopes are plotted, Ana— General Khadem will have everyone expend their ordnance ASAP."

He also suspected his squadron was not going to make it to the jump threshold intact. As if to make the point, the tactical display bloomed with red RDV indicators, rapid delta-v. At this range they'd be missiles and drones; the railguns and point defense grids would come later.

The lines stretched out in crimson webs from the Proximan force, the SDF defense posts, the Earth guard escort squadrons, and the missiles tucked in among Oswald's squadron.

Oswald's eyes glazed over as his mind processed the data on a level something below consciousness. Oswald adjusted delta-v and trajectory values, the slight motions of his fingertips in the gloves translated to the display on his visor. *Roland*'s projection track snaked around as the navigation computer recalculated each option.

The number of incoming RDVs from the Proximan force was too low. They were holding back to see which way *Roland*'s squadron would vector. There was no way to avoid the enemy attack envelope; they were too well positioned and there were too many of them.

But they might be able to spread out the attack, maybe only get hit by twenty missiles instead of fifty.

The display flashed yellow on Oswald's visor as MCC took remote control of *Roland*. He could feel the LANTRn pushing and watched her orbital vector shift. They'd be thrusting the entire way to the jump threshold.

Panning the display out, Oswald could see the projected paths of the rest of the squadrons. Anahita was pushing the two escort groups between *Roland* and the Proximan attack force.

As the navigation tracks played out, it became obvious the enemy was after *Roland*'s squadron. Two more waves of RDVs burst from the closing ships as final targeting envelopes solidified.

"Command, Tactical," Karpov said, his voice calmer. "MCC's loading up interceptors into the missile bays. And... they're away."

RDV tracks expanded from *Roland*, *Charger*, and *Triumph* to join the other crimson fingers of war on the tactical display.

"And now here are today's contestants on the Waiting Game!" Karpov sang over the net. He then launched into the theme song of the popular game show *Dikki's Dozenz*. It was decidedly not about waiting, but it was a catchy tune.

"Colonel, might I say the only thing more deplorable than waiting as a hapless passenger on my own ship," McFarren said, adding a loud sniff, "is having to do so while being subjected to a bad song sung badly."

"Don't worry about my feelings, Aux," Karpov said. "I'll cry later in my tube. Time to first-wave intercept is thirty-two minutes."

So they waited, watching numbers and icons race towards each other across the display. There was nothing to say, nothing to do, until the outcome of the first wave was determined.

Oswald spent the time analyzing the Proximans' movements. Their tactics were straightforward enough. They were using the most consistently successful tactics in history: numbers superiority and overwhelming firepower.

One of the first things a fleet cadet learned was that orbital combat is nothing like the adventure vids. There was nowhere to hide a thermal signature in space. Weapons were aimed and fired not by steely-eyed pilots but by powerful targeting computers. A starship couldn't evade a laser. As far as combat went, space warfare was pretty dull.

The real fight started well before commanders dramatically yelled "Fire!" Ships and drones maneuvered for the best attack vectors, and electronic countermeasures systems fought each other with range gate stealers, apparent-vector scramblers, and decoy signal generators. It was all about returning fire with enough accuracy and volume to make sure the enemy died too.

The calm Oswald exuded was a combination of experience and a grim, stoic acceptance that it was out of his hands now. Especially with Anahita's "crew" flying *Roland*. All the decisions—and mistakes—had already been made. They were now passengers on a great space coaster with little ability to alter their fates. It was quite possible to make no mistakes and still lose a fight.

Despite Oswald's external calm, the familiar aroma of his own terror filled his nostrils. It emanated from his skin, the breath of his mouth. He stank of it even after twenty years of experience. His was a subtle yet pervasive terror that often left him trembling when he woke from his night terrors. Even when he was safe on Earth.

Karpov spoke to the net. "Command, Tactical. One minute until first intercept."

"Squadron, make ready decoys," McFarran said. "Tactical, launch them in the interference window."

"Paper planes ready."

The lines of RDVs intersected, their icons replaced with tiny starbursts or question marks to show detonations and unknown changes in status. Interceptor warheads exploded, spraying kinetic kill clouds of spinning tungsten rods into the flight paths of incoming missiles.

Laser-burst warheads flared and sliced into enemy drones, igniting fuel and coolant. EMP generators fried guidance controls, targeting sensors, and main flight computers.

The space around the detonations blurred as *Roland*'s computers and sensors rebuilt the picture of the battle.

"Paper planes away," Karpov said.

Three modules fired away from *Roland* in a random scatter. They quickly reached their programmed distance and deployed large reflective sails. The sails, combined with spoofing transmitters and thermal-signature generators, would hopefully draw off some incoming missiles when they emerged from the interference and reacquired their targets.

As the tactical display updated, *Roland*, *Charger*, and *Triumph* were surrounded by their decoys. So were the Proximan craft. Almost one hundred ships now faced the SDF force on the display.

Within a minute, the MCC's Q-puters and large, local sensor-net erased all of the Proximan decoys except three.

"Incoming MCC instructions, Colonel," McFarran said, as the display flashed yellow.

More RDVs appeared as the two forces fired interceptors at the surviving missiles. *Roland* fired six more interceptors at MCC's command.

Oswald's heart raced while he watched the surviving Proximan missiles rip into the SDF escort formations. The display lit up with new tracks as their laser arrays switched to point-defense mode. Point defense was a relative term when incoming targets could be engaged at thousands of kilometers.

The tactical display blurred out again and when it resolved, every SDF starship in the defense squadrons showed red. Their velocity tracks were splitting apart and tumbling.

All dead.

The net was silent, as if someone had dropped the connection.

"Shit," Karpov whispered. "Just HVCs..."

"HVCs?" Luskin asked.

Oswald cleared his throat. "High velocity caskets."

If Anahita's plan for him had stuck, Oswald would have been leading one of those squadrons. He'd be riding an HVC right now.

The spike of paralyzing terror that froze his breathing was so overwhelming, Oswald couldn't process it. It left him numb, too numb to release the scream building in his chest as dozens of missiles continued rushing at *Roland*, closing in like red claws on the display. *Triumph* and *Charger* were also marked for death by the tactical display. With fingers of lead, Oswald activated the fear repressors in the crew's suits. The pinch of his injector barely registered.

The MCC fired another spread of interceptors and EMP warheads from Oswald's squadron. They hadn't even left the Earth system and *Roland* was down to fifty percent of her defensive ordnance.

There would be no reloads in Delta Pavonis.

The screen flashed yellow again and Oswald felt *Roland* pivot. His mind was clearing, growing calm once more. With quick twists of his armored glove, he zoomed in to see what Anahita had done with his ship. Then he noticed the changing flight tracks of the other two ships in the squadron.

"Colonel," McFarran said on the commander channel, "the MCC is using *Triumph* and *Charger* as a screen."

"Abort that maneuver, MCC!" Oswald's voice trembled with rage. "Anahita! Anahita! Don't throw them away. Give us a chance, dammit. Give me control of my squadron!"

There was no reply.

Now the first wave of SDF missiles flew into the Proximan formation. The enemy ships were flying close enough to support each other with point defense fire. Anahita had sent a sizable fleet of missiles their way though, and when the display resolved again, ten Proximan starships had been destroyed or crippled.

Thirteen were still closing the distance. And *Triumph* and *Charger* were now directly between *Roland* and the enemy squadron.

The next wave of Earth RDVs burst into deadly clusters of shrapnel. Another Proximan broke apart.

Three EMP generator warheads flared next to *Triumph*. Her telemetry indicator icon went from a green *Active* to a yellow *Connection Lost*. Oswald knew the ship's brains had been fried. The SDF might be able to recover her in a few years—depending on where inertia took her.

At least he wouldn't have to worry about Colonel Wright or his gear anymore.

"*Charger* is engaging with her laser array," Karpov said.

"Cindy, put the big-eye on *Charger*." Oswald was glad to see they at least still had control of the main telescope.

Oswald switched his displays to show a grainy view of *Charger*. The system digitizer swept across the image three times to resolve the ship's sleek lines in fine detail.

Plumes of plasma erupted along the ship's armored nose as enemy lasers, invisible to the eye, reached out to cut *Charger* to shreds. The sparkling death dancing across her plating was almost beautiful. An important rule of direct-energy weapons: if you can hit them, they can hit you.

Oswald hesitated for a second, then thumbed the squadron commander channel.

"*Charger* actual, this is *Roland* actual."

"Go ahead, Oswald."

"It wasn't me. It wasn't me, Paul. She won't give me control!"

"No worries, mate." Paul Gryphon spoke as if through gritted teeth. "And I know it. We should both be dead already."

"They should have given us control."

"Can't cash shoulds around here, mate. Look, just make sure my dolls know I went out fighting. Got to go, Pierce. Service."

"Service." Oswald dropped the connection and returned his attention to the spectacle of *Charger*'s death. "Thermal and spectral overlay."

The raw video of *Charger* became a combination of reds, oranges, and yellows. A constant barrage of white streaks struck the ship, leaving shining spots across the hull. One of the Rangers' landers exploded away from its cradle.

*Charger*'s thermal signature slowly shifted to a dangerous orange as the ship struggled to dissipate the heat buildup of the battle. They'd been burning the LANTRn, firing missiles and lasers, and were now being lanced with high-power directed-energy weapons. And that didn't include the heat generated by non-combat systems like life support and maintenance. Space didn't absorb radiant heat well.

The radiator panels were fully extended now, searing white on the scope. It was a well-known sign that the ship was at its thermal redline.

"She's hitting thermal threshold," Karpov said. His voice had grown tense, almost wavering.

The enemy lasers were now cutting long gashes across *Charger*'s frame, releasing ghostly clouds of superheated gas and plasma into space. Her life's blood spilled red from mortal wounds in the thermal display.

She kept firing though, but not at the incoming enemy starships. Anahita was using *Charger* to take out Proximan missiles—the ones targeting *Roland*. She wasn't letting Gryphon defend himself. As Oswald had done to *Bonwei* and Ululani.

A detonating Proximan warhead was translated into a bright yellow flower by the big-eye's spectral imager. Moments later, a kinetic kill cloud of shrapnel ripped across the *Charger's* hull and shredded her radiator panels.

No one could hear Oswald slamming his fist on the shell of his acceleration couch. An angry red stain of deadly heat spread through *Charger's* image like an infection.

"Goddammit, Anahita! Order *Charger* to stand down!"

There was no reply from the MCC. He understood there could be no answer, understood the sacrifice Anahita was making. And he hated it.

Oswald stared as the flashes on the hull became plumes of fire and the plumes of fire became silent screams.

One of the rocket boosters split apart and exploded, tearing *Charger* open, sending two clouds of debris twirling away in opposite directions.

Oswald shut off the big-eye. The operations net was silent. Anahita should have had them stand down. The Proximans might have left *Charger* alone if she'd stopped firing at them. Anahita gave them no choice. Anahita had sacrificed *Triumph* and *Charger* to save *Roland*. To save him. And he knew she'd had no choice; it was the only way to save the mission.

Oswald's eyes went wide as he felt a sudden push of acceleration. Their LANTRn was already firing at its full 0.5 g. The only thing he could think of that would push them like that was some kind of explosion.

Like *Charger*.

"Engineering, Flight. What the hell?"

"MCC fired off the boosters, Colonel," McFarran said. "They must be trying to get us to the jump threshold."

"And out of the kill cloud coming our way," Karpov said.

The push of acceleration was smooth and constant, easing Oswald's mind that it was the ship's booster and not some uncontrolled explosion.

"Point defense grid active."

Time slowed as Oswald's mind grappled with the countless new threat tracks, target prioritization, velocity envelopes, and Proximan positioning. Anahita was still in control, so there was no real use in concerning himself with such things, except to satisfy a morbid, intellectual curiosity. And the injection hadn't worn off either.

*Roland*'s weapons flashed red, yellow, and green on the display as they fired and recharged. The incoming warheads were disappearing, but there were still so many.

The green jump line lay before them, creeping closer. The nearest flight of enemy missiles sped towards *Roland*'s flank. It would be close.

The tactical display highlighted two damaged Proximan attackers as they pivoted to accelerate towards the jump line, limping away from the battle. Their thrust output fluctuated, an obvious sign of damage.

Oswald highlighted them on his visor. "Tactical, I want a targeting profile on these two."

"Roger that, FC. I think I can get them with one T-REX," Karpov said. The T-REX, or Thermonuclear Rod-Expended X-Ray, used a nuclear submunition to pump massive amounts of power through disposable lasing rods. It generated multiple hard x-ray beams, either at one target or many.

"Perfect. We've spent enough munitions already," Oswald said. A T-REX was just the thing for some chicken-shit Proxie bastards.

"They are retreating, Colonel," McFarran said. "They are no longer a threat. They are no longer attacking."

"Not for now," Karpov said. "They'll be back in the fight in no time. Guaranteed."

"What would we like them to do if we were in that situation, Colonel?"

"We—" Karpov started.

"I said 'colonel'!"

"I would like them to burn in hell, Aux." Oswald's voice was cold. "But if you want more opinions, maybe we should ask Gryphon. Or Baker. See what they say."

"Colonel..." McFarrran paused. "I'm simply pointing out we might need that ordnance."

"Yeah," Karpov said. "We need it to teach them not to fuck with us, Aux."

"We haven't authority for an independent ordnance expenditure, Colonel."

Oswald muted them both. Impact indicators and thermal spikes were registering on *Roland*'s armor. Someone was calling out hit locations, but Oswald could see them in his visor.

The red warning flashes came first in ones and twos, then in short barrages. Integrity sensors blinked red in two compartments. *Roland* had been breached.

"Flight, initiate roll," Oswald ordered. He was surprised Anahita hadn't done so already. It was a standard maneuver to spread damage around a ship's outer armor.

"Roll initiated."

Another flight of missiles was almost in detonation range and *Roland* was less than a minute from the jump threshold.

"MCC has released control, Colonel," McFarran said over the net. "We are ready to jump!"

"Hold," Oswald replied. He sounded almost sleepy even to himself. "Tactical?"

"T-REX is deploying, FC."

"Missiles in detonation range, Colonel! Initiate jump!"

"Tactical?"

"T-REX has cleared the launch bay," Karpov said, his voice thick with satisfaction.

"Astro, FC. Initiate jump."

"Jump in three..."

One of the Proximan missiles blinked to a yellow detonation icon.

Two more integrity sensors flashed red, one in the tailward machine shop. No jump critical systems alarmed.

"...two..."

"I hate this part," Karpov muttered.

"...one..."

A text message appeared in Oswald's visor. It was from Anahita on his personal channel.

*Sorry for everything. Please make it back, Pierce.*

"...jump..."

And the universe froze.

# Chapter 7

ANAHITA SLUMPED INTO her chair when *Roland*'s telemetry reported jump-tunnel activation and the ship disappeared from the holo-screen hovering in the MCC.

"*Roland* is away," the telemetry officer said.

Instead of cheers, there were heavy sighs followed by grim silence. The data chief had tears glistening in his thick red beard and the comms officer broke down sobbing in the corner of her station.

Eight starships lost. The SDF hadn't lost that many in a single battle in well over a decade. Losing drones was bad enough, and the Proximans had destroyed dozens of those too. Not to mention the countless warheads Anahita had expended.

And two-thirds of the mission squadron had still been destroyed.

Someone upstairs was going to want her ass.

And she would give it to them... to kiss. Twenty-three enemy starships? The Proximans had to have known the mission was important. Hopefully, it was just good signal analysis and movement observation. If it was a deeper intelligence compromise, a mole or spybot, the SDF was in real trouble.

"Status of the decoy freighter payload?" Anahita asked. The freighters sent ahead of *Roland*'s squadron had been secretly loaded with ordnance. They had been positioned as a reserve to intercept reinforcements, out of range of the first engagement. That had been her mistake. But they were close enough now to gut the fleeing enemy ships.

"First flight of missiles is thirty minutes out," the MCC tactical officer answered. "Looks like the leading edge will intercept the Proximans before they get back out to the jump threshold."

"Good." Anahita stared at the display for a minute. She lifted her teacup, but she'd known it was long empty. Just picking it up helped settle her thoughts. There was a drop in the bottom of the cup that rolled around in small circles as Anahita tilted it this way, then that. She needed to keep her thoughts in the right direction or risk collapsing into a shameful fit of blubbering like the comms officer. It wasn't time for that. Not yet.

"Transfer guidance to MCC 4 with instructions to engage with extreme prejudice," Anahita said. "Those bastards don't go home. Shift laser defense sats—the Proximans should be in range of some at least. And get the full telemetry report to orbital ops for a recovery options analysis." She wasn't hopeful, but there was always the chance of survivors who didn't drift into space or burn up before rescue.

Anahita grimaced at the spreading cloud of new navigational-hazard tracks. "MCC 7 and 11 are to start immediate tracking of battle debris. It's going to be double shifts until we get every piece's trajectory computed and logged. Hopefully, a lot of it will fall into atmo and burn."

"What about *Roland*'s T-REX?" asked the tactical officer. "Should we take over guidance?"

Anahita clenched her jaw. What the hell had Pierce been thinking delaying his jump? Didn't he have enough kills on his record? She'd sacrificed everything, everyone, to save the mission. To save him. And he'd almost thrown it all away. She'd seen *Roland*'s damage warning. With luck, the old warship wouldn't explode as soon as it exited the jump tunnel. What kind of fool had he become?

No. This wasn't the time for those thoughts either.

"Let the T-REX succeed or fail on its own. That way they can't blame us for everything." Anahita glanced at the weeping comms officer. She wanted to grab the woman by the collar and scream at her to pull herself together. She also wanted to join her. Today had been a disaster. "Good job, everyone. It may not feel like it, but we succeeded. The Proximans got the drop on us, but we still got *Roland* away through overwhelming odds. Colonel Oswald will pull it off.

"Once handoff is completed, enjoy your off shift. Work it out, drink it off, whatever you need. I'll make sure the mental health department has all of their counselors available. It's been a shitty day. But we made it through."

Once Anahita shut the door, she looked back through the transparent side of the cube wall. No one moved. No one tapped or swiped their screens. No one exchanged furtive glances. They were processing the battle, the lives lost. They were assigning themselves blame and heaping guilt upon their own heads. She couldn't help them with that, though she felt she should be able to. It only took a moment to send a priority request to the director of mental health.

Anahita surrendered to the hypnotic thrum of the elevator as it rose to her office. She rubbed away the knots in her neck, but they grew back the instant her hands left. Her office was only a few moments away and she couldn't wait to throw her jacket on the floor, down a few shots, and collapse on the couch before the oncoming breakdown took over. She might even get in a few hours of sleep before the inquest started.

Anahita got off the elevator and strode down the hall to her office. She came up short when she rounded the corner. Will Zaphrim was sitting in his wheelchair in front of her door.

He twisted his body to face her, his scarred cheeks folding in what he could manage for a smile. "Hell of a fight."

Anahita stopped in front of the wheelchair and looked down at him, hands on her hips.

"Can we talk?" he asked.

Anahita motioned to her door. "Not right now. When I walk in there, I'm done."

"OK." He twisted in each direction to scan the hallway. "Well, before you're done, give me your initial thoughts. We can write up the after-action report later."

"What do I think? I think twenty-three ships is a lot of fucking ships. They threw unreasonable resources into this attack."

"Assuming they were manned. The Type-12s always have been before, but it's a dangerous assumption. You can program a computer to do just about anything. Except maybe replace Anahita Khadem."

Anahita offered a wry smile. "Thanks. The recovery teams will find out if they were manned when they look for prisoners. I'm more curious about why they would send so many. They obviously saw through our tricks and knew the mission was important to us. But do they know why?"

"Good questions. We recorded five Proxie spy sats that self-destructed after sending their transmission. Special Ops suspected some were there, but I'm afraid they may have more eyes on us than we realize."

"I'd say. I just hope the Proxies can't field squadrons that size at a whim."

"I don't think so. They hit us hard, but I think they'll feel the loss too." Will took a deep breath and looked at his white-gloved hands. "Speaking of high losses..."

"Twenty-three."

"I know. Good thing you saved Pierce."

Anahita raised her chin. "*Roland*. I saved *Roland*. And for good reason. Though the guys in PSYOPS probably have other ideas."

Will's head bobbed, leaving her wondering which reason he believed to be true.

"Are we done, Will?"

"Well, Pierce's family is waiting in the VIP lounge." Will looked up at her.

"What are they waiting for?"

"You. I might have told them you'd tell them about Pierce."

"And why would you do that?"

"I thought you might want to share the good news? Your choice though. I can get a liaison to see them back to their rooms."

Anahita glanced at her door, then glared down at Will.

He plucked at the cuff of his glove. "Sorry."

"I'll talk to them."

"Thanks, Ana."

She stormed off without a word. Her neck ached. Exhaustion weighed heavier on her the further she got away from her office, from her couch. From her booze.

Anahita almost burst into the VIP room, demanding to know what the hell they were even doing there. She stopped in front of the door. It took five full breaths and a vigorous neck rub before she felt in control enough to enter. Anahita forced a smile.

The lounge was heavy with fear. Not the fear of immediate harm, or fight or flight, but of dread anticipation. Anahita called it watcher's worry, something mission controllers knew well. Pierce's family were no strangers to this terror, but that didn't make them immune to it. Misty wanted to know about her man. His daughters wanted to know about their father.

Except Ululani. She had no more worries.

Misty stood up as soon as the door opened. The woman's hair was long and golden, and her designer dress clung to her curves like a lover. Pierce's daughters were just as beautiful. Mary was holding hands with her handsome fiancé, and father of her child. A dream that would forever remain unfulfilled for Pierce's first daughter. Anahita wondered if he'd told his family about Ululani.

The room grew silent as everyone followed Misty's gaze and stood with her, waiting. All eyes were on Anahita, as usual.

Anahita forced her smile a little wider. "They made it away."

Pierce's family collapsed in on each other, as if their anxiety was the only thing holding them up. They clutched and whispered and wept. Anahita was glad to have been forgotten. The struggle to keep back her tears, to embrace her own rage and relief, was at a breaking point. Her own collapse was imminent. Anahita turned to go before the inevitable barrage of questions started.

"Did you hear that, Mummy? The lady said Daddy's OK." A little girl around six years old with bouncing brown locks jumped up from a chair behind the Oswalds. Her Australian accent was adorable, and her Rs and Ls were pronounced like Ws. She spoke to a woman, obviously her mother, with a delicate face except for the red, swollen eyes.

"Oh, thank God," the woman said in an accent thicker than the little girl's. She snatched up her daughter and sobbed into the child's hair.

Anahita tasted the bile filling her mouth, fought against her clenching stomach trying to empty itself. "I'm sorry, you are?" She knew already, but her numb brain had nothing else for her to say.

The girl beamed and hiked a thumb to her chest. She was missing one of her front teeth. "I'm Terrisa Annelle Gryphon and this is my mummy. And my daddy is Lef-ten-tant Colonel Paul Gryhpon and *Charger* is the best spaceship in the whole fleet."

Mrs. Gryphon looked up at Anahita and put a hand to her mouth. "Wait. Is... is Paul alright?"

Anahita didn't know what to say, was afraid to say anything. The edges of her eyes were beginning to sting. But Mrs. Gryphon's terrible grimace grew darker with the passing of each unanswered second.

She glanced at Misty, though she had no idea why. Did she expect help? Strength? Misty must have read the same thing as Mrs. Gryphon on Anahita's face. Misty put her hand to her mouth and looked at the little girl's mother.

"I'm sorry to inform you..." Anahita started before the room erupted in wailing.

Misty rushed over to Mrs. Gryphon and knelt next to her, and they bawled on each other's shoulders. Mara and Mary—or was it Mary and Mara?—peered with wet eyes at the little girl, who was now looking from Anahita to her mother and back in confusion.

No one heard Anahita's mumbled lies about recovery and rescue operations. She'd seen *Charger*'s catastrophic destruction; they'd never see Paul again. His body wouldn't even be part of the meteor shower that would be seen around Earth for the next few weeks.

"What's wrong, Mummy? Is Daddy OK?"

Anahita clamped her trembling jaw shut and spun on her heel. She wasn't sure if she'd kept from leaving the lounge in an all-out run, but she didn't care anymore. That was it. There was nothing else she could fucking handle. She rushed to her office, barely able to see through her watery eyes.

Prime Minister Tzun was sitting in one of the chairs outside her door.

Anahita stumbled as she stopped. She glared at him, trying to formulate something besides the primal scream working its way up from her heart. At least she managed a trembling silence.

Tzun's expression fell in sympathy. He stood and bowed. "My apologies, General Khadem. Please contact me when you are ready. Rest." The prime minister left her alone outside her door.

The familiar air of her office comforted her. Anahita locked her door, threw her jacket on the floor and stomped on it several times before dimming the lights. Tears were streaming down her face now. Almost ready.

"Computer." Her voice was thick and raspy, but the voice software still recognized her. "Set all access to do not disturb. Belay that, set them to out of office." She didn't check the screen to see if her scheduling status changed; she'd only have seen an electric blur.

When the wet bar didn't open fast enough, she slammed her fist on the desk. She reached for the Delamain and snarled when it wasn't there. Had someone stolen Pierce's...?

Pierce had it. Right. It would be whiskey then. She grabbed the bottle. And because she wasn't a barbarian, she grabbed two shot glasses. One didn't drink straight from the bottle, even if the world was ending.

Anahita staggered to her couch and fell into it face-first. She screamed and bawled and punched and kicked until all she had left were dry sobs. Sobs for the astronauts she'd flown to their deaths. Sobs for their families. Sobs for Ululani. Sobs for Paul's daughter and wife. Sobs for the lies she told herself. All for Pierce's sake. No, not all for his sake. His mission was for everyone's sake. But she could have saved Paul Gryphon instead if she'd wanted. He could pull the mission off too. Probably. At least then she wouldn't have had to seen the look on that little girl's face.

Then no more sobs.

Anahita didn't know what time it was when she emerged from the tear- and snot-covered cushion, and she wasn't really interested. She scooted over to the couch arm farthest from where she'd been bawling and poured two shots. They burned all the way down, but chased away the shit of the day—for a while. Each slug promised to chase it away for a little bit longer. She agreed to the lie.

The holo-cube flickered on the desk, casting a picture of her childhood mosque. She waited with a mix of grief and hope for the next picture. Ululani in her cadet uniform. Then the picture of Anahita and Pierce during the leave where Ululani had been conceived.

She should have listened to her father. But she hadn't, and found herself pregnant with a choice to make. Killing baby Ululani wasn't an option, but neither was abandoning her while Mommy gallivanted around the galaxy. And she couldn't bring herself to ruin Pierce's dreams. He was a good man and would have stayed, would have done anything for her. She'd been wrong not to let him make his own choice. Maybe.

And then he married Misty.

Anahita filled both shot glasses again. She tapped them together in a toast with herself and downed them simultaneously without spilling a drop.

"Fuck her."

When Pierce got back, she'd throw it on the table. She'd beg him to love her again. Little Miss Perfect officer's wife wouldn't even have to know. Anahita saw it in Pierce's eyes sometimes. He remembered being with her. She'd almost asked him several times over the years. It was on her mind every time duty put them together.

There'd been other lovers, but never another love. No man had stared into her eyes with the steely-gray intensity he had. It was those smoldering eyes that finally drowned out her father's lifetime of warnings.

"Oh, Papa," she muttered.

Had Pierce told Misty about Ululani? Maybe she'd ask Misty if Pierce still did that little thing when he kissed...

No. Misty was his wife, not her. And she had no one else to blame for that. Anahita held one of the glasses against her forehead.

There were many things in her life that could be blamed on no one else.

Time would tell if she could be blamed for Pierce's death too.

# Chapter 8

THE MYSTERIES SURROUNDING the jump tunnel phenomenon were deep and pervasive. Like many human discoveries about the universe, the uses were devised before figuring out all the fundamentals... or the repercussions.

Jump tunnels only formed if both ends were within a limited range of gravity values. These thresholds could not form too close to a gravity well, nor in deep space. This odd specificity led some to call the whole phenomenon God's cosmic game of connect-the-dots. To others it simply fell in line with the various forms of the anthropic principle, that the universe exists in such a state as to be compatible with any sapience that can develop, observe, or interact with it. To wit, if there are distant stars to explore, there must be some way to get to them.

The jump effect halted motion at some levels of local space for a fraction of a second: generators, pumps, a ship's inertia... biological hearts. Jump-capable craft had to be designed with specialized, instant-recovery failsafe systems or risk destruction upon arrival. Fortunately, the jump stop, as it was known, didn't freeze motion at the molecular level; it would be hard for humans to survive being flash frozen at absolute zero. No one knew where a craft's momentum went; it was assumed to be conserved somewhere. Possibly it went to imparting the craft with a galactic-relative velocity equal to that of the destination system.

They were questions Oswald sometimes pondered in his free time, but there was only one question he was asking as the jump counted down. It was the same question he'd asked for twenty years.

*Will my heart start when I get there?*

Oswald coughed, then groaned. The stab of pain in his chest was over in an instant; the suit's defibrillator hadn't fired. His ticker had started on its own again.

Spluttering curses drifted in over the net as the crew recovered.

"Someday," Karpov whispered, "they'll figure out how to stop that shit."

"Astro, Aux. Confirm jump status." McFarran belched. "Apologies, everyone. Life Support, get vitals and report. All departments begin post-jump checks. Forward the T3 report."

The department heads sounded as though they were recovering from an overnight bender as they reported back to the net. It wasn't too far from how Oswald felt. He didn't hear Luskin check in for the Rangers and fear clenched his already weak stomach. He muted his mic just before retching. He spat the small glop into the helmet's vacuum tube. It disappeared with a wet slurp.

"Rangers, FC. You guys alright?" Oswald frowned. "Luskin? Any Ranger on the net?"

"They can't all be jump cherries," Karpov said. "Could they?"

"We've never really had anything for gropos to attack," Oswald said. "I guess it's possible." He froze as a thought struck him. "Does their armor have defib units? Does it?"

"Most combat armor has an integrated trauma unit," Karpov said, his voice unsure, "so I'd assume that includes a defib. But I'm not really up on gropo stuff."

Oswald didn't wait for Dr. Hines to check in. He pulled up the crew vitals. The Rangers' telemetry feeds were dark. At least they weren't red.

"Medical team to Rangers' compartment," Oswald announced over the net. "Hines?"

"Already moving, Colonel. Someone will have the rest of the vitals report shortly. I've got someone else checking on Yninski. I'll let you know."

Oswald didn't have time to worry about the Rangers now. They were out of his hands. He'd only pulled up the vitals on the Rangers because of their silence. Now he saw the one red light on Yninski. She was strapped into a station in the tailward machine shop. He didn't have time to worry about her now either.

Reports from the department heads were filtering in. The initial T3 report indicated the local space was clear of navigational hazards. All systems had recovered from the jump. Four hull breaches were being repaired. No equipment damage. No extra reaction mass lost. Six defibrillators activated, all crew recovered.

Status on the Rangers and Yninski pending.

"Six is a lot, Colonel," McFarran said.

"Must have something to do with the distance of the jump."

"Command, Astro. It's the longest I've ever programmed," Lt. Major Breen said. "But the computer won't verify our location to me. We're here though, wherever that is."

Oswald grimaced as he watched *Roland*'s sensor picture expand with each sweep. He hated keeping info from the crew. But he'd fix that nonsense shortly. "Yep. Let's get under normal ops and I'll make an announcement. I'll unlock the nav report, but keep it to yourself, Breen."

A moment later Breen whistled low over the net. "Wow."

"Wow, indeed," Oswald agreed. He monitored *Roland*'s ship-status displays while he waited for a report from the medics about the Rangers and Yninski.

It wasn't long before the medics reported Yninski was dead. The Proximan laser that penetrated *Roland* right before jump had cut through her and her crew station. At least it had been quick.

"What's your status, Hines?" Oswald finally asked, his worry overcoming his patience. The doctor was one of the best, but Oswald needed to know. The sacrifice of the Earth squadrons would mean nothing if the Rangers didn't make it.

"Sorry, Colonel. Everyone's fine. For some reason their suits shut down. None of these young studs needed a jump start, but it is a mess. Most vomited all up in their suits."

"Colonel," Luskin said. His voice was hoarse and unsteady. "It was our... my fault. There's an interlock on our suit that trips during a jump."

"And they sent you in them anyway?"

"We're supposed to connect to ship's power. But we couldn't find the power ports, so we, I, thought there'd been an upgrade." He coughed into the mic. "I've now been shown where the ports are on *Roland*."

"Was this your guys' first jump, Major?"

"Yes, Colonel. Except Salazar. He's a former spacer."

"Did he puke?"

"Yes, Colonel. He says that's just one of the reasons he's a former spacer."

Oswald grinned. "Hines will make sure you guys get some cleaning kits. I want everyone in their cans until we stand down."

Ninety minutes later, all repairs were complete and the local navigation sphere was plotted to Oswald's satisfaction. They were ready to go. Except Yninski.

"All departments doff armor by watch section and begin standard duty rotations. Aux, log current T3 and turn down the net. I will address *Roland* in thirty." Oswald hoped his voice didn't sound as shaky as he suddenly felt.

"Understood, Colonel."

Oswald waited for McFarran to finish the reports and dress down. When the Aux was ready, he took the flight command watch and Oswald stowed his armor.

"I'll be in the staff room," Oswald said.

*Roland*'s staff room was spacious compared to other compartments only because it lacked the usual acceleration stations and armor plating. Eight normal people, or ten spacers, could crowd around the holo-table in the center. It was a popular rec room when not in use for official business and was the most popular place for crew to join the light-year club, the missile bays coming in a close second.

He wasn't a member himself, finding such hanky-panky unworthy of *Roland*. It never led to anything but trouble. But he was under no illusions as to the purity of his crew. What happened in space stayed in space as far as many astronauts were concerned.

Oswald rubbed his eyes with a thumb and forefinger. The helmet displays gave a rendering that fooled the human brain into thinking it was seeing a much larger image. But it tired his eyes. The larger hologram of the staff room was a welcome relief at his age.

A technician from Life Support brought him a rehydrated pouch labeled "Zero-Gravity Meal, One Each," and a sippy cup of vitamin water. These space rations, called space-rats or s-rats, had ingredients printed on them that read like an ancient Greek pantheon. The inscrutability of the contents bothered him. He often threw the empty pouches away unsure of what he'd actually eaten.

Replies from fleet supply to his inquiries concerning the ingredients of the space-rats, when answered at all, were usually just a reprinted list of what was already on the pouch. Pressing for more details as to what the additives and chemicals were for usually garnered a reply along the lines of, "Just trust us, they're good for you."

Oswald forced the s-rat down. For all their mystery ingredients, the space-rats were good. His stomach just wasn't quite ready to eat yet. Space travel was hard on the body. He tucked the empty pouch into the sealable trash bin and looked up to see McFarran float in. Oswald gulped and motioned for his aux to strap in to a seat across the holo-table.

McFarran sealed the hatch behind him as he entered. Oswald raised a brow.

"Everything is proceeding, Colonel. We should have navigation references worked up soon."

Oswald nodded.

"How much do you plan to tell them?"

"Pretty much everything. About the aliens, about where we are, about losing every other ship in Sol."

"That's not a good idea, Colonel."

Oswald shrugged. "Maybe not. But I think they should know."

"That's not keeping with need-to-know protocols."

"Says you. I think they do need to know."

McFarran shook his head. "You know I'll have to log a complaint."

"I've managed to survive all your other logged complaints." Oswald grinned and glanced at his aux. "What's wrong?"

McFarran scanned Oswald's face for a moment. "I'm also going to file a complaint concerning Yninski."

Oswald leaned back and let his arms float limp in front of him. "That's your right. But she's not the first casualty *Roland*'s seen."

"It was needless, Colonel."

"The damn Proxies were shooting at us."

"Yninski is dead because you delayed the jump to fire at two helpless targets."

Oswald crossed his arms. "I didn't realize that we considered enemy starships still under thrust harmless. I'll be sure to share that with Proximan HQ."

"I didn't say harmless, Colonel. I said—"

"Then you just killed your own complaint. It's the same damn thing." Oswald looked up at the reports displayed on the holo.

"We had no authority. It wasn't our job to engage them. General Khadem was very clear about that. MCC was obviously trying to get us out of there ASAP." McFarran swiped a hand through the holo display and it winked away. "That delay could have ended this mission. If it hit the jump generator or the reactor, we'd be dead."

"You didn't use to file so many complaints."

"You didn't use to be so reckless."

"I'm not reckless."

"I've been on *Roland* almost as long as you have, Pierce. Something in Barnard's Star changed you."

"Maybe it was losing the whole damned squadron while we were away?"

"It was before that. If I may be so bold, Pierce, Ululani's death has affected you more than you allow. You asked me about what you should feel after it happened." McFarran looked apologetic. "You've changed. You've stopped looking before you leap. You've stopped checking your answers before turning in the test, so to speak. Like turning down Sol duty for this.

"You've also become uncharacteristically harsh with the crew at times. I'm the auxiliary flight commander. I'm the one that's supposed to be the hard-ass. You know that. You get to play the good guy, I'm the bad guy."

Oswald stared at the hatch and drummed his fingers on the dark holo-table. He started to speak out of reflex, realized he didn't know what to say, and snapped his mouth shut.

"*Bonwei* was a hard call," McFarran continued. "Especially knowing she was on board. But it was the right call."

"They all died because of my orders, too."

"It was a tactical consideration. Even if it was the wrong decision—which I don't believe it was—there was a point to the risk, to the sacrifice. We could have lost the rest of the squadron if you hadn't. Trading Yninski for a random potshot was pointless, Colonel. Reckless."

Oswald glared at his aux. "Maybe. You file what you need to file then, Hashi. You'll probably be filing several on this mission. Start writing. I'm going to tell the crew our dirty secrets now."

"Colonel..."

Oswald ignored the protest and brought the holo-display back to life and connected to the interior comm system.

McFarran was right. The mission could succeed without divulging the full details. But it was too monumental to keep it all to himself. The SDF didn't even want him telling the crew what system they were in, but any spacer worth their O2 would want to know. And it was a new system for every astronaut on *Roland*. It'd be robbing them of a point of pride. It would be a travesty, a betrayal, of one spacer to another. Hardcore vets got electro-tattoos of the systems they'd visited. Bragging rights were no small thing to a military person.

He smirked, thinking of his aux busily tattling on him. Oswald was weary of protocols, reports, and senseless regulations. All those rules hadn't saved Gryphon or Baker. Or Ululani. He was suddenly weary of space, and separation from his family, and of dying friends. He was weary of the damned Proxies and their damned war. Earth's damned war.

Yet he'd insisted on coming, spitting in Anahita's face by refusing her rescue attempt. Maybe McFarren had a point.

"*Roland*, this is the FC." Oswald paused to give the crew a chance to shift their attention and listen in. "As is my custom, believing an informed flight crew is a ready flight crew, I will have the operations-net recording made available to all hands as soon as Cindy pulls it.

"Everyone should know that we were engaged by a Proximan attack force as we approached the jump threshold. It was the largest force I've ever seen. Twenty-three ships." Oswald paused to let it sink in. "Yes, twenty-three. According to tactical logs, *Roland* took out two of them."

Never mind that the MCC had fired everything.

"We'll have to wait until we get back to see if we killed two others." He paused to glance at McFarran, who looked placidly back. "We made it away, but at a terrible price. Yninski was killed as we jumped. Before we grieve the loss of a child of *Roland*, know that *Charger* and *Triumph* were lost with all hands, ensuring we could complete the mission.

"Add to that *Euphrates*, *Valkyrie*, *Birmingham*, *Spectre*, *Event Horizon*, and *Madrid*. All destroyed. We can't know for certain about rescue efforts, but every ship in our task force was destroyed except us. They all died protecting *Roland*.

"The fleet is a small orbit. We've all lost friends today. We shall toast their service and pledge to avenge them. But *Roland* has a job to do first and we'll make sure they didn't die in vain. And remember our Ranger brothers. They've lost their own family too, and now they are left to carry a heavy burden. Let us have a moment of silence for our lost comrades."

Oswald waited, thinking about the flight commanders. Especially Nunez. The man had thought himself safe in a home guard squadron. And for anything short of the flotilla the Proxies had thrown at them today, he would have been safe. After the pause, Oswald almost couldn't go on. "And now for something amazing. Welcome to Delta Pavonis. For those of you scrambling for a star chart to punch your cards, we are now twenty light-years away from Sol and, no, you haven't been here."

Oswald met McFarran's eyes. The aux was shaking his head. Not in desperation or reproach, just as a reminder that he didn't think it was a good idea.

"We are not alone," Oswald continued. "And by that I mean we are sharing the system with something completely alien. Yes, as in space alien. We are here to recover an artifact from a hostile alien world that the brains at HQ think will win the war. The artifact is guarded and humans have already died here.

"This is the most uniquely dangerous mission in my career. But we will do *Roland* proud and we will do right by those who died to get us here. Stay sharp and we'll make it back to Sol. Oswald out."

He turned to McFarran and yawned. "Get all that?"

"Yes, Colonel. Permission to return to my post?"

Oswald waved a hand towards the hatch. "Dismissed."

McFarran paused before opening it. "I hope we can go back to how it used to be between us, Pierce."

Did he mean before Oswald had ordered his daughter to her death? He stared until McFarran left.

He tossed his stylus like a tiny spear at the opposite wall and watched it bounce back in a slow tumble before catching it. Tumbling like *Triumph* had been when he'd seen her last.

Oswald wasn't ready to deal with the slaughter. Or that he'd made a bad call. Any commander had to deal with their own mistakes, and he might come to the conclusion that he'd been wrong. But McFarran was already there to point it out for him. Even if the aux was right, he could have waited. He could have filed it without the pontification. It didn't seem as if he was hoping things would be like before. More like kicking Oswald while he was down.

But it wasn't McFarran's style, and that was one of the things that made him a good officer, a good second-in-command. He did what he thought was right, held to his core beliefs and those of the fleet. And he talked to his FC about those things. Oswald was jealous in a way. He'd lost faith in the fleet long ago; and in himself more recently.

Oswald's stomach cramped, and it wasn't due to a bad space-rat. He'd had enough post-trauma evals to know that *Roland* was likely to have a crew filled with survivor's guilt complexes, him included. But it was too early for the booze and he hoped everyone else realized that too.

There was work to do. Oswald caught his stylus again and activated the holo-table to load up the latest situation reports.

# Chapter 9

OSWALD FLIPPED THROUGH the updated reports after coming on duty. Three sensor drones had been successfully inserted into a high orbit around Delta Pavonis V, now referred to as DPV, or "deep-vee" for the sake of brevity, in the logs and conversation. Once they had provided a full surface map, Oswald would bring them lower for more detailed sweeps of the landing sites. Nothing had shot at them so far.

The Rangers' suits were finally integrated with *Roland*'s systems after long hours put in by the engineering team. Since *Roland* wasn't originally slotted to be in the squadron, Special Operations hadn't tweaked the suits for her. That had been an alpha class fuck-up that was almost an alpha class mishap. Something else McFarran could shove up his report file.

They were pinged three days into their trip by an SDF sensor satellite that had been collecting EM and navigation data for the last five years.

There was nothing of tactical value in the logs they recovered, no EM signals or navigation tracks of note. DPV had been silent the entire time. According to the system intel, there were supposed to be three such satellites, but the other two weren't responding.

Once the data had been recovered, C'nD cleaned up the system files and requested permission to update the sat's firmware to the latest fleet release. The satellite seemed to be working fine and Oswald was reluctant to risk killing it with an upgrade. Or, as he preferred to call them, disimprovements. But he relented and the satellite status showed green after the final upgrade push completed.

"Well, tickle my tots," Karpov said. "That actually worked."

The upgraded system was able to process a cleaner data set and verified there was something undetected farther out in the system perturbing inner orbits. Oswald would see about naming it *Charger* when they returned. Anything else interesting he'd try to get named *Triumph*.

DPV was close to the size of Mars and shone green through the big-eye. Not the verdant green of jungles, but the pale green of verdigris, of decaying lifeless metal.

On full magnification, he made out two of the ancient sites. The feeds from the sensor drones had more definition, but there was something about seeing it through the big-eye. Even if it was projected onto a display. The details of the ruins were remarkably well-preserved by the vacuum. Had the aliens come before or after the loss of atmosphere? Had they stripped the planet of that atmosphere for terraforming or to make their jump beacon lighthouse work?

"Just fascinating." He'd been saying that a lot.

Two days from DPV, Oswald ordered the sensor drones into a lower orbit for detailed sweeps of the three target sites. There was still no reaction from the planet or the four inert alien satellites they detected in orbit.

Flight Sgt. Norris uploaded her final orbital insertion plan and drifted over to Oswald's station.

He pulled it up and compared the lines curving around DPV. A cloud of red, indicating a navigational hazard, covered a small section of one orbital band.

"Is that the debris field from the last mission?"

"Yes, sir. One of the sensor drones got a good sweep. Definitely an Earth ship." She ran a finger around the holo-projection. "And it was probably in a low orbit for a drop to Site Two. But there's nothing in the pictures of any drop."

Oswald had already worked out a set of orbital insertion burns, inclination, and eccentricity. He was pleased to see hers were close to his. Instead of having a ship and a Ranger platoon for each site, *Roland* would now have to attempt recovery of all the artifacts of interest alone.

Artifacts of interest, indeed. It was a ridiculous term for pieces of technology that had been crafted before humans stopped tossing feces at each other. But since they still did it in various, more civilized ways, maybe that wasn't a good benchmark. UXA was only a marginally better name. As if the whole planet wasn't an artifact of unimaginable interest. At least to those with a modicum of foresight.

Oswald highlighted one of the course projections. "That's the one, Flight Sgt. Initial insertion burn here, second one here."

"Roger that, Colonel." Flight Sgt. Norris floated back to her station next to Lieutenant Chun, *Roland*'s senior pilot.

Moments later, Oswald felt the slight shift in pitch and yaw as Chun adjusted *Roland*'s vector to match the selected plot.

It was close to change of watch, and Oswald swiped his hand to shut down his displays. He tapped his earpiece to change the comm channel and asked McFarran to meet in the staff compartment for passdown.

He arrived to find three crew playing a holographic board game called *Star Haulers*. Sleek rocket-shaped cars swerved and darted above the table's surface.

A lieutenant called out, "FC present!" and the digital cars froze in place.

Oswald grinned and hiked a thumb towards the hatch. "Scram."

The crew gathered their tablets and left with good-natured grumbles. McFarran arrived a moment later.

"Anything to hand down?" McFarran asked.

"Nothing much. Chun adjusted our vector and the initial deceleration burn should be in about six hours." He glanced at his tablet. "Then we'll start final approach and the fun starts." Oswald tucked his tablet into his flightsuit and frowned at McFarran.

"Something wrong, Colonel?"

"This whole goddamned mission is wrong, Hashi." In all of humanity's years of watching the stars and exploring extrasolar planets, even before the war, they'd found exactly one world that might hold an answer to Fermi's Paradox. And he was being ordered to ruin that chance. He braced his knees against the underside of the table so he could slam his fist on it a few times without flying away. He took a deep breath, slammed the table a final time, and pursed his lips. "What could we learn if we had scientists instead of bombs with us?"

McFarran shrugged, his face relaxing. "The fleet decided we didn't need scientists. Or maybe the last mission had scientists and it proved too dangerous."

It was hard for Oswald not to transfer some of his anger at the SDF to McFarran when the man defended all of their actions. Oswald watched the aux quietly as he considered his reply.

Everyone working in microgravity suffered some degree of swelling as fluids redistributed through their bodies. Hashi McFarran's black face, by some chance of his genetics or bone structure, became almost unrecognizably bloated. The effect was all the more striking because of the man's normally handsome African features. The crew sometimes called him Big Face McFarran behind his back.

"Have you read the reports of the initial teams? More to the point, who they were?"

"Sorry to say, Colonel, I have not. I read the summary but did not dig deeper. It seems the first ship was of a Chinese registry and the second some sort of Special Forces scout."

"The Chinese ship wasn't even SDF." Oswald ran his fingers across the table and a vehicle registry appeared. "Belonged to Lu-Pang Corp; it was a damned mining prospector."

McFarran raised his brows. "That does seem strange, Colonel. Perhaps it had advanced imaging scopes or geological sensors?"

"Just usual back-door dealing between the SDF and the national govs. There isn't a bit of useful detail in the full report to fleet command, even if it did have advanced sensors. It was submitted to Beijing and scrubbed. But what can you expect?" Oswald rapped the knuckle of his forefinger on the table. "I bet they didn't even bother to map the whole planet before sending back the OK. The first survey only found where the artifacts were. If they'd done any actual recon, maybe the second expedition wouldn't be slowly raining down on the planet."

"If that is true, Colonel, it is disturbing on many levels."

"It's bullshit." Oswald flipped to another report. "You'd expect to find some more useful details here, being an SDF military mission. Nope.

"Names, times, even the weapons loadout, all redacted. But that second ship? The report calls it a scout. It was a troop carrier. They tried to do a smash-and-grab and got fragged."

"So they sent us in, Colonel?"

"Yes. They planned on sending three platoons with three armed starships. But surprise!" Oswald held his palms towards McFarran and wriggled splayed fingers. "Just us. Just *Roland*."

"Are you thinking about aborting, Colonel?"

"No. Too many died. But I'm thinking about modifying our mission orders. Make this a research mission instead."

McFarran's look of horror amused Oswald.

"You can't, Colonel! We are not equipped with a research payload. And if we aren't going to do our mission here, *Roland* is needed back in the fight."

Though a good officer, Oswald sometimes wondered if his aux was imaginative enough to get outraged at fleet horseshit. Not that getting outraged was a virtue. Oswald had been getting outraged a lot lately; it wasn't helpful. Things he'd once acccepted as being business as usual, now chafed. *Amor fati*, to love your fate no matter what it had in store, as the Stoics put it, had once been how Oswald tried to live. He no longer loved his fate.

Not since Ululani. Probably even long before her death.

"Of course we can't." Oswald pulled up the most recent sweep from the drones. "But, still, we're looking at the mysteries of a race that could unlock so much. Have you considered that this might be the same race that transplanted the Proximans from Earth?"

"Or that transplanted them to Earth." McFarran grinned as Oswald rolled his eyes. "But, yes, Colonel. I have pondered that possibility. And that there are great mysteries below is no question. It just isn't our mission. Maybe Anahita can get you assigned after the war."

"If the war ever ends."

"All wars end, Colonel. At some point." McFarran shrugged. "Our own Earth wars have lasted longer than this one."

Oswald swiped his hand over the projection of DPV. The planet, sensor drones, and debris field spun wildly. Oswald let it spin for a moment before stopping it with a finger. In the center of the display was a satellite that looked like the bulb of a metallic flower.

"Thoughts on the alien satellites?"

McFarran considered the image before answering. "Who can know, Colonel? They look dead, no power, no signals, no thermals. But something destroyed our ship in orbit."

"Maybe they only awake when Prometheus steals the fire and tries to run." Oswald panned the image out. The satellites were in a cluster with only a few degrees of inclination to their orbits. Not much coverage for a defense grid. But it would be risky to ignore them. "Part of me wants to leave them alone so we can study them. When the war is over. The other part of me, the commander, the warmonger, says they have to go. Especially with the losses we've already taken. That part of me says better safe than sorry."

"I agree with the warmonger, Colonel."

"Me too, damn it all." Oswald shook his head and opened a comm channel on the table. "Karpov, Oswald."

"Yessir," Karpov's cheery voice answered immediately.

"Ambush being the better part of valor, can we get the alien sats with a single T-REX?"

"It seems like a waste of a T-REX, sir," Karpov said. "We could get them all with a well-placed kill cloud."

"I want as few deadly BBs in orbit as possible when we approach. Hopefully, the sats will stay more or less in their orbits if we zap them."

"I've got it plotted now, sir. We launch in two hours, fifty-two minutes, and T-REX Sierra-7 will engage the sats at their closest in about fourteen hours."

*Roland* had expended far more of its munitions in the escape from Sol than Oswald had anticipated. Not to mention Anahita firing the booster rockets. Hopefully, they had enough left to take off if it came to that.

"Program it and deploy, Tactical."

"Roger that, FC."

Oswald closed the channel. "He's always happiest when he gets to shoot things."

"He certainly seems to love it, Colonel."

"You have *Roland*, Aux." Oswald rubbed his eyes and left the staff compartment for the beehive.

But sleep would not come. Not with the aid of the thrust providing psuedo-gravity, not with the somnolence generator at max. Sometimes high energy particles made it through the magnetic shield, and when the third ray of cosmic radiation flashed deep in his closed eye, Oswald gave up and floated free of his tube.

Whispers echoed up from the Rangers' compartment so he decided to see if Luskin was awake. As he drew closer, the bawdy nature of the conversation became more apparent. A man and woman were trading vulgar barbs that cycled from whispers to raucous laughter and back to whispers. The Rangers must know how to sleep.

Oswald peered in to see a middle-aged man with a bald, wrinkled brow and an attractive young woman with a strip of short black hair running from her hairline to the back of her head. They continued to leer and insult each other as they performed function checks on the team's weapons and sensor gear.

"As you were," Oswald said, drifting in.

The Rangers looked up at him, still chuckling from their exchange. Oswald glanced around and saw how the sleeping troops were not disturbed.

"Does your team always sleep in their power armor?" Oswald asked.

The bald man, Command Sgt. Salazar, slapped the leg of a nearby suit of armor strapped into an acceleration couch. "Not always. But they're comfy and you can black out sight and audio."

"Good idea." Oswald turned to Specialist Mona Sharp. "Did you draw the short straw to have to pull a shift with this guy?"

"Oh, sir," Sharp said, grinning at Salazar. "You shouldn't talk about his manhood like that."

Salazar guffawed, covering his crotch with both hands. "It ain't true, sir!"

The two Rangers laughed aloud until Oswald raised a finger to his lips. His crew wasn't sleeping in armor.

Oswald held his palms out towards Salazar and looked away. "I don't think that's mission-relevant intel, Command Sgt. I take it the major is sleeping?"

"You want me to wake him up, FC?" Salazar asked. "I'd be more than happy to."

"I'm sure. That's OK. Just floating around, can't sleep."

"Yeah, I forgot how hard it could be," Salazar said. "I never could get any good sleep when I was a vacc-sucker. One of the reasons I changed branches; I need my beauty sleep." He spread his hands over the disassembled mine-detection drone on his lap. "And I still can't sleep floating. That's why I'm up doing this."

Oswald took leave of the Rangers and made rounds to the entertainment compartment. He chatted with other restless crew floating around *Roland*. Many were off-shift and admitted they couldn't sleep either. They talked about the chances of rescue for the ships destroyed in Sol, asked if there were really, really aliens, and cursed the Proximan bastards.

"If Karpov can survive what he's been through," Oswald told them, "anything is possible."

Some laughed, while others replied with perfunctory grunts or thoughtful nods. But being veterans, everyone was proud to be in Delta Pavonis. They could whip out their log books and show they'd been where none of their peers had. Hopefully, fleet command would approve releasing the info. Otherwise, Oswald might actually get in trouble.

After a good two hours of chit-chat, Oswald felt he might have a chance at some sleep. Then he'd be well-rested for the days of waiting. He was right, drifting off before he could secure his last sleep strap.

OSWALD WASN'T SURE if he was glad to be on duty and awake for the attack on the alien satellites or not. The T-REX dipped into DPV's orbit and detonated in a tiny white flash as the sats gathered. The display showed each of the satellites split into a cloud of debris, but not enough to make Oswald recalculate his orbit.

"I wonder how old those were?" Oswald asked no one in particular.

He hoped the small nuclear detonation used to pump the x-ray lasers hadn't set off any alarms. Without atmosphere, there wouldn't be any secondary EMP pulse generated. But it would be a hard thing to miss if someone below was watching.

The ordnance display was showing low. They did have the OR-BAM warheads, but those were designed to be fired from orbit at the planet, not at speeding interceptors. Mostly they were high-capacity laser batteries, useful due to DPV's lack of atmosphere. But there were a few bunker poppers and some good old-fashioned general-purpose nuclear warheads suitable for any occasion.

Whatever was below might be able to shoot them down easily with some alien death-ray. And *Roland* too.

With only one ship providing cover instead of three, he decided on a highly eccentric orbit that would keep *Roland* and the orbiting ORBAM platforms over the three Ranger teams. A geosynchronous orbit was out of the lasers' effective range. But keeping all the weapon platforms spread out would ensure at least some orbital coverage for each team for the duration of the mission.

Oswald and Luskin agreed to send them to each site simultaneously to avoid having to send other landers if the first mission activated a planet-wide lockdown. If they were going to smash and grab, he wanted to get *Roland* out of there ASAP.

The sensor operator detected no response from the planet.

"Pilot, please initiate flight plan Orbital Ops One," Oswald said.

"Roger, FC," Lt. Chun said. "ETA to first drop is nineteen hours, seven minutes."

"Set the clock. Did you hear that, Luskin?"

"Roger that, Colonel. Ready to stomp a hole in DPV." A hint of terror edged in beneath the man's bravado.

One of the most important skills of a combat commander was to be able to hide the terror in his voice. The way Oswald was doing now.

# Chapter 10

ROMAN KARPOV SAW THE dark bubbles gathering in his peripheral vision, as if space itself was trying to engulf him. It was a familiar darkness. He'd seen it just before his father died, and now he saw it in every corner of the ship. *Roland* was doomed. And so was he if he didn't prepare.

The years of psychological evaluation, or programming, had taught him that the darkness was really a psychosomatic reaction made even more vivid by an accompanying stress-related increase in blood pressure. His therapists told him it was a natural reaction to his fear, ocular illusions similar to those sometimes seen with migraine episodes.

It was all perfectly understandable, they said, given his many brushes with death. The SDF didn't give a medal every time he was almost killed by some damned Proxie warhead. He was not superstitious and knew it wasn't some kind of psychic precognition. But Karpov did trust his instincts.

And his instincts were screaming.

Karpov pulled a maintenance pouch from the cabinet. "I'm going to check missile bay two."

"Again?" Lieutenants Nora Gilweh and Vier Relor asked simultaneously. They looked and acted like sisters. Karpov assumed it was due to their working so well together in close proximity. He knew their menses were synced.

"And I checked it on my rounds too," added Relor.

"And I'm going to check it again. Preparation, ladies."

Karpov made his way to missile bay two, placing the "Secured For Maintenance" flag over the access hatch. He searched every corner of the bay. There wasn't supposed to be anyone in here, but such compartments were popular places for lazy stargazers to hide—and for those joining the light-year club. He'd joined the light-year club years ago in an auxiliary reaction-mass transfer tank. It was the only time he'd slept with a flight commander. Every time he thought of her, Karpov still got an erection. She'd died in a Proximan attack in Vega two years later.

Satisfied he was alone, Karpov pulled a control board from the spares locker. He ran his fingers across the other parts, looking for what he needed. Only one or two things at a time though. Never enough to be noticed. And he never took things they needed to survive or to kill the Proximans. That was the main thing, after all. Karpov's contingencies were only for if the Proximans won. Then it was every person for themselves.

He settled on adding a universal wiring harness. The rest would come later. Karpov then made his way to his vacc-armor. Keeping his actions hidden behind the acceleration station where the armor was stowed, he acted as if he were performing a preventative maintenance routine. The leg casing of his armor was a perfect place to hide a spare control board. The wiring harness found its way into Karpov's sleep tube locker. It was small and flexible and looked like something that might connect to a personal tablet. An easy cover story. Karpov prided himself on his cover stories.

The darkness receded as he closed the locker. Piece by piece he'd get ready. Piece by piece he'd fight for his life.

The Lucky Star patch made Karpov smile. Dumbasses called them lucky stars. If he'd been lucky, he wouldn't have been on those fucking ships in the first place. No, he thought of them as little gold stars like those he'd get in day school for eating his lunch. But these stars were for doing whatever it takes, for making his own luck.

That was the type of luck needed to survive a destroyed starship. It was the type of luck that didn't favor the unprepared.

But most lacked the brains or balls to truly prepare for the worst. It was preparation that saw his family through what history now called the Slavic Starvation. His father had seen the signs of the economic collapse, believed the predictions of the blizzards that would bury Zuberec for three years, and predicted the floods that finally washed the city away during the thaw. It was from his father that Karpov learned to prepare. Not just preparation of rations and allies, but how to ready his mind to do what needed to be done. Millions in the region died, despite so-called global unity. He had not been the first Karpov to kill for survival.

"Karpov," Major McFarran said from the hatch to the beehive. "Catching some rest for your upcoming off shift?"

Karpov's stomach lurched. He turned to zip his tube shut to give the shock a chance to leave his face. "No sir, Aux, sir." He racked his brain for one of those good excuses in case McFarran pressed the issue. Normally, coming up with a believable story came easy but the surprise had thrown him.

McFarran glanced down at Karpov's pouch. "Are you checking bay two again?"

"It did light a fault when we got hit, Aux."

McFarran glanced at the beehive and then at Karpov. He continued to stare at the tactical officer. Karpov smiled pleasantly while the aux chewed his lip.

"Is it still fixed, Lt. Major?"

"Yes, sir. Just being careful, you know. We'll definitely want our missile bays working."

McFarran nodded. "Good job on the sats. We might not have needed to, but better safe than sorry."

"Yup. Just like the FC said. But it was my pleasure. I might be the first person to shoot down an alien spaceship. How about that?"

"Excuse me?" McFarran laughed a nasally, French-sounding laugh. "We've been shooting down aliens for over twenty years, Karpov. Don't tell me you've forgotten about the war."

"They don't count. They're just human dickheads from another planet. Like the dickheads from our planet with a funny accent."

McFarran's brows shot upwards. "Excuse me?"

"They have a funny accent, Aux. The Proximans. I'm not talking about your funny accent. No need to get your gender-neutral underpants in a twist."

"The colonel may put up with your mouth, Lt. Major, but I will not."

Karpov grinned. "What're you going to do? Shanghai me onto a starship and make me fight?"

"I will get you reassigned. No more firing missiles. No more laser cannons. You're not the only one who can plot an intercept course."

"You'd cripple *Roland* just to make a point?"

"Discipline on a starship is far more important than stroking your ego. Leave that to your fans. Your loss certainly would not cripple *Roland*. And life-support is far more important than tactical, all things considered." McFarran sniffed and looked away, his expression dismissive. "Do you understand me, Karpov?"

Karpov narrowed his eyes. When McFarran looked back at him for an answer, however, the tactical officer was all smiles.

"Yes, Major. Perfectly." Karpov watched the aux float out of the compartment without another word.

"Bus—ted," came an artificially deep voice from the beehive.

Several voices burst out laughing.

Karpov chortled. He could feel the blush rushing across his face. "You guys," he said in his best "aw-shucks" voice.

More laughter.

"Shut the fuck up?" grumbled someone from the bottom row.

Karpov drifted away as the muffled voices devolved into shushing and name-calling. When he was alone in the main passage, he let out a slow breath. McFarran had almost caught him. Not that the dipshit was smart enough to realize what Karpov was doing, even if he found the wiring harness. But it might be best to pretend he'd been sleeping on duty. Everyone drifted off from time to time. That would certainly get him in less trouble than if McFarran suspected him of stealing parts.

It was time to be extra careful. The aux was too uptight for his own good. McFarran only wished he was half the FC Oswald was. No one, not even Karpov himself, killed Proximans like Oswald. It was the highlight of Karpov's career to have been with Oswald during his attack on the Proximan starbase that earned him that gold rocket.

McFarran was a fussbudget. A checklist tyrant. A boot polisher. It was a shame that laser hit Yninski instead of McFarran. Maybe Karpov should get prepared to do something about that.

For *Roland*'s good, of course. If it were McFarran in charge, they'd never survive, let alone complete the mission.

# Chapter 11

"TEAM THREE AWAY," LUSKIN announced over the net.

Oswald watched the video feed from the lander's external cameras and saw *Roland* silently fall away. Lander three would be in position for its final rapid drop in fifteen minutes by the mission clock. Then all three teams would fall to Delta Pavonis V in seconds.

*Roland* and her ORBAM platforms were in position to give the Ranger teams orbital support. Oswald ran the computer models again as an outlet for his nervousness. His crew had done their jobs and done them well. As always. *Roland*'s children made it look easy to be their flight commander.

There had been no response from the planet when *Roland* inserted into orbit, nor when the ORBAM platforms or landers were deployed. But Oswald refused to take that as a good sign; the sensor signal of the debris field from the last Earth ship in orbit wouldn't let him.

Hopefully, the rapid insertion drop, RID in the extensive and wearying lexicon of SDF acronyms, would keep them safe from ground batteries. Hopefully. But Oswald suspected any alien death-rays that could hit the landers could have already hit *Roland*.

"I sure wish *Charger* and *Triumph* were here," Breen said over the net. Despite being an expert programmer and mathematician, the astrogator's voice had a perpetual childlike tone.

"Astro, are you having a wonderful time with *le bavardage*?" McFarran asked.

Breen hesitated. "Sorry, Aux. I don't know what that means."

"It means that we're about to enter combat and to keep the net free of your blabbering, Lt. Major Breen."

"French is hard," Breen answered.

Oswald laughed and tension drained from his neck like a snake loosening its coils and slithering away. The vacc-armor had limited amenities and a neck massager was not one of them.

"Aux is right," Oswald said. "Time to gird your loins and button your lip."

"Yes, sir." Breen sounded dejected as usual.

The big-eye was designed to stare deep at enemy craft and celestial points of interest. Luskin's lander was a grainy blur bouncing in the display as the telescope tried to track and focus on it.

"RID commence in three... two... one, drop!" called Luskin.

A dull flare shot from the lander and it plummeted towards the surface. The Rangers' vitals all shot into the red. Oswald could only imagine what that ride felt like. Not having to fight a thick atmosphere probably smoothed the drop, but it would still be rough. He'd landed on Earth and a handful of other planets, but had never used an RID.

Fire erupted from the lander's braking rockets. As the lander's distance increased, the picture from the big-eye grew clearer. Landing struts extended moments before a greenish spray of dust blasted away from beneath the lander.

The hue of the planet had darkened as they approached. Instead of looking like a dusting of harmless verdigris, DPV now looked toxic. Diseased. Poisonous. Human blood had already been spilled below. And the first thing Oswald had done upon arrival was destroy artifacts they didn't understand. More bloodshed might be a foregone conclusion.

Oswald chuckled grimly, imagining a scene right out of a comic vid. *"Here come those humans again,"* the alien burbled. *"Maybe this time they've come in peace. Power down the death-ray, Xorblox."*

The planet had already changed for Oswald, aside from the color. It had lost its mystique of discovery. He had once hoped exploring the planet would be like finding ancient Incan ruins and delving into what lay hidden, learning what they'd learned so long ago. Now in his mind it was like the Sphynx of legend, presenting a riddle that led to death if not solved properly.

Yet Oswald hoped they could complete their mission and leave the scene of the crime relatively untouched. The Rangers were well trained, equipped, and knew where the UXAs were.

It could happen.

Oswald flipped through the camera feeds, watching the Rangers set up perimeters and unfold the small, open-framed rovers that would take them into the ruins and back. A missile battery was already deployed next to each lander.

"Any response from DPV?"

"Nothing, Colonel," McFarran said. "Maybe their batteries wore out since the last visit?"

"Could be Special Forces redacted the fact that they blew up all the bad guys," Karpov said.

"Let's make sure we're scanning a wide area around each team. We don't want any surprises." Oswald gave the reminder in case the sensor operators were being drawn into the Rangers' video feed as much as he was.

Flight Sergeant Norris was remotely piloting the drone covering Major Luskin's team. With no atmosphere, the drones weren't the usual winged or propeller-driven models. These drones looked like spiders with thrusters on the ends of their legs, flying in slow arcs in the low gravity using bursts of compressed gas.

The Ranger teams rode well into the ruins and disembarked at the assigned rally points. From there they bounded in alternating two-person teams, one covering with their weapons while the other moved in low bounces. Threat assessment and recon were their orders, not xenoarcheology. The mysterious buildings blurred by in the video feeds without a second look.

It was all Oswald could do not to order Luskin to stop and pan his camera feed to capture the details of the ruins. Their sensor package was capturing 360-degree optical and lidar readings, but those would not be made available to Oswald until they returned to Earth, if ever.

Oswald pulled his eyes away from the ground game and back into his own sphere. No aerospace threats, no signals, no response from the still-silent planet. He watched his tactical screens in the visor, and listened to the Rangers' net with one ear and *Roland's* with the other.

As the teams approached the UXA locations, they slowed to a walk and scanned their surroundings more cautiously. Oswald could see more details of the alien cityscape. The structures were built at strange angles and in uncomfortable proportions. Though odd-looking, it was also very familiar. A door is a door and a wall is a wall, even in ancient alien ruins.

One of the Rangers scanned down dust-strewn stairs that led to a tiny set of ossified doors. Oswald pictured an old clown car, since the doors were so out of proportion to the much larger buildings. Perhaps more than one species of aliens had lived here together.

Luskin's camera feed swept across what looked like an eroded fresco.

"Luskin, pan back to that picture." Feeling the need to justify his order, Oswald added, "I just want to see if it might show us what we're up against."

If Luskin felt put out, it didn't show in his voice. "Roger that, *Roland*." His camera showed definite outlines and geometric shapes on the wall, but nothing useful or interesting.

Team Two signaled they were on station and Oswald switched to Command Sergeant Salazar's video feed. A spherical structure was nestled beneath an impossibly thin spire that rose out of sight into the star-filled sky.

"It looks taller than on the display, Colonel," McFarran said. "Surely it must be some type of antenna. It would make sense for a beacon."

"Or a lighthouse," Breen said. "Uh, sorry, sir."

Oswald grunted. The structure looked abandoned and crumbling, not the type of place for important equipment. But how much of Earth's critical systems were built on layer upon layer of rotting infrastructure? There was no way to know if someone might still be using this lighthouse.

The center of the building contained a circular opening. The other two teams reported on station and, while they established security, Oswald marked the directions of each site's opening relative to one another. They were slightly off, as if triangulated to some distant point. There was no time for the calculations, but he wondered if they were aimed at something important.

"All teams begin recovery," Luskin ordered.

The Rangers spread out around the spheres. Neither the drones nor the Rangers' sensor nets detected any motion or signals. Oswald watched as the tactical support frame detached from hardpoints on the back, shoulders, and limbs of Luskin's armor to enter the portal. The other teams' videos showed the same.

"Tinman has entered the structure," Luskin said.

When separated from the combat armor, a tactical support frame, or "tinny," looked like a headless mechanical skeleton. A power pack attached in the middle of the spine, and small spherical sensors clustered at the top of its neck. The cluster was too small to really look like a head. The tinny switched between bipedal, tripedal, and quadrupedal locomotion as needed, every section connected by robust ball joints. Each appendage ended in three grippers that allowed it to walk, run, climb, or jump any obstacle with ease. And it could manipulate every Ranger weapon in the arsenal.

Luskin's tinny approached and swiveled its sensor cluster to get images from several angles. Something hovered in the center of a vaguely crystalline frame. But no matter the angle of the camera, Oswald couldn't assign a shape to what he saw. It was as if his mind slid around the object that must surely be the UXA.

"*Roland*, can you make that out?" Luskin asked. "Use some kind of filter or sensor or something else techno-fleety?"

"Cindy," Oswald said. "Can you make anything of it?"

"Negative, Colonel. It's... like I can't bring myself to look, but I am looking straight at it," Lt. Trese, division officer of Comms and Data, said. "I'll see if we can do something, but since Luskin is looking at it straight through his visor and seeing the same, I don't think it'll be a feed issue."

"Do what you can." Oswald repeatedly switched between all the feeds of the alien artifacts. None showed a clear picture. "Now that's damned strange."

"The artifacts?" Mcfarran asked.

"No, that the top of Salazar's tinman is painted like a penis."

"Good attention to detail on that paint job," Karpov said. "Care to bet on what that tinny is named?"

"No."

"All teams begin recovery." Luskin's tinny reached out and plucked the object from the air.

It was hard to compare the object to the tinman's size, but it looked about one meter tall and half a meter wide. Oswald held his breath, waiting for some defense system, some monster, to attack them for taking the fire from their lighthouse.

The other two tinnies reached out.

"Team Two, abort!" Oswald cried. "This is *Roland* actual. Abort recovery, Team Two."

"Abort!" repeated Salazar instantly. "Back to rally point."

The tinny caught up with Salazar in an instant and jumped on the Ranger's back, attaching to the armor on the run.

"Command, Tactical."

"Go, Tactical."

"That was pretty fucking slick."

The other tinnies carried the artifacts out of the domed rooms and took position next to their squad leaders, scanning the buildings.

Everyone's vitals spiked when Oswald aborted Team Two.

"Don't see anything, *Roland*." Salazar's video feed was panning back and forth so quickly it was making Oswald queasy. "At the rally, but no activity."

"Roger that, Salazar. Best speed back to your recovery vehicle," Oswald said.

Teams One and Three stayed in a security formation as they waited for any response from the planet. Norris's drone drifted over Luskin's team and clamped onto a tall building. She panned the camera around and pinged the sensors. Nothing.

"All teams best speed to recovery vehicles," Luskin started. "What the hell is that?"

His view swept around to show a small creature or robot. It reminded Oswald of a horseshoe crab. The plates that ran down its body looked both chitinous and metallic. The reports had used the term biomechanical. Given the complete lack of atmosphere on the surface of DPV, Oswald guessed more mechanical than bio. Perhaps it was a meaningless distinction to the builders of the ruins.

It crawled from a small panel on the spire building. Two long eye-stalks—or sensor pods—extended from between the front two plates. The Rangers locked onto the thing as it skittered towards their defensive perimeter.

"Hold fire," Luskin said in a shaky voice.

The crab stopped three meters away, the eye-stalks bent towards the artifact in the tinman's hands. Oswald bet that thing could see the UXA clearly.

A similar creature stared at Team One, though its rear half dragged limply behind it, leaving a trail in the dust. A green patina dappled the edges of its plates.

"All teams cautiously return to the recovery vehicles," Oswald said.

Luskin's voice was now steady. "Roger that, *Roland*."

Ranger Team One rounded the corner and their dilapidated alien escort followed. When its eye-stalks pointed towards the tinny holding the UXA, it rushed forward, its flaccid, broken tail bouncing and kicking up sprays of dirt that drifted slowly back to the ground.

"Hold fire," Luskin said, still focused on the alien thing charging at his own team.

Despite being broken, the alien after Team One reached its target first. It raced around the tinny and extended a claw-tipped arm towards the artifact.

The tinny lifted the UXA in the air like a child playing keep away and stomped the crab's head. Reddish gel spurted from the beneath the tinny's foot.

In the strange light of DPV, it could be some sort of hydraulic fluid. Or blood.

"Here we go," Karpov muttered.

"EM and thermal readings are spiking from all four sites!" the sensor operator called.

"Drone's motion sensors are keying on something, Colonel," Norris said.

"All Ranger teams make best speed to launch sites." Oswald panned out to see what *Roland* was seeing now. "Move it!"

Luskin and Salazar were repeatedly telling their Rangers to keep their jumps low and to come down in cover. The other team was jumping as hard and fast as possible, the team leader saying nothing. City and sky flashed by in the Rangers' feeds.

"Aux?" Oswald said.

"Recovery vehicles are ready for launch and support artillery is ready, Colonel." McFarran said.

"Tactical?"

"All ORBAM modules are actively scanning, *Roland*'s laser capacitors at full and ready."

Norris gasped. "Holy shit."

"Something useful if you please, Flight Sergeant," McFarran said.

"Holy shit," she repeated.

Oswald pulled up her drone's display. "Holy shit."

"Like a giant millipede," Karpov said.

"Millipede doesn't do it justice," McFarran said, his prim voice filled with awe. "Gigantipede."

"I like that," Karpov said. "Nice, Aux. Nice. Oh, and let me add a holy shit."

The gigantipede was a terror-inducing biomechanical construct over one hundred meters long racing towards Luskin's team. It didn't have the stubby legs or wide plates of the crab-like thing. It looked like an armored vertebrate spine with countless spidery legs that weaved between each other like a nightmare sewing machine as it ran. Two menacing orbs waved from the front of the thing.

Sprays of dust shot up where the legs struck the street and surfaces of the buildings as the gigantipede crawled between, over, and through them. One of the giant orbs rotated towards the drone, and the video feed was replaced with a blinking yellow "Signal Lost" an instant later. The other two drone feeds died in short order.

"Activate ORBAM," Oswald said, his voice growing cool as the battle began unfolding in his mind. He was taking in the firing coverage, line of sight, angles of attack, and the recovery timelines, folding them all into a semi-conscious haze that made its own decisions. "Tactical, get laser one on Team One and laser two on Team Three. Aux, get the ground artillery in the air—the Rangers can designate targets."

He didn't hear the replies as much as register them somewhere in the back of his mind. C'nD produced an enhanced computer video from the feeds of the big-eye, the targeting optics from *Roland*'s lasers, and the ORBAM modules. Oswald's mind used this information to coordinate support fire. McFarran and Karpov were issuing navigation corrections to the Rangers to help them avoid the monsters.

Gouts of plasma erupted from the streets and buildings as the orbital lasers found their range and calibrated. The massive attackers moved with incredible speed and agility, their spiked legs able to dig in and push off without bouncing in the low gravity. But a monster one hundred meters long could only avoid a sustained rapid-fire laser battery for so long.

Gigantipedes began bursting apart in showers of sparks that severed their bodies, legs, and heads. There was no atmosphere to cause the lasers to defract or scatter and whatever the alien things were using as armor wasn't strong enough to protect them from the orbital attack. It gave the Ranger teams enough time to make it to their rovers.

But more gigantipedes kept appearing on the scope.

"They must be coming from underground, Colonel," McFarran said. "Or maybe from within the buildings. But I don't know from where! They're so fast."

Oswald watched as more of the writhing aliens closed in on the fleeing Rangers. Even Team Two, which hadn't taken an artifact, was being pursued.

"First round of artillery on station," McFarran said. "Rangers, designate targets."

Salazar shrieked and his feed showed clawing spindles reach over a building in front of them, followed by a pair of orbs that turned towards him.

A missile streaked in from the direction of the recovery vehicles, a thin trail of glowing smoke trailing into the darkness behind. The monster and the building it was perched on exploded, showering the Rangers with debris.

A celebratory whoop became a strangled gargle, then a scream. Two more orbs rose over the adjacent building. An intense pinpoint of light flared in each orb.

"Cover!" Salazar cried. His video feed became a blur of dust, crumbling buildings, and black alien sky.

When the picture jostled to a stop, the unmanned rover was still rolling down the street. A red haze enveloped it, followed by a flash. When the glow faded, the rover was gone.

The Ranger vitals display flashed yellow. Specialist Kovac's telemetry grayed out.

*Signal Lost*

Salazar locked onto the gigantipede, but it shattered under a fiery flower as a laser from orbit burned through it. Glowing segments of the giant bounced slowly through the alien cityscape.

A gigantipede snaked out from between two more buildings, its huge frame scraping down both sides of the alley. Salazar's feed switched to the weapon sights of his suit's portable laser cannon. The aiming reticle paused over one of the giant orbs. It burst into sparks and the monster's head whipped back and forth as if in pain.

Another missile streaked in from behind, and the front half of the gigantipede disappeared in a silent explosion. Shrapnel tore divots in the streets and buildings around the Rangers.

"*Roland*, Team Two is danger close!" shouted Salazar.

It took a second for the term to register. Oswald had never used artillery. Everything was space battles; the SDF had never found a Proximan planetary colony to attack.

"Roger that, Team Two," answered Karpov.

"Where's Kovac?" Salazar was yelling to his squad. "Get eyes on, now!"

"Negative, Team Two," McFarran said. "Kovac is gone like the rover. Continue to recovery."

"We don't leave a man behind," Salazar said.

"There's no one left behind," Oswald said. He hoped a firm but calm voice would convince the Ranger who'd just lost a man. "Proceed to recovery."

"Go!" Luskin called. "Go-go-go!"

Oswald watched a desperate, bouncing run from the Rangers' cameras. Gigantipedes appeared over and around buildings like monsters in a haunted house ride. Missiles streaked across the sky and lasers cut down from above.

The Rangers burst into the open, dust-filled plains around the ruins. Gigantipedes raced after them.

A Ranger from Team Three flashed off-line an instant before Luskin guided a missile into the attacking monster. The Ranger hadn't even had time to scream as the alien weapon burned her away.

The teams were getting closer, but the alien defenders were multiplying behind them and gaining.

The computations, as much instinct as formulae, swirled in Oswald's mind. There were too many enemies moving too fast. The

Rangers weren't going to make it without concentrated fire support.

Most weren't going to make it no matter what *Roland* did.

The odds were with Luskin's team and that's where Oswald would focus his fire.

He'd hoped the aliens would leave Team Two alone, but now he was going to abandon them because they were no longer mission critical. It was easier to make such decisions in his state of tactical disassociation.

"Whoa," Karpov said. "Explosion at Site One. A big one."

Oswald switched his feed to view the site from orbit. "Us?"

"Nothing I launched, FC."

"Look at the defenders in that sector," McFarrarn said. "They've all stopped, Colonel."

Oswald zoomed the visual display on a glowing crater in the center of the site. Gigantipedes hung expectantly and began silently collapsing in ones and twos. The city filled with flying dust and debris as the monsters fell.

"Maybe something couldn't take the load of all those robots," the engineering officer, Major Bowens, said. "Like an ancient substation or control facility. Power surge would explain it better though."

"Whatever it was," Karpov said, "it sure killed them bugs dead."

Oswald considered the layout of the sites. He'd studied them for hours, looking for the best insertion and extraction routes for the Rangers. They were the experts and made their own plans, but Oswald liked contingencies. Contingencies upon contingencies. Twenty-six light-years from the nearest base was not the best time to run out of ideas.

"Tactical, shift ORBAM coverage from Team One to Team Two, and see if you can pinpoint the same structure in Site Three." Oswald took several deep breaths. His stomach turned to mud and he almost vomited as he said the next words. So much for limited collateral damage. "And drop a TNP there."

Karpov sounded like an excited child. "Yes, sir!"

"What about Team Two, Colonel?" McFarran asked.

Oswald paused, hating his aux for a moment for even asking, for forcing him to consider. Was it possible anyone still used this beacon? Did it even work now that they'd stolen two of the artifacts? There was no way to know.

More importantly, was the risk to Team Two worth the possibility of saving some theoretical alien navigator? There was no way to know.

"Negative, Aux. I don't want to risk damaging the UXA if someone has to come back and get it."

The thermonuclear penetrator, or TNP, launched from Team Three's artillery battery. Each team had been equipped with one as a final contingency. Oswald had hoped not to use it.

"Team Three, nuke inbound," Karpov said. "Bound two-five meters at one-one-four degrees and brace."

The missile dove at the heart of Site Three. A flash filled the sky as a powerful explosive ejected the nuclear penetrator at hypersonic speeds. There would be no atmospheric shockwave, but detonating underground would be devastating. An instant after the TNP punched deep beneath the ruins, a jet of radioactive debris spewed upwards. Buildings canted madly as the ground below them bubbled and rolled. Debris and dust rose kilometers into the sky, obscuring the city. Despite the destruction, it looked wrong to Oswald without a billowing mushroom cloud, almost unimpressive. But the gigantipedes still visible beneath the edge of the debris field froze and toppled.

Oswald shifted all ORBAM coverage to Team Two. The laser capacitors were getting low as they continued to cut down the pursuing monsters. But his focus was still on Teams One and Three—they had the goods.

"Team Three is ready for launch," McFarran announced, excitement or hope creeping into his voice. "And Team One is boarding."

Oswald switched to Luskin's view. The three Rangers faced inwards in a circle and tested each other's restraints. Each of their feeds kept drifting to the empty seat. Luskin reached for the launch button, then withdrew his hand.

"Launch, Team Three," Oswald said.

"Negative, *Roland*. Not until all teams are ready."

Oswald sighed. "Aux, launch the recovery vehicle." He'd spoken over the commander's channel so Luskin wouldn't hear the order. He didn't want to give the Ranger a chance to bravely abort the launch somehow. Oswald didn't need any audio to know what Luskin was screaming into his mic as his team blasted away from the surface of Delta Pavonis V.

Oswald ignored the pleas and curses from Team One, and ordered McFarran to launch them, too, minutes later as soon as they reported ready.

The flames from the boosters detonated the landing module and artillery system by design. Oswald wondered what alien explorers one hundred thousand years in the future would make of the strange human debris. He couldn't help but smile as the two recovery vehicles, UXAs on board, escaped the murderous planet.

Team Two continued their mad buddy rushes on foot, bounding to their own escape. The Rangers looked back only to designate targets for incoming ordnance. Gigantipedes burned and collapsed across the green desert as ORBAM batteries drained to minimal levels. From above, they looked like drowning earthworms.

*Roland*'s sensor display flared red as five new tracks rose from the planet's surface over the horizon. Oswald listened as Karpov listed off their tactical information and ran the targeting numbers.

"So they're probably from Site Four," Oswald said. "Too bad we won't get a chance to blow that up before they get here."

"I guess someone wants those beacons to stay, Colonel," McFarran said.

"Detecting strong ECM, FC," added the sensors officer. "Having trouble getting proper nav values."

As if to prove the point, one of the new tracks ran straight out from the planet, 139,939 kilometers from where it had been a second before.

"Extrapolate their last known position and launch a kill cloud warhead," Oswald said. "See if we can't blast it towards the planet and out of our orbit."

The big-eye finally got a good look at the new arrivals, just before the whirling cloud of tungsten rods ripped the lead craft into scrap. To Oswald it looked like a giant cockroach with a rocket shoved up its ass. They shared the same biomechanical ambiguity as the horseshoe crabs and gigantipedes below.

"They look like turds," Breen said. "Uh, Command."

"Thank you, Astro," Oswald replied.

The remaining cockroaches turned and sparkling plumes ejected from what Oswald assumed were their thrusters. It looked beautiful, like a fireworks celebration.

One skirted the edge of the kinetic kill cloud and shattered. The other three evaded, corrected course, and moved to intercept.

They'd bought the recovery vehicles some time, as the alien interceptors would have to change orbits again to catch them. Depending from how far away they could attack, that is.

"Team Two lift off, Colonel," McFarran said.

"Keep *Roland* covering landers one and three," Oswald said.

The plan had been for the landers to climb to staggered altitudes so *Roland* could pick them up while still accelerating and increasing her orbit. There was no contingency plan for picking up a tardy lander; they'd have to recalculate and make another trip around DPV to match orbits with Team Two.

For now, there was nothing left to do but watch as *Roland* fired potshots at the radar-scrambled alien drones. Oswald was grinding his teeth. Every minute they'd gained by forcing the three surviving roaches to change orbit evading had been wasted as the laser batteries failed to score a single hit. The alien interference was too complex to overcome.

One of the alien interceptors finally split into a cloud of dancing embers that tumbled towards the planet.

"Numbers don't lie, but men lie about what the numbers mean," Oswald's father used to say whenever someone threw a study or statistic at him. In space, unlike politics or economics, the numbers meant what they said. These numbers told Oswald he wouldn't be able to save all the landers. Time to prioritize his... assets.

"Sorry, Luskin," Oswald whispered. "Tactical, get all laser batteries covering Team One. Get a kill cloud in matched orbit with Team Two. If they get hit, give the attacker the scattergun treatment. If Team Two survives, we'll have to come back around to get them." Oswald fought back the urge to explain or apologize to the crew. But the numbers left him with nothing else to say.

There was a morbid comfort in mathematical inevitability, though. There was nothing he could do against the solid reality of delta-v, specific impulse, and orbital vectors. Maybe in Star-Captain Yasmina's world; not in the skies over DPV.

The cockroaches turned to burn retrograde into new orbits, one that would match course with landers one and three, the other to drop towards lander two.

Oswald switched from the video feed to the digital representation of the tactical screen. He didn't want to see the death of the Ranger teams in real time, though part of him said he owed them at least that much.

If *Charger* and *Triumph* were here, all the Rangers would probably have made it home.

An energy spike registered from the alien craft and recovery vehicle two flashed red. Its navigational track split into three branches, falling back towards the surface of the planet.

Three *Signal Lost* notifications appeared on the Rangers' vitals display.

"They are lost, Colonel," McFarran said.

Flight Sergeant Norris gasped and almost muted her mic before a sob escaped her mouth.

A warhead detonation indicated on the display, and the kinetic kill cloud spread out before the shifting icon of the alien attacker. Minutes later, the remains of the cockroach were raining down after Team Two.

"KKC detonation successful," Karpov said, his voice now subdued. "Interceptor four destroyed."

Now it was *Roland*, a handful of mostly spent ORBAM modules, and two unarmed launch pods against an alien interceptor with a weapon Oswald had no doubt could cut his venerable starship in two.

The remaining cockroach initiated a burn and rose up towards recovery pod three. *Roland*'s lasers still could not find their mark. Being in a stable orbit awaiting pick up, the recovery vehicle had no chance. Luskin's craft, Rangers, and presumably valued cargo, spread across Delta Pavonis V's image like a bloody smear.

*Signal Lost... Signal Lost... Signal Lost...*

The alien sped towards the last recovery vehicle. Once it had destroyed the recovery vehicle, there was no doubt it would come for *Roland*.

There was another energy spike on the tactical display. Oswald blew out all his breath, his head lolling forward as if he'd deflated inside his armor. New tracks of debris replaced the single dot of the destroyed vehicle.

*Signal Lost* times four.

They'd lost. Eight starships. Thirty-six Rangers. Yninski. All lost for nothing.

And *Roland* was next.

"Hell, yeah," Karpov cried. "Interceptor five is down in flames. Finally got that fucker."

Oswald perked up and studied the display. Recovery pod one was in one piece and it was the damned cockroach falling in pieces. The telemetry signal must have been jammed by the alien interference.

Oswald allowed relief in his voice. "Perform docking evolution with recovery vehicle one. Then get the hell out here."

He scanned the debris field that had once been Luskin's team. It looked like a shattered mirror. There were no pieces larger than a meter across.

Oswald thought he could make out the remains of a tinny and one of the Ranger's helmets; possibly a laser rifle. But he couldn't find a sign of the artifact or the thick safe it had been stored in. That could have been because it was destroyed or because it was already impossible to see. Either way, he wasn't inclined to try to recover it. He'd mark it for a later mission to try. Let the fleet send someone else if what they brought back wasn't good enough. It tasted like cowardice, but Oswald had his fill of death. He had shook the hands and offered platitudes of encouragement to each of the now-dead bodies on or around DPV before he sent them out.

If there was a way to kill every Proximan, he would. He didn't care if he'd be remembered for his genocide. But there wasn't a way to kill them all and he was now done with this war. Fucking done. The SDF could challenge him, but he'd served two decades. If anyone had earned the right to muster out, he had. State of war or no.

He'd even be willing to make the PR circles, buff his golden rocket on the news feeds for the patriots, and dehumanize the enemy however the leadership wanted. There had never been a day in his life when Oswald could remember feeling like this, but he never wanted to go back into space. Ever.

Screw the black. Screw the fleet. He'd done his time.

McFarran spoke over the net. "Capsule one has been recovered, Colonel."

"Roger that, Aux. Flight, give us a roll to put the Rangers facing away from DPV and initiate exit burn."

Like the humans before, *Roland* fled Delta Pavonis, battered and bloodied, leaving their dead behind. Unlike those trail blazers, however, Oswald had escaped and inflicted his own wounds on the alien world. And he'd stolen the fire from the gods, had retrieved command's holy grail. He hoped it would be enough, hoped that he could be done. Suffer a few virtual parades and go home for some well-earned rest.

But as his father was wont to say:

*There ain't no rest for the wicked, boy.*

# Chapter 12

"STILL NOTHING?" OSWALD asked.

"Nothing, Colonel," McFarran answered.

"Any response from the Rangers?"

"No, Colonel."

Oswald shifted in his suit. "Let's get a life-support team down there. Make sure Hines is on it. I'm starting to get a bad feeling."

Delta Pavonis V glared at him in the big-eye, like a predator that sees its prey and decides chasing it down isn't worth the effort. There were hundreds, if not thousands, of the gigantipedes that had crawled up from their long-forgotten garages to attack the Rangers. It wasn't reasonable to think the planet could only offer five space vehicles.

Of course, those roaches had done their share. Surely DPV had a stockpile of missiles that could atomize *Roland*.

Oswald wasn't going to complain though. They'd recovered a lander, two ORBAM modules, and one mysterious alien artifact of interest. The remaining Rangers, landers, ORBAM, and artifacts would have to stay put until the SDF decided they needed to be recovered. General Zaphrim would want his Rangers' remains returned to Earth if possible. It probably wouldn't be.

It would be hours before they reached the jump threshold. *Roland* had been on battle standing for almost two days during the approach. The defenses on DPV were far more advanced than those of the SDF, but not invulnerable. They still obeyed the laws of physics and if the planet decided to swat at them, *Roland* would have some warning. Hopefully.

Oswald keyed his mic to address all hands. "This is the FC. All department heads resume normal duty rotations. Duty stations will remain armored up until further notice. Everyone else pop your tops and get some rest."

McFarran replied on the commander's channel. "Yes, Colonel. I have command."

Oswald removed his armor and just floated, rubbing his eyes until he saw spots. A quick wash and a nap was what he wanted, but he needed to check on the Rangers. Then he needed to update the ship's flight package with the new numbers for the expended reaction mass and ordnance. And of course the logs and after action reports needed to be written and filed. A flight commander was never off duty. But first the Rangers.

He was barely out of the flight control pod when his comm chimed. "FC here."

"FC, Hines. You should come to the recovery vehicle."

"I'm already on my way. Bad news, Doc?"

"Come and see."

When Oswald arrived at the docking ring, Dr. Hines waved him over and motioned towards the hatch. Team one had not suffered a communications failure, they had suffered enemy fire. Since the whole craft hadn't shattered like the others, Oswald assumed it must have been a glancing shot. This glancing shot had done the Rangers in.

Four rictus faces grinned up at Oswald through split faceplates. The spider web of cracks extended around the helmets and down the armor plates of the suits. Rivulets of blood seeped from lifeless eyes, pulled slowly down by *Roland's* acceleration.

The recovery pod was missing sections of frame below the Ranger's seats. The UXA container drifted near one of the breaches, still inside only because it was slightly larger than the nearest hole. The cage it had been secured in was reduced to a warped metal outline in the tiny cargo compartment. It had been too close.

"Shit," Oswald whispered.

"Probably didn't even feel it," Dr. Hines said. "You know, a human body exposed to vacuum will go unconscious in a matter of seconds. To shatter the armor and the pod like that, their internal organs were probably instantly pulverized anyway. Might not even have had time to suffocate." The doctor looked at Oswald and nodded, as if the information made everything more acceptable.

Oswald stared back, glad the Rangers' loved ones didn't have to speak with the good doctor. He let the comments go. Turning his attention back to the recovery vehicle, Oswald saw just how close they'd come to losing their prize. If another section of the pod had given way, the UXA container could have fallen out the back and into the LANTRn's radioactive plume.

Oswald couldn't imaging going back.

*"Hey Xorblox, did you see where my jump tunnel beacons got off to?"*

*"Why yes I did! Those pesky humans came by, smashed up the place, and stole them."*

*"How rude. Do you know where they got off to?"*

*"Well look at that. They're coming back. They must have dropped their wallet or something."*

*"Maybe they're coming back to apologize and make reparations, Xorblox."*

Oswald chuckled.

Dr. Hines frowned. "It was probably very quick, Colonel, but very painful. Nothing to laugh at."

"Not that." Oswald shook his head. "Not them. Nevermind." He spoke into his tablet. "Aux, the Rangers didn't make it. Cut thrust until the recovery vehicle is dealt with. We'll have to jettison it."

Oswald watched as technicians bagged the bodies and secured the UXA. It looked like everything in the capsule was ruined. Being a structural hazard, Oswald ordered it searched, just in case, and set to drift. It would enter the Delta Pavonis Oort cloud in about three-hundred years.

The forms to be filled out were ponderous, their questions invasive and accusatory. Oswald dictated the answers to his tablet until his voice suddenly grew hoarse. He grabbed a space-rat and a pouch of coffee on his way to retrieve his Delamain. After slurping down a supposedly protein-derived faux turkey breast, Oswald stowed the trash and called McFarran to gather the department heads for the dreaded PAA, the Post Action Analysis.

The officers on duty had removed their vacc-suits, as the conference room was too cramped for them to fit in while armored. Hines and Karpov drifted in last, the doctor having autopsies and Karpov recording expenditures and post-battle weapons readiness checks. After the PAA, the tactical officer would have to adjust the ordnance mass and balance.

"Close the hatch please, Karpov," Oswald said. "Just in case you haven't heard, the entire Ranger platoon is KIA. We'll have formal ceremonies back in Sol for them and Yninski. Until then, we'll toast our fallen."

He lifted the Delamain and with an expert hand left a honey-colored globule quivering in place in front of each officer. Fleet tradition called these space-shots. The smell of the cognac filled the small compartment, providing its own tiny pre-buzz.

"*Ad Astra*," Oswald intoned.

"*Ad Astra*," the officers responded.

Karpov put his lips against his portion and smooched it loudly until it shrunk to nothing. Breen tried sucking his in but instead inhaled the burning spirits and began hacking, which sent him bouncing and flailing. Fortunately the compartment was so crowded the astrogator didn't get very far. Hines slurped his drink out of the air an instant before Breen put his elbow through it.

McFarran wasn't so fast. His brows raised and his lip stiffened. On his swollen face, it looked like a child pouting. Oswald grinned and squeezed out another drop in front of McFarran. McFarran looked at Breen and sniffed before sipping his shot.

Breen was still coughing and the compartment was filled with raucous laughter. Oswald savored the moment as the Delamain spread warmth through him. The rich aftertaste tempted him to dribble out another round. He decided to save seconds for any hard feelings after the discussion.

"Before we get started," Oswald said, "what's the latest, Aux?"

McFarran offered a hopeful grin. "No change, Colonel. Still nothing from DPV. After the meeting, I'll light the LANTRn back up, and we should be safely past the jump threshold in three hours."

"Excellent." Oswald tapped the table surface and it projected the PAA forms above the officers. "Recording. Alright, everyone knows drill.

"The point of the PAA is to identify weaknesses in our processes, the things that worked and those that didn't. It isn't a place to air personal grievances or engage in general whining. If you have a complaint, express it and explain what actionable item you think might address it." Oswald tugged at his straps and smiled at each officer.

His gut churned as Dr. Hines started. It was a difficult mission, complex, with too many moving parts, and had started with a shit-storm and the immediate loss of two-thirds of the mission assets. There was going to be a nasty investigation by nasty investigators. *Roland* would be windicated in the end, he was sure, but until then an FC was guilty until a political ally proved him innocent.

It was not the first combat PAA these men had gone through together. *Roland* was a forward-deployed starship; she was a killer down to her schematics. The crew had a camaraderie forged in vacuum and radiation. But they were also intelligent and driven warriors who spoke their minds.

Being professionals, they managed to keep most of their comments in their own departments. One complaint, that Oswald agreed with, was the amount of pointless chatter on the net. Lt. Gresh, the sensors officer, complained that it was hard to do her job if flight, meaning Oswald, kept commandeering the big-eye. Oswald had seen that one coming—she mentioned it in every analysis.

The problem with the idea of presenting a solution for every problem was that the problems were often not in their control. Command had selected the loadout and delta-v parameters. It would take someone in fleet planning to address those. The meeting went on for over an hour, in part due to the chatter brought on by the officers' residual excitement from the battle. The war stories had already started.

The officers took the deaths of the Rangers hard. They gave themselves harsh critiques about what they could have done to save them.

What if the drones hadn't been taken out so quickly? Could *Roland* have prepared a better countermeasures suite against the alien jamming? Why hadn't the recovery pods been equipped with some sort of space defenses? What the fuck were those gigantipede things and why weren't we told?

"I agree," Oswald said at length, hoping everyone else's batteries were as low as his. "They should have told us something about the defenses. But the first expedition didn't meet anything and the second didn't survive. They could have at least shown us a fake alien autopsy."

That brought a chuckle from the department heads. Good, they sounded tired. It would soon be over. He needed a nap—and another shot of booze.

Karpov waved his hand in the air. "Ooh, ooh. Me next, Colonel."

McFarran looked away and pursed his lips. Oswald motioned for Karpov to speak.

"I just want to say, FC, that *Roland* kicked some major alien ass today. Yeah, it sucks about the Rangers. They were good people. Hell, I even took one those fine ladies up to missile bay two to polish the old warhead, if you get my drift." He winked at Breen, who blushed bright red.

McFarran inhaled deeply, but deflated when Oswald caught his attention and shook his head.

"But they didn't die rescuing some dipshit colonists that wandered off the reservation and got lost, or fighting some crazy anti-Earth terrorist cell.

"They died fighting giant alien death-bot monsters on a planet covered with ancient alien ruins. And *Roland* was right there with them, kicking alien ass. Right?" Karpov held out his arms to encompass his fellow officers. "We came, we saw, we kicked their asses. Yeah, we got a bloody nose, but you should see the other guy. And they had disintegrators!"

"You can't actually disinteg—" Engineer Bowens started.

"Yeah, yeah." Karpov waved a dismissive hand over his head. "I'm sure we'll figure out the pure and accepted science behind what the bug-weapons were doing. Until we get the proper name for that devilish phenomenon, I'm just going call them disintegrators, OK? Though I am willing to concede to death-ray for the sake of syllable count.

"Anyway, we blasted them to hell. And I plan on putting recommendations in for my gunner-gals. Gilweh and Relor were lining them up and burning them down." Karpov mimicked pistols with his hands and made as if shooting at the other officers, adding his own special effects as he did so.

Bowens tried again to speak, but Karpov gave him a double shot of pistol fingers and continued over him.

"And we used the lander artillery. And ORBAM munitions. In actual combat. We've never had a chance to use those things against the Proxies. But we blasted the minions of the galactic overlords. We. Kicked. Ass."

"Yeah!" Breen said, pounding his fist on the table. He seemed surprised by his own outburst then nodded at Karpov. "Yeah."

"Fucking interstellar," Karpov said, pointing his fingers at Breen and making laser noises. One of Karpov's fingers reached forward as if to poke Breen in the eye, then it touched a rogue bead of De-lamain. The tactical officer noisily sucked his finger clean.

"Thank you, Tac," Oswald said.

"Just one more thing," Karpov said. "We did well. *Roland* did well, pissant mistakes and all. But you really saved our asses, Colonel. If you hadn't ordered those kill clouds, I'm not sure we'd have managed to bag all those bug ships before they split us open like the landers. Good call, FC."

Oswald fought down his blush by picturing the smiling corpses of the Rangers staring up at him through the docking ring. He didn't take compliments well, but rebuking Karpov now that the other officers had started clapping seemed peevish.

"Yes, *Roland* did well," Oswald said once the room quieted. "Good points, Mr. Karpov. Now whose turn was it before they were so rudely interrupted?"

A few more comments were made about trivial things, mostly because when an officer didn't have anything useful to add they were prodded until they added something, anything.

Oswald let out a breath and extended his finger to shut down the table. "Very well. If there are no other comments..."

"Just one more thing, Colonel," McFarran said, smiling ruefully at the chorus of sighs, snorts, and *tsks*.

"Yes, Aux?"

"Why did you abort Team Two? I see no reason. And if we'd have destroyed Site Two's power grid, they might have made it. Probably not, but it seems we should have given them every chance possible."

And there it was, the question Oswald hoped would remain unasked for now. He wanted to reach out and stop the recorder, but the eyes that had been rolling at McFarran's last-minute question were now all focused on him. Curiosity replaced the irritation in their faces. McFarran would file a report anyway if he turned off the recorder early.

The problem was, he didn't know. Not really. The decision had come straight from his gut, lacking even a pretense of reason. Commanders sometimes had to make decisions on a best-guess level. He had no doubt that Team Two would have been just as doomed. But he'd made the abort call before any threats presented themselves. There was no solid reason he could point to. He couldn't even credit a commander's educated guess.

It was hope, he realized. Nothing more.

Hope that there was something or someone out there that might still need the jump beacon. And hope that if they were there, DPV would still function with just one remaining. Otherwise, he'd fucked the hypothetical aliens and Team Two. And maybe, ultimately, the whole Earth.

Oswald looked at his officers in turn, holding Breen's eyes for a long moment before finally facing McFarran.

"I didn't want to blow out the last candle in the lighthouse."

# Chapter 13

OSWALD STARED AT THE artifact not two meters away, and his brain would still not assign a shape to it. By way of experimentation, he'd ordered all his senior officers to give it a good hard look and log what they saw independently. No one could make out what it looked like.

To Oswald, it was like a 3-D stereogram that refused to reveal the hidden picture he could almost see, no matter how long he stared or how hard he crossed his eyes. A xenophobic strand revealed itself, a primal fear of the great unknown, the dark reality of a universe that cared little for his primate sensibilities. He wasn't sure he even wanted to see it.

"Try turning it this way." Oswald mimicked the motion he desired with his hand.

The tinman holding the UXA had survived the recovery vehicle's damage, along with a few weapons. It would have joined the capsule on its journey to the Oort cloud if not for a request by a junior technician to try to bring it back on line. Oswald signed off on her request. He was no robot activist, but it felt like saving the last Ranger. He was grateful the sole-surviving tinny hadn't been painted like a penis.

The tech had written *Rocketman* on the side of the tinny's neck in indelible marker next to a simple drawing of *Roland*.

Rocketman braced against the bulkhead with two limbs and held the UXA with the other two. It turned the artifact as indicated, its small sensor cluster staring lifelessly at Oswald and awaiting further instruction.

Oswald frowned and rubbed his eyes. "What about you, Aux? See anything?"

McFarran shrugged. "Sorry, Colonel. I suffer the same frailties as the rest, it seems."

"Almost like security feeds where they blur out someone's face. Almost."

"But it doesn't blur it all the way," McFarran said. "Like you could make out who it is if you just stared a little... harder."

"Exactly."

Oswald had Rocketman bring the UXA closer and turn it again. Perhaps he could see it if he ate some crazy tribal mushroom or pharmacological equivalent. The tinny hung motionless, its views on the artifact a mystery. Even though the strange visual effect was passed through the robot's optical sensor, it was able to grasp the UXA.

He wasn't willing to let anyone touch it with their bare hands. SDF command was going to have to solve this mystery. Oswald was just the getaway driver.

"Rocketman, stow the item in the container and stow the container in the safe."

The robot complied with machine precision, then folded itself into a cube. Oswald placed his eye over the safe's retinal scanner. The deck vibrated with the impact of the locks.

"You hear that?" Oswald asked. "Not the lock slamming, but that."

McFarran grimaced as if he'd bitten into a lemon. "Yes, Colonel. It's almost worse from inside the safe. Like it's screaming."

"That's it." Oswald slipped his tablet from its pouch and looked at the ship's summary screen. *Roland* was all green. It seemed the strange alien thrumming should be setting off some kind of alarm or maybe burning a hole in the ship. But it didn't seem to be bothering *Roland*.

"Everything is prepped for jump to Sol, Colonel. Shall we send a jump comm?"

*Roland* had passed the jump threshold nineteen hours ago, but Oswald didn't know what they'd find on their return. He couldn't assume the Proximan fleet had been taken care of or that they wouldn't jump in when *Roland* did. He wanted the crew well rested.

"Yeah. Have Cindy work it up and make ready to jump in one hour."

"Very good, Colonel." McFarran nodded and drifted coneward towards the comms and sensors pod.

Jump comm was discovered when Dr. Beth Valki of Ford-Tanshi Aerospace noticed unstable jump tunnels still generated a minute signature at the far end before collapsing. By generating a series of unstable jump tunnels that instantly collapsed, binary signals could be sent to anyone listening on the far end.

A binary, unidirectional signal required complex cyphers and codes to achieve any level of security. Each ship used a single mission cypher, a random character replacement template that was destroyed at the end of the mission. Sending a simple message required several pulses. *Roland* was sending just such a message now.

*Three stars spinward.*

Which translated into something like, "Incoming with one item."

Oswald hooked his toes into a handhold and pushed down towards the beehive. He usually changed in the common area, his modesty worn away by years of service. But he wanted a sip of Delamain so struggled into a new flight suit in the confines of his sleep tube.

After taking a final, small pull of the bottle, Oswald made it to his station in time for the outgoing jump comm. The cycling of the jump engine produced a dull buzz.

"Thermal spike in jump engine," Bowens reported over the duty channel.

As the jump pulses continued, the internal temperature reading increased. It was a small amount, barely two percent past acceptable variance, but it was unusual.

Oswald was about to abort the jump comms when Lt. Trese reported the message was complete. Jump temperature fell back into range within a minute.

Stray radiation was well known for causing random sensor spikes, false target readings, and even the occasional LED flash. Depending on which LED lit, it could be quite disconcerting.

If not for the action they'd seen, Oswald would have ignored it. Successful jump tunnels were inherently stable and wouldn't form except under well-understood conditions. Statistically, it was safer than operating standard reaction-mass propulsion.

But things overheating in space could quickly cascade into disaster. Oswald ordered a complete system check of the jump drive software and hardware. Sol had sent the single jump pulse indicating they'd received *Roland*'s transmission. They'd have to wait though.

Thirty minutes later, Bowens declared the jump system and the main reactor good to go. Oswald was not a great believer in coincidence, even though he'd experienced it many times in his career. Space could be a strange place.

McFarran reported that all crew were in their vacc-armor and all systems were green. Oswald double-checked the same screens and called for the department heads to check in on the ops net.

His stomach clenched. Remembering how he'd felt after the long jump to Delta Pavonis, Oswald questioned the wisdom of that second drink. And the first.

All warheads were ready and the laser capacitors charged. The reactor was still good and the LANTRn was ready for burn on the other side. They had plenty of delta-v to get back to Earth from wherever they popped back into Sol.

Though safe, SDF jump tunnels were known to scatter, forming seemingly at random within a wide target area. It was the reason Oswald's daughter was dead.

There was no way the Proximans should know where they'd jump in, or when, since they were half an hour late already. Still, it would be nice to have an escort. Had *Triumph* and *Charger* survived, they'd have been a formidable squadron. Oswald wondered what Anahita had managed to hobble together while they'd been gone.

The jump clock hit five minutes and McFarran issued a ship-wide notification.

Oswald considered how he'd deliver his resignation. What he'd say and how he'd feel when he did. Or how he'd feel a year later. There had been nothing but war for him for almost twenty years. It had been a priority over even his family. There was always a new campaign, a new incursion, a desperately needed patrol to stop the Proxie bastards from nuking the Big Blue.

"Ten," came Breen's voice over the ops net.

Oswald felt the usual urge to scratch his nose right before a jump. He scanned the ship status screens for any change, ready to abort the jump if needed. All clear.

But his breath came in short, panicked gasps. Forcing himself to flip through the data pages projected on his visor again, he still saw nothing.

He'd only shit himself once in fear, what was known as "combat evacuation" in the more polite circles of the military. When he'd been a junior pilot on CPR-33 *Barrgos*, they'd been hit by a Proximan penetrator that ripped through the secondary flight compartment he'd been manning. He shit his suit when he saw the black hole where the auxiliary flight commander and senior navigator were supposed to be. His bowels were now gurgling the same way. And it wasn't the space-rats. Fortunately, the new suits had better combat evacuation systems if it came to that.

Oswald itched all over and couldn't help but squirm in his armor, trying to scratch everywhere at once. His thoughts grew sluggish and he struggled to focus on *Roland's* summary screen. Cheery green icons smiled back at him, telling him all was well as the countdown progressed.

Someone grunted over the net.

"Three..."

Had he finally cracked? It could take years after a particular trauma for someone to lose it. He'd seen it happen to better men than him. But it was just his nerves.

"Two..."

Who'd grunted? And why? Maybe someone else was having nerves. Or that Delamain had gone bad. Can cognac go bad? Who was whimpering on his ops net?

"One..."

There was something he was supposed to do when things were going wrong. Oswald couldn't remember. But he wasn't going to let someone freaking out keep him from Misty and his girls. Even if every spacer on *Roland* crapped in their cans.

"Ju—mp..."

The word came in two long, slurred syllables. It sounded stupid. He would have to talk to that guy about being stupid on his ship. As soon as he could remember the name...

A deafening crash echoed through the hull, audible even through Oswald's vacc-armor. Pain flared in the middle of his spine and radiated out through his body until his toes and fingertips burned. Oswald screamed in pain, but his scream was drowned out by someone else's scream in his right ear. He tried covering his ears with his hands, but only succeeded in slapping his helmet repeat-edly.

Then he recognized the scream. It was the alien artifact, the hum he'd heard earlier amplified to deafening levels.

The display on Oswald's visor swirled, the lines melting togeth-er into a sparkling whorl of wondrous colors. They shattered into countless dancing embers, angry at the night for some reason. Or they might have been happy.

The visor on his helmet wavered and poured away like liquid. McFarran's black super-fat French face was shoving its way in where the visor used to be.

"Colonel! Colonel! Colonel!" McFarran shouted in a cheerful but endless loop.

The man's breath smelled like thunder and he kept getting clos-er. Oswald thought about telling his friend to get back in the kitchen, but neither of them spoke Swahili.

Finally, the fat face was sliding away. A look of deep consterna-tion flashed there, and McFarran's face tried to keep its purchase by hooking a long, purple tongue on the rim of Oswald's helmet. But the visor returned, severing the tongue.

McFarran's face stretched out impossibly towards *Roland*'s cone. Oswald watched two starfish in vacc-suits randomly pushing buttons on a control panel.

Being at least a million kilometers away, they ignored Oswald's screams.

Oswald felt as if people and overdue fuel bills he couldn't see were walking back and forth across his ship, judging him.

The laser arrays extended and retracted in time to one of those stupid songs his daughters loved to listen to while they shaved pigs.

Oswald realized the grim red light flashing in his face for the last century still took itself quite seriously. It split into two, then four, then eight flashing red lights. He could feel the heat of the lights on his face, but fanning his hands had no effect. The lights grew more insistent and were joined by that familiar alien throbbing.

Another jolt slammed Oswald's teeth and spine. He screamed again, spraying spittle on the inside of his visor. The red lights solidified and he recognized them.

Critical system alarms. A lot of them.

He couldn't stop screaming and pounding on his helmet, even as his mind came back into focus. Others were screaming over the net too. Oswald's helmet felt as if it was filled with fire. He couldn't breathe, as if he was burning alive.

The helmet needed to come off.

*Roland*'s critical heat indicator was flashing red, along with the primary heat sink and external radiators. Systems were going offline. People were still screaming. He was still screaming.

Oswald tried to call out on the net for the engineer to jettison the primary heat sink and coolant. To scram the reactor, but his throat would only issue the same warbling, mindless noise. His voice commands to the computer went unrecognized.

He fought his fingers to input the commands in between his terrifying efforts to remove his helmet. Oswald saw a dip in the heat level as the display verified the heat sink had been jettisoned and the coolant purged into space.

The reactor was not responding to the shut-down command. Oswald hoped it was only a comms or software failure and not warped control-rod channels. The reactor scrammed on its own as safety protocols kicked in. Emergency batteries took over. They flickered yellow on the status screen to indicate some problem, but at least they weren't red.

Oswald didn't know why he was still struggling to remove his helmet. The air was hot inside his suit and it burned his lungs to breathe. But he could breathe. He flipped through the views of several compartments, looking for fires or hull breaches.

Other suits of vacc-armor struggled with their helmets too. Some had managed to get them off. Those lay rigid and unmoving, their faces twisted and blackened, armored hands clutching at their throats or silently screaming mouths.

"Life Support!" Oswald could recognize snatches of his words now. "Override. Sedate! Full sedation! Hines! Sedate everyone."

He wasn't sure if the doctor had heard him or if the system had recognized the command. The doctor might be one of those who'd removed their helmets. Just when Oswald was sure the doctor was dead and the computer hadn't heard his commands, his arms went numb. He was thankful that the incessant clanging of his own glove on his helmet had stopped. Oswald's head lolled and he could feel drool running down his cheek.

It shouldn't be doing that, though he couldn't think why not with all this bliss.

"What if... Proximans?" McFarran tried to ask.

"Dead anyway..." Oswald choked out before all the angry red lights faded to black.

# Chapter 14

ANAHITA HADN'T HAD much spare time to worry about *Roland* and knew it was a pointless exercise in any case. What happened in Delta Pavonis was completely out of her hands. She'd done what she could and now it was up to Pierce.

Still, what scant time she had that could be called spare was spent worrying about him.

"Looks like *Xinglong* finished off that Proximan straggler by Io," Will Zaphrim said. He looked up at Anahita.

She could see the concern in his eyes for her. For the fleet. "Yeah, I saw that. Now that Jupiter station is rearmed, it's one less thing to worry about. And when the next batch of drones gets finished on Luna, we should have Earth covered again."

"You're going to recommend sending the loaner ships back to their theaters?"

"Some, I think." Anahita looked to the holographic war map that now constantly rotated on the wall across from her desk. Many systems were red, indicating active Proximan operations. "But they're not all worth saving. I'm suggesting pulling out of some. Including Vega. That place is a death trap even without the Proxies."

Will gave a low whistle. "General Sanchez won't like that."

"Sanchez is an idiot who doesn't realize he's losing."

"But he's an idiot with an SDF congresswoman for a mother."

Anahita waved her hand in the air. "Which is why he's a general in the first place. Sanchez is one that would help us if he got spaced."

"Addition through subtraction?" Will smiled and shrugged.

"He wouldn't be so bad if he ever listened to any of his flight commanders. Any time someone offers reasonable advice, it seems he ignores it on principle. Or convinces himself it was his idea in the first place."

"He's an idiot."

"And that's why I'm going to suggest abandoning Vega." Anahita leaned back in her chair and rubbed her eyes. "Not that it matters. None of these systems are really worth fighting over except to keep some of the Proxie fleets busy and out of Sol."

"If Pierce makes it back, and the eggheads deliver, we'll be able to start tracking them back from those systems."

Anahita glared at Will. "Oh, he'll make it back. Don't know about the eggheads though." She zoomed the war map onto Delta Pavonis, one of the few green systems.

Will raised his white-gloved hands. "You know what I mean. Pierce'll get it done."

Anahita chewed her thumbnail. "Sorry. He's a few days past due."

"He may have jumped farther out than expected or decided to alter his approach or—"

"I know all that. Of course, if someone hadn't redacted so much of the relevant data on the planet..."

"Not my call and you know it."

"Whoever made the call is an idiot too."

Will snorted. "I think it was Tzun."

"Then he's a fucking idiot."

Will's snort turned into a stiff laugh. "I pushed, but between Special Forces paranoia and Chinese face-saving, command wouldn't let me."

"Aren't intel mistakes bad enough? Now we're making those mistakes on purpose."

"You're just as guilty," Will said. He slid fingers across his tablet, idly scanning reports without reading them. "You just hate being on the other side of it."

Anahita brought up the latest MCC status reports. Two more Proximan spy sats had been destroyed and one of their squadrons forced to jump away near the Trojan asteroids. Now all she needed was Pierce's jump signal. "This goes well beyond need to know and you know that."

Will shrugged. "Your FCs might disagree. Pierce would definitely disagree. No one likes being kept out of the loop. When you're putting your life out there, it's hard to let someone else decide what you really need to know. Besides, it's not like we had much info to start with."

"And some armchair general wouldn't understand that?"

Will blew out loudly. "Get over it, Ana. I know you understand it. You weren't always a general, in case you forgot. I'm just trying to remind you before you decide to go march off to Tzun's office and give him another piece of your career."

Anahita stared at him, then chuckled. "Why, Will, I didn't know you cared."

"I just don't want to get shoved into your job."

"At least you aren't an idiot."

"I wouldn't go that far."

"Trying to be nice here..." Anahita returned to her reports. Will now seemed to be paying attention to his, but she only cared for one report. The update on *Roland*'s status.

Pierce wasn't her only concern. In fact, Pierce was one of the few who didn't need her input at all. He was making his own calls and perhaps referring back to what he considered her suggestions. Despite the official SDF stamp that said flight *orders*, not suggestions. But when the MCC is 20 light-years away, the FC will play.

And who was she to second-guess Pierce Oswald, anyway? That damned RoV of his sometimes made it hard to argue with him. She hated to admit that his constant reminders that he was a war-hero and that she was essentially a spectator affected her. Her job was hard enough without Oswald's sanctimonious attempts to shatter her confidence. But she did her job, she always did her job. And he could go to hell. Her orders had killed more people than his... especially after what she now called The Battle of Twenty-three.

The display hovering over her desk blinked red for a priority message. She saw it was from Major Thomason, the comms officer for Mission Control Center 3. Anahita started to jump to her feet, saw Will, and tried to play it off by reaching for her bottle of water and taking a drink.

Will chuckled.

"This is General Khadem," she said into the comm panel.

"Incoming jump comm, General. Content of message not cleared for this channel."

"On my way." Anahita secured her terminal and strode to the doorway. She stopped and turned to Will. "You coming?"

"I'll catch up. You look very eager."

"So are you," she said, walking behind his chair and pushing it into the hallway before Will could object.

They didn't speak on the elevator ride to her master MCC. Anahita bounced on the balls of her feet and tapped her thighs. She made sure to stay behind Will so as not to see the humor in his eyes, as good-natured as it might be. The guards silently scanned them through.

She let go of Will's wheelchair as soon as they were in her MCC and snatched up two headsets. Handing one to Will, Anahita clipped hers on and powered up the interface. The main display from MCC 3 now hovered above them.

"General Khadem on the net," she said. "What's the message?"

"Decoded, it reads they are incoming with one mission item. Would you like the raw pulse data from *Roland*?"

"Yes, please." Anahita sighed. A hopeful smile played at the edges of her lips as she looked at Will.

"One's better than none," Will said.

The smile left Anahita's face. "But not as good as three." If Pierce Oswald had not taken all three, *Roland* must have run into trouble. Something bad. "So help me, if something's happened because that intel—"

"I know, you'll eat my eyes." Will sounded weary. "About the only part of me not overcooked."

"It might not even be Pierce."

"If *Roland* is alive, Pierce is alive."

"Not necessarily."

"Well, he'll be here in any minute, so you can ask him." Will gave a scarred grin. "Over a secure channel, of course."

*Roland* was not there any minute. There were any number of reasons an FC might delay a jump, such as a maintenance issue. The pulse could alert local hostiles, but there weren't supposed to be any Proximans in Delta Pavonis, so maybe there wasn't a problem at all. Pierce just wasn't feeling rushed.

After twenty minutes, Anahita was in a near panic, and she didn't give a damn what Will thought. She glared at him, daring him to make some comment. Any comment that would give her a pretense to release some stress at him. The look of worry mirrored in his own eyes made her whimper instead.

She hoped he hadn't heard it.

"What the hell, Will?"

"Just... be patient." His voice carried the tone of a man who didn't believe his own words.

"So what could cause that delay? It's usually five minutes max between the comms and the jump."

"True."

"Well, you were an FC. Why would he do that?" Anahita hoped Will wouldn't give the obvious answer. She had that one covered.

"Mechanical issues for one," Will said. "If some final checksum failed after the jump comm, Pierce would want it checked out. Could be a computer glitch requiring a system reset, an off-normal sensor reading, something broke loose in the cargo compartment." He counted them off on his gloved fingers, but his face was emotionless. "And I probably wouldn't send a follow-up pulse unless I knew I had to completely abort."

Anahita paced around the wheelchair. She nodded and took a deep breath. Will had obviously just pulled those things out of his ass. But they at least sounded plausible enough to give hope. "Fine."

But hope had let her down repeatedly. She'd hoped she wasn't pregnant. She'd hoped to command a starship. She'd hoped Pierce would leave Misty. She'd hoped the Proximans would catch some Earth flu that wiped them all out. Nope on all counts.

"Just in case every jump detector in Sol failed simultaneously," Anahita said to the crew of MCC 3, "get as many optics as we can spare scanning that return sector. And forward me a list of ships prepared for a jump."

"You sure we can afford that?" Will asked.

"We can't afford not to," Anahita said. "If something has happened," she paused to clear her throat, "we still need the UXA. And hopefully we can rescue survivors."

As the minutes passed, hope withered and a grim calm settled over her. It made the task of selecting which ship to send to Delta Pavonis easier. *Vasterness* had an expert flight commander, but it was too cramped for extended operations. *Fan Tai Do* was perfect, but the last flight commander had recently been killed and the new FC was a good officer but too junior for her liking.

"Jump tunnel detected," MCC 3 reported. "But it's strange."

"Strange how?" Will asked.

"The system is flagging it as both a jump comm and an incoming tunnel." The sensor officer forwarded his screen to Anahita. "I've never seen this before."

Anahita slapped the desktop until her hand stung. "Get me a visual! Get the scopes scanning!" The system distance estimate would put the light lag at just over twelve minutes. But the anomalous readings meant anything might be possible.

The twelve minutes dragged on. Anahita didn't trust herself so she kept quiet. She wasn't able to concentrate on anything she pretended to study so she gave up. Will offered her a hand and she took it.

He winced and she realized she'd been squeezing. She apologized and Will patted her hand. They waited together in the silence of the master MCC.

"There it is," the sensor officer said. "Coordinates confirmed between optical and jump detector."

"Show me," Anahita said. "Start at first observation."

A star field replaced the tactical map on the far wall of the cubicle. The tiny points of light gave a false impression of the magnification level. The jump tunnel appeared from the darkness to fill half of the screen.

She'd seen countless jump tunnels in her time. Though novel and beautiful in their own way, they flashed a bright white and were gone the next instant, replaced by whatever had gone in on the other end.

Not this one.

A shower of red sparks exploded from the white star. Anahita stood, putting her hands over her mouth. The sparks raced away in every direction. But the glaring star of the jump tunnel stayed.

The net was silent. Everyone was waiting for the tunnel to collapse. It had to, after all. They always had.

This one didn't.

"What's going on?" Anahita whispered. "Is that...?"

"A persistent jump tunnel?" Will finished. "It might explain the fuzzy readings, but let's not jump to conclusions."

Anahita looked at Will. "We've never gotten much past the theory. How?"

"We need to get the science guys on it to make sure." Will twisted his body to look back at her. "I can't even guess how. But I can guess why."

"The UXA."

Will nodded. "I'm afraid that might have been *Roland* scattering. Which now breaks two rules. That debris had momentum exiting a jump tunnel."

Anahita walked to the display and put her forehead against the wall. It was really over. Pierce had completed his mission and brought back a poison pill that killed him and *Roland*. A pill she'd put on his ship.

She knew that part of her would always expect him to return until his body was dumped on her desk. The other part of her knew better though. Pierce hadn't really made it back from Delta Pavonis. And the war had changed in front of her eyes again. First Ululani. Now Pierce.

*Roland* would not be forgotten. Colonel Pierce Oswald would not be forgotten. And she would have to tell his family. A minor SDF lackey wouldn't do. The dread she felt when Paul Gryphon's wife and daughter had unexpectedly been in the VIP lounge that day sent Anahita's stomach flipping.

"Divert squadron Alpha Six to fortify that space before the Proximans show up to investigate." Anahita collapsed into her chair. "We won't be able to hide that thing."

"Or what we've found on Delta Pavonis," Will said. "There'll be lots of fun questions to follow."

Anahita had already moved beyond the inquests and head-chopping that would come. Those things were out of her hands, too, and that brought a strange peace. So did the idea that she might be replaced. That would change after hours of political showboating and righteous indignation by the very people who already knew about the UXA and the mission. Or by those who were too dull to even understand the implications. Those VIPs would only worry about how to spin the PR repercussions.

In truth, she couldn't accept being replaced. Not now. She had to survive the upcoming circus. Anahita needed to keep her position, needed to stay in the fleet. It was the only way to make the Proximans pay. To make all Proximans pay for *Bonwei* and for *Roland*.

# Chapter 15

OSWALD STARED AT THE thirteen vacuum-sealed body bags lashed to the cargo compartment's bulkhead. It was a final charnel formation of *Roland*'s casualties on this mission so far. The vacuum process left the twisted bodies and screaming faces imprinted against the plastic. He could recognize some of them. Three, whose hands had moved postmortem, looked as if they were trying to claw their way out.

The chemical embalming fluid pooled and gurgled in the zero-g. Freezers for the dead were a luxury a mass-conscious starship couldn't afford. The chemical-vacuum body bag worked well enough, but a corpse could pop, its liquefied putrescence filling the bag and expanding if not taken to a proper mortuary eventually. But he didn't want to space the bodies so close to home.

The bags storing Yninski and the Rangers had melted onto their bodies in the extreme heat of the failed jump. Oswald and McFarran re-interred the polymer-shrouded corpses into new bags, unwilling and unable to remove the melted plastic first. Fortunately, the lockers with the unused body bags had been protected from the catastrophic heat. Some grim and forward-thinking mission planner had made sure *Roland* held extra interment bags for the Rangers.

Oswald coughed on the acrid fumes still being cleaned by the air system. "It's like one of those legendary cursed diamonds that brings death to everyone who owns it."

McFarran nodded, glancing at the shattered safe that once held the UXA. "Are you sure you want to jettison it, Colonel?"

"No. But I want to be able to. If I ever hear that scream again..." Oswald pantomimed pressing a button with his thumb. "Whoosh."

Two crewmen floated past in their skivvies, taking air samples. It was still stifling in *Roland* and Oswald had given permission for the crew to strip down. He and the aux were in flight suits unzipped to the waist.

McFarran grasped a handhold and sneered at the black smudge it left on his hand. He wiped it on his flight suit but the stain remained. Or it was replaced with one of the stains already covering both of them.

*Roland*'s interior was now dark and gloomy, filled with ash, soot, and death. Even the lenses of the emergency lanterns had been scorched, casting gloomy shadows in every direction. Conduits had ruptured and deck plates had buckled. The blackened scars of the flash fire were everywhere.

Especially on the survivors.

Oswald blew out a breath and gagged on the thick air. "Eight, including Bowens." He read the report from Dr. Hines on his tablet. "Three from heart failures that didn't recover after defib. One broken neck." He paused to stretch his back and caught at the sudden pain. "I might have busted something myself."

"You should go see Hines, Colonel."

"Medical is already full of burns and broken bones. I'll go later."

"Maybe he can explain why a crew of veteran astronauts tried to take off their helmets in a crisis situation. Myself included." McFarran sniffed and watched a cluster of crewmen drift by with another emergency air filter.

Oswald nodded, remembering his own inexplicable efforts to pop his top. Two crew asphyxiated on their own vomit in the throes of panic—or possibly while sedated. Four managed to get their helmets off, roasting alive as they clawed at their split, charred faces. Including Lt. Chun, *Roland*'s senior pilot.

Oswald pursed his lips. "All he could tell me was they died quickly from the superheated gases in their lungs. Probably didn't even feel their skin burning."

"Not very reassuring, Colonel."

"I wish I could pretend that the doctor was trying to be reassuring."

Oswald's muscles trembled as he pulled along the main passage. Looking coneward, he was reminded of the inside of a chimney. He didn't want to know how bad the air recyclers were. Pieces of split conduit, snapped fasteners, and strips of peeled insulation still drifted in the gloom. They would have to perform a full FOD, floating object damage, inspection.

"That was close, Hashi. The whole frame almost failed." He imagined it was close to the last thing Gryphon saw before *Charger* died.

McFarran coughed up a black and red glob. He looked around for some container or recycler.

"Just spit it there," Oswald said. "The whole place needs cleaned."

"Colonel!" McFarran turned his nose up. "The very thought." He grabbed a piece of floating insulation and blew the glob out of his mouth onto it. "*Roland* is hurt, but she deserves better than that."

Oswald chuckled, coughed. "Apologies to your sensibilities, Aux."

McFarran made a slight bow. "You saved us, you know. If you hadn't dumped the heat sink and sedated everyone... we wouldn't be here to worry about where to spit. Command will have quite an investigation. I've never seen or heard of anything like this."

"I should have aborted the jump. That would have saved everyone."

"Maybe, Colonel. But there is no way to know. We had to come back somehow. This is very strange."

"That thing"—Oswald hiked a thumb back towards where the UXA awaited being jettisoned—"changed everything we know. Which probably means we didn't know all that much to start with."

He pushed into the flight control compartment and McFarran followed. Flight Sgt. Norris was at her station, wearing a bulky sound-powered headphone set. One earpiece was hiked up on her temple to keep an ear free.

Norris turned as Oswald and McFarren entered. Her eyes were red and her cheeks smeared black from where she'd obviously been wiping away tears and soot. She started to announce his presence, but only coughed and tried again.

"As you were." Oswald moved towards the flight station and offered her a warm smile. One he didn't feel.

Norris laughed and wiped her eyes. "Sorry, Colonel. All this smoke."

"Of course. It was smoky down in the cargo bay too." Oswald hooked his toes under the console. The lights were barely bright enough to see the juggler, so-called for the cluster of three oil-suspended spheres, red, blue, and yellow, used to indicate acceleration changes along the relative X, Y, and Z axes.

Below the colored spheres, six diamond needles recorded those changes by etching spikes on a slowly moving plate of nano-constructed glass.

When used in conjunction with a manual flight computer, basically a circular slide rule, and the navigation charts for each system, basic orbital plotting was possible as an emergency backup.

The manual flight computer was a series of tough metal disks. Unfortunately, the system navigation books, while liquid- and tear-proof, were now a single, melted, polymer blob.

Oswald produced a small light and focused it on the etched glass. Though under a magnifier, the gauges had been fogged by the heat and were hard to read. "Look at the juggler. Two acceleration spikes." He spat on his thumb and rubbed the glass. "We're moving alright. Maybe wobbling a bit. Is that what you make of it, Norris?"

"Yes, sir. I thought I might have seen a third spike but, you know, the smoke."

"How is that possible, Colonel?" McFarran moved closer, squinting at the juggler.

Oswald shrugged. "Maybe we never actually jumped, so we never lost our momentum. But we'd still have to account for the acceleration. These seem to be more than malfunctioning maneuver thrusters. If I'm reading this right, the first spike shows an acceleration of 10.2 g. The LANTRn can't even come close to that. I'd say we're moving at a pretty good clip."

"And I'd say the UXA is still to blame, Colonel."

"Yup. Hopefully that means we're in Sol and something strange just happened. Even if Danner can't get the systems back up, we should get a rescue." Oswald clicked his light off and put it away.

"Danner is a good assistant, Colonel."

Until the main computer was online, they were flying deaf, dumb, and blind. So Oswald started gathering bits of FOD still in the flight compartment. It was about the only thing he could do. McFarran did the same. Once they could no longer see any debris, Oswald plugged a headset into the sound-powered phones and listened to the repair crews work.

He was less concerned about what they were saying than how they were saying it. *Roland* had taken a beating before. This crew had lost members to enemy fire. But nothing like this near-destruction. Oswald was glad they were in Sol—at least, he hoped they were in Sol. The tone of the workers was grim. Grim and angry was

OK. Grim and humorous was better. But what he heard was grim and despondent. Defeated. They needed to get home, quickly.

It had to be more than the casualties and the damage. Oswald often bragged about having the toughest crew in the fleet. And he believed it. But there was something about the jump, something about the attempts to escape their suits. When he tried to remember the strange things he'd seen, no images came to mind, only an acute dread. Something dark had happened to their psyches.

Oswald looked down to see his hands trembling. He noticed McFarran watching him and shoved his hands into his pockets. McFarran's hands were already in his.

The main lights flickered. Oswald pulled the tablet from his flight suit. It shook in his hands and the screen glowed in the gloom as he watched the progress of the main computer reboot.

"It seems Danner was paying attention," McFarran said.

Oswald nodded and moved towards his couch. The surfaces were curled and blackened, except where he'd been covering it in his armor. He'd have to use his tablet until the integrated monitors were replaced. A chime sounded when the reboot was complete. Subsytem recovery indicators appeared to climb across the screen as they progressed.

Oswald held the push-to-talk button on the sound-powered phone mic. "Clear channel for the FC. Pass on to all department heads that navigation processing and navigation sensors are top priority. I say again, pass to all department heads that nav systems are top priority. That is all." He took off the headset, reeled the cable back into the bulkhead, and stowed it.

They hadn't hit anything yet, so Oswald figured the chances of hitting anything were low. Jump tunnels didn't form close to gravity wells, but this jump had broken the rules already. He couldn't count on the way things used to be.

OSWALD SLID OVER AS Dr. Hines took his seat at the conference table. The environmental control systems were still struggling so Oswald left the hatch open. "I know there's still a lot of red on this display and you've all got things to do. How's the aux doing, Doctor?"

"He'll be fine. Just low oxygen from too much particulate in the air." Dr. Hines flashed an awkward smile and looked around. "The real damage won't come for at least a decade. That's when—"

"Thank you, Doctor." Oswald looked away, his eyes wide. He suddenly didn't feel very well, either. "While you've been piecing *Roland* back together, I've been trying to piece together what the hell happened.

"For those that don't know, *Roland* lost nine children in that jump, including Chun and Bowens."

The officers looked down at the table. Some hadn't known, but there were no sobs or gasps. Just stony silence.

"What the fuck did happen?" Karpov looked around the room with an expression as if he'd bitten a lemon. He rubbed the polymold cast on his left arm.

"Leave that alone," Dr. Hines said. "I don't have time to set it again."

Oswald shrugged. "I can only blame it on the artifact. Can't tell you the how, only that we apparently don't know as much about jump physics as we thought. Like the fact that we underwent a 10.2 g acceleration upon exiting the tunnel."

"That's not even possible," Gresh said. She raised her palms and looked around. "Right? I mean, that's not how it works."

"I saw the juggler readout," Breen said, wonder in his voice. "I verified the time stamps—as best as possible."

"Which is why we need the nav sensors up, Gresh. We've been flying blind and we're not exactly sure how long. It'd be a shame to have escaped the Proximans, raid DPV, and survive a near-catastrophic meltdown, only to nosedive into Neptune."

"The reactor and LANTRn are up and ready," Danner said. "Battery one is down. It fried and won't hold a charge. We can fire everything up, but without the main heat sink I wouldn't suggest it."

Oswald tapped a note about battery one on his tablet. "I want to see where we are before spending any delta-v. We might be going in the right direction for all I know." Oswald doubted it, but it would take a lot of reaction mass to come to a complete stop.

"Nav and targeting radars should be up within the hour," Gresh said. "Most of the damage looks to have been blown power feeds. Most of the spares were damaged, but we have enough."

"Good. I want a navigation plot ASAP. Once we verify we're safe on our vector, we can get our bearings and head to Earth."

"Assuming we're even in Sol, right?" Karpov asked. "Don't get me wrong, FC. I hope we're in Sol. But that jump... I still feel like I'm about to shit myself. And not just from those dreams."

Oswald nodded. "Any thoughts on this mass hallucination, Doc?"

"Nothing but guesses," Hines said. "But I wouldn't toss around the term mass hallucinations just yet."

"What the fuck should we call them?" Karpov asked. "Daydreams? Everyone I've talked to saw some shit. Except the dead ones. They didn't talk back, fortunately."

"Yes, yes," Dr. Hines said. "I'm sure you conducted a very strict data experiment. Everyone I asked who admitted to remembering anything, said they felt like they were trapped or smothering. Like a bad case of claustrophobia."

"Like spacer fever," Breen said. He looked around, as if apologizing for speaking. "Someone spaced themselves on my first flight. Just walked right out the airlock. Well, I mean he had to get past the safety interlocks and all that, but my flight commander called it spacer fever."

Hines nodded. "Close to what I was thinking. But everyone got it at once. Too short a time to expect a single case, let alone multiple. At this point, I'll have to blame it on the artifact's effect on the jump too. Some kind of short-term psychosis. If you hadn't issued the sedation order, Colonel, we'd all be dead."

Oswald motioned for Karpov to speak.

"As far as tactical goes, laser array two is toast. The main reflection tube is warped to shit and the primary optic's cracked. I robbed it to fix laser one, which wasn't in very good shape either. Two isn't getting fixed; it needs replaced. We also lost about half of our remaining delivery vehicles. I am happy to report, however"—Karpov spread his arms magnanimously—"that none of the warheads detonated."

"Obviously," Breen said.

"Obviously," Karpov agreed. "Where'd all that heat come from? The reactor or LANTRn or what?"

Danner shook his head. "The reactor scrammed and took the LANTRn down with it. No logs of it firing off. Must have been some reaction to the artifact."

"I'm getting pretty fucking sick of that artifact," Karpov said.

Oswald agreed.

"At least one thing didn't change," Dr. Hines said. "It still stopped everyone's hearts."

Oswald pursed his lips at the doctor, who shrugged back. "It's always been assumed that the conservation of momentum and heat got dumped into the jump tunnel somehow. I guess it got dumped back on us this time. With interest."

"Crazy," Breen said. "I hope we'll be home soon."

"I have no reason to think otherwise, Mr. Breen." Oswald smiled at the astrogation officer, again wondering how such a man could remain so unchanged by the battles he'd been in. Breen was just as straightforward, innocent, and optimistic as ever. "Let's get back to work. We've got a starship to fix."

# Chapter 16

NORRIS SAW CHUN'S FACE everywhere she looked, hovering before her like the after-image of a brilliant flash. It always started off with his smiling face and those twinkling eyes. Then it shrank to the charred ruin with shriveled pits floating in his eye sockets that had been peering in through her visor when she awoke. That was the face that now appeared the instant she wasn't focusing on a specific task. It was the face that stared back at her from the reflection in the tablet screen.

Most of the crew didn't remember what they saw during that jump. She did, at least in part, though she couldn't delineate between the jump dream and the sedation. It was all mixed together in her memory. In that dream, she was being eaten by a planet full of writhing yellow worms. They were devouring her cell by cell, but she never ran out of cells.

Her groans had echoed in her helmet as she woke. It took long seconds for her eyes to focus. When they did, she still didn't realize what she'd been seeing at first. Smoldering black cheeks were pulled back in a rictus smile. The heat-withered gums made the teeth look elongated and crooked.

She'd reached out then, as if touching the unidentified mess outside her helmet might help her recognize it. Chun's shriveled eye didn't react when her armored finger jabbed into the socket. Then she'd realized it was Chun. And then she'd screamed, vomited, and passed out again.

It wasn't the professional reaction someone with her experience should have managed. She would do better now. How much she'd wept and cried disappointed her. She was the senior pilot now and *Roland* didn't need weepers. *Roland* needed warriors.

Norris was glad for the overpowering smell of burnt plastic that still hung in the air around her station. It covered up the smell of Chun's flesh.

Her hands shook if she didn't ball them into fists. It wasn't the first time she'd almost died on *Roland*. But that jump... her chest still ached from the defibrillator.

And those hallucinations? Worse than when her husband, Nolan, scored that vial of escrow. It had taken her two days to recover and her other husband, Cliff, almost had to go to a medical station. It would have ruined her career, so they all agreed to wait it out. Nolan had worked hard to make amends for that bit of stupidity.

Cliff's eye was peering at her through Chun's charred visage. The picture of Cliff and Nolan was ruined save for Cliff's one smoke-damaged eye. The fire had robbed it of its beautiful green hue. She only knew it was his from its position within the frame.

Yet there it was, as if peeking at her between black fingers. It asked, as always, why she kept flying off into space. Why she wasn't there to keep her husbands warm at night, and dance, and sing, and watch vids with them, and do all the things she promised when they'd become a triad.

They knew the answer to those questions, of course: they just didn't like them. It was the military life, her duty. They hated it. She lied when she told them she didn't like it, either. And they knew she lied. She didn't love being away from them, but she loved every second of flight duty. At least, she used to.

Norris started when Oswald cleared his throat behind her.

"You got this?" he asked.

"Yes, sir."

"You don't sound so sure."

Norris bit her lip to keep it from quivering. Goddess, she hated being so weak. "Why did Chun do that? Take off his helmet, I mean."

Oswald took a deep breath. "Doc's looking into it. I really don't know. I almost got mine off too. Do you need some more time? I can man pilot watch if you need it."

"Sorry. Yes, FC. I mean, no, FC. I'm ready. My quals are up to date. I can fly *Roland* wherever you need to go."

"That's what I like to hear, Norris." Oswald smiled down at her and squeezed her shoulder. He tapped his tablet to hers. "While we're waiting, run these nav plots. Someone has to figure out where we are. Start with Sol and see what you make of it."

The warmth from his hand lingered. The touch felt good, but she couldn't take any comfort from it. The FC was not one to make physical contact with his crew. That he had touched her only warned Norris how stressed he was, despite the kind smile.

Her stomach flipped. She could do this, had done it. Hours of the pilot log showed her as primary. But Chun had always been there double-checking her. She wasn't sure without him.

She decided to trust Oswald. He obviously thought she was ready, despite her own uncertainty. Or he didn't care if she was ready and was trusting her to rise to the occasion.

He joined the ops net and immediately demanded updates from the departments. Even his normally confident voice was sounding haggard and exhausted. It was too bad he was happily monogamous.

No, it was best that he was. Norris rubbed the tattoo beneath her navel and thought of Nolan. It had been a peace offering to him because people weren't perfect, and even in a mature triad feelings got hurt.

Norris focused on the system map *Roland's* nav sensors had put together. Jupiter's red eye was a relief. Even though the planets were all in the wrong place, she knew they were somewhere in Sol. It had to be a matter of position or system calibration. They simply weren't where they thought there were. Norris dragged the rocket icon representing *Roland* across the solar system map, looking for a relative match of where the planets looked to be and where they actually were.

The rocket's icon updated to account for its velocity. That terrified her. She knew they weren't going to hit anything now that the sensors were up. But they shouldn't be moving at all. Jump physics were no longer working as advertised, and she didn't know what that meant, if anything.

Norris took deep breaths. She wouldn't panic. She wouldn't cry. Fear was clinging to her like a wet towel since the jump. Normally, it would come and go, especially after a good breakdown. But it was still there in her night terrors and bouts of trembling.

She rubbed her navel and gazed into Cliff's ruined eye. They'd almost lost her.

"Shit," she muttered.

She'd zoned out while the nav simulation was running, and it continued beyond her model parameters. *Roland* was back in its assumed position, and the virtual planets had been spinning for centuries. She let them spin while she considered the next model to use.

It would be helpful if they could get the comms working. Then she could download a positional update from SolNav. Trese said everything was up, but that obviously wasn't true.

They hadn't even been able to find Earth with all of its EM noise. It would have to be on the far side of Sol. But Jupiter was Jupiter and Saturn was Saturn, and they could see them, though they were eerily silent too. Each had a sizable SDF space station, plus facilities on the moons.

Norris tapped her lips and decided to run the next model relative to Jupiter. She gasped at the screen and stopped the simulation with a jab that hurt her finger.

All the planets matched except Earth, which couldn't be directly verified because it would be masked by Sol in the model's timeframe.

Norris's breath came in short gulps. It couldn't be. There was something else going on—she was jumping to conclusions or had modelled the simulation wrong. It wouldn't be the first time.

Yet her breath would not come. The model was right. The parameters matched what Oswald had given her. It came back with the same results three times: *Simulation Validated*. She struggled from her seat and mouthed to Oswald that she was leaving her station.

Oswald muted his mic. "You OK?"

Norris inhaled deeply through her nose. "Yes, sir. Just need to freshen up."

Oswald eyed her with a mixture of concern and suspicion. She was afraid he would push the issue. Then he nodded and returned to the ops net.

The main shaft echoed with the pops and groans of still-cooling materials. Backup air filters hummed outside compartments that suffered from the worst damage, or contained more pungent or dangerous materials. Norris heard a single sob over *Roland*'s background noise. At least she wasn't the only one.

She was glad to find the head empty. The water from the cold faucet was still warm, but it felt good as she scrubbed her face raw. She used the small vacuum that sucked up the globules of stray water to pull the tears from her eyes. Chun stared back at her from the mirror.

Norris drifted back to her station, careful to avert her gaze from Oswald. The nav computer presented a message that the latest simulation was complete.

Her finger hovered over the screen for a moment before she could force herself to push it.

*Simulation Validated.*

She slid *Roland* around the map and ran the timestamp forward and back.

*Simulation Validated.*

She prayed to the Goddess that Oswald had been given bad data, or had given her bad data by mistake. If the models were correct, they'd all lost everything and would never get home.

Norris buried her face in her hands and hoped her flight commander didn't see her crying again.

# Chapter 17

OSWALD RUBBED HIS EYES with one hand, then slid it down his cheeks. The stubble rasped against his fingers loud enough to be heard on the net. "How can you not fix our position? We're in Sol." He hadn't been able to either, but it wasn't the FC's job.

"Sorry, sir," Major Kirsk said. "Cindy insists the sensors all pass diag. And they do. I saw it. But the planets don't line up. Of course, I can give you straight line to Sol and the angle over the ecliptic..."

"So we're not picking up any signals? Nothing?" Oswald didn't care to badger people, but he'd learned long ago that sometimes people needed to be prodded over and over before they thought a problem through fully.

"Are we even sure it's Sol?" Karpov asked.

"The spectrum-analysis profile matches almost perfectly," Kirsk answered. "Unless we're in some bad sci-fi horror story, I'd say we're pretty sure about that."

"Maybe something happened and command ordered system silence?" Breen said.

"We should still see something from Earth, Breen," McFarran said. "No way to shut down everything. And those homesteaders in the belt don't care what the SDF says. And WalStar doesn't listen to anyone."

"I'm not sure the SDF even has the authority to shut off SolSat One or Terra Nav Prime," Oswald said. "The US and SoAm Collective certainly wouldn't approve. Anyway, I guess we'll just have to figure it out old-school. Danner, what about the heat sink?"

"Just about finished. Fortunately, no coolant channels got warped. We're doing final pressure checks with the replacement coolant. The exterior panel is wrecked though, still tumbling along next to us. We'll have to wait to get a new one."

Norris pushed against her station a few times before being able to free herself. She turned and mouthed, "Leaving station."

She looked ashen, her eyes wide and wet. Oswald muted his mic. "You OK?"

Norris inhaled deeply through her nose. "Yes, sir. Just need to freshen up."

Oswald wanted to say something, to offer some comfort. But he didn't have any to spare. He nodded.

"Even if they could turn down everything in Sol, Colonel," McFarran said, "command just sent us a jump confirmation a few hours ago. With light lag, we should still be seeing some signals. It has to be something on our end."

"Every radio and radar?" Kirsk asked.

"Then it must be something with the software or core." McFarran's voice was curt. Oswald heard the frustration mirrored in his own voice. It wasn't from being contradicted, it was that nothing made sense.

"Even the handhelds and EVA suits aren't picking anything up," Trese said. "The suits should be able to pick up nav beacons. It's fucking strange."

Karpov raised his brows. "There's no way the Proximans could have rolled through Sol and wiped out everything. No way. Not in the time we were gone, at least."

"Not in the time since the jump comms, certainly," Oswald said.

"Maybe it was a trap," Breen said.

Karpov laughed. "Not a very fucking good one. We're still here."

"Just brainstorming," Breen muttered.

"Storming part's right." Karpov snorted at his own joke.

Oswald muted his mic and blew out a slow breath. Snapping at anyone, even Karpov, wasn't going to help. "Knock it off, Tac. Alright, people, someone needs to give me some answers. I'm leaving the net up, but everyone get back to work."

Oswald scratched his chin. Nothing made a damned bit of sense. There had to be something wrong with *Roland*. But the handhelds and EVA suits worked independently. He'd seen some strange technical gripes in his time, but nothing quite like this. One thing he had learned though, if it was really strange, it was always software.

And they should be able to see Earth on the big-eye from the sector they were supposed to arrive in. And if Earth was in Sol's umbra, then Jupiter and Saturn shouldn't be where the nav computer said they were.

Oswald shook the problem from his head. A dull throbbing started behind his right eye and he needed to shut his brain down for a bit. Something he'd never been good at.

"Sir?"

Oswald started at the voice above him. He looked to see Norris had floated up there without his notice. She was holding her tablet. He smiled. "Yes, Flight Sgt?"

"Can I speak with you?"

Oswald motioned to her tablet with his chin. "Figure something out?"

"I hope not, sir."

He raised an eyebrow. "Problem?"

She let out a single sob and dabbed at her eyes with the cuff of her flight suit. "I just want you to tell me I'm wrong."

"About what?"

Norris shoved her tablet at him. Oswald tapped his tablet to hers to download what she wanted to share.

The navigational model she'd been working on appeared on his screen. He grunted. *Roland* slipped between planets as Oswald manipulated the time progression. The final position matched perfectly, including Earth being on the other side of Sol. "What did you do here?"

Norris tapped her screen and the timestamp on Oswald's display blinked.

*05NOV2618*

It couldn't be right. The current date on *Roland's* master clock read:

*21JUL2195*

"No fucking way, Norris," he whispered. He coughed to summon back his voice. Oswald smiled up at her. "No, you've set up a bad parameter somewhere."

They hadn't been gone 423 years.

"Goddess, I hope so."

"Has to be bad input."

"Show me." Norris dabbed at her eye. "Please." She floated back to her station and strapped in.

Oswald skipped through decades and centuries on the map. There were minor variances between the projected and measured planetary positions, but not enough to provide any hope from mistakes in the simulation. The differences were within the margin of error of *Roland's* scopes, especially considering the massive damage the starship had suffered.

The more he looked, the more it matched. The positioning lined up. The time involved could fit a number of explanations for the loss of signals, none of which Oswald wanted to contemplate at the moment. Where would the missing 423 years have gone though?

The artifact, of course.

Oswald accessed Norris's private channel. "Have you told any-one else?"

Her voice was hoarse, full of sobs waiting to burst through. "No, sir."

"Don't. Understood?"

Norris didn't speak, but Oswald saw her nodding at her station.

"I'll get Astrogation to run it against some extra-solar reference points. And we'll figure out why it's wrong. It has to be..." He tried a comforting smile, but it felt more like death's grin to him. Oswald was glad she wasn't looking.

# Chapter 18

SATURN LOOMED ON THE monitor as *Roland* approached from the outer system opposite Sol. Its obsidian rings cut across the gas giant, reminding Oswald of a black, lidded eye. The visible moons were as implacable as their father.

"Any sign?" Oswald asked.

"No sir," Kirsk answered. "We should see Saturn Station by now."

"Unless Norris is right," Breen said.

"That's all some bullshit," Karpov said. "There's something going on, but..."

"But what?" Norris asked.

"But just no to all that," Karpov said. "For now, anyway."

"Well, I hope we find something," Oswald said. "We spent a good bit of delta-v to match orbits."

"Would it even still be in orbit if it's been that long?" Breen asked.

Oswald panned his view from the big-eye, looking for anything. Saturn Station should be surrounded by comm and nav sats. But none could be found and there was still no answer to *Roland*'s transponder.

"It's pretty high up," he said. "And it was set to be pulled along by perturbations from the moons. But there's a lot of rock and ice around here, so who knows."

Oswald watched three moons transition across Saturn and into darkness, to be silhouetted by the sun. Sol was so distant. And too quiet.

"I think I might have it, Colonel," McFarran said.

The scope's focus swept right and zoomed in on the edge of the outer ring. After two minutes of digital enhancement, Saturn Station came into view among the rings of frozen debris. It fully looked the part of an SDF battle station with its heavy armor plates and weapon ports. Antenna clusters reached far above and below the main toroidal center structure. From this distance, it looked intact.

"Spectrum and thermal overlay," Oswald ordered.

No thermal signature. No EM signature. No transponder. Saturn Station was dead. But it would have some answers. It had to.

"Plot a docking orbit and power up the magnetic field. I'm not sure our radiation map is accurate." Oswald put his thumbprint on the last three reports for the shift and floated from the flight pod.

He drifted in *Roland*'s main shaft, deciding if he should inspect the ship, go sleep, or brainstorm in the conference room. It would be four days before docking.

He was exhausted and restless, which made trying to sleep unappealing. His head hurt, which wasn't the best time to figure things out. The rest of the crew felt just like he did and would appreciate an inspection like a meteor through the hull. So he just floated there, rubbing at black smudges until he either cleaned something up or decided nothing more was coming off. The task brought focus in the tiny repetitive motions of his thumb. He wouldn't do an inspection—he'd see how his crew was doing. Just chat with them.

"FC present," Breen announced as Oswald entered the astrogation pod.

"As you were," Oswald said. He looked around and only saw Breen and Trese. "Anyone else on duty in here?"

Trese spoke without looking up from the terminal he was installing. "Just us, Colonel."

"Everyone else is working on inspections before we get under radiation restrictions," Breen said. He looked as if he wanted to add something.

"What is it, Breen?" Oswald asked. "Speak your mind."

Breen exchanged glances with Trese. "What are we going to do if it is really the future?"

Oswald latched onto a handhold and rubbed his shoulder. That would be a damn fine question to brainstorm. He'd only focused on the best way to solve the riddle. The bias in his thinking had been to figuring a more mundane explanation that, however strange it might be, would see them return to their normal lives somehow.

But Saturn Station was dead. No one in Sol was talking. One way or another, there was a new normal and they'd have to adapt to it.

Oswald shook his head. "Don't know. What do you think? Trese?"

"I think we better start remembering how to farm and get to Earth," Trese said.

Breen's face went pale. "We have to find it first. What'll we do if we can't?"

"Whatever happened," Oswald said, "Earth will be there. Planets don't just disappear. Don't worry, we'll figure it out."

Breen's smile was rigid and unconvinced. But he was trying.

"Carry on." Oswald nodded to the men and slipped out of the pod. There were no good answers to those good questions. If they could find the master clock on Saturn Station, they'd know something, at least. Until then, he didn't know any more than the crew. A cleaning before radiation ops was a good idea, followed by a long nap where no one could ask him questions. No dreams either, please.

SATURN STATION FLOATED like a dead titan under Oswald's boots, so rimed with ice that it looked like a natural part of the rings. The main dock was too damaged for *Roland* to use. The lack of other visible battle damage, and the slight wobble detected in the station's orbit, led Oswald to believe the docking ring had been hit by an asteroid or ice chunk after losing power.

*Roland's* magnetic shielding extended around the station and Oswald's team. Ghostly waves of electricity danced around them as charged particles became trapped in the field.

Saturn filled Oswald's visor, the icy rings spreading into infinity beyond the capabilities of his human sight. Even now on the sun side, it wasn't so colorful without the enhancements of astro-photography. But it was certainly majestic.

"That's beautiful," Breen said.

"Yes, sir," Corporal Tadashi Gaho said. "Like a jade viper."

Oswald waved his team forward. "The radiation fields here aren't as bad as Jupiter's, but it's no time for stargazing. Let's get inside."

He clamped his suit onto a cable an EVA drone had attached to the nearest airlock. The drone now drifted above them, ready to assist as needed. Oswald pulled himself along the cable, constantly scanning for debris ready to rip open his suit. The EVA suits were tough, but not like their vacc-armor.

The team made it to the central maintenance airlock. Gaho pulled a yellow-striped emergency recovery kit from Breen's back. He attached four clips from the box to rings positioned around the airlock hatch and pulled a lever on the side. A gear extended from the recovery kit and slid into a slot labelled *RECOVERY*.

It spun slowly for a second, then stopped. Breen pulled a long slide hammer from Gaho's back and fitted the feet of the tool against the edges of the hatch. He clamped his belt to the airlock, slid the striker up, then slammed it against the hatch. It seemed strange to Oswald to see the hammering and hear nothing. Still hovering over the station, he didn't even feel the vibrations as Breen repeatedly worked the hammer against the hatch.

Breen moved the hammer to a spot on the opposite side of the hatch and, after three strikes, the recovery kit gear spun again. Everyone on the team braced for any outgassing, but there was none. The airlock crept open into darkness, a clockwork maw screaming silently at the violators. Gaho and Breen recovered their tools and Oswald led them into Saturn Station.

Ice crystals and clumps of frozen dust floated everywhere, lighting up like motes in a window sill as the astronauts' lights swept through the darkness. There was no battle damage inside. No charring. No emergency shoring. No floating bodies clutching at the intruders with accusing fingers.

For all of its size, the passages of Saturn Station were as cramped as *Roland*'s. Oswald led the team through the pitch black towards the central hub. The SDF logo was displayed on the wall, the dates of the station's commissioning and changes of command engraved on a faux-granite plaque.

At the bottom of the plaque, someone had neatly written with a maintenance marker:

*Surrendered to Proximan Forces. 18FEB2207 Colonel Linda Cornin commanding. R.I.P.*

"Is everything OK, Colonel?" Breen asked.

Oswald had to swallow twice before he could speak. "Yeah. Just getting my bearings." He pressed against the plaque, and waved Breen and Gaho past him so they wouldn't be able to see the writing. He'd never heard of Colonel Linda Cornin. The year 2207 was over ten years after their jump to Delta Pavonis. But how long ago had it been written?

Gaho spun to face Oswald. "How can this place be so empty? Even if they evacuated the second we left..."

Oswald held up a hand. "That's what we're here to find out. You're the one most recently stationed here. Command capsule is down three levels?"

Gaho was shaking his head absently as he took in the lifeless surroundings. He looked back at Oswald. "Sorry, Colonel. Yes. Those hatches there."

"Right. Let's get them open." Oswald remained in front of the plaque until Breen and Gaho moved to the hatches. It wasn't rational to try to hide anything from them. He'd shared about the aliens, no problem. There was something holding him back about this though.

Their passage cut dark slashes into the thin sheen of frost that covered the bulkhead and hatches. The lifeless eyes of unpowered emergency lanterns reflected the team's lights back at them. These lanterns were designed to run on batteries that could last decades and charged not only from solar arrays but from Saturn's own magnetosphere. They should be at least glowing dimly.

The internal hatches opened manually, after a few knocks from the slide hammer, without needing the recovery kit. Oswald pulled through the hatch into more of the same mote-filled darkness. The team came across a sign labelled *POWER PLANT*.

"Let's take a quick look-see." Oswald tugged the latches and spun the wheel to open the hatch. Breen and Gaho followed him through.

"There's why it's so dark," Gaho said. "The entire battery bank's missing and the main breakers have been pulled."

Oswald followed the corporal's light beam. There were gaping spaces where equipment used to be. Even if the solar arrays were working, there was nothing to hold the charge. He toyed with the idea of setting an engineering detail to see what they could power up, but decided against it. That was just asking for an explosion without knowing more. Maybe the SDF—or whoever—had powered everything down for a good reason.

"Let's go," Oswald said.

He continued to sweep his light through the darkness before them. His breath was growing louder in his helmet and his brow grew moist. A quick check of his EVA status panel showed all green.

It was merely nerves. But he could feel the gloom pressing in on him. It reminded him of the deep-water excursions he'd done in spacesuit training. If he was starting to develop claustrophobia, it was time to muster out. If it wasn't too late already.

A flash of color appeared in the beam of his light and Oswald grabbed a conduit to stop. "Hold."

"That's the hatch to ops," Gaho said.

Oswald focused the beam on the colored patch. It was still there, but from the angle he couldn't tell what it was.

"Take it slow," Oswald said and tugged on the conduit enough for a slow glide.

An aquamarine-colored sign was set across the hatch labelled *OPERATIONS*. The sign was made from a sheet of some type of polymer with blocky glyphs printed on it. Whatever adhesive force had been used to attach the sign had worn off long ago; it was held on now only by a corner.

Oswald's heart thundered and his guts turned liquid. "Proximan," he whispered.

He scanned the hatch for signs of a booby trap, knowing that he'd already be dead if there had been one. Oswald tugged the sign free and held it in front of his helmet camera. "Aux, get this translated. I barely remember my Proximan insults. Aux?"

"Sorry, Colonel. Yes. I'm on it. Have it for you in a moment."

"Discreetly," Oswald said over the commanders-only channel.

"I'm always discreet, Colonel."

Oswald grinned. "Remember that time at Olympus Mons—"

McFarran cleared his throat. "I have always appreciated your own discretion on that matter, Colonel."

Oswald's team floated in the icy darkness, continually scanning with their lights as they waited for the translation.

After three minutes, McFarran spoke over the commander's channel. "I... I don't know what to say to this."

"Start with telling me what it says."

"Presenting to your visor, Colonel."

Holographic letters formed in Oswald's helmet.

*Conquered by Zon-Bri-Kon, Bellick War Group. 18FEB2207 No Admittance*

"It took longer to convert the date from Proximan, Colonel," McFarran said. "It is a rather pretentious language."

"Nothing worse than a pretentious language."

"I'm glad you agree, Colonel."

Oswald grabbed a handhold and wedged the sign between two nearby pipes. Turning to the hatch, he jerked on it until it swung open, still half-expecting to find some Proximan nastiness.

He wasn't disappointed.

Three desiccated corpses stared back at Oswald with black eye-sockets and faces stretched into grins of ancient death.

He bit back a scream, and braced himself in the hatch to shield Breen and Gaho from whatever had killed these people. The bodies didn't move. Nothing exploded. Oswald hadn't died this time. Though these poor souls had obviously died long ago, there was no telling how long a trap might lie in wait for its next victims. It was apparent no booby trap had killed these people. The corpses' hands were lashed to the upper deck and their feet to the lower, stretched out like skeletons in a medieval dungeon.

"What is it, sir?" Breen asked.

Oswald entered the control center and the others followed. When Breen saw the bodies, he shrieked into his mic and scrabbled to get back into the passage. All he managed to do was fling himself against the wall in a panicked, spiraling conniption.

"Get ahold of yourself, Breen," Oswald said. He and Gaho grappled with Breen's flailing limbs until Breen stopped struggling.

"Sorry, sir," Breen said. "I don't know... I just wasn't expecting that. This place is so creepy. And dark." He turned slowly and gaped at the bodies. It was dead silent except for the sound of Breen's heavy breathing over the mic.

Oswald patted Breen on the shoulder and moved closer to inspect the corpses. The blue and gold uniforms were stiff, a spiderweb of cracks reaching out from the seams and across the fabric. One flight suit wore colonel's bars. Oswald tentatively brushed the ice from the faded name tape. The whole left breast of the flight suit fell into crumbling fibers, but he could barely read the worn letters.

*L. Cornin*

The motion set the strung-up corpse to spin slowly on its restraints, revealing the back of the withered skull. In the bone beneath the remaining clumps of hair, a clean-cut hole about the size of a thumb could be seen.

Oswald leaned between the corpses as best as he could without bumping into them. Each had the same ancient wound.

"Laser burn," he said. "Close range."

Breen turned away. "Executed?"

"That'd be my guess."

Gaho moved to try to read the names on the other corpses. He reached out to dust one, but pulled his hand back at the last second. "I've never heard of a Colonel Cornin on Sat-Stat. Colonel Hays was still commander when we jumped to Delta Pavonis. I messaged a few friends there—here—when I was still on leave."

"If they executed everyone," Oswald asked, "where would they have put those bodies?"

"Maybe only the command staff was properly executed, Colonel," McFarran said. "The Proximans love their ceremony."

Oswald ran his fingers against a nearby wall, the tips of his gloves leaving slashes in the thin ice. "It looks like the station was taken without a shot. I find it hard to believe the crew would let themselves be executed without some kind of fight."

"Maybe the command staff traded their lives for those of their crew, Colonel. There might be POWs somewhere," McFarran said. "Or life support got hacked and no one had the chance to fight back."

"POW skeletons, maybe," Oswald said. "At this point, I'm not interested in a deck-by-deck to see what happened. We're here for the clock." With everything he'd seen, he'd almost forgotten their mission.

The control panel Oswald wanted was on the other side of the corpses. He tried squeezing between the bodies slowly, but felt something give. Cornin's face knocked against Oswald's visor, sending her nose and three teeth spinning away with a cloud of skin flakes. Her hands twirled in their restraints on the upper deck like a pair of tiny ceiling fans in a horror show.

"Sorry," Oswald whispered. Having already desecrated the body, he shoved through to the controls. The instruments were dead. The juggler balls were still tilted slightly in their freeze-proof liquid. The recording needles had reached the end of their glass long ago.

Above that was the master clock, powered by a minuscule atomic battery with a half-life in the thousands of years. Master clocks were designed to survive all but the most catastrophic damage and keep running beyond even the expected life span of the Sol

Defense Fleet. In this case, it looked like the engineers had delivered.

Oswald hesitated as he reached out to brush the ice from the clock's analog display. After a moment, he wiped the display, looked, and averted his eyes before he could read it. He was glad his back was to Breen and Gaho so they couldn't see his childish antics.

He shook his head and read the display, this time unable to turn away.

*18DEC2618*

He brought up the display from *Roland* and stared.

*02SEP2195*

Oswald pressed the master clock's calibration test button. It blinked yellow for a few seconds, then shone bright green. He pressed it three more times—each time the result was the same.

Calibrated. No errors. Saturn Station's master clock had faithfully kept counting for 423 years while *Roland* was... what? Where?

Bile burned Oswald's throat and he couldn't breathe. Sweat poured down his face, pungent and slick.

"Colonel?" McFarran called, his voice high. "Sir. Your biometrics are going into alarm. Colonel?"

The room swam and then spun. McFarran's voice became a distant buzz as darkness swallowed even the beams of Oswald's lights. Apparently, his mind wasn't quite ready for the truth.

"Breen! Gaho! Get the colonel..."

# Chapter 19

OSWALD IMAGINED HOW satisfying it would feel to smack Danner upside the head and watch him cartwheel away in the zero-g. Instead, he crossed his arms and took three deep breaths. The astronauts reeked of sweat, smoke, and cleaning solvents. He eased the muscles in his face, trying to look more pleasant than he felt.

"Maybe the Ancient Ones came and opened a dimensional rift?" Danner's voice roared in the small conference room. "Or alternate universe doppelgangers? Space Vampires, even?"

"I get it," Oswald said. "Now how about offering up something useful."

"Useful?" Danner looked at each of the other officers with an incredulous, almost mad, smile. "Useful, Colonel? We're already off in fantasy land. Time travel and stasis fields? You want useful? Here you go. We're all just computer programs in a huge mainframe and this is a big-ass glitch."

Karpov looked wide-eyed at Danner. "I know! We can slingshot ourselves around the sun and open a time warp. And *bam*, we're back for dinner."

Oswald rubbed his temples. "Karpov..."

Karpov clapped Danner on the back. "No, no. I really saw it on a vid once. Lots of pretty colors too."

"I've had enough pretty colors," Breen said.

Karpov scratched his chin. "Now that you mention it, that vid did kind of look like what I saw during the jump."

"You saw the master clock yourself," Oswald said. "You know how those things are calibrated. You know how they work."

"Let's find another then, FC. We can't go on pretending it's 2618 just because of one clock." Danner pointed into the air. "We can find Earth. Or Luna. Or another station."

"But we can't find Earth," McFarran said. "And it's not just because of one clock. Everything else matches. Even if you don't trust the clock, Danner, you have to account for that."

Danner turned away. "Not everything else matches."

Oswald understood. The whole damn thing was crazy. No one had come up with anything like a reasonable explanation as to how or why it had happened. But Oswald knew it had. The twisting in his gut gave him the certainty his reasoning could not. "Is everyone else agreed that at least it seems we've returned 423 years after mission start?"

A few officers shook their heads. Oswald knew they weren't disagreeing with his suggestion. They simply couldn't believe they were actually considering the idea. Knowing the most reasonable explanation was something impossible could be hard for technically minded people to accept. As long as they didn't think about it too hard, the crew should be able to overcome their cognitive dissonance.

Danner spoke over his shoulder. "But the planetary model *doesn't* fit, Colonel. Where's Earth? Hm? By this model you want us to believe, it should have cleared Sol by now."

Oswald nodded. "True. But Earth should have cleared Sol by now in any model. So you're just shuffling mysteries here. But the pulsar references do match. I can't explain Earth, but everything else fits that data—"

"Well, then, maybe fleet command figured out how to make the planet invisible while we were gone."

"That's enough, Danner. I'm eagerly awaiting your solution. Because we should have seen Earth by now no matter what the date is."

Danner turned back to face Oswald. "I don't know. But I do know we didn't time travel."

Karpov leaned close to Danner. "For someone versed in the mysterious intricacies of jump tunnel generators and how they violate physics as we used to know it, you are particularly close-minded. We're traveling through time right this instant."

Danner put a finger on Karpov's chest and pushed him away. "Back off. And don't be stupid. You know what I mean."

"I'd like to throw something out there," Doctor Hines said. "Why everyone went crazy. It might fit with the four-hundred-year thing."

Oswald waved him on. Anything to get Karpov to shut up.

"Shall we go back to our discussion of the experience resembling a mass case of severe spacer fever? That might lend credibility that we were in some manner of stasis, or time warp, or jump hibernation, or whatever we wish to call it. Maybe something in our subconscious felt that passage of time. And when we woke up, all our brains wanted to do was get out. To escape."

"It would match," Breen said.

Danner shook his head.

Hines looked at Danner and shrugged. "Just a thought. Might be hogwash. I do think it would be a good idea to find Earth though. We know, at least, where it should be, right? We could find another clock and some friends. Or at least someone who'll tell us what happened before executing us."

"Maybe we're still in the hallucination," Karpov said. "We could be in one big three-ring circus of crazy." His smile waned as the doctor stared back.

"I've considered that. If we can get to Earth, someone there can tell us for sure," Dr. Hines said.

Danner glared at Karpov as he spoke. "The hydrogen tanks from the station nearly topped off our reaction mass. And the heat sink panel has been replaced. I'm go for finding Earth."

Oswald traced his finger along the tabletop. Troubleshooting processes usually started with the assumption that there was a single root cause. One CPU had failed. One database was corrupt. One circuit path was open. Any other issues would be related to a single fail point.

It was time to consider multiple, simultaneous glitches. Navigation was tracking Mercury and Venus with no trouble. They should be able to find Earth. Tales of alternate realities and parallel dimensions filled Oswald's head. But he couldn't go there. Not yet.

"Earth it is then," Oswald said.

"We should send a transmission out there," Gresh said. She looked around the table, nodding. "It's not like anyone we need to worry about didn't see the plume from our LANTRn already. And we're going to have to fire it again."

"Maybe, but there's a chance they weren't looking in our sector of the sky. If we send an omni-directional RF signal, someone will hear that. We'll maintain EM discipline for now." Oswald unstrapped and pulled away from the table. "Plot me a high-efficiency burn. It might be a while before we can top off. Anything else?"

"Just one more thing, FC," Karpov said.

Oswald took a small measure of pride that he'd kept from groaning, unlike some of the other officers.

Karpov looked around and shook his head. "Try to do good for some folks, I tell you what. In the spirit of accepting the times in which we live..." He pulled what looked like a red sock from his pocket and slipped it over his head. The tip of it was topped with a white, fuzzy ball that drifted next to his left ear.

Oswald examined the makeshift cap. "Is that—?”

"A hastily sewn-together pair of socks topped with a fluffy ball of aerogel?" Karpov interrupted. "Why, yes. Yes, it is, FC. Merry Christmas. According to the master clock on Saturn Station, it is now 25DEC2618. And I come bearing gifts!"

Oswald smiled despite himself. He didn't care for Karpov's usual shenanigans, and he didn't care for his briefings to get derailed. But he had to give it to his tactical officer: the man thought outside the proverbial box.

Karpov beamed, pulled out his tablet and held it over the table. "For just this occasion, my entire book bundle is free for download for my beloved crew."

The offer was met with a chorus of groans and boos, but some pulled out their own tablets and accessed the download. Oswald already had them all. They were well written, if not exactly accurate.

Karpov bowed. "And that's not all, my good fellows." He reached over to open the hatch and clapped twice. A pair of hands handed him a serving container, then closed the hatch.

Karpov rubbed the adhesive strip on the container and stuck it to the table. With a wild flourish of his hands, he opened the lid to reveal what vaguely resembled a baked chicken made of dough. "Voila! I made it myself."

"From what?" Danner asked.

"Why, from space-rats, of course. You don't think we have real turkeys on *Roland*, do you?"

"Of course not."

Karpov rubbed his hands together over the table. "With loving hands, I painstakingly crafted this beautiful, albeit smallish, Christmas turkey out of the unidentifiable mush contained in no less than six space-ration packages. It was quite a messy chore, but I used Danner's sleep tube so as to not make a mess anywhere important."

Danner glared at Karpov before shoving his finger through the faux turkey. "Fuck you."

Karpov slapped Danner's hand. "Hey. Now there's some fucking yuletide joy for you." He pulled a bundle of galley forks from the lid of the box and tossed them to those around the table. Danner threw his back.

"Fine, more for me," Karpov said. "FC, would you like the first bite? There's not much, so it will be your first and only bite."

Breen was laughing so joyously, so unashamedly, that Oswald had to join in. Soon, they were all laughing except Danner.

"I'd be honored, Mr. Karpov." Oswald dug into the mushy stump representing one of the faux turkey's legs. He raised his fork as if in toast and ate the bite. "Just like Mom never made. Thank you, Tac."

"Oh, I want the other drumstick," Breen said. "My dad and big brother always took the drumsticks."

"Sorry, man," Karpov said. "That depends on the aux. He gets next dibs."

McFarran offered a tight smile and took a small bite from the sculpture's breast. "You are quite the *chef de cuisine*, Mr. Karpov."

"It's all in how you mash things together, Aux. And making do with what you got." Karpov slapped Breen on the back. "Guess you finally get your drumstick."

OSWALD KEPT THE BIG-eye scanning along Earth's orbit, occasionally swinging back to verify the positions of the other planets. And each time the other planets were where they were supposed to be—in 2618.

But the Big Blue remained hidden from them. No sighting. No beacons. No emergency signals. No hope in sight.

Oswald was growing numb to each new disaster. He rubbed his forehead as he reviewed the report on Corporal Odvyg one final time before thumb-printing the approval tab. His headaches were growing worse.

At least she'd only vacc'd herself in the airlock, instead of leaping into space. Leaving one of *Roland*'s children behind would be another blow to the crew. Despair already filled the modules of Oswald's ship, growing heavier with each day they couldn't find Earth.

The commander's stateroom stank of Oswald's sweat and the astro-tape used to strap the makeshift replacement cushions in place. Oswald craned his head and rubbed his neck. It would still take months to match orbit with where Earth was supposed to be. Jumping was out of the question. He'd have to make sure everyone was getting their required exercise. Himself included.

"Colonel?" Flight Sgt. Norris stuck her head in through the hatch. "Do you have a moment?"

Oswald slid his tablet in the receptacle on the table. "Sure. Come on in."

She entered and opened her mouth twice, trying to start. "I wanted to apologize, sir."

"For?"

"For blubbering like some jump-cherry."

"I don't follow."

"When I presented my findings, sir. About the time lapse. I cried like a baby, sir. I've always hated people like that. Especially women. Like some weepy housewife."

Oswald frowned. "I happen to love my housewife very much and she is not the least bit weepy."

Norris blushed. "Sorry, Colonel. I wasn't... I mean, your wife. Sorry."

"No worries. It's been a hell of a mission. I have a feeling we've got more shit coming." Oswald smiled. "We've lost good people. And if you are worried about crying, you'll be the only one doing so."

"Crying, sir?"

"No. Worrying about it. Everyone else will be too busy crying themselves to worry about you crying."

Norris nodded, a grin touching her lips for second. "Permission to leave, FC."

Oswald waved and watched her go. Things must really be getting to her. Norris was not one to usually waste his time with matters like that. There were enough real problems to keep up with.

He retrieved his tablet and thumbed comms connection for the duty net. "Sensors, anything new?"

"No, Colonel," answered Gresh. "But we are about to get a fix on Fairday colony on Mars. It's rolling into our line-of-sight now. Pretty sure what we'll see though."

"Alright." Oswald pulled up big-eye's feed. A magnified Martian plain slid by. At this range, the telescope was able to distinguish the rocks and canyons of the surface, but not with much detail. The outlying domes of Fairday colony were sunk in black-rimmed craters. Panels and shattered dome glass were strewn about the collapsed buildings. The damage grew worse as more of the colony came into view.

"Just like the rest," Oswald said. "Just like Ceres."

"Shall I go back to scanning for Earth debris, FC?"

If Earth had been destroyed somehow, there would have to be debris somewhere in the planet's orbit. They hadn't detected any and Oswald wasn't sure if he should be happy about that or not.

It had been long enough. They had been sneaking around Sol for weeks now and were still no closer to solving anything. "Cindy, do we still have a good uplink to the nav-sats we've dropped?"

"Roger that, FC," Trese said. "Both sync'd up less than an hour ago."

Oswald brought up the Solar display on his tablet. Except for a small minute of angle on the far side of Sol, *Roland* and her nav-sats should be able to pick up any transmission in the system.

"I think it's time to ring the doorbell and not worry about who answers. Trese, send out a high-power transponder ping."

"Transmission sent, FC."

"Shout it loud and proud," Karpov said in a poor attempt at a Texan accent.

"What will we do if there is no reply, Colonel?" McFarran asked.

"One failure at a time, Aux." Oswald chuckled, but wished he hadn't said it. This wasn't the time for a flight commander to show negativity. There never was a good time. Even joking. But it was hard to be concerned with others' morale when his own was starting to flag. It could only make things worse.

"How long shall we wait, FC?" Trese asked.

"Until something happens, I guess," Oswald said. "We should be able to detect reflected signals from some objects, so we'll know our signal made it there. But someone out there might not answer right away."

"Or at all," Karpov said.

"Or at all," Oswald agreed. "But we'll see in twenty-four hours."

They got a reply three hours later.

"We've got a hit, FC," Trese called over the net. "There's a definite carrier signal. Standard SDF frequency. But there's no modulation or data attachment. No info."

"Like a beacon someone forgot to encode, Colonel," McFarran said.

"Actually," Trese said, "that reference carrier frequency is for emergencies, quarantines, or radiological warnings. There should be a voice component and embedded data packets."

"The lights are on but nobody's home," Karpov said.

"I hope somebody's home," said Breen. "I don't even care who at this point."

Oswald felt relief and dread warring in his stomach. There was some artifact, some piece of Earth, still operating out there. It wouldn't be good news, but it was something. "Where's the direction finder put the source?"

"Looks like somewhere above the ecliptic and starward, sir. I've put the search arc into the big-eye."

Oswald watched the big-eye telescope pan through dark space. If the source was between Sol and *Roland*, it would be dark and more difficult to detect optically. If the signal was a warning beacon, it would be omni-directional. One or both of the other nav-sats should detect the signal and be able to triangulate.

"Triangulation from nav-sat two," Trese said.

The telescope's display shifted and magnified, revealing a dark sphere.

"What's that?" Oswald asked. "I'm not seeing any planetoids in that orbit that match."

"Applying discovery filters," Gresh said.

The planetoid shifted colors on the screen as Gresh focused and ran spectrometer overlays. The cloak of darkness melted away as *Roland*'s imaging software translated what the big-eye saw.

A familiar face stared back at Oswald.

"Is that... Luna?" he asked, already knowing the answer.

# Chapter 20

OSWALD GLANCED AT THE tablet McFarran held out towards him.

"We're approaching the end of the flight envelope if we plan on diverting to Luna, Colonel," McFarran said.

It seemed a ridiculous thing that Luna would be so far out of place. Oswald couldn't imagine the tidal forces the moon would suffer to be pushed out of orbit. He couldn't imagine what point there'd be in pushing it out of orbit, let alone the how.

"Still no Earth debris?"

"No, Colonel."

Oswald pushed off the table in his stateroom and rotated slowly in the zero-g. "I don't know which way to jump, Hashi. If we go to Luna and all we find is rack and ruin, proof that everything is gone, I'm not sure how the crew will take it. Myself included.

"If we continue looking for Earth and don't find anything... well, we'll have to stop looking sometime. Either way, morale is in the shitter. And I don't know if I can do anything about it."

"This whole situation we find ourselves in stretches credulity, Colonel. I don't know if anyone could do anything about morale. It's too huge. Yet, a choice must be made."

"Yep. What do you think?"

"Luna. It's all we have. And if nothing is there, we might find more reaction mass like we did at Saturn."

Oswald grabbed two handholds and crouched against the wall, pushing hard with his feet to stretch his back. "Maybe."

The emergency lights began flashing, followed by three resounding blats of the klaxon.

The duty officer's voice came over the ship's speakers. "Maintenance crews to airlock one. Medical team to airlock one."

Oswald's heart sank. He pushed off the wall too hard and clipped his forehead on the rim of the hatch to his stateroom. He reached out with a hand in the main passage to stop his spin. The other hand, which he pressed to the throbbing impact point on his head, came back red with blood. "Shit."

"Are you well, Colonel?" McFarran reached out towards Oswald's injury.

"Forget it. Let's go." He pushed off towards the airlock, keeping pressure on his cut so there wouldn't be a trail of floating blood globules bouncing around the ship.

Oswald propelled himself through distant hatches with a reckless accuracy born of two decades in zero-g. Airlock one was tailward through the central shaft. He splayed his feet to catch the edge of an internal hatch left open by the responding crew.

It was too late.

Dr. Hines floated between two bodies. Their eyes were shriveled, and their lips and fingertips were blue. A medical analyzer was wired to a patch on each of their necks. There was no emotion on the doctor's face as he read the display.

Behind him, two repair crew were disconnecting a tablet from the airlock's maintenance port. One of them manually closed and locked the internal seal, while the other plugged in a test set. The lights on the airlock hatch and the test set both turned green.

"What the fuck," one whispered. He shook his head, looked up at his partner and saw Oswald. "Sorry, FC."

"What the fuck is right," Oswald said. "Doc?"

Dr. Hines looked up over his tablet and shook his head. "Andy Patel and Deirdre Donnelly. Death by asphyxiation and internal damage due to vacuum exposure. Andy should have emptied his lungs first. If you don't they—"

"Thank you, Doctor." Oswald narrowed his eyes at Hines, who shrugged and looked back to his scanner. "Airlock up-and-up?"

The technician tapped his test set. "Yes, FC. They rigged it to run a test cycle. Didn't even set off any alarms. Their unit was on this side of the hatch. No way to stop it from the inside. Airlock is still functional though."

Oswald pulled on his lip and nodded. "Alright. Lock that damned hatch. Set all the airlocks to commander-only access until we come up with something."

"Sure thing, FC."

Dr. Hines and two medics started patting down the bodies. They had nothing on them. The medics each unfurled an embalming bag and looked at Hines, who looked at Oswald.

Dierdre's corpse rolled slowly until her shriveled eyes seemed to lock with Oswald's, begging for forgiveness. He glared back at her. The expected pity and sorrow weren't there. Instead, a rage was beginning to rise in his belly.

Rage at the cowardice of these two. They had abandoned ship when *Roland* needed them most. Betrayed their brothers and sisters. He didn't know if they had been lovers or just came to the same conclusion at the same time. And he didn't care. She wanted redemption? Not likely. Not from him. The audacity. He'd thought better of them all.

Oswald looked away from the bodies and snorted, flicking his hand dismissively as if shooing away flies.

McFarran raised his brow.

Grief came in stages. Maybe he'd feel differently later, but he only felt contempt for the pair now. He kept it to himself, as if speaking the words would transform him into the monster he should feel like, but didn't. He should read the *Sol Defense Fleet Suicide Awareness for Commanders* manual again.

Later.

Oswald led McFarran back to his stateroom. "I should have locked the damned airlocks after the first one. Set a watch. Something."

"If someone wants to kill themselves, Colonel, they don't need an airlock."

Oswald saw the compassion on his friend's face and nodded. "What do you think? Two-person teams? Permanent suicide watch?"

"They were a two-person team already, Colonel."

"We need to start somewhere. What if the next one decides they want to take a few people with them?" Oswald rubbed his eyes until stars blossomed in his vision. "I have a hard time thinking any of my crew would do that, but..." He waved a hand in the direction of the airlock.

"Then we should put commander-only codes for all the obvious stuff, Colonel. Small arms locker, ship's ordnance, engineering chemical bay."

"Atmospheric controls."

"That goes without saying, Colonel."

"What about Karpov? He's got so many Lucky Stars, he won't kill himself. Might miss the next media contract." Oswald smirked.

McFarran didn't return the smile. "He might not kill himself, Colonel. But someone else? I still don't like not having access to his psyche eval after his last ship was destroyed."

"You just don't trust him."

"That's true, Colonel. Nor do I like him, though he is a competent tactical officer. He lacks a strong group ethic. I believe him, in fact, to be a bully, even though he couches his disdain for others in humor. That's not good for morale."

Oswald blinked. In the years he'd known Hashi, he'd seldom heard the man express such a direct dislike of one of the crew. "Yeah."

After a moment of staring at each other, McFarran cleared his throat. "Yes, well, I'll set the hazardous compartments to commander-access only, Colonel, and forward you a list."

Oswald nodded and McFarran left.

Would he ever kill himself? Oswald had flown knowingly into engagements with a high probability of getting vaporized. And ordered others to do the same. Like his daughter. But that was always for the sake of a mission, and there was usually some hope of survival. He'd never had a death wish.

Would he ever feel that level of despair?

Luna might hold answers that would impart hopelessness to others in the crew. Maybe even him. Despite his war record, Oswald was under no illusion of immortality. In the long run, he might even come to think of Patel and Donnelly as the smart ones.

But not today.

Oswald made his way to the flight control pod and strapped into his station. His display had finally been replaced, but even the spare from the parts locker was singed around the edges. It was better than constantly using his tablet; his eyes were too old for that.

"Is it true, FC?" Norris asked over her shoulder. "About Patel and Donnelly?"

Oswald considered asking Norris if Patel and Donnelly had been in some sort of relationship, but found he didn't care anymore. "Yes. They overrode the test system and vacc'd themselves."

She turned back to her screens without a word. Thankfully, she didn't start crying. Anahita would never cry like that. Neither would his weepy housewife.

"Flight, plot orbital insertion around Luna. Altitude 5 klicks. Light the LANTRn when ready."

"Affirmative, FC," Norris said.

McFarran called on the command channel moments after the gentle push of the fusion thruster began.

"To Luna then, Colonel?"

"Yup. What kind of shape will Earth be in without Luna? And vice versa?"

"The very seismic stresses of breaking orbit would likely be catastrophic to both, Colonel. Hardly livable, barring some miracle of science or deity. Though I'm no geologist. Or priest."

"Let's hope for some miracles then, Aux."

What made some people consider suicide and others not? There were, of course, religious or moral objections, but even with that consideration it seemed a crapshoot. People were fuzzy, not like numbers. But even simple equations needed a certain amount of information to be solved accurately. People were seldom so simple.

He imagined Patel and Donnelly exchanging final glances, clutching each other as they gasped their last breaths, then floating motionless save for the angular momentum imparted by their death throes.

These weren't the first crew he'd known to vacc themselves. It always left him curious about why so few actually cast themselves into the endless night. He thought it might be that staring out of an open airlock gave death a physical avatar, banishing the metaphor with a visible endless black silence. A spacer may want to die, but rarely did one want to drift alone forever. Oswald shared that sentiment.

He could be guilty of thinking only in the short term to avoid examining the finale. Had Patel and Donnelly seen how it must play out and decided to face death on their own terms? Had they considered him a coward for clinging to a life whose impending end was a foregone conclusion?

What would his reaction be when the universe dragged him kicking and screaming off his mortal coil? When he accepted in his heart, as he knew he must, that Misty, Mara, and Mary, his grandchildren and great-grandchildren died centuries ago? What would Colonel Pierce Oswald, Rocket of Valor awardee, do when his path led inexorably to the grave?

Hopefully, he'd be murdering Proximans. And if they had destroyed Earth, somehow he would kill them all.

Somehow.

For now, he would take his crew to the moon, their reactions be damned. Oswald didn't know what awaited them there, but he didn't think it would be an augmented-reality parade in honor of *Roland*'s return.

# Chapter 21

THOUGH LUNA'S CURRENT estimated orbit was now closer to that of Mars than of Earth, it was still almost nine Astronomical Units away from Saturn. The LANTRn's efficiency mode provided a constant, low-power acceleration that would take months to get them there. But any discussion of using the jump tunnel generator was met with instant opposition, bordering on mutiny. Oswald enforced standard starship operations in the hopes that the routine would calm the crew and keep their minds off the situation. It was difficult for Oswald to play the part, given his own dark thoughts. He hated to admit it, but it had been McFarran who carried most of the load of keeping *Roland* in shape and the crew in line during the four-month trip.

*Roland*'s approach kept Luna between her and Sol, leaving the big-eye only able to see the moon in shadow. The filters were able to make out some of the terrain features, but the images were dark and the resolution lacking. Luna's orbit and rotation were erratic, preventing detailed mapping without a closer orbit. Norris announced commencement of orbital insertion. Soon they'd be able to see who'd sent the answer to their ping.

Despair filled Oswald as he watched the blackened craters that were once Luna's settlements roll by beneath *Roland*. They stared up at him like empty sockets in a sun-bleached skull. He'd expected to find destruction; Luna had been ripped from its birth orbit, after all. But the signal had given him just enough hope to be dashed.

Some craters seemed to be from stray shots, positioned over coordinates with no associated facility in the computer's records.

Though they could be structures built after *Roland*'s departure, or maybe SDF secret facilities the Proximans had ferreted out and destroyed. Only one surviving site appeared over the lunar horizon. It wasn't in the database either.

A large landing pad and track led to a complex of four sublunar access hatches—one hatch was large enough to fit a standard lunar tractor. Regolith-covered solar panels lay in a rectangular pattern in the center of the complex.

"That's got to be the place," Oswald said.

"There could be other hidden or buried places," Karpov said. "This is just the one we can see."

"I can send a low-power transponder signal, FC," Trese said. "I should be able to figure out if this is the place or not based on the reply signal's power."

"Do it."

The response was immediate. Oswald heard the click of the carrier but nothing else, as if someone had keyed a mic but refused to speak.

"Confirmed, FC," Trese said. "Signal's from beneath us. Oh, look at that."

About half the landing lights around the pad flickered to life. They began flashing in a standard landing pattern, though, with so many having failed, the pattern looked haphazard and barely recognizable for what it was.

Oswald watched for any other reaction from below. "There's power, at least."

"Think there's someone down there?" Breen asked.

Oswald hated it when Breen spoke with such earnest hope. His own hope hadn't recovered yet. He, or someone else, inevitably had to deliver the bad news. But not everyone hated that job.

"The haunted caves of the Moon People," Karpov said in a warbling voice and laughed.

"Keep it professional on the net, Karpov," McFarran said. "This isn't the time for your jokes."

Karpov affected a hurt tone. "You always say that, Aux."

"Secure that shit, Tac," Oswald said.

Now sounding cheerful, Karpov said, "Roger that, FC."

Oswald watched the landing pad slip out of sight. The ruins of Luna City rolled by; the nearest edge to the pad was a little over five kilometers from the city's perimeter. "Breen, we'll just have to see. But don't get your hopes up. It looks like an automated transponder."

While *Roland* was capable of landing, it normally required a fully equipped SDF infrastructure and external boosters to launch again, except in very low gravity. She had only landed once in her twenty-one-year career, to hide in a crater on Callisto to conduct a passive search for a Proximan strike force in the area.

The mission was a success, but *Roland*'s crew suffered severe radiation poisoning when her magnetic-shield generator failed. The Jovian radiation field was thousands of times stronger than Earth's own Van Allen belts. *Roland* outlived her crew and became Oswald's first assignment as a flight commander.

But the LANTRn was not designed for takeoff in a gravity well, even one as weak as Luna's. The reaction mass it spat out would leave the complex a toxic, radioactive waste. The landing would be impossible if not for the boosters affixed for the mission to Delta Pavonis V.

Oswald drummed his fingers on the armrest of his station, now uneven from the heat damage. He had no way of knowing if this pad was rated for the thrust the boosters would apply. Most lunar craft were simple suborbital hoppers. A full-sized starship might be too much.

There was no choice with the landers all destroyed. He'd have to hope—they were flying on a lot of that these days—that Norris could land them without collapsing the pad. It would be tricky. Luna's orbital profile was completely different now that it was free of Earth's fetters and wobbling above the Solar plane.

"Flight, put us down on that landing pad, please."

"I wish Chun was here," Norris said.

So did Oswald. "He never landed *Roland* either. Just plot it and go hands off. Make sure we use the chemical boosters only. If abort is called, initiate escape orbit."

Oswald ordered the crew into their armor. If *Roland* crashed and went fireball, it wouldn't save anyone. Better safe than sorry though. At least any survivors of a lesser catastrophe might make their way to the lunar hatches. Though that might not help either, depending on the condition of the tunnels beneath.

The surface of Luna sped by in the landing cameras as *Roland's* altitude dropped. The ship was now nose-skyward in relation to the surface. Norris was guiding them on their third flyby. They were at two thousand meters and falling. Maneuvering thrusters fired in rapid bursts to make last-minute corrections.

One small crater raced by, then another. The edge of the landing pad appeared in the camera screen. The landing boosters roared to life and Oswald felt the force push him down into his station.

His heart thundered in his chest as the lights of the landing pad came directly beneath them. "If anyone sees that pad crumble, call abort," Oswald said through clenched teeth.

The spray of exhaust and flying regolith obscured the landing camera's view. The pad's lights disappeared. No one would be able to see if it was coming apart.

The boosters cut off and, a second later, *Roland* hit the platform. The impact echoed through the ship and Oswald cringed, expecting his back to spasm in pain. It didn't.

He could feel *Roland* scrape along the platform for an instant before the landing stabilizers unfolded. There was a slight leaning one way, then the other, and the ship settled in place.

Oswald waited for the platform to collapse. The lunar dust had been cleared away by the rocket's thrust, revealing the pad to the landing cameras. The platform looked solid and *Roland*'s landing fins were secure.

Oswald's neck and shoulders relaxed. He smiled and tried to hide the breathlessness in his voice. "Good job, Norris. Damn fine flying. Chun would be proud."

"I feel like he's watching over everything I do," Norris said in a shaky voice.

"STILL NOTHING FROM the complex?" Oswald knew the answer already. He'd been watching the same screens as everyone else for the last hour.

"No signals, no movement, FC," Trese answered over the duty net. "Do you want me to send the transponder code?"

"Do it," Oswald said. "Milliwatt range. Let's make this a local call."

The response was instant again. The same empty carrier frequency with dead air. The surviving landing lights started blinking again.

"From right here, sir," Trese said. "Now I guess we just need boots on the ground."

There were only eighteen of them left. Eighteen. It was hard for Oswald to grasp. Starships seldom suffered so many casualties without the whole craft exploding. The Rangers all dead at the hands—claws? tentacles?—of the aliens of DPV. Three cowards had committed suicide and the rest had been killed by that damned alien artifact. Except Yninski, killed by the Proximans. Or by Oswald, according to McFarran.

Everyone on *Roland* had been to Luna and walked several EVAs as part of basic training. But Oswald still had no idea what was going on or what they might find, and he was reluctant to put boots on the ground. *Roland*'s surface scouting drones had all been destroyed on Delta Pavonis V, and they had no surface rovers. The EVA drones had only basic cameras and provided nothing *Roland* couldn't already see. He wished the Rangers were still with them, and not only so he could send them in to investigate the base first.

But he did still have one Ranger, he realized.

Oswald slapped his helmeted forehead. "Danner, get a crew to unfold Rocketman and let's send it out."

"Rocketman, sir?"

"That combat frame from the Rangers. Get it online and sync it up." Oswald decided to keep everyone strapped in and suited up in case they needed to blast off. It would make it harder for the engineers to work with the robot, but they'd lost enough people. Caution was worth a little inconvenience.

Twenty minutes later, Rocketman was pushed out of the cargo bay hatch by Danner's team. Its video feed and a graphic interface came up in Oswald's visor. He had only interfaced with the robot through voice commands. Now he saw a command menu that listed a series of autonomous and semi-autonomous mission modes.

The menus were simple, designed for ease of use in fire fights. He selected the *Autonomous Recon Patrol* and then *300 meters* when prompted. *Acknowledged* flashed on the screen, then shrank away into the corner with the rest of the robot's statistics.

Rocketman's feed panned a slow 360-degree view; small analysis windows winked in and out as the robot's tactical computer noted and analyzed features of the surrounding moonscape. Then it loped out in an expanding circle, stopping every fifty meters for another 360-degree scan.

Oswald issued orders for close examinations of the access hatches and the solar panels.

"Look," Norris said. "Footprints."

Oswald saw them and his heart raced. The edges were crisp and the tracks led straight to one of the hatches. But there was nothing to erode the prints in this vacuum except for falling micrometeorites. The original tracks of the astronauts in the Sea of Tranquility were almost as pristine when put under a heritage dome as they had been when first made two hundred years before.

"Don't mean a thing," Karpov said. "Probably four hundred years old."

"Panels are in decent shape," Danner said. "Maybe seventy percent look good, from the outside at least. No power to the hatches and the seal indicators are red."

"Vacuum inside," Oswald said. "Danner, get a crew in EVA suits, and see if we can get inside and take a look. We'll leave Rocketman out there to help out."

"Yes, sir," Danner said.

"We might want to get a view of *Roland* while that thing's out and about, Colonel," McFarran said.

"Good call." Oswald selected a direct-control option and pointed Rocketman's sensor cluster back towards *Roland*.

Karpov let out a low whistle.

The old girl was beat-up. Her silver skin was streaked with scorch marks as if she'd been held over a giant lighter. A bubbled, serpentine patch of ash-gray was all that remained of the starship's giant red-shark mascot. It had been repainted only a few months before. At least the outer hull plates were still flush.

Oswald swallowed. He'd known from the sensor logs and repair reports how badly *Roland* had been damaged. The deaths of the crew and the interior scars he saw every day were visceral reminders of the same. But seeing the whole picture from a distance added a deeper appreciation to how narrowly they'd escaped Death's clutches.

"That was pretty damn close," was all Oswald could say.

OSWALD HADN'T SET FOOT on Luna in over five years, relatively speaking. It was much cheaper to ferry crews to the moon for leave and training than it was to fight Earth's gravity well. But rank has its privileges and Oswald was able to get flights down to the Big Blue when he wanted, in addition to the medically required rotations on Earth all astronauts underwent to help their bodies recover from the deprivations of life in zero-g.

He looked up at the black sky. Earth should be hanging there now, peeking down on him like a loving mother. Puffs of lunar dust spilled out in every direction from Oswald's boots with each step.

Rocketman bounced along beside him, its bulbous sensor cluster rotating slowly. When the engineering team had set out to inspect the structures five hours ago, Oswald set the robot to Semi-Autonomous Escort mode. With the help of a sparse FAQ file and some random button pushing, he designated Danner's team as Rocketman's wards. Hopefully, that meant the robot was scanning for external threats and any other signs of distress in those he was guarding.

Oswald added himself to that list for the excursion to the site. Being unfamiliar with how Rocketman functioned in any great detail, Oswald couldn't bring himself to select any of the autonomous mission profiles. He wasn't sure just how autonomous the robotic combat frame would get.

The hatch opened as Oswald approached. He climbed down the ladder into the airlock and Rocketman followed. The airlock cycled and the inner hatch opened. Danner stood there with a tight smile, his helmet and gloves off.

Oswald stepped through and Danner closed the hatch once Rocketman had entered. The atmospheric display on Oswald's visor shone green. He looked and saw two other engineers down the corridor with their helmets off too.

A waft of stale air rushed against Oswald's face as he unsealed his helmet. He took a few deep breaths. The familiar smell of old oil, plastic, and spent gunpowder mixed in his nostrils. The gunpowder smell of moondust had been explained years ago during orientation, but Oswald had considered it academic, forgetting the details almost as quickly as they'd been presented by the eager young steward. He'd never smelled actual gunpowder on Earth, so it meant nothing to him.

Oswald rubbed his ears. "Pressure's a little high in here."

"Yes, sir. I pumped it up to help find a few of the last leaks." Danner reached over and tapped on a cluster of hoses along the wall. "The place was in total vacuum, but the air storage is full. All we had to do was throw the breakers and the air handlers came on line."

"Like setting up a summer cottage."

"I guess so. We did have to replace a few filters, patch a few cracks, but we could live here a good while, FC."

"Only if you found some food stores."

Danner's smile faded. "No food. But we did find something weird. Not sure what to make of it."

"Show me."

Danner swept a vacuum hose over Oswald and Rocketman to get as much of the clingy moondust off them as possible. After he'd finished, he motioned with his head for them to follow. "All four of the external hatches lead to a central hub. There's a lot of bunks and standard habitat equipment, you know, monitors, routers, that sort of thing. And a visitors' book."

"A visitors' book?"

"Yes, sir. Like at a wedding."

"Anyone sign it?"

Danner chuckled. "No, sir."

"Bizarre."

"Wait till you see the vault."

Oswald lowered his voice. "You doing OK?"

"As well as anyone."

"Your brother was stationed on Luna, right?"

Danner glanced at Oswald, then away before answering. "Yes, sir. He's... or was... officer in charge of a missile battery. Brandon really wanted to get assigned to a starship. He passed all his tests and was just waiting on word about his submission when we jumped to DPV."

Oswald turned away to inspect a random power coupling to give Danner the chance to wipe at his eyes.

"The site he was stationed at was slagged," Danner said. "I saw it on our flyby. But, if this time thing is true, who knows where he was when it went down."

Oswald nodded and they walked in silence down the passage. The same could be said of Misty, Mara, and Mary. His grandchild. Anahita. Who knew where any of them were when it went down? But it didn't matter where, it was the when. Even if they had survived whatever happened, they were long dead.

Hell, the details didn't even matter now. Only that it had happened.

The walls of the passage were smooth, with hoses and conduits running the length overhead. The dim lights served more to cast dark shadows than to light the way. Danner led Oswald to what he'd called the hub, and it was filled with the amenities the engineer had described. Oswald walked to the central table and there was the visitors' book, with a stylus attached by a length of purple ribbon. The pages flipped slowly in the low gravity, but there was no writing.

"Maybe they forgot to send the invitations," Oswald said, closing the book. "Is that the vault?"

Danner nodded and pointed a finger at Rocketman. "I think that thing checked for explosives and such, if I used the menu right. I'm guessing it has some sort of chemical sniffers. Not sure how good they are up here though."

The door looked to be made of black obsidian and stood three meters tall. The lights of the room were reflected in its dark surface, which was completely smooth except for a large handle and an aquamarine plaque across the top.

Danner shone his light on the plaque, revealing a column of writing, each line in a different language. "And that's why we didn't go in there."

Proximan hieroglyphs topped the list. Then a block of Chinese, and beneath that English, Spanish, French, and then some other Arabic- and Oriental-looking scripts Oswald didn't recognize. He assumed they all said the same thing as the line in English.

*Earth Peoples Given Honor Memorial*

The plaque and bonding were much more sturdy than what he'd found on Saturn Station. Oswald removed his gloves and examined the edges of the door and handle, before cautiously brushing his fingers over the surface. It was smooth as a so-called frictionless coating and painfully cold.

He reached out and pulled on the handle. Danner jumped back, and Rocketmen fell into a crouch and pointed its sensor cluster at Danner. It scanned the area and stood back up.

"Sorry, FC." Danner flashed an embarrassed grin. "Just surprised me there."

Beyond the door was another airlock. The vacuum indicator was red. If the pressure was holding in this section of the complex, then the seal must be good. Oswald slipped his helmet and gloves on, turning so Danner could verify his suit integrity.

"I don't know what's back there, Colonel," Danner said.

"I'll take Rocketman and find out." Oswald stepped to the airlock and cycled through it. On the other side was an even darker cave, illuminated only by the weak beam of light from the airlock window.

Oswald switched on his suit's lights and hopped forward, careful not to catapult into the low ceiling. Ten meters in, he came across a stack of airtight containers labeled "Emergency Rations" piled into a deep shelf cut into the wall.

Oswald smiled. He'd have to get Dr. Hines to inspect them, but SDF space rations were supposed to have an indefinite shelf life if stored properly. *Roland* had lost almost half her rations, but it hadn't concerned Oswald initially. They were supposed to have been back at Earth by now. Food would be a concern if they didn't get there soon.

Past the ration crates was another obsidian-looking door that opened into a natural cavern. A metal scaffold ran from the door across the top of the chamber, parallel to a wall made of pink granite. It was some ten meters tall and thirty meters across. A pattern of one-meter squares with reflective disks in the center covered the wall.

Oswald grabbed on to one of the handrails and watched dust drift down to the cavern floor. Leaning over, he saw there was a stairway at the midpoint of the scaffold and two more walkways beneath; one walkway for each row of squares. The granite wall extended to the bottom of the cavern, the disks winking like eyes in the darkness as Oswald swept his light back and forth.

He tested the scaffold by shaking the handrail, but nothing shifted. With a cautious first couple of steps, Oswald moved onto the scaffold. "Stay put," he told Rocketman.

A fine layer of dust covered the surface of the granite wall. Oswald leaned in to examine the first square. There was writing engraved in the rock, and the shining disk turned out to be a small holographic picture. He gently brushed the dust away.

He knew that face.

*Supreme Leader of China Sheu Tzun*

*Given Honor 23JUL2210*

The message was repeated in a column in the same order as had been on the door, Proximan at the top.

"Fuck," he whispered.

Oswald trudged down the walkway, passing names and faces of presidents and prime ministers of Earth. Most he'd never heard of. But they had all been "Given Honor" on that same date.

A mass execution of the leaders of Earth? Like the commanders of Saturn Station?

His feet grew heavy as he took the stairs to the second level. It was lined with the names and images of admirals and generals. He couldn't figure how they'd been arranged, not being in order of rank or the Anglo alphabet. It might make sense in Proximan.

He saw her face glaring up through the dust.

*Supreme Commander of Sol Defense Fleet General Anahita Khadem*

*Given Honor 23JUL2210*

Bile rose in his throat and burned twice as hot as he swallowed it back down. An image of Anahita's face, rotting like the commanders at Saturn Station, came unbidden to his mind. Is that what they'd done to her? Strung her up and blasted her brains out? Had they done that to all of these people?

Oswald's knees buckled and he fell into a sitting position, his legs sprawled out. Anahita's stern image stared at him from between his feet.

He sat there staring back, ignoring the radio calls. Her bones were in there. The woman he'd spoken to, the mother of his dead child, had died four hundred years ago. Had been executed four hundred years ago.

Which meant all the mothers of his children, and all his children, were dust too. He didn't even know if their bones still existed. Whatever had happened to Earth had happened to them, had happened to everyone.

Oswald started as Rocketman's sensor cluster pressed against his visor. The robot's external speaker vibrated where it made contact with Oswald's helmet, producing a buzzing, mechanical voice.

"Colonel Oswald, are you OK?"

Oswald blinked up at Rocketman. He'd never heard the robot speak. Then he heard the calls over the radio again. All they'd seen was his collapse. He couldn't afford to be weak in front of his crew or Anahita. Not now. "Yes, I'm fine. Just stumbled. Help me up, Rocketman."

Mechanical arms lifted Oswald to his feet, strong but careful in the low gravity. Oswald looked at Anahita's image again and wished her peace wherever she was now.

He didn't really know if she was in there. It could be a memorial, or it could be ashes, or her desiccated bones could be behind that facade. She could be a nanobot-rendered collection of molecules. Whatever the case, it wouldn't be right to leave her covered in dirt, so he brushed the dust from the entire surface of her square.

A faint outline of a smaller square appeared beneath the script, visible only after the dust was gone. It was the same color as the granite but, on closer investigation, it lacked the streaks and whorls of the rest of the stone.

Oswald pushed it gently and felt the give. He pushed a little harder, and the square receded two centimeters with a *click* he felt through his glove. When Oswald removed his finger, the square extended into a cube protruding several centimeters from the surface of the stone.

He pulled it free. The cube was only pink on the one surface; the other faces were black. Another, smaller holo-image of Anahita was on the face opposite the pink. A variety of data ports and power connectors were set into one of the other faces.

Oswald recognized some of the connections as standard SDF types. He shoved the cube into a leg pouch on his suit.

"I'm heading back, *Roland*." Oswald's words came in short, excited pants as he scrabbled up the stairs. "I think I've found a datacube from Anahita. General Khadem, I mean. Let's see what she has to tell us."

# Chapter 22

ROCKETMAN LIFTED OSWALD to his feet. Again. This time they were on the lunar surface, heading towards *Roland*. Oswald brushed at the regolith on his visor but it clung in place. When he'd finally managed to push most of the dust out of his direct line of vision, Oswald continued.

"Colonel," McFarran said over the radio, his voice bemused. "Perhaps you should slow down. If you go flying into *Roland* head first, you might tip her over."

Oswald imagined the scene and chuckled. He fought the urge to make another long leap, and probably another landing on his face, and shuffled along instead. The amount of dust on his suit was already going to cause the duty tech extra work. "Roger that, Aux."

For all of his rush, Oswald didn't even know what the cube was. It had a data port and power connections, but would it tell him anything useful? Would it merely confirm Anahita was dead? It was probably only a recording of her funeral and a generic fleet eulogy for persons of staff rank or higher. But it was something. The only thing they'd found so far. His enthusiasm was curbed by the fear that this discovery would lead to more unanswered questions.

McFarran was waiting for Oswald at the airlock and helped him off with his suit. "May I take a look, Colonel?"

Alarm raced through Oswald at the thought of handing Anahita's cube over. But he unzipped the pouch in the EVA suit and offered it to McFarran. The duty technician set the EVA suit in the cleaning locker and looked with dismay at the coating of moondust on the suit and the deck.

"Sorry," Oswald said. He held his hand out to McFarran. He wanted it back already.

The aux turned it in his hand a final time and passed the cube back to Oswald. "It certainly looks like a datacube, but it's so big, Colonel. You can fit the design specs for the entire fleet in a nano-drive."

Oswald shrugged. "Maybe it's built rugged. But I plan on finding out. Have Danner see about pressurizing the rest of the complex except the vault. And make sure they swap out work crews soon; they've been over there five hours already."

The climb up the central ladder was a struggle even in one-sixth gravity. It hadn't been that long since their Space Recovery and Physical Training routine on Earth. But it was easy to get used to the pampering of null gravity.

Oswald closed the hatch to his stateroom. He stumbled into his seat, rushing to examine the box. The drawer that contained the room's cables wouldn't open, and Oswald jerked on the handle furiously until the small latch he'd forgotten to undo snapped.

"Calm the fuck down," Oswald muttered to himself.

He found the power and data connectors and unrolled them from the drawer. They caught when he pulled too quickly. Oswald lost his grip and knocked the data cube across the table. He froze until the cube stopped, took a deep breath, and waited for several more seconds.

"Calm the fuck down."

He set the cube with Anathita's image facing up and plugged in the power connector. A green LED lit up beneath her face. Oswald reached forward with the data connection, but stopped just before plugging it in. Even in his excitement, he knew C'nD needed to run the data connection through the combat firewall. There was no way of telling what was on the cube and, while Oswald didn't know what was going on, he did know the Proximans were sneaky bastards. This whole place could be nothing more than a honeypot to lure in SDF survivors and get them to download from a cube. Not all traps involved explosions. But he could take a look without connecting to the ship's systems.

The green LED started to blink. Oswald jerked back, thinking that he deserved to get blown up for his stupidity. He reached forward to unplug the power in hopes of avoiding whatever bomb was about to go off. Instead of exploding, the cube projected a holo-keyboard on the surface of the table. Each button had a word on it. One said "English" and Oswald placed his finger over the projection.

The keyboard reformed into a menu with each selection written in English. Words appeared in the air over Anahita's image.

*Honor Chest of General Anahita Khadem*

The selections on the keyboard were *Last Words and Testament, Records and Data, Genealogy and Family History, Career Achievements, Role in the Earth War*, and *Interactive Personality Module.*

Oswald tapped *Last Words and Testament.*

A life-sized bust of Anahita appeared over the box, almost eye-to-eye with Oswald. The clarity and solidity of the image explained the cube's size. It was a high-definition holo-projector. The traces of the projector's beam were almost invisible. He fought the urge to reach out and touch her cheek.

It was Anahita, no doubt, but her expression held a desperation he'd never seen before. Her face was thick with age, and wrinkles gathered at her eyes and jowls. If the dates were correct and this really was her last testament, she'd been close to sixty when this was recorded. White streaks ran through her hair. But her eyes still held their sultry fire.

He stared into those holographic eyes, dreading what she would say, wanting her words to make everything better somehow.

Nothing happened and Oswald looked down. The keyboard had changed once again, this time into standard audio-visual control buttons. He hit play.

"I am Supreme General of the Sol Defense Fleet, Anahita Khadem. I'm told I've been given a great honor, that my last words will be recorded for all time. I don't really have much to say at this point. We've lost the war and I believe the Ay-Yon plan to exterminate us all.

"So if you are some sort of Ay-Yon tourist or history student, may your mother burn away the eyes of your siblings to save them from seeing your face.

"If you aren't Ay-Yon, that was basically the cultural equivalent to a giant 'fuck you.'

"I'm supposedly allowed to say anything I want for history, for posterity. I'll start by saying the Ay-Yon started this war with their unprovoked attack on our station in Proxima Centauri. So if any of you are little Ay-Yon kids, don't let your teachers lie to you. Your ancestors were fully responsible for this war. I've spent my entire adult life fighting it, and have lost countless friends and loved ones to your people's bloodlust. Including my daughter and her father."

Anahita flipped her hair and drank from a small silver flask with the Sol Defense Fleet logo on it. "I'm not really sure I want to help the bastard Ay-Yon, but I don't have much else to do here under house arrest. So I'll talk to my long-lost friends."

Oswald pressed his thumb and forefinger to his eyes as Anahita proceeded to address her dead friends. He didn't recognize most of them. When she addressed Will Zaphrim, who apparently died during a reconstructive surgery, a tear slid from beneath his thumb.

"Hey, Pierce."

Oswald started when the recording called his name. Anahita was smiling and her speech had slowed, probably from whatever was in that flask. "Hey, Anahita."

"Just where did you get off to, Pierce? Obviously, you'll never be able to answer, since we're both dead. It's been close to what, twenty years?"

Anahita frowned, then sighed mournfully. "What really happened to you? We needed you. If you'd been here... well, I wouldn't have fucked things up so bad in Delta Pavonis.

"None of the eggheads could ever decide why that wormhole formed. A permanent jump tunnel between Sol and Delta P. Most guessed it had to do with the UXA." She shook her head and snorted. "What a stupid name. Ooooks-Ahhh. But the Ay-Yon sure knew what it was. They came in force, and we fought around that hole and at Delta Pavonis Five. It was a regular game of hot potato, fighting over the ruins and the artifacts."

Anahita raised her flask in a toast and took another pull. Oswald wondered if it was Delamain.

She hiked a thumb to the golden Rocket of Valor on her chest. "I got my RoV and Comet, just like you. I led the Delta P squadron from a new command ship, like an armed, flying MCC. I remembered what you said about the MCCs in space so I insisted it be mobile. But they still sniffed us out.

"It didn't end well. We actually won, but it was a Pyrrhic victory. We didn't have enough ships to hold off the Ay-Yon counterattack."

Oswald dug his fingers into the padding of his seat. Why the hell did she keep calling them Ay-Yon? They were Proxies. They were damned murdering bastards. They didn't get to use their fancy name.

"By the time we got back with the squadron I could scrape up," Anahita continued, "they had an orbital blockade. Not a strong one, but too strong for us.

"I filled Delta Pavonis with sensor drones, looking for any sign of you, Pierce. You were supposed to come back to me."

Anahita broke out in sobs for a few seconds, before she reached out in Oswald's direction and the recording froze for an instant. When it began playing again, her tear-streaked face was replaced with one of steely resolve.

Oswald reached out for the white stripe in her hair. The fingers passed through air and he put his hand on the table. He stared down at his hand as he listened.

"We kept on fighting for almost fifteen years after you went MIA or KIA, Pierce. But Earth fell like so many empires have, through bickering and backstabbing. I suppose it was inevitable, deserved even. I wish we could have done better.

"But the SDF was in shambles. We barely had enough ships to clear Earth's orbit, let alone Sol. We never recovered from Delta Pavonis. Then the American Block got into a trade war with Europe. China actually fired on a Japanese merchant convoy. And GlobalComm contacted the Ay-Yon directly to offer a business arrangement.

"The Ay-Yon had to retreat too. But they were the first ones to rebuild their fleet. They had been licking their wounds, while we were pouring salt in ours. We didn't have a chance when they returned.

"Then the bastards got smart. Well, smarter. They actually started dealing with the nation blocks and corporations directly, bypassing the SDF and even that sham of a UN. Support for the war eroded and the fleet was defunded. Dumbasses."

Anahita lifted the flask. She considered it for a moment, shook her head and put it down somewhere out of frame. "I think that's enough of that.

"Anyway, there was excitement about being part of an interstellar alliance, and hope and cooperation and all that shit. Just a bunch of people not willing to realize that we'd lost the war and the enemy was blowing smoke up our thrusters to calm us down. It worked.

"Oh, watch this." She reached down off screen and, when she spoke next, her voice was magnified in a thunderous echo. "I was Supreme Commander of the Sol Defense FLEET-Fleet-fleet!"

She laughed and, for a second, she looked like the cadet he'd loved. Like the woman he knew before Ululani's death.

Her voice returned to normal. "I love that. Anyway, I'm Supreme Commander for one more day. Our last hope was *Tagono*'s attack at Jupiter. She was partially successful... before taking a thruster hit and tumbling into the atmosphere.

"I'm ashamed to admit I welcomed our surrender, Pierce. My whole life was spent in this goddamned war. There were a few hold-outs, a few would-be heroes. But like you always said, life isn't an episode of Captain Yasmina. There are no heroes. No room for childish fantasy. It's all delta-v and momentum and entropy and enthalpy.

"And it would have possibly been the last of it, except for one of you damned Americans. Captain Harold Harmon of the orbital defense submarine USS *Circe*. He hid in the ocean for months, while everyone else was busy surrendering.

"Then he popped up from nowhere and burned a hole through the Ay-Yon command ship. Not *a* command ship, mind you. *The* command ship. He sent a brigade of ambassadors, high commanders, and princes burning in atmo. He fucking killed us all, but it was a nice shot. And he evaded the counterattack. An American task force found and destroyed *Circe*, declaring her rogue. But no one bought it. I think it might have been true though. Hotshot captains and flight commanders tend to do their own thing." Anahita's projection raised an accusatory eyebrow at Oswald. He laughed.

"That was about a month ago, and the Ay-Yon have been gathering up Earth's leaders since. All surrender agreements were declared null and void, and every remaining space and military asset in the system was targeted for destruction or capture."

She buried her face in her hands and wept for a full minute, not bothering to shut off the recorder this time. "Tomorrow I'll be 'given honor' and be allowed not to witness what they plan on doing to Earth. Intel says the Ay-Yon execute those they honor." She made a pistol shape with her fingers and put it to her head. "Zap. Instant honor. I'm so fucking scared, Pierce. Oh, Allah, so scared.

"Speaking of doing your own thing, Pierce. That last T-REX you fired before your jump from Sol killed two. Not that you were supposed to fire at all, but what the fuck, right? You never did listen very well." Anahita reached forward and the recording flickered to a stop.

Oswald hit the pause button and leaned back in his seat. He stared into the distance as he struggled to absorb it all. He couldn't. It was too much. They'd lost and they'd lost it all. He jammed his fists into his eyes as the sobs came. With a final ragged breath, Oswald got a grip on himself and pressed play.

Anahita's hair was now put up tightly and her jaw clenched. She glared straight ahead instead of looking directly at the recorder as she had previously.

"I'm told my honoring will be within the hour. All I can hope for is that I won't have a breakdown. I want to be staring my executioner in the eye when he pulls the trigger.

"Again, for you Ay-Yon students, I've found out what I'm being spared from seeing. Your brave ancestors are dropping biological weapons to wipe humanity from the face of the Earth. But the viruses are designed to die after sixty years. How magnanimous.

"This, of course, negates my being spared. Just another Ay-Yon betrayal. Whoever was so important in that ship, I hope they are burning in *Jaheem*, or wherever you assholes go. By the way, I know the genocide ship was already part of your fleet, so don't let them tell you they weren't already planning on killing us all. Nothing but pretense and lies."

Anahita took a long, quivering breath. She again spoke to names Oswald didn't recognize. Jealousy bit at him as Anahita relived memories with strangers she'd grown close to in his absence. From the tone of the messages, she'd been closer to some of them than she had been with him.

For the sake of his jealousy, he allowed his mind to wander. The messages were of a personal nature and held nothing useful for his situation. Despite his assumption, it was actually possible, if not likely, that she could have had other children. Children that could have grown to adulthood just in time to watch the world end along with his own family. Anahita's voice jerked him from his reverie.

"I know you're not here, Pierce. But I wanted to say I forgive you. It took me a long time. Like it did to forgive you for marrying Misty. The irony is that both of those things were really my fault.

"And I hope you forgive me for Mara and believe me that it wasn't revenge. She joined the fleet after you went missing and insisted on being assigned to Delta Pavonis. I think she still held hopes of finding some trace of *Roland*. I know I did.

"In the final throes of the Delta Pavonis campaign, I ordered *Gigante* to lead an attack wing against a drop-ship convoy. Mara was the tactical officer. They completed the mission, but they didn't make it back. Like father, like daughter, I suppose."

Oswald rested his forehead on the table. Of course, the bitch had done it to get back at him. Did she really think he was that stupid? He knew, better than most, how well Anahita Khadem could hold a grudge. She was like a python strangling a lamb.

No. No, she wouldn't have harmed Mara and he knew it. Even if she had grown to hate him. Just as he hadn't ordered *Bonwei* to her death because she'd kept their daughter a secret. He hadn't. He wouldn't. It was the fucking Proximans that killed Mara, not Anahita. Just like they'd killed Ululani, not him.

And even if Mara had survived the war, she'd be dead now.

Anahita took a deep breath. "There. I said it. Maybe there is something to this final testament thing. But still, fuck you, Ay-Yon.

"And don't think ill of me for not crying as I talk about these things today, friends. I've shed my tears and I'm trying to steel my soul. I can hear the politicians being gathered in the corridor, whimpering and crying the lot of them.

"I watched them take Prime Minister Tzun. For an old, career politician, he walked with them head held high. I have to give him that, even if he failed to keep the SDF together. So much depended on him."

Anahita went rigid and turned away until her face was out of frame. Her eyes were wide and her upper lip was trembling when she turned back. Clutching her hands together over her chest, Anahita cleared her throat. "My time has come. The Ay-Yon have summoned me to my murder. I will die as I lived, a soldier. Though betrayed by twelve billion ingrates below on Earth, I die for them.

"May the stars look down on the Ay-Yon and their generations and curse them for what they've done. May they taste the bitter fruits of what they do to us today." Defiance flared in her eyes.

It was her fierce face. A wild desert dervish. A bloody-fisted shield maiden. It was Captain Yasmina, wicked and beautiful, made real.

Anahita loomed in, as if leaning in to offer Oswald a parting kiss. Her hand covered the recorder for a second and the image vanished, leaving Oswald feeling suddenly, desperately alone.

A sense of disconnection from reality washed over him. He couldn't believe what he'd just seen, but knew he had to. His vision wouldn't focus. There were no tears in his eyes this time. He hoped he would meet his end as steadily as Anahita Khadem had.

# Chapter 23

OSWALD WATCHED THE message five times, skipping the parts addressed to strangers. It helped him to absorb what Anahita said, to wrestle with the reality of what happened. Every time he thought he'd accepted the truth of their strange situation, internalized it, another supporting fact of that truth would shock him all over again. He would have to share the message with the crew, or at least the department heads, and he didn't want to lose it in front of them. Each replay numbed him a little more.

But something else must have happened to Earth. Even if the Proximans had sterilized the whole planet, it should still be there. Anahita would have said something. Unless the Proximans lied to her. And that seemed pointless, since they were executing everyone anyway.

How could they physically destroy an entire planet?

Oswald rubbed his hand over his stubbled scalp. Maybe they'd always had the ability and the loss of all their VIPs was the final straw.

But where was the debris?

He pushed his palms out, not ready to go flying through that black hole again. There wasn't enough new information to start another round of educated guessing. Anahita explained how the war had been lost. Now the question was—the question had always been—what to do next?

Oswald returned to the main menu traced out on the table by the holo-cube and selected *Records and Data*. Twenty minutes of expanding file directories and subdirectories left him wondering how the Proximans decided which files were interesting or relevant. Most were trivial details: travel receipts, evaluation reports, 2,312 fleet bulletins and memos, staff digital correspondence...

As he browsed, he decided they hadn't found these things interesting, they'd simply copied Anahita's terminal file by file. With that in mind, Oswald searched as he would any standard SDF computer system. In minutes he found the copy of the sector Anahita had allowed herself for personal files. Each node in the directory was labelled with a person's name. Many he recognized from her message. With a brief hesitation, he tapped the node named "Pierce."

The projected keyboard shifted to display the files in the directory. Most were images, their thumbnails now drawn on the tabletop. Some had names like "Misty12" or "Wedding," but many were simply strings of numbers incorporating a date and time.

Oswald didn't know if he wanted to see. Surely Anahita wouldn't have kept a bunch of pictures showing the terrible fates of his family. Though it might be worse seeing their smiling faces knowing that they were ignorant of the death the Proximans would mete out.

Already he was fighting back the images of his family's terror as the world ended around them, calling out to him for help. Would they have called for him? His family believed him dead twenty years before it would happen. Part of him hoped they would have, even though it was futile.

Simple curiosity won out and Oswald tapped the first image with Misty in the name. An image of her standing beneath a holo-banner that read "Remember *Roland* Third Anniversary" appeared over the table. She was surrounded by other families he recognized. McFarran's sons. Norris's husbands. Engineer Bowen's wife and children.

The next image was "MistyWed", followed by other similarly named image files. The time stamps on the files were five years after *Roland* and crew disappeared.

Oswald took a deep breath and drummed his fingers on the table. To her it had been five years; he had to remember that. And it had been over four hundred years since, though only months to him. He feared what the images would show. Oswald tapped the thumbnail.

The image of Misty in a simple but elegant peach-colored wedding gown appeared over the table. She was smiling. Oswald knew that smile—it was the relaxed smile that made her eyes twinkle. It was her really happy smile.

Next to her stood a man in a casual suit, his hair slicked back, and his arm around Oswald's wife. He looked familiar. It was finally the bright green eyes Oswald recognized. Cliff Norris, one of the flight sergeant's husbands. At least she wasn't marrying them both.

Oswald's stomach clenched and he couldn't bring himself to open any more "MistyWed" images or films he found there. He understood—she had suffered the life of a military spouse and widow—but he couldn't watch any more. Maybe later, but not now. For now, he'd just try to be happy for her. She'd always been a good wife and mother. She deserved to be happy.

He opened the files named after Mary and Mara, and watched a video of Mary and Brent walking down the aisle. They'd waited three years to get married according to the date in the lower left corner. Mara, Misty, and Anahita stood in a row next to Mary as the bridesmaids, each beautiful in their matching gowns. He didn't recognize any of the young groomsmen, but behind them was a service-holo of Oswald, looking on with a benevolent smile.

Someone must have altered the picture. He never smiled in his service-holos.

A precious young girl dressed in white toddled down the aisle behind Mary and Brent, clutching a silk ring-bearer's pillow. She looked just old enough to be the unborn baby he'd said goodbye to on his last day on Earth. When Mary turned to smile at the girl and wave her forward, Oswald could see the swell of her belly. Another one on the way.

He squeezed his eyes shut. Mary and Brent would be close to his age when the Proximans murdered them all. His beautiful grandchildren would have just enough time to grow up before dying.

The Anahita in that video with her bright smile probably still thought Earth would win. She didn't know that her enemy would eventually burn the brains from her skull. Maybe she even hoped he would still turn up and save the day.

"Surprise," Oswald whispered as he shut down Mary's folder and opened Mara's.

Mara's academy graduation-holo looked like one of the super-model pictures the SDF used in their recruitment ads. There weren't as many pictures of her as there were of Misty and Mary. They were all of her duty assignments; sometimes she was smiling and other times she stared into the camera with grim defiance. He knew that expression all too well. She'd been born with it.

Somewhere in her military adventures, Mara had acquired a burn scar on her left cheek. In her uniform, she reminded him of Ululani, but her features were all Oswald and Misty; no Anahita. The final picture was of her in combat vacc-armor, with major's bars, and *Gigante* stenciled on the breastplate. He wondered how soon before her death it had been taken.

He switched the cube off and connected to the duty net. "All department heads report to the conference room in one hour."

OSWALD SAT WITH HIS arms crossed, staring past the holographic projection as Anahita's last testament played through the second time for his officers. He was proud of them. They hadn't started blubbering like he had, not even Breen. There were wet eyes and quivering lips, to be sure, but their shocked silence was much more dignified than his display had been.

"Leaders of the world, my ass," Karpov said at length. "We know we're officially fucked, at least, but it still doesn't tell us what happened to Earth. Unless their bio weapon turned out to be some sort of nanobugs that ate the whole planet."

"Even then the constituent remains would have clumped together," Danner said. "Even if they ate it at the atomic level, there'd be some kind of detectable cloud in orbit."

Oswald turned to McFarran, hoping for encouragement. He saw only his own stunned despair reflected back at him. "Trese, I want you to set up an isolated sector in the database so you can scrub this of threats, then run an analysis on it. There are a lot of files on here, mostly from General Khadem's terminal. Maybe something got put on there after her execution that might tell us what happened."

Trese stared at him a moment before answering. "Yes, FC."

Oswald slid the data box in close. "Danner, how's the complex coming?"

"Three of the access passages are sealed off and holding pressure, including the garage. Two rovers inside needed new batteries, but both at least start. There's lots of storage space and enough bunks for everyone. It'll take a few more hours to heat up enough not to need an EVA suit. It'll be more comfortable there than in this bucket."

A wave of grumbling rolled around the table and Oswald held up his hands. "Mr. Danner, that's no way to talk about *Roland*. But the point is taken. It's been a rough mission."

"All we need is some food, Colonel," McFarran said. He smiled and held his hands as if holding a plate. "I could go for some steaming bouillabaisse. Oh, *magnifique.*"

Breen rubbed his eyes and laughed. "I was thinking this morning about some deep-dish pizza. Real Chicago-style."

The talk of food animated the officers, and Oswald let it continue because it was real talk of home. He hoped the tentative laughter and furtive smiles would ease them. *Roland*'s children had hard work ahead and even harder choices. Oswald needed to be vigilant—it might be days before what Anahita's message truly meant sank in.

"Too bad it's just space-rats for us," Karpov said.

Oswald offered a wry smile. "Well, I can't promise any banquets, but there are some sealed crates of food and water past that vault door."

"What's back there, FC?" Breen asked.

Oswald tapped the data cube. "I found this back there. It's a mausoleum full of dead VIPs. Including General Khadem."

"It's like a memorial, Colonel," McFarran said. "To the leaders of Earth. Do they all have such cubes?"

"I didn't check. Everything was dusty. Anahita's was the first one I saw. You can go check."

Karpov scoffed. "More like a trophy collection. Come see the extinct Earthers what we killed."

"Possibly part of the honoring ceremony?" McFarran asked, looking around the table.

"Fuck their honoring ceremony," Karpov said. Several heads nodded in agreement.

"I'm merely suggesting that to them"—McFarran held out his hands to placate the other officers—"this is how you honor fallen enemies. Like giving a proper burial."

"What?" Karpov said. "More like how a taxidermist honors a dead goat by stuffing it and putting it on display."

Oswald leaned forward to break the icy glare between his aux and his tactical officer. "Anyway, Doc, you'll have to test the rations. The cavern's pretty deep, but four hundred years is a long time to bake in radiation."

Danner slammed the table, causing everyone to start back. "It hasn't been four hundred years—"

"Will you secure that shit, Danner?" Karpov rose from his seat, as far as the cramped space allowed, and brought his fist down. "Even if it's only been twenty years, or one year, something happened. We're not in Kansas anymore. And if you won't shut up, at least stop saying stupid things. It's bad for morale to have such a fucking idiot as flight engineer—"

It was Oswald's turn to slam his palm on the table. "Enough. Tac, stop jumping on everyone's back. If you can't act like a fucking department head, name your replacement. You got me?"

Karpov fell back into his seat without looking away from Danner. "I got you, FC."

And just like that, the camaraderie was gone. Like air sucked out a hatch. That's where they'd all be going if he didn't get things back under control. "Danner, we are officially operating on the assumption due to overwhelming evidence—"

"Circumstantial—" Danner started.

Oswald lifted a finger and continued, "Overwhelming evidence that somehow four hundred years have passed. I can't make you believe it, but you will perform your duties in accordance with that scenario. And you will stop arguing about it."

"Yes, sir."

Oswald glanced at each of the other officers. "Now we have to decide what to do. The way I see it, we either stay here or we take off and search for something else.

"If we stay here, the crew might get too comfortable and not want to leave. I might not want to leave. And if we leave, who knows what we'll find? If we find anything at all. After all, how long was it before we detected Luna? Maybe there is some other base or colony out there."

"I say we definitely stay, Colonel," Danner said. "I can get the complex looking like a hotel. It has power, an air processor, and plenty of food."

"It *might* have plenty of food," Oswald said. "We have to see."

Danner's voice grew hopeful. "It's probably good, FC. And even if not, we'll be able to get a decent sleep."

"And when we run out of food, Danner?" McFarran asked. "What then?"

"Then we decide. We might have found some other answer. Who knows?"

Karpov raised a finger. "FC?"

Oswald narrowed his eyes at the tactical officer and noticed Danner doing the same. "Yes?"

"My thoughts, for the record, are that we allow our esteemed engineer to fix up the base, and we garrison here while we analyze the data cube. I haven't gotten a decent bit of shut-eye since the fucking accident myself. Like he said, we might find something. Set the big-eye scanning, and maybe even start scanning the cubes from the other stiffs."

Oswald clenched his jaw and felt the heat rising from his neck.

Karpov held his hands up. "Sorry, FC. Sorry. Bad choice of words. But if the other crypts or coffins or whatever have cubes like that, there's no telling what we might find."

"It sounds reasonable to me, Colonel," McFarran said. "We don't have the delta-v to jump blindly. I mean figuratively, of course. I don't want to jump at all. Ever again."

Oswald looked around. "Anyone else?"

Dr. Hines raised his hand. "I agree with staying, FC. This crew needs a rest. This isn't home, but it's probably the closest we're going to get for now. We should be careful how we disseminate these findings to the crew, as well."

"Hell, Doc," Oswald said, "half the crew's in this room."

"Well, then, we don't want to send the other half into a panic," the doctor replied. "Give them a soft landing, so to speak."

"I'll fix the place up so nice, no one will want to leave," Danner said, his voice sure.

Oswald shook his finger. "I'm not sure we want that."

"We can explore the ruins too," Breen blurted. "I mean, maybe something's survived the attack. Luna University is less than twenty clicks according to our last reference map. You never know."

"That's a good idea, Breen," McFarran said. "Colonel, I must concur. I believe we should stay for now. Rest. Give the outer hull a good inspection. Take some time to decide what to do. There should still be plenty of ice in the dark craters, so air and water shouldn't be a problem."

Oswald steepled his fingers in thought. This couldn't become their new home, no matter how cozy Danner made it. Air and water might not be an issue, but food would be. *Roland* wasn't equipped with an aeroponics bay, and there was no way such a thing had survived the frozen centuries on dead Luna.

But he hadn't slept well either since the jump into Sol. And not only because of the ghosts of Yninski, Luskin, and Ululani. The Delamain hadn't helped. How the hell was someone supposed to sleep while the world you knew was ending?

"So be it," Oswald said. "We'll divide into sections. One to work on the base, the other to put *Roland* in standby mode."

"We could just shut her down," Danner said.

"She's still a warship. And I still plan on taking this war to the Proximans." Oswald shrugged. "When we can find them."

"Fucking right," Karpov said.

McFarran rolled his eyes. "We don't have enough EVA suits for everyone to be in the base, Colonel."

"If we store the vacc-armor in the vehicle bay," Danner said, "everyone should be able to stay in the base."

"Let's get to it then," Oswald said. "Aux, write up the duty schedules and get them to me by end of shift. Everyone, dismissed."

The tone of conversation was lighter as the officers filed from the conference room. Sometimes, the troops just needed direction, any direction, to feel less hopeless or helpless. Oswald felt a little better too; he was as tired as they were of aimlessly flying around Sol.

Once the other officers had left, Oswald climbed back down to his stateroom. He'd start scanning the files in the cube, files not in the "Pierce" directory, while Trese readied the security protocols.

He set the cube in the center of the table and activated it again. As he was about to select *Records and Data*, Oswald decided to tap *Interactive Personality Module* instead.

An image of Anahita snapped into existence in the air above him. The expression was less severe than it had been on her last day. She also looked tidy. Too tidy. Every crease was perfect and not a single strand of hair waved out of place.

Oswald snorted. "Just some avatar." He jumped when Anahita tilted her head down to look at him.

"Hello," she said in a precise tone that emulated Anahita's perfectly. "Have you come to learn about me, Honored General Anahita Khadem?"

"I know more about you than you do." Oswald leaned forward to exit and dig into the files.

"Excellent," she said cheerfully. It had been years since he'd heard Anahita be cheerful, but that, too, was a perfect imitation. "What's your name?"

"Pierce, not that it matters."

"Pierce Oswald, is that you?"

His jaw went slack as he looked up. It shouldn't have shocked him. Any face-recognition software could analyze his face and assign his name to a data array. But it still felt as if he'd been slapped. Oswald shut his jaw with a snap. "You know me?"

"I couldn't forget the father of my child, Pierce."

# Chapter 24

OSWALD GAPED AT ANAHITA's image. Her face loomed over the table, forcing him to crane his neck. He didn't see a zoom option. Finally, he put his finger and thumb at the edge of the keyboard and made a pinching motion. Anahita's face shrank. "You're not Anahita."

"Of course I'm not." Her expression changed from cheerful to placid disapproval, her voice became icy. "And you're not Pierce Oswald. He died over four hundred years ago. But I am programmed for entertaining interaction. Would you prefer a more pleasant attitude?"

Anahita beamed. Her eyes twinkled. Years and worries melted from her face. "Is this better?" she asked in a voice bubbly to the point of vacuousness.

Oswald grimaced. "She never sounded like that."

The image blurred and was replaced with a video of a much younger Anahita, nursing a baby Oswald assumed was Ululani. "Oh, there's a little one. Oh, there's my yam. Ooh-ooh-ooh." Her words devolved into indecipherable cooing. The voice was a perfect, bubbly match.

Oswald held his hands up towards the holograph as it went blurry. "Fine. She never spoke to adults that way that I ever heard. Use the previous voice and image."

"Information noted, Pierce," Anahita said in her dour voice. He preferred that.

"What is your function?"

"To simulate conversation with the Sol Defense Fleet's supreme commander, General Anahita Khadem."

"You said that already."

"Yes, I did."

Oswald pursed his lips. The simulation was doing a good job simulating how difficult Anahita could be. "I mean why? What is the point of this program?"

"So future generations can learn about honored people from Earth and meet the villains of the Freedom War."

Oswald chuckled. Villains of the Freedom War? Those were lofty, guilt-assuaging titles coming from the people that started it. The Proximan rulers might not have been that different from Earth's after all. "How many people have come by to learn this great knowledge?"

"I have never before been activated."

"Sounds like the educational program failed."

"The knowledge is still here, Pierce." Anahita leaned forward to rest her chin in one palm. "And you're here. Getting educated."

Oswald couldn't help staring into Anahita's eyes. But it wasn't Anahita. It was a damned good imitation though. Her, no its, right brow arched exactly like Anahita's when she grew impatient. The image's left eye was barely higher than the right. The difference was so slight that only someone intimately familiar with her face would notice.

"I'm not Proximan."

"Of course you aren't if you're Pierce." Anahita waved a hand at him. "You're learning about your own Earth honored leaders."

"There's nothing about you that couldn't be a book."

Anahita straightened. "Excuse me? I'm not merely a data collection. I'm the product of Ay-Yon experts not only in software interface but also psychology and machine learning. I can give you the experience of what it would be like to actually talk to Honored Anahita Khadem."

Oswald paused to verify that the vein on the left side of her neck was throbbing as it always had when she was pissed. It was. Her Proximan handlers must have put her through some heated interrogations designed to produce every biometric reaction a human can make.

"Like a dead Earth wax museum."

"I suppose."

"Are you AI?"

Anahita smiled. "Not like you mean it. But I do have rudimentary sensors to help me detect emotional reactions from those I'm conversing with. Mostly facial muscle-twitch analysis, with biometric and thermal detection."

"A toy."

"In companion mode, my emotional responses are designed to react to emotional cues with my own emotion emulators." Anahita shrugged and looked around the cramped compartment. "It makes some people uncomfortable, so units like me aren't allowed without express permission. Funerary simulations are a popular tradition among the Ay-Yon. It allows grieving people a chance to say those final farewells and hear stories of the deceased from the deceased. It was decided to do the same for any Earthers who might have survived the war."

"I'd rather have a single severing of those ties."

"Very well, I will deactivate—"

"Wait-wait."

Anahita raised her brow. "Yes?"

"I didn't say deactivate. This is... it's not a custom of my people."

She winked. "Right. Of you Earth people."

"Yes. Just wait a minute."

"Waiting."

There was more this program could tell him, maybe more than what could be found from reading the files alone. Was it possible it might let something slip while in its Anahita persona that was otherwise classified? Probably not. There'd be no reason to give some memorial program current military information. And that current intel would be four hundred years out of date.

"How was the planet Earth destroyed?"

"The human population was eliminated after their heinous crimes with a genetically tailored biological weapon. According to the documents of Anahita Khadem and the current date, the planet should currently be safe once again for human settlement."

"Earth is gone. It is no longer physically in its orbit around Sol."

Anahita broke out laughing. Her arms crossed over her belly and the image rocked back and forth. "That is a very funny joke, Pierce. It must have been aliens."

Oswald balled his hands into fists. It wasn't the first time some program had laughed at him. Hacker-bots, joke sites, and countless advertising holos had done the same over the years. But this Proximan simulation laughing about Earth had him gritting his teeth. "Stop laughing."

Anahita straightened and her expression became apologetic. "I'm sorry, Pierce. I detect that you have grown angrier. The non sequitur nature of your comment made me assume it was an attempt at humor."

"Look for yourself. You won't see it."

"I can't see it. I don't have the capability of analyzing astronomical data." She shrugged. "I lack the external sensors and proper applications. But I do have the ability to entertain theoretical content."

"You can pretend."

"Yes, though the accuracy of Anahita Khadem's responses decrease significantly due to increased extrapolation requirements."

Oswald drummed his fingers on the table. He knew it wasn't her, but it sure felt like her. At least, a version of her. Avatar assistants had been popular in Oswald's youth, 3-D representations that learned to manage schedules and were supposed to know what their owner would find important. Like digital chamberlains, that could discern real connection requests from the countless marketing avatars that could be just as convincing. The av-assistants fell out of favor when people had difficulty telling if they were talking to the real or digital version of their friends.

That's what this was. An av-assist programmed by the Proximans. It was hard to imagine the aliens being able to incorporate Earther nuances, but they'd done a decent job. This Anahita probably couldn't have a real conversation about why she'd hidden his daughter. But maybe.

"Did Ululani know I was her father?"

Anahita's image paused for a second and grew stern. "Of course she knew who you were, Pierce. I didn't tell her, but she figured it out. She worshipped you, the war-hero astronaut father. Couldn't stop talking about you. Me? I just worked in an office. I was just Mom."

The image halted another moment. "I urged her to tell you when she was assigned to *Bonwei*. But she was too wonderstruck to tell the great Lieutenant Colonel Oswald."

"Did she know I didn't abandon her? That you hid her from me? That I didn't know?"

"Yes, Pierce. But I don't know if she ever realized what I gave up for both of your sakes. It was always about you." Anahita's face grew placid again.

Oswald looked away. Ululani had been afraid of approaching him, and he'd been afraid of approaching her. He'd faced down Proximan squadrons and alien monsters, but he'd been afraid of his own daughter. His heart ached with the desire to go back and talk to her, to get to know her. Even if only for a short while. Too late now.

"Tell me about this honoring ceremony," Oswald said.

Anahita's image was replaced with a video. The real Anahita, jaw set and eyes defiant, back to being sixty, was walking stiffly in front of two Proximan officers. They all stopped and one of the officers drew a laser pistol from his belt.

Oswald looked away and scrambled to cover the cube with his hands. "No-no-no. Just tell me. I don't want to see."

"I have the historical event on file, Pierce Oswald. What better way to learn?"

"No." Oswald waited a moment and lifted his hands.

The Anahita simulation was scowling at him again. "When a person, Earther or Ay-Yon, or presumably any sentient, achieves recognition but is to be put to death, they are given the opportunity to share their last testament. In ancient days, the honored statements were kept on scrolls which were guarded by the local leaders. As technology advanced, so did the capabilities of the testament.

"It started as a way to show respect and calm hard feelings after wars, political executions, and even euthanasia or self-terminations. Many followers of influential people feel less inclined to revenge if honor is given. Civilians are given painless toxins, leaders and soldiers are given a final wound."

"What if a soldier doesn't want to get their brains blown out?"

Anahita's voice had taken the tone of a teacher, though a cold one. "It would be an insult, but it is not unheard of. Ay-Yon have a variety of beliefs. Anahita Khadem was—"

Oswald held up a hand. "I know. That's enough."

"Is there anything else you would like to discuss?"

"What is this immersive mode you were talking about?"

"I will interact using Anahita's extrapolated personality in all situations and speak in the first person. This grants a more personalized educational experience."

There was no reason to think the personality module would have access to more information if in this immersion mode. That would be foolish from a security standpoint. She would merely try to sound more like Anahita instead of a computerized subject-matter expert.

But maybe it would give a hint about how Anahita felt about things, which might in turn give him something to go on. At least, that's what he told himself. He wanted to hear how this program, this Anahita, would talk. He wanted to talk to her. To it. To her.

"OK. Activate immersive mode, or whatever you called it."

Anahita's image went rigid and her eyes flashed electric blue twice. "Done." Her expression morphed as wrinkles spread across her face and her jowls thickened. White highlighted her black hair. It was a perfect image of Anahita from her last testament.

Oswald couldn't think of a thing to say. The projection was so lifelike. She looked so different from the last time he'd seen her on the shuttle pad. But it was her—it looked like her. "Hello."

"Good to see you, Pierce." Anahita's face had softened from a scowl to mild amiability. "Why so glum?"

"It looks like we lost."

"We did what we could. You give up?"

He still wasn't hopeful he'd learn anything more, but Oswald knew he'd have to play along. "Not yet. We got back and everyone's gone. No SDF. No Proximans; not here, anyway."

"What are you going to do about it?"

"What can I do about it?" Pierce exhaled and held up his hands. "We don't have enough reaction mass to go jumping from system to system. And if there are any Proximans here, they're keeping quiet."

"Try their home system, Beta Hydri."

"No shit? I remember Will guessing that was a good candidate years ago."

Anahita lifted a brow. "Will?"

"Will Zaphrim."

"Yes, Will Zaphrim. I worked with him for years. He died on the operating table during reconstructive surgery."

"Right. I don't suppose you have the jump tunnel information for Beta Hydri? I'm pretty sure *Roland* doesn't."

"Of course I do, Pierce. I'm not some cadet."

Oswald sneered as he imagined jumping in on the Proximans and transmitting something like "We're back," or "Guess who, assholes!" while he rained nuclear fire on the largest targets he could find.

It was a dark feeling, but a warm one. He embraced it. He usually felt the overwhelming relief of survival or the fiery pride of victory after winning a battle. And occasionally, grim satisfaction at being able to avenge his fallen friends.

Now Oswald was filled with ecstatic bloodlust as he imagined the murderers of his family burning. He rubbed his hands together and looked up at Anahita. "I guess I know what I'm about to do about it."

The barest smile touched Anahita's lips. "Come back at the helm, come back in a bag, or don't come back at all."

# Chapter 25

THE MASSIVE PROXIMAN starship, designated *Titan* before Oswald destroyed it in Barnard's Star, hung in the blue sky. It was larger than he remembered. Billowy clouds drifted by, obscuring it momentarily. Purple mountains stood silently watching in the distance.

Far below the ship, two young girls giggled as they swung higher and higher on a brightly colored swing set. The red chains squealed in protest with each pass. On opposite sides of the playground stood the girls' mothers, faces wearing warm smiles as they watched the children play. One wore a curve-hugging floral dress and the other an unadorned SDF officer's uniform.

They turned their smiles to him. The women wanted him to choose. He understood this because in dreams things were sometimes simply known. Unexplained knowledge was part of the dreamworld, and the participants didn't need to know how they knew anything.

He knew, in this dream, that he was wearing his vacc-armor. The sense of restriction and the gleaming display on his visor were as realistic as they would be in the real world.

But knowing he was in a dream hadn't helped him escape it once in the last three weeks.

The weapon ports on *Titan* opened and lances of swirling fire reached down to the Earth. The beams were the product of an action-adventure creator, not a real-world laser emitter.

The friendly clouds burned away and the mountains melted into the horizon. The flowers and grass surrounding the park wilted, blackened, and blew away in the dust.

A beam fell from the looming alien ship towards the playground. It raced down in slow motion as can only happen in dreams. The girls and women looked up at it and ran towards Oswald. His screams were muted by his helmet. He tried to reach out for them, to grab them, to jump in the way, but his armor was too heavy.

The beam evaporated the swing set, then chased after the girls and their mothers, scorching the ground in its path. The runners were almost to him, reaching out for help, when the beam caught up. Their clothes burst into flames and their flesh melted from their bones. Oswald could hear their screams through his helmet. They didn't even have radios; how could he hear them? Because in this dream, he was supposed to.

The ground beneath them exploded, and the girls and their mothers flew into the air above him. He reached out desperately, screaming mutely into the useless mic. Each body cartwheeled by just out of reach, leaving a trail of smoke behind it.

The speaker in his helmet blared to life.

"Come back at the helm, come back in a bag, or don't come back at all."

Oswald jerked awake, fighting to free himself from the blanket wrapped around him. Terror froze his blood. It wasn't a blanket, but his vacc-armor. He had to get out of his suit before he suffocated. *Roland* was burning around him, but he had to get his helmet off. He couldn't breathe—

Oswald jerked awake with just enough wherewithal to bite back the scream this time. The duty watch rushed in each time they heard the flight commander shrieking. Everyone knew about his dreams, but he wasn't the only one screaming during their sleep shift these days.

He sat up panting, almost bouncing out of his bunk in the low gravity. The blanket slid from his trembling hands three times before he was able to get it around his shoulders. Blood pounded in his ears and terror turned his guts to jelly.

It was several minutes before Oswald didn't feel like screaming anymore. He sat in the darkness of the tiny lunar cabin, staring at McFarran's back. Even in the weak glow of the room's tiny indicator lights, Oswald could tell his aux was not asleep. He couldn't explain why, exactly. The rhythm of his breathing or a tension in his shoulders, maybe. Oswald hoped McFarran wouldn't try to talk to him. After several more minutes, Oswald felt a measure of relief. McFarran was earnestly trying to go back to sleep or offering Oswald a pretense of privacy. Either was fine with him.

It was just after 2:00 a.m. by *Roland*'s reckoning. Oswald leaned forward and put his face in his hands. He could barely keep his eyes open, but there was no getting back to sleep now. In such cramped spaces, though palatial compared to his rack in the beehive, it would make it harder on his aux to get back to sleep if he just sat there staring. Slipping on his socks to keep his feet warm on the cool stone floor, Oswald left McFarran to his own nightmares. He grabbed his tablet and the holo-cube on his way out.

Danner had done a good job. The crew had been living in the lunar complex for almost three weeks now and spirits had improved marginally. It was all he could hope for since around-the-clock scanning with the big-eye still hadn't turned up Earth. Or any fucking thing at all.

At least no one else had killed themselves. That was something. But a few of the crew spoke as if they'd found their new home, Danner being the most vocal. And that was going to be a problem, one he didn't know how to fix. Announcing that, no, Luna was not going to be their home because they'd run out of food and would die soon wasn't going to help morale. It was a true statement, but not useful at this time.

The duty rover bounced by and offered a quick salute. Oswald returned it and made his way to the closet that had been repurposed into his office. He slid the door closed, set the holo-cube on top of the air-tight crate that served as his ad hoc desk, and turned it on.

Anahita appeared on the other side of the crate as if sitting opposite him. In the weeks of working with the cube, he'd learned how to reposition the projection, change the visuals, and tweak the personality module's responses. The Anahita sitting across from him now looked like the Anahita he'd seen on his last day on Earth.

But he could only modify her personality in small ways. It drew from its own database and algorithms. Oswald had even tried flirting with Anahita, and the experience left him excited and uncomfortable at the same time.

"Pierce."

"Ana."

"You know I hate being called that."

"I do."

Anahita pursed her lips for a second. "So it's going to be one of those types of talks, is it?"

Oswald shook his head. "No. Sorry. I'm not looking for a fight."

Anahita lifted a holo-graphic tablet and glanced at the screen. "Another dream?"

"Yep. Same thing. You, Misty, Ululani, and Mara in the park."

"My father would have called it witchcraft, but there are many who believe dreams have meanings. That they can be harbingers of things to come."

"I don't believe that," Oswald said. "But I do believe they can mean I'm going crazy."

"You have an unfulfilled need to avenge the death of your family."

"Oh, do you have a psychoanalysis suite too?"

Anahita raised a brow. "I know what you mean by that but, as you know, I'm a general, not a psychologist. A general who is wondering why you haven't attacked the Proximans yet."

"Because the jump data you gave me is four hundred years out of date."

"And what are you doing about that? The Pierce I know wouldn't just sit back on his ass when there are Proximans to kill."

"Then you don't know me very well." Oswald rubbed his scalp. "Look, I'm not here to fight. You were telling me about going to Wolf 1061. I was never deployed there. What's it like?"

Oswald lost track of time as he chatted with Anahita in the privacy of his little office. On some level, it was easy to forget she was a simulation. When he remembered, it didn't really matter. He was talking to the Anahita he knew. When they were deep in conversation, he barely noticed her non sequiturs or Turing Test slips.

The door slid open while Oswald was laughing and McFarran stuck his head in.

Oswald froze, choking on the laughter from his gaping mouth. He slapped at the holo-cube's controls until Anahita blinked away. It felt like the time his mother had caught him masturbating. He cleared his throat. "Aux."

McFarran frowned at the cube for an instant before entering. Oswald picked it up and looked for a pocket to tuck it into. He was still in his sleep suit, which had no large pockets, so he put it back on the table.

"The memorial is in one hour, Colonel. I know you didn't sleep well last night and wanted to remind you."

Oswald cleared his throat again. "Yes. Thank you. Sorry I woke you. That same nightmare."

McFarran glanced away for a second. "Perhaps, Colonel, you should return the cube to the monument. I don't think it's helping with your sleep."

"And what's that supposed to mean, Aux?"

"Only that you need more sleep, Colonel. Nothing more. And it seems that instead of trying to go back to sleep or getting some sleep aids from Dr. Hines, you're playing with that." McFarran smiled and inched closer. "I don't mean to lecture, Colonel, but I had a similar situation with my oldest and his video games."

"This isn't a video game."

"Yes, Colonel. But we have important decisions to make and your mind needs to be clear. In any case, the shower is currently empty. You might feel refreshed if you avail yourself of it."

OSWALD CLOSED THE OUTER hatch to the airlock after McFarran had joined him on the lunar surface. Pausing to verify the positive-seal indicator was green, Oswald waved a hand for his aux to follow.

They moved with slow bounces towards the landing pad. The crew waited in two rows on the far side of *Roland*, facing away from the base. It was such a small formation compared to what it had been on their day of departure from Earth.

Oswald and McFarran took up position in front of the crew. There weren't enough of the more agile EVA suits for everyone, so the crew all wore their combat vacc-armor for the sake of uniformity and ceremony. It was difficult to see the ditch containing the funerary fireworks that had been dug one hundred meters in front of them. Especially with body bags lined up shoulder to shoulder before them in the regolith.

The Proximans had left behind a large crate of the standard fleet funeral rockets. Anahita said they'd been made available to perform SDF memorial services after the honoring. That there were so many told Oswald that the Proxies either reneged on their promise after they'd murdered everyone, or that they had never planned to use them in the first place.

The hole dug by Danner's crew held seven rockets for each of the dead, with a few spares in case of failures. With as much military bearing as they could muster in the bulky suits, Oswald and McFarran turned to face one another. Sharp drill and ceremony techniques were often impossible in space. Approximations were the best the astronauts could offer. The remote control interface for the rockets flashed ready on Oswald's visor. He nodded to McFarran.

"*Roland*, attention!" McFarran called over the crew channel. "I shall read off the names of our fallen fellows with pride and remorse."

Oswald and McFarran tottered in military fashion to face back over the bodies. "*Roland*, hand salute!"

"Major Jeremy Bowens," McFarran intoned.

Oswald twitched a finger and seven sparkling streaks of red raced into the dark sky. They flared bright, then disappeared in a silent flash, burning into dust that wouldn't contaminate the surface or reach escape velocity. According to the *Basic Orbital Operations Manual*, the BOOM, they burned brighter at first to remember the life of the departed and burned out with a flash to light the way into whatever lay beyond.

"Lieutenant Yun Chun."

Seven rockets into the dark.

"Lieutenant Sally Krace."

Seven streamers of life into death.

"Major Terrance Luskin."

Seven.

"Command Sergeant Kenneth Salazar."

Seven more.

"Specialist Monique Sharp."

Seven more silent death candles flew away in the vacuum.

A name. Seven rockets. Another name, another seven. Oswald watched barrage after barrage fly into the star field above them. Only a few of the ancient rockets sputtered out of control or failed to launch. It was an easy matter to launch the spares.

He should have added rockets for Anahita and Mara. And Ululani. No, they'd already had their sending-off day long ago. Ages ago. Today was for *Roland*'s children. McFarran read off the last name, Yninski. The last by name but the first to die.

Maybe he should show McFarran's report on Yniniski's death to Anahita now. See what she had to say.

"Colonel?" McFarran asked over the commander's channel.

"Of course. Sorry." Oswald fired off the last set of rockets. He'd been lost in thought and missed his cue. Once the rockets had faded away, Oswald opened the crew channel. "*Roland*, ready, two!" He dropped his salute and tottered back around.

He'd performed memorials many times in the past, but never so many at once. Never on Luna. Never so utterly alone. Maybe their souls were looking down on him with pity from wherever they were. Oswald suddenly felt like lying down and sleeping.

"On behalf of the Supreme Commander of the Sol Defense Fleet and a grateful world," Oswald said. The words made him want to vomit. There was no fucking world and it had never been grateful. Only greedy. And stupid. But he still missed it, still needed it. Or at least needed to find out what had happened to it. It struck him that the people on the ground before him had all died in vain.

Oswald swallowed hard at the lump in his throat, hoping the sound hadn't been heard over his mic. "On behalf of the Supreme Commander of the Sol Defense Fleet and a grateful world, we offer this fiery display in memory of the faithful and honorable service of our fallen companions.

"We go on to face challenges and mysteries without their guidance, without their wisdom, and without their hands to steady our faltering steps.

"*Roland*'s lost children will live on with us, having forever forged a part of our lives." But they wouldn't, they were all dead. "We have stars to move and their presence, their support, and their strength will be missed. *Ad astra*."

"*Ad astra*," the crew replied in unison.

Oswald tapped a finger and select verses from "Will Sol Cry For You?" by Marilyn Gordon played over everyone's headset. It had been written as a memorial for the Joint Mars Venture colony ship, *Future's Hope*. The colonists were to move into the habitats built by robots, but burned up instead due to a last-minute mechanical failure during landing. The fiery crash was caught from three separate high-definition satellites. *Future's Hope* had rained across Mars as the Rangers' landers had across DPV. The fleet adopted the ballad as its official ceremonial dirge.

*...Traveler, will Sol cry for you...*

Oswald scanned the faces of the crew through their visors. Nearly every eye was wet, even those with clenched jaws trying to keep it together. Others didn't try to hide it, wiping running noses on the scratch sponges in their helmets. There was something comforting about the sense of isolation a space helmet gave. His crew wouldn't have normally carried on so freely in formation. Of course, he'd never seen a formation of spacers that had literally lost their whole world.

When the song finished, Oswald stepped as solemnly as possible to stand at the head of Bowen's body as McFarran stopped at the engineer's feet. They lifted the body and carried it to the vehicle bay.

Despite the low gravity and McFarran's help, it was difficult work. Walking in step with someone to share a burden could be difficult enough. Trying to do it without bouncing too high or tripping on Luna's rough surface, while wearing vacc-armor and carrying an uncooperative corpse in a bag, was much harder. Oswald fought back an image of him falling on the body bag somehow and ripping it open. He couldn't even think of what he'd do then.

The crew paired off and each pair acted as pallbearers until all the body bags were in the bay. Breen had suggested having Rocketman move the bodies, but everyone else thought it would be disrespectful. Once the bodies were all inside, Oswald and McFarran led the procession to the VIP mausoleum. It took an hour to lay out the bodies at the bottom of the cavern.

Oswald and McFarran watched the mausoleum airlock cycle red, then green as Norris and Trese went back to the main hub of the complex. McFarran opened the hatch and stepped in. When he realized Oswald hadn't followed, he turned.

"Are you well, Colonel?"

"Yeah. I just need a minute. I'll be out."

McFarran saluted and cycled through.

Oswald leaned over the railing. From the high angle, he could see the dead laid out all at once. If not for the stretched imprints of the reaching bodies in the bags, it would have looked like a row of pillows. There were so many.

Part of him threatened to tear up again, to lament the charnel scene beneath his feet. But that part was dead now. After two decades of dealing out and suffering death, that part of him that felt remorse finally bled its last drop. That part of him had committed suicide, casting itself into the void. He felt that should terrify him, should destroy him. It didn't.

Yet rage was gone too. Rage at SDF stupidity, at Anahita, even at the Proximans. All he had was an icy, logical certainty that they had to pay. Or was it numbness from weeks of pain and emotional turmoil? He couldn't tell.

Exhaustion threatened to pull him over the railing and drop him with the corpses. And maybe he'd let it. Maybe if he lay down with the dead, he could sleep without dreams. Maybe he wouldn't have to wake up.

But who'd take care of Anahita?

With a final, lingering stare over the edge, Oswald pushed away from the railing and staggered through the airlock.

He made it to his room and stacked the pieces of his vacc-armor outside the door. McFarran's suit was against the wall on the other side. He winced at the smell of his clothes. It had been sweaty work. His armor was designed to protect from external heat and shrapnel, not body odor.

Peering around the corner, Oswald saw the long line he expected to the single shower stall. The crew was subdued, but there were a few timid smiles among the wet eyes and drawn faces.

He could wait. When he came around the corner, a few of the crew moved to let him in line. Oswald waved the offer off with a soft smile and slid into his office.

Anahita sat on the other side of the table, frowning. Oswald's tablet was before her where he'd left the video feed from his helmet for her to watch. Now it was black, except for a blinking, yellow *No Signal.*

"What'd you think?" Oswald asked.

"It was nice. I always hated funerals, though I never had to do one quite like that." Anahita shifted in her virtual seat. "You look like you need to talk. Tell me what's on your mind. What's really on your mind."

ROMAN KARPOV CLOSED his eyes and enjoyed the heat from the drying booth as it washed over his body. He'd had the foresight to make straight for the shower stall after the ceremony. Those in the line behind him wore expressions of sorrow and confusion. Hopelessness. Some looked lost and others stared into the distance somewhere beyond the rock walls of the cramped lunar base.

They disgusted him. Everything that happened had sapped their will to fight. So many were still weeping, carrying on only because they didn't know what else to do. Not that he hadn't teared up; the dead had been his friends too. But the mourners were missing the point.

They should be looking to their rage for direction and strength. Instead, they were embracing their weakness. He hadn't come up with any answers about the jump accident, but it was obvious they had lost centuries somehow. Danner was the weakest. A fool. Though he was a good engineer, and had fixed this shitty little base up, the man couldn't even accept what he saw in front of him.

That was alright. As long as Oswald kept it together. That man knew what they had to do. But Oswald had too many voices talking to him. Karpov was afraid his FC was getting distracted, that he would soften up and listen to the whiners. Especially that asshole McFarran. There was only one choice. The Proximans, and their collaborators, must die.

Someone pounded on the air booth. "Come on in there."

Karpov rolled his shoulders and slipped into his clean flight suit. He cast a final look at the line and shook his head. At least someone in this sorry lot had enough gumption to get on his ass for stargazing.

This weakness was not going to bring it home to the enemy.

Karpov made his way to the vehicle bay. He'd convinced the FC to let him bunk in the small, attached tool room. With a bit of commandeering and jury-rigging, Karpov had set up a hammock made of cargo netting between the hatch and the parts locker.

The tiny room reminded him of the shanty his family lived in after Zuberec was washed away during the big thaw. His father's preparations had saved them where many had died, but there was only so much one family could do against such a disastrous flood. Isaac had been carried away, never to be found. The image of his brother's thrashing arms the second before they slipped beneath the roiling, muddy waves still visited Roman some nights.

They'd rebuilt their home from washed-up wreckage. They slept on shelves or hammocks to keep off the floor; the makeshift walls could never keep out the rats. It was a shit-hole compared to what they'd lost, but it had become their home, and the hardship brought his surviving family closer together. His father kept building on the new home, even up to the time Roman was accepted into the fleet academy.

The cluttered, gunpowder-and-grease smell of the tool room brought a grim nostalgia. Without the rat shit and reek of stagnant marsh, fortunately. Those were hard years, but long behind him now. Dwelling on them would be as bad as weeping in the shower line.

Karpov pried open the side of the tool cabinet and reached into the narrow gap. The igniters he'd taken from some of the spare funeral rockets were still there. Three small bottles of reactive solvent hid behind the battery charger.

Smiling, he set everything back in place and shuffled to the hub. The large table near the vault had become the de facto conference room. McFarran, Breen, Kirsk, Trese, and Norris were seated around it.

A few people were still in line for the shower, the rest having retired to their makeshift bunks and their own thoughts. The whole base was quiet. Even those talking around the table spoke in subdued voices. Norris waved him over.

"Danner still hiding?" Karpov asked as he took his seat. One-sixth of a gravity wasn't much, but it felt good to be able to sit without your arms floating everywhere. "His thruster must still be puckered."

"This is a time when it's very important for us to get along, Karpov," McFarran said. "He's done an excellent job taking over for Bowens and fixing this place up."

Karpov shrugged and scanned the room. "Where's Oswald?"

"He saw the line for the shower and went to his closet," Breen said.

"Off talking to his girlfriend," Karpov said.

McFarran pointed a finger at him. "That is no way to talk about the Colonel. He's using it to get info."

"There's a lot of those cubes, supposedly," Karpov said. "He could ask some of them too."

"You could go get one," Trese said.

"It's way too creepy in there," Breen said. "Some of the bodies were still moving when I left."

"That's just the liquid and the low-g, Breen," McFarran said. "They'll settle."

"Still creepy."

Karpov clucked his tongue. "Not as creepy as Oswald and that cube."

"It was a nice ceremony," Norris said. She smiled at Karpov and McFarran. "I'm glad we found those little rockets."

"What really made it nice was the lack of prime ministers or senators going on and on after the reading." Karpov smiled and tapped his Lucky Star patch. "I watched the replays of two services where they read my name."

"Just twice?" Norris asked. "I see two extra stars on that—doesn't that mean you were on three destroyed ships?"

"They didn't know *Swift* was KIA until the rescue, so no early ceremony."

Breen leaned forward to inspect the patch on Karpov's chest. "How did you even survive? I mean, I know people have, but how? Did you do something special?"

"Yes, Karpov," McFarran said with a sidelong glance. "Tell us how you survived. Some helpful advice might do us all well."

"You really want to know, Aux?"

"Only what you're comfortable telling, Karpov."

Breen smiled. "I'm free for the rest of the evening."

Karpov drew air in through his teeth. "Well, to be honest, most of it is just dumb fucking luck. At least, to start with. You ain't surviving anything if you take a direct hit."

"What ship?" Breen asked.

"The first was *Julian Brevard.*"

"You were on the *Julie B.*?" Trese asked. He sounded impressed, and rightly so. "I don't know how anyone could have survived that. What I saw looked nasty."

"Oh, it was a mess alright." Karpov leaned back and looked at each of the listeners in turn, before continuing. "I was near the reactor on a repair team. We'd already taken a hit that basically blinded us. Another warhead snuck in and cut *Julie* to pieces.

"I happened to be on the other side of the heat sink, and it was a heavy-duty C-3 model. That's the only reason I didn't get slagged right off."

"She was out there for a while though," Breen said. "Even with a full suit of air—"

"I had to jump around the wreckage. Very carefully, of course. Set up some zip lines between the closer chunks. I gathered O2 from wherever I could. Had to even tap into some dead folks' air tanks."

"Oh, Goddess," Norris whispered.

Karpov smiled. "I didn't see *her* there. But that's not nearly as bad as *Sao Paulo*."

There really was no reason to tell them. They'd never understand. The SDF flight psychologist hadn't understood, either, but he'd threatened to keep Karpov off flight status if he didn't cooperate. It wasn't hard to figure out what the doctor had wanted to hear. So Karpov told him just enough to get reinstated... with a few tactical omissions.

"You don't have to," Norris said.

"No, it's alright," Karpov said. "It's just not one of the war stories I tell at parties."

"You told it in your book," McFarran said.

"Not all of it. But the good doctor might say it's cathartic to talk about it from time to time. To bare my soul, so to speak."

McFarran was staring at Karpov. "I had a good friend on *Sao Paulo*. Fabrice Baschet."

Karpov snorted. "Figures."

"Because he was French?"

"No. Because he was an idiot."

"Oh, so you did know him."

Everyone at the table started laughing. Karpov had meant his comment to be a simple insult of the asshole aux's asshole friend. Who was, in fact, an idiot. Not to be outdone, Karpov laughed along.

He cleared his throat. "Doroteya Ilyinishna Vikasheva. Dot to her friends. She was the woman I killed to survive."

The remaining chuckles dried up as soon as the words left his mouth. That would teach McFarran to laugh it up at Karpov's expense. "We were at full burn, trying to evade the parting shot of some Proximan ship we'd fragged a few hours earlier. Not sure what hit us, but I think it was with something like our T-REX.

"We, I mean Dot and I, were life-support techs on that run. We were strapped into the kibitzer bench, waiting for a call for a damage-control team. We took it right up the ass. Burned through every core compartment. Everyone else fried, even two others with us in the same space." He tapped the star on his uniform. "Again, just luck."

It did feel good to talk about what happened. And it always did, somehow. Talking about it, or at least accepting that he needed to talk about it, made him feel weak. He hated that it helped. Which was why he was thankful there were so few people he considered worth telling.

"We were out pretty far and, like I said, we were burning up delta-v like Cerberus was trying to eat our ass. When we got hit, we were a high-velocity coffin, total HVC. No reactor, no thruster, no controls. We didn't even know our vector.

"But most of the life-support supplies were good. Rations were a little irradiated, but still edible. I had a hand-cranked generator in my tool kit, so we could even power the remaining water recycler that hadn't been fried."

"Man," Breen muttered.

Karpov shrugged. "It still wasn't enough. That became apparent after two weeks. Dot suggested a lottery. I won and I shot her in the head because she couldn't bring herself to do it."

He closed his eyes, hoping to hide the wetness there. Willing himself not to let even a single sob escape, Karpov continued, "It was a mortal sin to her, suicide, that is. She was in essence asking me to take that hit for her, I guess."

"I've heard of sin-eaters in some religions," Breen said.

"I never asked her if it would be a sin to kill me if I'd lost the draw. I've often wondered if I had to kill myself, would I be able to.

So I shot her in the back of the head and turned off the air to her suit so it wouldn't leak out. It was... hard."

Karpov stared at his hands for several moments. He'd liked Dot. She was like him: tough, not willing to let things get her down. She'd always done what needed to be done. Except that one last thing. Would he have been able to? Would he be able to now?

Norris reached out and rubbed his shoulder. "I'm sorry. We shouldn't have asked you to talk about it."

He smiled at her. "Might as well finish. Six months later, some SDF scout latched on, looking for the flight recorder. That thing even got fried. Instead, they found a half-mad, shit-stained, blabbering skeleton, wearing my vacc-suit. I put the cost for rescuing my sorry ass at fifty million solars. Even though they weren't looking for me."

McFarran furrowed his brow. "Half-mad?"

Karpov flashed the crazy smile he'd practiced for just such occasions. The fans loved it. "Oh, yes. But don't worry, Aux. SDF flight psych division cleared that half."

Everyone except McFarran looked away in obvious discomfort. His smile grew as he bit back the laugh and returned McFarran's stare. It was a good reminder that not everyone was his friend. Not that it mattered; Dot had been his friend back when he allowed people to get close. He'd still blown her brains out.

The Proximans had taken everything from him. Even the ruins of Zuberec were gone now. And everything he'd built for himself: a career, his celebrity. All gone. But that kind of thing was temporary. It all was. Even he was temporary.

But he could do something that wasn't temporary. It was Oswald who could help with that, if he didn't get distracted by that damned cube or the mealy-mouthed aux. McFarran didn't have the vision or balls to wipe out the Proximans. Karpov didn't know how to do it. But Oswald would. Or he'd figure it out. No one killed the fucking Proxies like Oswald, and someone needed to watch his back.

"And the last one?" Breen asked. He noticed the glares from the other crew at the table and looked around helplessly. "What?"

"That one... well, I'm not ready to talk about it. Not yet."

"That's OK. No worries." Norris shot Breen a disapproving glance.

Karpov turned his smile to McFarran. "All that to say, Aux, that I'm not sure I can give any advice on how *you* can survive."

# Chapter 26

BREEN LAUGHED AS THE lunar rover bounced over a small ridge. He felt a long "Weeeee!" was in order and vocalized it... but only with his mic off. He knew most of the crew thought he was a simpleton, an idiot savant. "Sargeant Spectrum" is what some had called him in the academy. And maybe they were right, even if his medical record was clear.

But he was the one they called to program their toys. No one had scored like he had in advanced astrogation. Not even Colonel Oswald. Breen had laughed at graduation too, when the commandant pinned the honor student medal on his chest.

The gray of the moonscape was in stark contrast to the black sky above it. With no atmosphere, it looked like the clearest starry night possible. He could almost imagine he was camping in the desert with his grandfather. It was a far better view than the blackened craters and smashed rubble of the remains of Luna City going by on the other side of the rover.

The rover jostled Breen and he barked another laugh, before remembering to cut off his mic again. He loved the moon, had since his earliest memories. When his next orders were set to come up, he'd planned on putting in for a lunar post. He'd miss *Roland*, but this was much more fun than staying locked up in his cramped flight pod all the time. Breen needed some elbow room.

"What was that, sir?" Corporal Wells asked.

She was beautiful in a way that made him nervous. And she was nice. He knew it wasn't how an officer should think, but it was a struggle not to stammer when talking to her. "Just wondering if we'll find anything today."

"Haven't found anything so far," Trese said. "I think the old man's just sending us outside to play, like my granny used to."

"The colonel knows what he's doing," said Breen. "He always does. He'll get us back home."

"What if this is our new home?" Wells asked. "Oswald's good, but this is some crazy shit. We're not talking the war, we're talking about the laws of the universe changing here."

"Only as we know them," Trese said. "It was probably always that way, we just never understood as much as we thought we did."

Breen hated not being able to look at people when he spoke to them, but the EVA helmets and the seat restraints kept him from seeing Trese or Wells as the rover trundled along. "He'll get us home somehow."

"Sounds like he wants to keep on fighting the war." Wells didn't sound so nice now. "I'd just rather stay here, thanks."

"We can't stay here," Trese said. "We'll run out of food soon."

"I'm hoping we can find some ag-system," Wells said. "Something that got missed. I know they had some xeno-agricultural ecologies that were self-sufficient once they were established. And we'll run out of food on *Roland* too."

"The Proxies were pretty thorough," Breen said. "I mean, I'm sure they missed something, but even those xeno-ag modules need power and heat."

Wells sniffled and her voice grew wet. "I don't want to fight anymore, sir."

Breen wasn't sure if she meant the war or if she thought he was fighting with her. He hoped it was the former, since he was ready for that to be over too. If she thought he was trying to fight with her, he'd have to explain what he meant and apologize. He was used to that.

The navigation-change alert chimed in his ear. Trese turned the rover and the ruins of Luna City appeared before them. The destruction was right there and it upset Breen's stomach. He couldn't escape the view except by closing his eyes, which wasn't very officer-like.

Blackened structural girders lay twisted in the wreckage, their jagged edges reaching out for the astronauts like talons. Shards of melted surface dome were strewn around like shattered beer bottles in a gutter.

Breen shuddered. He didn't like the utter silence when no one was transmitting. There was no movement except for the dust his team was kicking up. Breen knew they'd have to be careful exploring. They were pretty far from the base and emergency repair patches could only do so much. The edges on the debris looked razor-sharp.

"Look at this," Trese said, motioning to a toppled sign with his arm. "Luna University. Might be something interesting there if we can get to it."

Breen agreed, and they spent the next half hour carefully pulling and prying rubble from the mouth of an open corridor that disappeared into the rock. The tunnel beneath would never hold air without extensive repair, but it looked stable enough to enter. The display screens lining the walls, that had once shown ads, class schedules, directions, and articles from the university press, were all shattered. Regolith clung to their boots and left tracks in the frozen tunnels.

Breen set the mission timer to the agreed two hours. Most of the passages were choked in rubble. They managed to get into the cafeteria, but the food stores looked to have been emptied before the attack. Considering how notoriously awful the chow at Luna University was, Breen was glad. If they'd found some, they'd be ordered to bring it back and eat it. LU food was always a mission fail.

Wells insisted they find the xeno-ag wing, but the tunnel to all of the life sciences departments was collapsed beyond excavation. They made some progress digging towards the physics department. Breen hoped to find some tools, sensors, or test equipment. But three meters in, the passage opened up into a ravine at least ten meters across and fifty meters deep. A direct hit from a Proximan warhead. The opening on the other side was filled with rubble.

"Let's go," Breen said, trying to keep the defeat out of his voice. "There's plenty to explore tomorrow."

"What's the point?" Wells asked.

"I don't know," Trese said. "But we did see some places that survived. Granted, they didn't have anything useful inside. Surely there's some compartment around here with something we can use."

"Maybe in here." Breen stopped at a door labeled "Storage" and pulled on it. The frame looked slightly twisted, and it took Breen and Trese with a pry-tool to get it open.

Breen flashed a light around inside. Frozen dust motes sparkled on the floor and other surfaces. There were rows of stacked chairs, a collection of dome-shaped cleaning bots, and what looked like standard SDF servers stacked almost two meters high.

Trese grunted. "Nothing."

"Yeah, let's go." Breen swept his light around the room a final time. He lit up what he'd thought was an open cleaning locker. But the cabinet wasn't open and empty like he thought. He was seeing a black monitor screen.

Breen squealed and rushed into the storage room. He ignored Trese's objections over the radio and started brushing the icy dust from the cabinet's surfaces. It was undamaged, at least externally. This would help them solve all their problems, if they could get it out of here and back to *Roland*.

OSWALD LEANED BACK against the wall of the bunk room he shared with McFarran. His aux officer sat on his own bunk, facing Oswald. They'd spent the last two hours going over reports on air consumption, power levels, work-crew activities, and duty rotations. But these reports focused more on the small lunar base than *Roland*.

Oswald rubbed his eyes and set his tablet on the bunk. "Not pretty."

"No, Colonel," said McFarran. "Three months at our current rationing level. I'm not sure why the Proximans left the food here at all, but it wasn't to support the crew of a starship."

"I'm guessing they left it for visitors. Like the book. Speaking of which, who do you think drew all the penises?"

"Karpov, Colonel. No doubt. Only he would have the persistence to put such puerile work on every page with such attention to detail." McFarran grinned, shrugged. "Of course, he didn't write all the profanity in there. I don't think he dots his letters with little hearts."

"Not usually."

"So, what do we do, Colonel? Three months is a short time. We weren't stocked for a full year's patrol. The salvage teams haven't found any usable food."

Oswald didn't want to look at McFarran, so he kept pressing on his eyes. The pressure felt good. He entertained the fantasy that if he rubbed hard enough, it would all go away. His eyes would open and he'd be back in Anahita's office, having dozed while she spoke. Dots floated and flashed in his vision, but he could still see all their troubles in his mind's eye.

"I don't know. The way Saturn Station was stripped, it would be pointless to fly out to any of the other stations. I thought about

Mars or Ceres, but they were both blasted as badly as this place. And we'd use most of our food just getting anywhere."

"What about other colonies?" McFarran asked. "Surely there are some left. *Roland* has all the jump coordinates."

"They're as out of date as the data for Beta Hydri. And most of them were already abandoned when we left. They all still needed support from Earth to survive."

"The Proximans left this place for visitors, Colonel. They must have expected someone."

"And my aunt always left a spare table setting for Elvis or something like that." Oswald shook his head and looked at McFarran. "He never came, and it looks like no one ever came here either. If they had, they'd have left something, or taken food, or a note saying 'Visit Rigel III for a good time.' Danner may get his wish. It looks like we're grounded."

A look of defiance crossed McFarran's face. The never-quit expression of an officer of the SDF. But when he started to speak, McFarran's eyes darted around the room as if searching for an answer. There was none. McFarran let out his breath.

"Maybe something will come up, Aux. Trese, Breen, and Gresh have all gone over the data in the cube, but whatever happened, happened after those recordings."

"Colonel, we can jump across Sol to explore."

Oswald raised his brows. "Are you ready to jump again?"

"We leave the UXA here, Colonel. And we can leave some personnel if we need to. We can't just quit, sir."

"I'm not quitting, Hashi. But we're at a point where, if we jump the wrong way, we die. All of us. There's only enough left in the booster for one landing and takeoff into any sort of gravity well."

McFarran held up his palms. "Then what, Colonel?"

"I said I don't know. Not yet. But I will say I'd rather die taking as many damn Proximans with me as I can than starving in this little hamster cage."

"I don't think the busy work is going to distract the crew much longer, Colonel. Maybe the big-eye will find something soon."

"Maybe." Oswald picked up his tablet to start going over the remaining reports, then tossed it back on the bed. "Fuck it. I heard Breen's team found Luna University. Maybe there'll be something in the cafeteria."

"*Mon dieu*, I hope not, Colonel." McFarran wrinkled his nose. "The Proximans did us a favor if they destroyed that abomination against man and God."

Oswald laughed and McFarran joined in. It felt good. It turned into a full belly laugh that bounced Oswald on his bunk in Luna's one-sixth gravity. And the only people who might get their feelings hurt were dead centuries past. They laughed and laughed until McFarran's tablet chimed.

McFarran wiped at the corner of his eye and took a deep breath. "Aux here."

"Breen's back in, sir," said Norris. "He's very excited about something. Heading your way."

"Thank you, Norris." McFarran set his tablet in his lap.

Oswald was still grinning. He watched the hatch while he waited. The scuff and stomp of EVA boots drifted in from the passage, growing louder with each step. Oswald grimaced expectantly; the steps were moving too fast. He heard a dull thud, followed by a yelp and muttering. Seconds later, Breen bounced off the edge of the hatch, spun into the small room, and came centimeters from falling on McFarran. A trail of moondust drifted to the floor behind him.

"Uh, permission to enter, Colonel." Breen winced as he rubbed the top of his head.

Oswald waved a hand in front of his face to fan away the dust. "Granted. You OK?"

"Oh, Colonel," Breen said, ignoring the question. "We hit the mother lode! Luna University."

"Did you find the cafeteria fully stocked with delicious rations, Breen?" McFarran asked. "You must really like them to be so excited."

Oswald and McFarran looked at each other and started laughing again.

Breen's face twisted in disgust. "That's gross. I don't think I'd even tell you if I found that."

Oswald laughed even harder and slapped his knee.

Breen looked at his superiors, a hesitant grin on his face. "Sirs?"

"Nothing, Breen," McFarran said once he'd gotten control of his laughter. "What, pray tell, have you found?"

"Most everything was smashed. Wells wanted to get to xeno-ag, but that was cut off. So was physics. I was hoping to find maybe some batteries or test equipment or some useful data cubes. They always have some kind of observations running, so maybe they saw what happened to Earth—"

Oswald held up a hand. "Please just tell us what you found."

"Oh, yes, sir. I was getting there. Anyway, the physics labs were cut off. On the way out we found a storage space. Lots of desks and chairs and things like that. But tucked in the back was an old HL-47 Q-puter cabinet!"

"Interesting," Oswald said. He looked at McFarran, who shrugged back. "Does it work?"

"I hooked up a universal test set and it at least powers up. I'd like permission to get a larger crew to bring it back and plug it into *Roland's* coolant system and see if she'll come online." Breen's smile faltered. "Don't you see?"

Oswald shrugged. "I like Q-puters as much as the next guy, Mr. Breen."

"We have the navigational info from General Khadem's files—"

Oswald slapped his forehead. "Of course! We can extrapolate the jump data." Oswald stood and grabbed Breen by the shoulders. "This is exactly what we needed. Good work. Excellent work! Do you know this model?"

Breen was beaming now. "Yes, Colonel. It's the twin sister of the HL-45A I trained on. If it works, I should be able to program the new jumps. It'll take a week or so probably to get things started."

"We could look for surviving colonies, Colonel," McFarran said.

Oswald glanced at McFarran, but said nothing. "Breen, rest your team. The aux will assign another three to you, at least one from engineering, and you get that on *Roland* ASAFP."

"Yes, FC."

"And take Rocketman."

"Yes, FC."

Oswald stood and slapped Breen on the back. "Good job, Breen. Good job. But get rested up."

"Thank you, sir." Breen was still beaming when he turned to leave.

Misty often said that sometimes the best thing to do was wait for the universe to present an answer. God, Creator, Jehovah, Allah, Kali, Fate, Coincidence; the god of the universe had been given many names. He/she/it/they had never told him which name was preferred though. Oswald was not one for prayer, finding his wife's universal consciousness to be peevish, specious, and sometimes downright malignant. But he gave thanks now to whatever might want to take credit for their find. Perhaps the makeshift holo-shrine Norris set up in the hub had paid off.

"Our new purpose in life is to take it to the Proximans while we still can." Oswald grinned at McFarran. "That's some busy work they'll enjoy. And we can find food."

McFarran looked away.

"What?"

"Colonel, we don't know what we'll find in Beta Hydri. But perhaps we should consider options that don't include us going out in a blaze of glory."

Oswald smirked. "Are you suggesting we turn ourselves in, Hashi? Pop in and say, 'Hey, guys, we're the only Earthers you didn't kill. Can we get some croissants, pretty please?'"

"Of course not, sir. Nothing so simple. We don't know what to expect. Maybe supplies, maybe battle. I just don't want us to have an inevitable ending in our mindset." McFarran looked up at Oswald. "You are the most successful combat FC I've known, Colonel. But even *Roland* only has so much fight in her. And these Proximans are four hundred years more advanced. I simply want to throw it out there. To them, the war is over. Something their great-great-great grandparents did. We may not have to fight anyone."

"Thank you, Aux. Dismissed."

McFarran stared at Oswald for a long moment before standing. With a sharp salute, McFarran turned and left the room.

Oswald closed the hatch and retrieved the holo-cube from under his bunk. He lay back, set the cube on his chest, and activated the display. "What'd you think about that?"

"It sounds a bit subversive to me, Pierce." Anahita tilted her head at the hatch. "Like he doesn't want to fight anymore."

"I don't want to fight anymore."

"Who does?" Anahita asked. "But all it takes for evil to win is for good people to do nothing. These people destroyed Earth, killed everyone we loved. If what you say is true. Don't tell me you're thinking of surrender? That's not the Pierce I said goodbye to."

Oswald stared into those dark eyes. It wasn't her, the woman he'd always loved. But it was now. *She* was now. It was Anahita in spirit and no different than talking to her over a holo-comm.

The way he'd acted about Ululani was boneheaded. He knew that now, had known it then. What right did he have to talk to Anahita that way? A grieving mother and grieving father who'd both made hard choices. She'd done him wrong by lying all those years, but he should have talked to her, not fought her.

"Sorry." He reached a hand out to stroke her cheek. Anahita leaned into it and closed her eyes. His hand passed through air, as he knew it must. But in his mind he conjured up the memories of how warm her dark skin had been, how smooth. An erection pushed against his flight suit. She might help him take care of that later, if he asked nicely.

"Don't you worry, Anahita," he whispered. "We'll fight those fuckers with our dying breath if it comes to that."

# Chapter 27

OSWALD WATCHED THROUGH the hatch of *Roland*'s cargo compartment. The Q-puter from Luna University was bolted to the frame, with power conduits and a coolant line running behind it. Breen's back was to Oswald, his shoulders rolling as he swiped across the Q-puter's programming screen.

"That should do it, FC." Breen turned to face Oswald, beaming. "Final checksum passed, astrogation program is online and ready to plot jumps whenever you like."

Oswald couldn't help but return the astrogator's smile. "Plot for Beta Hydri then, Mr. Breen."

Breen tapped through the Q-puter's menus. A window popped up that read, *Calculation Running*. "Beta Hydri's the tail of the Serpent constellation."

"Appropriate for such a genocidal race, I'd say."

"Yes, sir."

"Twenty-four light-years," Oswald said.

"Even farther than Delta Pavonis."

"Yeah, that jump didn't turn out so well. This one will go better."

Breen looked away.

Oswald touched Breen's shoulder. "I'm a bit nervous about jumping too. But we won't have the UXA this time. We'll be fine."

"Oh, well that's good to know. But... what are we going to do when we get there, Colonel?"

"Won't know till we get there." Oswald leaned back against a stack of crates. "What do you think we should do? Should we even go?"

Breen shook his head. "Oh, I don't know, sir. Some are ready to nuke any Proximans we find. Make them pay for Earth. Some say it'd be pointless and we're better off surrendering. Karpov says he'd rather eat plasma than be some Proximan's bitch." Breen looked apologetic. "His words, FC."

"Sounds like it. But what do you think?"

"I've even heard a couple say they'd just as soon die here than get blown up. But me? I don't really know. It's... too big."

"Welcome to the flight commander's ball." Oswald brushed a patch of moondust off the bulkhead. "Really, I want to find out what happened to Earth. Maybe it's tucked away in some pocket dimension. Who knows? But I know who probably does."

"The Proximans?"

Oswald nodded. "The fucking Proximans. We may have to crack a few heads, or databases. But we'll find out what they know. Hopefully get some food along the way."

"Their food tastes funny," Breen said.

"Tastes better than vacuum. Get my jump plotted, Astro. Then update all the jump plots in the database. Never know how long this Q-puter will keep working. It's pretty old."

Oswald was feeling pretty old himself.

OSWALD LOOKED AROUND the passages of the little complex. They were silent now. The areas near the airlocks were covered in spills of moondust. Footprints and drag lines along the floor gave testament to their departure preparations.

It had become a home, despite Oswald's admonitions. To a veteran of the fleet, home was where you recirculated your air. He had grown accustomed to the conversations and songs. A starship doesn't have large, open compartments like those the hub of this base possessed. There was little chance for more than seven or eight crew to gather together on a deployment. Everything was done over a net, seldom face-to-face. Only during leave on a larger station or planetside was a gathering possible.

In contrast to that homey feel was the dread of it turning into their tomb. There were already something like fifty corpses in the vault. The newly dead lay at the feet of the ancient, freeze-dried husks. Oswald assumed they were frozen husks, anyway. No one had opened the stone wall. No one had even wanted to go in and grab another holo-cube.

He hadn't needed another one.

Danner and Wells walked around the corner, and both looked up in surprise.

"Everything OK?" Oswald asked.

Danner gave a nervous chuckle. "Oh, yes, sir. I thought it was only my team still here."

"Just giving the place a last look."

"We made it pretty comfy, FC," Danner said. "Sure you don't want to stay?"

"We'll starve here, Danner. But you did do this place up right." Oswald turned a slow circle, taking in the details. "I'm heading back to *Roland*. Make your final checks and get the rest of the rations on board. We've got a jump to make."

Danner and Wells exchanged glances.

"Problem?"

Danner shook his head. "No, sir. Just going to miss it here. *Roland*'s not the most comfortable place."

There was something going on between these two. Danner had isolated himself for the last few weeks when he wasn't on duty. Oswald hadn't minded. He didn't care for Danner, and it kept the engineer and the tactical officer away from each other's throats.

But Danner had stopped sulking about the lost four hundred years and worked hard to make this place livable. So Oswald let the man be. It made sense that Danner didn't want to leave. But *Roland* needed a flight engineer and they would starve if they stayed.

Oswald nodded. "Understood. Make sure the place is in good condition. We might have to come back." Oswald smiled, but it felt false to him. There were contingencies, but he didn't think they'd see Luna again.

"Yes, sir," Danner said. He and Wells saluted.

Oswald returned the salute, donned his helmet, and shuffled to the airlock. The urge to rush to the ship was strong, but he took short, careful steps on the way. It reminded him of the last time he'd walked through his neighborhood before shipping out. Not the landscape, but the feeling of a coming change that couldn't be undone. That realization that you could never go home. It wasn't home, not really, but they wouldn't be back.

His true home rose above him, reaching into the starry night. *Roland* had been his home, even before the Earth met its mysterious fate. She waited for him now, ready to escape the shackles of her lunar prison. She was a huntress, not a nursemaid. Dying sitting on her ass like this was not what she was destined for.

*ROLAND* was ready to launch. The boosters were warm and set for ignition, the reactor was critical and ready for full load, the warheads secured, and the crew armored and strapped in.

Except for Danner and his team. All they needed to do was remove the UXA and load the rations. Just as it had been thirty minutes ago when Oswald joined *Roland*.

"Danner, this is the FC. Is there a problem down there? We have a jump window." Oswald waited for a reply. He heard the empty hum of a keyed mic with no voice. It cut off. "Danner, get up here now."

Danner's stuttering voice came over the channel. "Negative, Oswald. We're, uh, staying here."

The insolence in the tone made Oswald's belly ache more than the words. He closed his eyes. "Say again?"

"I said, we're not leaving, Oswald." Danner's voice was more decisive now. "You go, we stay. Simple."

"Simple mutiny? *Roland* needs those rations. Your ship, Danner, needs those rations and an engineer."

"Not mutiny. If this place died four hundred years ago, so did the SDF. Your commission and command are over. We don't want to go off and die chasing your war."

"You'll die here."

"And you'll die there. But we'll die peacefully. You'll get everyone burned to ashes. The six of us are staying here, thanks."

Bile burned Oswald's throat. A mutiny? A mutiny from people he'd been living with elbow to elbow. A mutiny he hadn't seen coming. How had he missed it? He turned his mic off long enough to clear his throat. "Think this through. Even if we allow you to keep the rations, they won't last you long. We don't know what we'll find in Beta Hydri."

"Yes, we do." Danner's voice was growing frantic, almost angry. "We'll find nothing or we'll find more death. We'd rather die here than in some fireball or Proximan gulag. And you're not getting our food, by the way."

"You will gather those supplies and board this ship now or—"

"If anyone comes off that piece of shit, no one is leaving Luna! No one." A video feed from Danner's tablet appeared in Oswald's display. A small remote control was in his bare hand.

"Is that a control for the funeral rockets?"

"Yes!" Danner shrieked. "I did what you wanted. *Roland* is in as good a shape as I could make her. And I added a few extra surprises. Those little rockets aren't much, but they make great detonators. Your *warship* is full of them.

"I hit this button, and she dies. And you can't scare us. We're dead if we listen to you or if we stay. And I don't give a shit at all where you die, here or there."

"He's bluffing, Colonel," McFarran said.

The remote shook in the camera's view. "Just go away. And when you make your jump, you won't have to worry about us blowing you up and we don't have to worry about you screwing with us."

"I'm not leaving my crew or that food." Oswald kept his voice firm, authoritative. Textbook military leadership. But he knew it rang hollow. Danner had sucker punched him. And if anyone knew how to kill *Roland* from the inside, it was Danner. And somehow he'd snatched a third, a fucking third, of the remaining crew. How did he miss it?

"If anyone leaves that ship, you're done." Danner sighed and muttered something incomprehensible. "Look, Colonel. I don't blame you or even the fleet for... for whatever happened. But we're screwed, we're dead people walking. And I, we, don't want to spend our last days strapped into a ship and screaming in terror. I've got the power management systems on automation. You won't even miss us."

Oswald thought of those who'd committed suicide and didn't think Danner was bluffing. He'd destroy *Roland* even if Oswald ordered Rocketman to go back out and kill them all.

How had such a putz gotten people to follow him? Engineering skills aside, Danner was not well-liked. He probably couldn't have. That meant they felt the same way, strongly enough to betray their crew and their flight commander. "We need to get the UXA off-loaded."

Danner's finger pointed at the large red button on the controller. "If anyone leaves *Roland*, I hit this button."

"Then we're not leaving," Oswald snapped. "We're not jumping with that thing. I'd rather take my chances trying to kill you."

"Stand by." Danner's video connection dropped.

Oswald waited quietly, willing to take all the time Danner would give him. He racked his brain, but no great tactical plan came. They weren't in their armor, so he couldn't sedate them. Which was probably why they'd taken it off. *Roland*'s one working laser array was facing away from the base. Not even Rocketman could breach the little base before Danner set off the bombs. Oswald didn't even know how many bombs there were.

"Danner?"

"Wait," Danner said. A minute later, he added, "Drop the UXA in the hole we dug for the rockets. And if you send out that robot, you're toast."

"OK," Oswald said, "McFarran—"

"I got it, FC," Karpov said. "I'm already on the way."

"OK. I've unlocked the mag-lock in the cargo bay," Oswald said. "Just do the job and get back, Karpov. Don't fuck around this time. No jokes."

"You hurt me, FC."

Oswald wasn't in the mood for any of the tactical officer's inane babbling, so he didn't answer. When he noticed it had been several minutes and Karpov hadn't made it to the hatch, Oswald keyed his mic. "What's taking so long, Tac?"

"Sorry, FC." Karpov was panting. "I forgot how clunky this armor is, even in this low gravity. Almost there."

Oswald watched Karpov grab the UXA case and struggle out of the cargo hatch. Karpov bounced to the crater. No, he wasn't bouncing. Oswald clenched his teeth. Karpov was skipping like a child across the lunar surface. He tripped as he reached the rim of the hole.

"*Sacre bleu*," McFarran whispered.

"I'm OK," Karpov said. He was obviously struggling to get back to his feet, his flailing arms sending regolith flying. "I'm OK. I just really buried myself, here."

After two minutes of watching the dust from Karpov's struggles, Oswald was about to order someone out to help. Then Karpov's dust-covered helmet popped into sight.

"Sorry, FC. I wasn't fucking around, just being clumsy." Karpov climbed out of the crater and returned to *Roland* with a more cautious gait. He paused once to raise a middle finger towards the base.

"Colonel, Trese here. I've found one of the bombs. It's bonded to the main comms-processor housing. If it goes off, so does the big-eye and anyone nearby not armored up." Trese clucked his tongue. "Looks like some wires along the side too. Maybe a tamper switch."

Oswald waited for Karpov to clean off his armor and get locked back into his station. "Anyone on that base who wants to join their crew will be allowed, no repercussions. Don't throw your lives away like this. That includes you, Danner. Burn with your ship, or burn alone."

"That shit doesn't apply anymore, Oswald. Like you said, you have a jump window. And if you light the LANTRn on us or bring the laser around—"

"I know, we're dead. Got it."

"If you got it, you wouldn't bother going," Danner said. "We all died a long time ago. It just hasn't gotten through that thick, flight commander skull of yours."

"Last chance, Danner."

"Leave. Now."

"Burn in hell, Danner. Fucking cowards, all of you." Oswald dropped the connection.

"We can't let them get away with this, Colonel!" McFarran said. "We must do something. Jam them, something. Anything."

At least McFarran had the sense to sound angry. And he should. Losing six crew members was going to limit *Roland*'s ability to kill Proximans, let alone run standard duty shifts. "I'm open for a plan that doesn't kill *Roland*." When McFarran didn't reply, Oswald grunted. "Norris, begin launch sequence."

KARPOV WATCHED THE four tiny airlocks on Luna's surface through the big-eye. They were the only visible signs of the complex below where he'd lived the last several weeks. At this resolution, he could make out the ant-sized boot prints the crew had left behind and the disturbance he'd left in the regolith, hiding the UXA.

But all the airlocks were still in place and undamaged. It seemed, unfortunately, Danner had enough sense not to retrieve the UXA case before *Roland* jumped. Karpov wouldn't have let them unload the UXA. He'd have told Oswald to get it off Luna too, to jettison it in space on their way out of Sol. He wouldn't have let anyone off *Roland* as Danner had. But, then again, Danner was a dumbass.

Hopefully, a big enough dumbass to miss what Karpov had buried and just grab the UXA case.

"Tactical, go no-go?" McFarran asked over the duty net.

Karpov jumped to the tactical systems status screen. He didn't need to, his systems were always ready, aside from being over half out of ordnance and laser array two being destroyed. Green lights across the display. "Tactical, is go."

He could still smell the burnt-gunpowder stink of the dust. The complex would slip over Luna's horizon and out of big-eye's line of sight any minute. The chance of seeing a catastrophe was passing away. Karpov regretted not being able to see Danner burn.

A smile crept across his face as he imagined Danner dying, on his back in the regolith, staring back up at Karpov. Maybe the coward would fall back and flail his arms in a panic, trying to get them to come help. That would leave an interesting death angel in the regolith.

It would be a fitting end for a traitor.

But he had to give Danner his due. Aside from being a decent engineer—though nowhere near as good as Bowens—Karpov never would have guessed Danner had the balls to lead a mutiny. It would make everyone's life more difficult as they tried to take the slack of six more losses on the duty roster. But that was OK. It was also six more people gone that Karpov knew couldn't have been trusted. And six more he wouldn't have to compete with when the time came. The bubbles in his vision were growing more frequent... and darker.

But not all the cowards had left. More of *Roland*'s children seemed to have lost their fangs because some general or president wasn't around to give them orders. Oswald was good enough, and the FC would need Karpov's support. Oswald knew what needed to be done. Unlike McFarran, who might need to have an accident.

He'd considered getting rid of the aux on Luna, but McFarran shared quarters with the FC. If they lost Oswald, they'd lose their chance. Karpov hadn't been willing to risk that. Oswald didn't yet see the aux's poison, but he would with Karpov's help. It was unfortunate. All things being equal, McFarran used to be a decent officer, and good in a fight. Karpov had worked with worse.

Being a coward was different from being a bad officer though. McFarran was constantly planting seeds of surrender, suggesting how the war was over, how the Proxies of this generation might let bygones be bygones, and shit like that. It wasn't true. The war wasn't over. Karpov had to keep reminding Oswald of that fact until their final run. If they got captured, so be it. But he'd be damned if he went in with hands up and pants down.

Oh, how he'd have loved to see Danner's face. But it was probably for the best. If Oswald noticed any trouble at the base, he'd have to indulge his savior complex and mount a rescue mission. That would lead to some awkward questions. Karpov would have to let his imagination supply the image of Danner's dying breath.

"Too late for you, either way," Karpov whispered as the base slipped out of sight.

"What was that, Tactical?" McFarran asked.

"Sorry, Aux. Didn't mean to go over the net. Just thinking about paying back the Proximans. You know, for murdering everyone on Earth."

Karpov shifted in his armor when McFarran didn't snap back with his usual reprimand about net protocol. He knew the aux didn't like him or trust him. But had he grown suspicious? Maybe he should have taken the aux out on Luna. Maybe it was too late for that too.

"Roger that, Tactical," McFarran said at length. "We'll be there soon enough."

# Chapter 28

CORPORAL DANIELLE WELLS rocked in her chair, rubbing her arms. Her eyes stung, though she'd run out of tears an hour ago. Danner was looking at her, his expression seeking permission to come over to comfort her. Again. Wells shook her head.

"They can't hurt us, Danielle." Danner hoisted the remote that controlled the bombs they'd placed in *Roland*. She was sure Danner thought the smile he was giving her was reassuring, exuding confidence and leadership. He looked like a puppy who'd pissed on the rug and was waiting for his owner to find out.

Wells had placed one of those explosives. Right above the lower main-relay assembly. The housing was armored, but she thought Danner's bomb might penetrate it. She couldn't keep him from talking, but at least he was keeping his distance.

Mgumbe, Thomas, Ahmed, and Richter sat in silence, staring at the green comms indicator on the station's computer panel. It was phase-locked with a small transmitter Danner had hidden in a maintenance panel on the ship. When *Roland* left the system, the connection would drop.

It was taking a long time to drop.

"They won't try anything." Irritation filled Danner's voice. "We'll know when they leave and we'll take care of them if they don't."

Richter shook her head. "And if Oswald decides to drop an ORBAM on us? Got anything to tell us about that?"

"Oswald wouldn't do that," Danner said.

"You so sure?" Wells asked. "You just led a mutiny, you know."

"We're all mutineers," Mgumbe said. "But he's right. Oswald won't attack us. FC's better than that."

Danner frowned. "Not so good that he wouldn't lead us to our death chasing his war."

"It's what he's supposed to do," Wells said. "It's what we're supposed to be doing."

"Then why'd you come?" Danner asked.

Wells flipped him off and looked away. Going to Beta Hydri was stupid. A waste of lives. She took her vows to the SDF and Earth seriously. But the war was over. And Danner was right when he explained that Oswald was going to go out fighting, no matter what happened. She'd seen it in the FC's eyes too. Everyone here had. How anyone could miss it was beyond her.

Ahmed cleared her throat. "Maybe we should call them back. Oswald needs us. He'd take us back."

Danner threw his hands in the air. "They won't come back for us. Even if they wanted to. The boosters only have so much propellant, and they'd have to burn enough for another landing and take-off. Oswald needs that so he can plant the SDF flag on the Proximan capital's lawn."

Danner steepled his hands over his lips. He turned in a circle, making sure he caught each person's eye. Wells thought it was something he'd learned in one of those crappy officer leadership vids. It didn't make him look any less terrified.

He stopped, staring at Wells. Ogling her, more like. "I guarantee they die first. We don't want to go back. We're all dead. Get it? They're dead. We're dead. Just like I told the old man, you can die peacefully in your own bunk, or you can die screaming and on fire."

Mgumbe scoffed. "You don't know what's there any more than the FC does."

Hysteria was creeping into Danner's voice. Wells felt for the wrench in her pocket. "If you know better, why the hell'd you leave?"

"I think they'll die." Mgumbe shrugged. "But if they don't, I hope they come back and get us."

"Yes, to take us to some wonderful new Eden just waiting in the Proximan home system," Richter said. She stared at Mgumbe with bulging eyes. "The only ones coming back are going to be pissed-off Proximans looking for *Roland*'s home base. After they've blown her up."

"They won't know where they jumped from," Wells said. "Will they?"

"They might if they managed to find an UXA we left behind and figured out how to use it like the SDF wanted to use it," Ahmed said.

Danner shook his head and hands violently. "Enough. Like it or not, we're here for the duration. We all have our own spaces, food, and entertainment systems."

Every head turned when the signal light went out.

Wells rose, her hands over her mouth. "Does that mean they're gone?"

Danner bounced to the comms array and ran a self-test. It passed. He tried connecting back to the hidden radio on *Roland* and couldn't. "They're gone."

"Maybe they just found the transponder," Ahmed said.

"I doubt it," Danner said. "It was deep. They'd have to open up some heavy panels. They're gone."

They stared at one another in silence. Wells drifted back into her seat. It felt like the beginning of her vacuum-suit emergency training, where the instructors tossed her in a dark maze with no atmosphere and locked the door behind her. She'd always had a good head for zero-g and she'd managed to escape. That time.

Now they were all alone on a lifeless moon, surrounded by the wreckage of a city that had been built before she was born. Just the six of them, ruins, and a crypt full of dead people next door.

A chill ran across her arms. She hadn't really considered being stuck here with a bunch of corpses. She wasn't sure which creeped her out the most, the ones executed centuries ago or her recently departed crewmates. Speaking of creepy...

"What does the UXA look like?" Wells asked. "I've never even seen it."

"You can't really see it," Danner said. "I looked at it twice while we were trying to figure out what to do with it. It's the damnedest thing." His eyes widened. "You want to see it?"

"Is it safe?"

Danner waved off the question. "Sure. Bowens had rad sensors on that thing the whole time. Didn't do anything until the jump. And now that *Roland*'s gone, it should be inert like when the Rangers found it. I'll go get it."

Wells started to reach out, but didn't want Danner getting the wrong impression. She wanted to see it, but he wasn't getting into her flight suit no matter what he did. That was the real reason she thought he'd started chatting her up about leaving Oswald. Not because she was an expert hull technician and rated for extended, unguided EVA.

To be fair, she didn't know if that was true. He obviously found her attractive—most men and women did. But maybe it was more about his fear. Many men sought comfort from women, much as women did the same. Danner was right about Oswald, but looked like a man who only now realized the magnitude of his fuck-up. Of their fuck-up.

Wells and the others watched the display from the base's single surface camera. Danner bounced across to the ditch, leaped out with the large case she remembered from the cargo bay, and was back inside within twenty minutes. He set the case on the table in the center of the hub.

"It used to hum," Wells said. "I remember that from my duty watches."

Danner nodded. "Yeah, it did. Must be because there's no jump gate generators nearby. Check this out."

He popped the latches open and spun the case towards Wells without looking inside. Set in the packing was a solid black canister. A folded piece of paper was tucked in next to it. She pointed a finger at it. "What's that?"

Danner peeked over the edge of the case. "That looks like a... condenser bottle. What the hell?"

Wells grabbed the note and unfolded it.

"A good luck note from the FC?" Mgumbe asked.

"More likely some kind of threats," Danner said. He held out his hand to Wells.

Her hands trembled until the note drifted to the floor. She couldn't breathe. She couldn't scream. The tremor in her hands spread until her knees buckled and her arms quaked. They wouldn't move for her. All of her words came out as whimpers she couldn't even understand. A warmth spread from her crotch. She'd pissed herself.

"What's it say?" Ahmed shrieked.

Danner stared wide-eyed down at Wells for a second, before snatching up the note. A smiley face with crosses for eyes was scrawled across the top. Danner's voice cracked in a mad laugh.

"What's it say!" someone cried. The voice was distant and Wells didn't recognize it. She reached out to claw across the floor. To go somewhere. To get away. Her arms merely flopped.

Danner read the note in a scream. "Dear dickhead, you're not the only one who can make a bomb."

Ahmed leaped to the nearest hatch, but slammed her head into the ceiling. Someone else started groaning in terror. Two bodies at the edge of Well's tunnel vision fell over the box as they clawed at the canister inside.

A primal scream filled the air. It was ripping free from Well's own throat. She'd found her voice just as the blinding flash and deafening explosion ripped her quivering body apart.

# Chapter 29

THE JUMP COUNTER GLARED a red *+10 seconds* in Oswald's visor. Before their fiery entrance into Sol, he would have been on Breen's ass for missing the jump timer. Despite the time that had passed since that deadly jump, he knew many on the crew still had nightmares. Himself included.

"Is there a problem, Astrogation?" McFarran asked.

"No, sir. Systems are green. I just need to, uh..."

Oswald tried to sound calm. His hands were shaking in his vacc-armor, but not in anger. "The UXA is gone. Please initiate jump procedure."

"Right away, FC," Breen said.

The jump timer soon showed a red *+32 seconds*. "Breen, activate jump. Now."

"Yes, sir!"

Oswald watched the timer reach *+60 seconds* past the scheduled jump. There was extra time built into a window's calculation; they weren't so accurate that a minute or two would ruin the jump. And they weren't coordinating with other starships. But it was time to go. "Breen, you stand relieved. I'll take it."

"Yes, sir. Sorry, sir." The relief in Breen's voice told Oswald the astrogator was not sorry.

Oswald logged into the astrogation subsystem as flight commander and brought up the jump tunnel generator menu. Everything there was green. Deciding it might be a good idea for a final, eyes-on check, Oswald opened *Roland*'s status display. All green.

"Colonel?" McFarran asked.

"Just a final check, Aux. Prepare for jump." Oswald grimaced as his own finger hesitated over the initiate command. He snorted. Twenty years of space flight and even he was struggling like a jump-cherry.

His breath grew ragged and his sphincter clenched as his finger fought against his brain. He was glad he hadn't dressed down Breen.

*+150 seconds*

"Here we go!" Oswald shouted for his own benefit, trying to psyche himself up. The initiate button winked in acknowledgement.

"Oh, God," someone whispered. Someone else whimpered. The precursor gurgle of vomit came over the net.

Everything stopped.

Everything started.

Oswald opened his eyes. "Give me a T3 report." His voice came out in a cough and he repeated his order.

Data started scrolling in from *Roland*'s sensors. Temperature readings were nominal. Navigation reported zero relative angular velocity. All systems that were green before the jump were still green. No immediate threats showed on the navigational or tactical displays.

"Oh, thank the Goddess," Norris breathed.

A light flashed red on the crew vitals page. Gilweh's suit was reporting unsuccessful defibrillation. A medical team was already en route. They'd still be recovering like everyone else, but they were on the way.

The reports came in as the remaining crew regained their senses and *Roland* continued to decipher the sensor readings of the Beta Hydri system. It would take hours to put together a useful tactical map of a system they had blind-jumped into. There were still no immediate threats, but they'd have to wait to see if anyone had noticed their entry.

"FC, Medical," Dr. Hines said, his voice heavy. "Sorry, Colonel. Gilweh didn't make it."

"Fuck," Karpov said. "And then there were eleven. We're going to miss her when the fighting starts. She knew those laser arrays."

"It has to be something about the jump distance, Colonel," McFarran said. "These heart failure rates are too high."

"Something the experts missed," Oswald said. "We never had many jumps this far. No way to know until it's too late. I guess we can't blame everything on the UXA. Nothing about long jumps in the data cube."

"Perhaps we should have examined more cubes, Colonel."

Karpov chuckled. "Yeah, I'm sure the holograph of the Argentinian Secretary of Agriculture would have had a lot to say about new findings of the SDF Flight Surgeon General."

"I wonder if the Proximans could jump straight to Sol from here," Breen said.

"A question for another time," Oswald said. "For all we know, they might not even use jump tunnel generators anymore. But we'll get them hopping one way or another soon enough."

The Proximans would surely know someone had jumped in system. Even if they were using some new travel technology, which he doubted, they'd still have jump detectors. But he didn't even know where Earth was, so what the hell did he know. If the Proximans had regular jump traffic, and if the war was over and they'd grown complacent, *Roland*'s entry might go unnoticed. The question now was where to go first.

And to know that, Oswald had to know what was in the system. "Let's work on that map. Hazard stations for another hour, then we can all slip into something more comfortable."

BETA HYDRI CAME TO life over the course of the next five hours. The question of the Proximans and jump drive was answered quickly when *Roland* detected several bursts of jump comms. They came in steady intervals, giving Oswald no reason to believe their arrival was the cause of those messages.

The orbital plots of the two planets they'd observed so far circled the inner system of Beta Hydri's yellow-orange G2 star .

They didn't detect the telltale thermal signatures of quick-reaction squadrons—which didn't mean they weren't coming. Four high-power navigational beacons and a constant stream of background RF chatter blared on the scopes. It was a noisy place.

Oswald grinned. They'd dropped into a target-rich environment. "Our main priority is working up an accurate nav-map. I want orbital profiles for everything we find, Norris. All of our plans are going to be jump, run, jump. We'll need Oberth envelopes and whatever cover we can find."

"Yes, FC."

Oswald flipped to the astronavigation overlay. "Breen, I need in-system jump thresholds plotted ASAP. I'm not looking forward to it, but we're going to have to jump around. We're too outnumbered to try running on the LANTRn alone."

"Oh, no," Breen muttered.

"What was that, Lt. Major Breen?" Oswald asked. He had to put just enough bite in the words to snap Breen into action without making him upset. He needed Breen at his best.

"Yes, FC." Breen's words were clear and loud. "Jump thresholds will be worked out."

"Better. Cindy, I want the chatter put through signals analysis. There's no telling how much their language has changed. And their encryption protocols certainly have."

"Maybe too much," Trese said.

"Probably," Oswald said. "We might get lucky and they're so laid-back, now that all the Earthers are dead, they don't bother. And speaking of dreams, begin duty rotation. I'm getting some shut-eye. McFarran, you have *Roland*."

"Roger that, Colonel. Sleep well," McFarran said. "And for what it's worth, I've updated the crew travel logs to show Beta Hydri."

Oswald did not sleep well. No matter how he adjusted the sleep straps, or how high he put the somnolence generator, his racing mind drove rest away. The tiny cot on Luna seemed like a luxury hotel, compared to the heat-warped sleep tube in the beehive.

They were in too much danger to risk seeing the doctor for a stronger sedative. So he took the holo-cube from the locker and made his way to his stateroom.

"Now you're in the belly of the beast," Anahita said. Her grin hinted at hidden danger. "You've got to go big or go home. *Roland* doesn't have the support for a drawn-out campaign."

Oswald snorted. "If I had another home, I might not be here. *Roland*'s the only home I have. Like a hermit crab crawling through space."

"Like a pissed-off hermit crab." Anahita brought a hand into view and snapped it like a crab claw. "You just need to figure out where to put the knife."

Oswald nodded and projected the growing system map above the holo-table. He and Anahita sat in companionable silence as more details were added with each update. The computer rendered two more planets and their orbital tracks. Each of the four planets had icons for a nav beacon, at least one space station, and several satellites.

The inner planet was a cacophony of signal noise. Long strings of lights sparkled on the dark side, revealing large cities spread across four landmasses. The surface water percentage was estimated at less than twenty percent with an arid, Earth-like atmosphere, according to *Roland*'s spectrometer. It orbited at the inner limit of Beta Hydri's estimated life zone.

"So I guess that's Ay-Yon. Home world of the victors."

Anahita furrowed her brow at the map. "For now."

"For now, what?" Oswald asked. "Victors or home world."

"Either. Both."

"We don't have enough nukes to do any real lasting damage. Even with the ORBAM package."

"We've got to hit them where it hurts."

"Where?"

Anahita smirked at Oswald. "Where it hurts."

Oswald pursed his lips and turned back to the map of Ay-Yon. No, it wasn't Ay-Yon any more than the Proxies were Ay-Yon. This was Beta Hydri I and the enemy lived there. Data scrolled along the information window with estimated power usage, temperature variations, atmospheric density, pollution levels, water percentage, and orbital defense threat ratings. Population estimate: 4.3 billion.

Oswald thumped a knuckle on the table hard enough to make the cube bounce. Anahita's image didn't jitter at all. "We hit the water. But even with that level of water scarcity, we couldn't give it a proper case of radiation poisoning or destroy enough infrastructure to matter. It's too distributed."

Anahita looked back to the map. "To provide for billions with that little water, there must be a complex distribution system. Networks. Monitoring."

Oswald traced his finger in circles on the tabletop while he thought about it. "EMP. High-altitude detonation. It would cover more area and maybe have a better chance against whatever missile defenses they have. Probably won't wipe them out, but I'll settle for starting an apocalypse."

"You'll probably only get one pass, you know."

"Yep. Maybe not even one. They might have some crazy nuclear force dampeners or tractor beams. Who knows."

Oswald yawned and tightened his restraints. He closed his eyes just for a second, before his tablet rang to wake him for his shift. Anahita sat there, smiling at him across the table.

"You need more than four hours' sleep to be at peak performance, Pierce."

Oswald smacked his lips in a vain attempt to get rid of the taste of garbage in his mouth. "Good morning to you too. There's no way that was four hours."

"Four hours and eight minutes, actually."

Oswald grunted, turned Anahita off, and floated to his locker for a fresh flight suit. The tube bed looked inviting, and he considered skipping his hygiene and exercise routines for a few more minutes of sleep. He wasn't likely to ever be planetside again, except as a Proximan prisoner. And in that case, he'd get plenty of exercise doing whatever their equivalent of breaking rocks was.

He grabbed a flight suit, labored through his mandated hour of exercise, and rinsed. By the time he had a package of space-rats and tepid coffee, things looked a little better. He'd done it all out of mindless routine, but he felt slightly less dead when he relieved McFarran. If he lived to see another sleep cycle, Oswald was sure he'd crash hard.

He caught himself dozing twice during his watch. Audible alerts would have woken him in an emergency, but sleeping on duty was a cardinal sin in the fleet. No Proximans jumped in to attack, so they were either unaware or unconcerned. Both worked for Oswald.

By the end of the watch, *Roland*'s navigational map included two gas giants in the outer orbits, three rocky inner planets, and a large planetary body with an undetermined orbit out past the gas giants.

The data from the outer planet piqued Oswald's interest enough to focus one sleepy eye on it. Large rocky planets that far out weren't unheard of, but they were uncommon. If it hadn't been for the nav-beacon pinging in orbit, *Roland* might not have detected it yet. Its negligible orbital velocity and lack of spin were what caught his interest.

It was just sitting there. That indicated it might be a captive rogue planet. Anything born in this system would have fallen into some orbit during its creation. But even a captured body should have more movement.

He had too many mysteries to solve already. The pressing ones were tactical, not scientific. Were things different, he'd take *Roland* out there at first opportunity and see what was going on. They probably weren't going to be around to get the chance.

# Chapter 30

OSWALD PROJECTED THE tactical display above the conference table. "I'd say we got lucky. One hundred hours and no response. No ping, no scouts, no increased activity, or detectable rocket burns heading our way."

Nine of the remaining eleven survivors were jammed around the table. The other two were manning duty stations, but listening in over the net. Oswald didn't even think of the crew in terms of divisions or departments now. Everyone did everything, including Oswald.

"That's assuming," Karpov said, "they still use thermal rockets. Maybe they moved onto anti-grav drives or dimensional phase-shifting."

"Then they should have been here by now, smart-ass." Oswald blew out a breath. "We've seen torch drives, just none coming our way. Regardless of what they use these days, they would have jumped in on us by now."

"Guess the assholes got lazy after killing all the Earthlings."

Oswald was weary of Karpov's vitriolic jocularity. But he agreed. They had detected little in the way of identifiable military comms or movement. Only a network of transport convoys. The ships had a higher thrust output than *Roland*.

That likely meant they were unmanned, but if it meant their standard, low-priority engines were more powerful than *Roland*'s at combat burn, it would make the fight that much harder.

Oswald highlighted two objects speeding in-system. "These are several kiloton chunks of ice set to find orbits around Beta Hydri

Two and Three. Their origin point is Object Omega at the outer part of the system. It's a strange one, but we'll have to have to worry about it later."

"Maybe they're using the ice for terraforming, Colonel?" McFarran said.

"Maybe they'll forget to carry a one and accidentally kill a bunch of their own colonists," Karpov said.

"There are still many unknowns, and we'll never be able to answer them all. We just have to proceed with certain assumptions. Now—"

"Colonel, please allow me to interrupt," McFarran said.

Oswald knew that look. McFarran's jaw was set and his eyes hard. The aux would not settle until he'd spoken his mind, and Oswald had an idea what what was coming. "Go on."

"While we're on the subject of assumptions, Colonel, I'd like to point out we're operating on the assumption this must end in violence. That the war is still on."

"No shit," Karpov said. "That's because the war *is* still on."

"It's been over four hundred years. These aren't the same people we were fighting. Attitudes change. Ideas fade away. Do you hold Napoleon's attacks on your ancestors against me, Karpov? We're talking about a similar time frame between those wars and the forming of the SDF, where we now work together. Insults are forgotten and, in time, enemies can become friends."

Karpov's head jerked back as if slapped. "What? Insults? Insults! They genocided Earth, for fuck's sake. We're not talking about an enemy that *only* killed fifty percent of the children on Earth and went home. Or wiped out fifty percent of all the sweet old grandmas. They. Killed. Everyone. On. Earth. And then destroyed the Earth just to make sure all their bases were covered."

McFarran slammed his fist on the table, causing everyone to flinch. "Including my sons! My mother. Yes, I know that, Karpov.

I get that. And nothing we do here can ever change that. But who knows what the future will bring if we explore our options. Maybe you can find an audience for more of your fiction."

"Why so eager to cozy up to the monsters, Aux?" Karpov held his hands up. "Why so eager to surrender?"

"Stop thinking like a child, Karpov." McFarran turned to Oswald. "We can parlay. Use diplomacy. Seek clemency. To them, this is all ancient history. They may even view us as archeological treasures."

Oswald frowned. "As soon as we try anything like that, we'll lose our one advantage. Surprise."

"And I put it to you, Colonel, that it might not be a bad thing. It may show them we aren't bloodthirsty barbarians seeking retribution for atrocities that happened generations before they were born."

"Did you mean to stay on Luna with Danner and just forget?" Karpov asked. "Because that sounds like the shit they were spewing."

"You'd have liked that, wouldn't you?" McFarran asked.

Karpov guffawed. "Oh, yes. Very much."

Oswald held up his hand. "That's enough, Tac."

Karpov crossed his arms and narrowed his eyes at McFarran.

"It is something to consider," Dr. Hines said. "But would they even believe us? It'd be like ancient Vikings showing up in London and saying they'd been frozen in ice for a few centuries. But now they're willing to live and let live."

"And if we do surrender," Trese added, "and don't live happily ever after, they get away with what they did. I don't think they'd just let us fly away with our nuclear arsenal to run wild and carefree in their universe."

"I am not saying that they will welcome us," McFarran said, spreading his hands out in an attempt to calm things down. "But they might. We might go to prison. Maybe we could work as free traders. They obviously have need of transports and have colonies outside of Beta Hydri.

"I will absolutely follow my orders to the bitter end." McFarran glared at Karpov. "I just don't want us to be gored on the horns of a false dilemma. Colonel, we have contingencies for many ways to die. I simply ask at least consideration for some contingencies to live." McFarran bowed his head and placed his palms on the table.

Oswald pressed his finger and thumb into his eyes until he saw spots. It was one thing to consider options, but McFarran was peddling hope. Hope in salvation delivered by not following through with the battle plan. The aux could try playing it off with assurances of obedience, but he'd just blown a huge fucking hole in morale. Oswald could already see doubt dancing in the eyes of some of the crew that hadn't been there before.

"Sounds like sedition to me," Karpov muttered to no one in particular.

"I said I will follow my orders—"

Oswald's hands shot out over the table. "Enough. Both of you. Maybe next time we'll pretend this is a democracy, Major McFarran. But for now, let's go over the plan outline again."

McFarran didn't look away from Karpov. "Of course, Colonel."

Oswald expanded the map far enough to show *Roland*'s position and the orbits of the inner planets. "We haven't managed to crack any codes, but Trese thinks we can replicate the transponder signal of one of the transports we observed jumping out of system.

"We'll jump to waypoint Alpha over their home world and fire the LANTRn. We won't be able to respond properly and they'll see the drive signature doesn't match anything they know. Hopefully, they'll be confused long enough to let us pick up some velocity using the booster rockets and deploy the ORBAM."

The display zoomed in to show *Roland* over Beta Hydri I, launching warheads in accelerated time. "The warheads will detonate and generate EMPs that should bring down their infrastructure network, especially the water system. We'll also drop our laser orbitals to target space stations instead of ground targets. Atmospheric attenuation would make them useless against anything down there."

The display then showed *Roland* accelerate towards the planet and slingshot around. "If Norris has her Oberth equations right, we should be able to speed out of range of these bases here and here, and fly out to the jump threshold and keep our distance until the jump generators are back online. Then we jump to waypoint Bravo and repeat.

"If we survive Alpha, Bravo will be a breeze. There are only a few small stations in orbit, probably monitoring their supposed terraforming project. *Roland*'s laser can cut them to pieces." Oswald scanned the faces, but he didn't see much change. At least the expressions hadn't grown any more doubtful. Karpov actually looked excited.

Kirsk shook his head. "That's a lot of jumping, FC. Not to mention a long time to survive in between. Especially if their jump tunnels have capabilities we're not aware of."

"If the Colonel says it will work, it will work," McFarran said. "This is the man who took down the Proximan station and *Titan* in Barnard's Star. It will be hard to catch *Roland* once we escape our initial attack run."

"We can do this, Colonel." Norris nodded and smiled at Oswald from across the table. "And we'll see where the universe takes us after that."

"*Roland* will ride into the fray, cutting a swath of bloody retribution," Karpov said in a dramatic tone. He flourished his hand as if wielding a sword. "And she'll go out with the wrath and fire of an exploding star."

Oswald grunted. "We'll try to avoid that last part, Tac. Time to mission start is eighteen hours. Get rested. Work your simulations. Pray, if you think that helps. Dismissed."

He watched them float out of the conference room and went back to studying the tactical map. It required months of surveillance to analyze enemy assets in a system like this, let alone develop an accurate gravitational influence map.

But he'd had to make plans quickly. A single starship couldn't do it alone, anyway, so planning was effectively a pretense. The only thing he could do was get as much detail on the immediate mission area and take their best shot.

Oswald buried his face in his hands. There was no genius plan to come up with. The few crew that still believed in him rested their hopes on his past successes. But nothing came. He hadn't found the plan to wipe out the Proximans. They were too many and *Roland* was too few.

His chest tightened. Death was coming and he knew it. Maybe McFarran had a point. Oswald put a hand up in rebuke. No. He'd rather die taking as many of them with him as possible. McFarran might ask which *them* Oswald meant. The struggle was to accept that fate, to love it. *Amor fati.*

Not seeing anything develop, Oswald shut down the map. He pulled the holo-cube from his flight suit and set it on the table. He wasn't in the mood for talking, so pulled up a static projection of Anahita. She glowered down at him and he glowered back, letting his mind run idle.

"She's lovely," said Norris from the hatchway. "In a severe kind of way."

Oswald froze. He'd forgotten where he was. This wasn't his stateroom and he'd left the hatch open. Not that he was doing anything wrong, but the crew wouldn't understand. She was an inspiration, a springboard, a database. Nothing more. It wouldn't do for morale if they thought he was infatuated with a hologram.

He shot his hand out to shut off the image. "Sorry, Norris. I didn't see you there. I hope I didn't ignore you too long."

Norris smiled at him and locked the hatch.

"What are you doing?"

Norris kept smiling as she unzipped her flight suit. Her body was lithe and her bosom, swollen by zero-g, floated before her, as if reaching out for him. Kabbalistic letters and other arcane symbols ran along the curves of her hips and shoulders. A holographic skin graft, an e-tattoo, of a bright red butterfly flapped its wings delicately beneath her navel.

Her flight suit drifted past Oswald.

"Look, Lisa..."

"I'm following you to my death. And I'm happy to do my duty. And join my husbands, fighting to the last. But give me this. I can see you need it too."

Oswald averted his eyes. "You're a member of the SDF. I'm your flight commander."

Norris slid onto the table. "What does that even mean now? Let me be Anahita to you—"

Oswald glared at her. He grabbed her wrists and pulled her face-to-face. "You're not Anahita." He drew a breath, ready to bellow at her in no uncertain terms that she was not Anahita and never could be.

But the smell of her hair filled his nostrils. The warmth of her body washed over his face. An ache was building in his crotch and his eyes lingered on her breasts.

"Anahita is dead," Norris whispered. "And so are our partners. But we're here, and warm, and alive. Today."

She pulled her hands free from his grip and slowly unzipped his flight suit. Oswald slipped his arms from his suit and pulled her close. Her breasts burned against his skin, and he kissed her deeply as he kicked the last of his uniform away. He took his hands off Norris just long enough to slip the holo-cube into a drawer and out of sight.

After over twenty years, he finally joined the light-year club. Not a bad way to spend his last night in the universe.

THE MEMORIES OF MAKING love to Norris generated too much heat to allow Oswald to sleep. He looked at the mission clock and wondered if the flight sergeant might want to hook up with her FC again. The possibility stirred his groin.

A thickness grew in the back of his throat, the ache of it driving away his desire. It was Misty. He'd cheated on her. After all the years of deployments. The oft-repeated adage of "What happens in the dark, stays in the dark" was a promise of mutual silence among the sinners. And he'd finally given in.

Yet, Misty was centuries dead. There was no doubt in his mind. But in his heart, he'd kissed her goodbye at Xichang only a couple of months ago. They were expecting their first grandchild together.

His throat burned and it was growing hard to breathe. Then it struck him. He'd sobbed and cried some, but never truly examined his loss and grieved it. There hadn't been time. The FC jumps from disaster to disaster, from decision to decision. Grief was an indulgence for other officers, not him. It was something you talked about with the flight psychologists in their soft offices long after the mission.

He'd lost so much. Reason counted off his losses even as emotion overwhelmed him. He'd shed no tears for the woman who'd shared his life for twenty years. Who'd been there for him. Who had cried on his shoulder, and on whose shoulder he had cried.

No tears for Misty. No tears for Mara or Mary. No tears for Ul-ulani. Should he cry for Anahita? He didn't know. He could ask her. But he wished by the universe he could take back the things he'd said the day of the briefing.

But he had cried for them all, hadn't he? He couldn't remember. In any case, now wasn't the time to cry. It was too close to mission start to lose it. Keeping it together was a lost cause, though. Like trying to choose not to be pulled down in a gravity well, or choosing to not go unconscious when given anesthesia. The breakdown was swelling up inside.

So he grabbed his oily-smelling pillow and bawled into it. He screamed and wailed and sobbed. Maybe he had cried like this already. He couldn't remember. It was all he could do to keep from punching and kicking the walls of his sleep tube.

He cried for his lost family and friends. He cried for Anahita, who'd met her end so bravely. Cried for his own mistakes and for billions of dead he'd never known. Oswald cried for the death of Earth and his failures that had led to it.

The dampness of his pillow brought him back to an awareness of the passage of time. How long, he didn't know. His breath was still coming in ragged gasps. The pain in the back of his throat eased. Oswald now realized his throat had ached for days. He'd just grown used to it.

Someone tapped on his sleep tube and Oswald started, knocking his head. His breath caught three times before he could answer. "What?"

"Colonel?"

"Yes, Breen." Oswald wiped his eyes with his blanket, before unzipping the flap and sticking his head out.

"Were you asleep, sir? Your eyes look very red."

"Never mind. What is it?"

"Sorry, FC. Well, I was updating the jump threshold estimates and I've been very curious about that outer body, you know the one—"

"I know it. Get on with it."

"Yes, sir. Well, we didn't spend much time looking at it since it wasn't a mission target. But it's strange, so I did my own image-rendering on the Q-puter and..."

"Breen!"

Breen stammered, clearly unsure what to say, but trying anyway. Finally, he thrust his tablet at Oswald forcefully enough to send him drifting the other way. "You gotta see it."

Oswald sighed and pulled himself out of his sleep tube. He reached a leg out and Breen grabbed it to pull himself back into place. Oswald studied the tablet. He zoomed in on the image, rotated it, and zoomed back out. What he saw didn't make sense, so Oswald rubbed his eyes and vigorously shook his head.

It couldn't be. He shot a quizzical look at Breen. The look on the navigator's face said that he was seeing the same thing. Oswald looked at the display, then back at Breen.

"What the fuck?" Oswald whispered.

"I haven't shown anyone else."

Oswald shook his head again. "How the fuck?"

Breen flinched. "I don't know, Colonel. But you see it? Right?"

"Oh, yeah." Oswald handed Breen the tablet. "Abort the mission, Breen. Get everyone in the conference room on the double."

# Chapter 31

OSWALD WATCHED THE faces gathered around the conference table oscillate between disbelief and horror as they stared at the holo-image of the outer planet slowly turning above them.

Karpov rubbed his jaw. "That's the Gulf of Mexico or I'm a pair of Proximan panties."

Breen's rendered image of the planet was overlaid with a thermal map. Two massive ice formations covered the poles of the planet, leaving an exposed midriff of geological details centered on the equator. There was no freestanding surface water detected.

Oswald couldn't explain the huge ice caps, but that was definitely the Gulf of Mexico. Some geological disaster looked to have altered the coastlines. Sections were missing, as if large seas or bays had been carved into the outlines of the familiar landmasses. But they were recognizable. The coasts of Mexico still ran down to the slender neck of Central America. Florida's toe peeked from beneath the ice shelf.

McFarran traced a finger along the tip of India and around Sri Lanka. "This is... impossible, Colonel. But, seeing is believing?" He shrugged.

Oswald nodded. "We've got the what and where of Earth. Maybe we'll find the how and why. How the hell do you move a planet?"

"Does it fucking matter?" Karpov asked. Anger replaced his usually unflappable sarcasm. "What matters is Earth is dead. Unequivocally, right fucking there, dead. And we have the who. Unless someone in here thinks it's just a strange coincidence that our dead planet is in the Proximan home system."

"It matters greatly, Karpov," McFarran said. "We're now dealing with an enemy that can move planets between star systems. Do you still think our little rocket can do much against them?"

"I'm not surrendering." Karpov glared at the aux.

Breen spun the displayed globe with a swipe of his hand. "They must have jumped it somehow. But how? However they did... just, wow."

"I aborted the mission because this changes things. Maybe." Oswald saw Karpov shake his head from the corner of his eye, but ignored him. "Do we want to investigate Earth, possibly dying anyway? If we do, we'll be revealing our presence and cutting our chances of carrying out a successful attack.

"Or do we decide it doesn't really matter what happened to Earth, since she's obviously dead, and proceed with the attack while we still can. Thoughts?"

"We can do both, Colonel," Norris said. "If we plot our investigation right, the Proxies won't necessarily start shooting right away. They might consider us harmless until we attack. It'd be nice to know what happened, but we'll just find more questions and a dead planet. Really, I don't know."

"Maybe they're in stasis, like we were." Breen smiled hopefully around the room. "If we could figure out a way to get them out—"

"Then they'd all wake up and immediately flash-freeze," Karpov said. "We need to stop these wild-goose chases and start kicking footballs sideways up the Proximans' collective asses." He looked at McFarran. "American footballs, of course."

McFarran offered a mirthless smile. "That's about all American footballs are good for."

"I wonder how the Luna City Steelers did," Breen said. "You know, while we were gone."

"If they didn't get rid of Breckenridge," Relor said, "probably as shitty as usual."

Breen turned on her, a shocked smile on his face. "You leave Breck alone!"

Relor pointed a finger at Breen. "They've never been the same since leaving Pittsburgh."

"They never left," Breen said. "They still practice Earthside." He looked up at the holo-display where Pittsburgh should have been and hung his head. "Used to."

Oswald guessed Breen and Relor were the types who had memorized sports statistics since childhood. They were both excellent officers, but he'd worked with astronauts who knew more about their favorite team's trivia than their jobs.

He didn't mind the banter. It gave him time, gave them all time, to absorb what they were seeing. McFarran was right. What could they do to an enemy that could move planets? But so was Karpov. Oswald wasn't ready to surrender... yet.

Another life-or-death decision. His shoulders sagged. If they weren't in zero-g, Oswald was sure he'd have slumped all the way to the deck. If he made the wrong decision, they were dead. If he made the right one, they were probably just as dead. There was no going home regardless of what he decided.

He let out a long breath. "Speaking as the highest-ranking member of the Sol Defense Fleet, this decision is above my pay grade. So my decision is to put it to a vote.

"Then we'll set to do the best job we can at what we all decide. So, investigate Earth or start our attack run?"

McFarran raised his hand. "Colonel, if it is truly to be a vote, then we must be able to vote on the option of reaching out to the Ay-Yon."

"Ooh," Karpov said. "Now it's the Ay-Yon, eh? Getting ready to lick some boots, Aux?"

Oswald jabbed a warning finger at Karpov, then turned back to McFarran. "That choice isn't on the ballot."

"Then it's not much of a vote, Colonel. With all due respect." McFarran looked around the table. "But perhaps we may find suitable answers on Earth to make a more informed decision."

"Or maybe we'll give ourselves away and get smoked before we even start," Karpov said.

Oswald set his tablet to float in the air next to him. "Everyone, please send me a private message with your vote."

It was a hard decision. He felt like a chickenshit for not making it himself. At least they'd all discuss it. Karpov voted immediately, crossed his arms, and glared at McFarran. Oswald stayed, mostly to keep Karpov, and McFarran to a lesser degree, from coercing votes. His presence wouldn't otherwise be helpful, since he didn't know any more than the crew. He listened to the discussions. Karpov and McFarran behaved, spending their time silently staring at each other. It took two hours for the final vote to be cast.

Oswald read the results and burst out laughing. Nothing was easy. It seemed he was not going to catch a single fucking break. Perhaps it was the universe's way of reminding him not to shirk his responsibilities. That he couldn't, even if he tried.

McFarran, Breen, Norris, Relor, and Hines voted to investigate Earth.

Karpov, Kirsk, Trese, Stungart, and Devlin voted to begin combat operations.

"Goddammit," Oswald whispered. He traced small circles on the tabletop with his finger. This option hadn't crossed his mind so he hadn't considered having to decide. He'd counted on following the crew's decision. Instead, they'd tossed the hot potato back at him with a tied vote.

Tactically, he knew the right answer: complete the mission. It didn't really matter what they found on Earth. The Proximans needed to pay. If they adopted a new mission, the main mission would suffer. *Roland* wouldn't get a second chance.

So far, he hadn't saved Earth. He hadn't jumped in at the last minute to rescue his family. The only hope of redemption for these failures was to slay the dragon that had devoured them. Earth's last hurrah would be the echo of his failure, quickly fading into the void.

Oswald saw Norris looking at him. Their eyes met for an instant and they both looked away. He glanced back, following the curve of her neck and breasts. He didn't love her. She wasn't Misty or Anahita. And she cried too much. But she was at least the possibility of something good. Like McFarran said.

"We'll go to Earth."

McFarran bowed his head to Oswald. Norris smiled and mouthed "Thank you." Karpov beamed at him and gave him two thumbs-up. Oswald could see the sarcasm flashing in his eyes.

Oswald glanced at McFarran and Karpov. They represented *Roland*'s warring conscience. Shame washed over him; he should be *Roland*'s conscience. Somehow he'd put it on them. Had he meant to? They were both right in their way. He hoped the trip to Earth would be worth it, that they would find something to make the right course obvious. Oswald had no idea what that would look like. Everything was slipping away from him.

"Norris, Breen, plot the jump," Oswald said. "I want to come in on the far side of the station around Earth. There might be other sats we can't see, but we go with what we have. Dismissed."

Back in his stateroom, Oswald reviewed what Norris and Breen had put together. It looked good, simple enough. He thought of Norris again and activated the holo-cube projector.

Anahita's face appeared, wearing a bemused smile. "A vote, Pierce? Truly? Are you a flight commander or a flight poll-watcher?"

"I didn't say we wouldn't go in guns blazing," Oswald said. "Maybe we'll find some answers. Maybe what we see will piss everyone off enough to want to fight. Either way, we're not going there to beg."

Anahita scoffed. "Well, I guess as long as you're doing what everyone else wants to do, you can't go wrong, right?"

# Chapter 32

"NEGATIVE, TACTICAL," Auxiliary Flight Commander Hashi McFarran said. "You cannot run another diagnostic on the submunitions."

In order to conserve energy and atmosphere, McFarran ordered some of the flight pods powered down and scheduled the crew to work closer together. He didn't know if it was worse to be stuck in the same compartment as Karpov or to have him skulking around *Roland* out of sight.

"Afraid we'll kill too many of your alien buddies, Aux?"

"You ran a complete series two hours ago. I seem to recall everything was green. Unless you doubt your job last time, it seems to be more of a nervous tick than preparation." McFarran knew engaging in the man's games was a fool's errand. But he couldn't resist the chance to put him in his place. "You aren't getting nervous are you, Karpov?"

"I don't get nervous anymore, Aux. But if you don't want me to do my job, I'll hit the rack."

"Stay at your station, Mr. Karpov. Your job is monitoring our tactical situation and weapons condition. If you are getting too fidgety to do that, I can ask the Colonel to come finish your watch for you."

Karpov glared at McFarran over his shoulder. The expression was dangerous and full of malignant promise. McFarran knew he needed to watch the man closely. It was a delicate balancing act. As aux, he couldn't afford to appear weak to Karpov or any of the crew.

But McFarran didn't want to push him over the edge either. Things were already about to snap apart.

"Yes, sir, Aux, sir." Karpov smiled and turned back to his station.

McFarran stared at the back of Karpov's head for a minute, before returning to his displays. Norris offered him an almost imperceptible nod.

"Mind your own station, Flight Sergeant," Karpov said, without looking up from his screens.

Norris turned to face Karpov and flipped him off.

They reminded McFarran of his sons, Clement and Robert. Of course, neither of his sons was a psychopath like Karpov. But Clement had brought no end of troubles to his family. The boys were still fond of exchanging vulgarities, though now it was with a measure of fraternal jocularity.

Or it had been, four hundred years ago.

He had little enough to do, in truth. Since the crew was so small, everyone now watched everything. Schedules were merely a matter of putting bodies in seats. He was not fond of the idleness, but it allowed him time to reminisce.

Personal files didn't belong on one's station during duty hours. He had been a much stronger enforcer of that than Oswald. But there on his display, Clement and Robert stood in front of Notre-Dame de Paris. Its survival was seen by some as an act of God, when much of the rest of Paris had been reduced to rubble by an Ay-Yon mass-driver attack. His sons had been part of the relief efforts.

McFarran was not a religious man, but he was thankful that his sons now loved each other and showed such compassion. And he was grateful they had not followed his steps into the military.

He laughed. Karpov and Norris both glanced at him, but they caught sight of each other looking and turned back to their posts with matching sneers.

Clement had been so afraid of telling his father he didn't want to join the fleet. He said he wanted to build space stations, not blow them up. The boy had been shocked when McFarran embraced him.

"Good," he told his son. "We need more builders than breakers in this world. Build me a new world, Clement."

He told Robert the same when the boy said he wanted to be a zookeeper. And a tour guide. And a yoga instructor. And a digital store owner. Anything but a soldier was fine with McFarran. But each time, Robert was so afraid of hurting his father's feelings he cried. McFarran's eyes were stinging.

"Armor drill," he said. "All duty stations don vacc-armor."

Karpov turned from his screens. "Give me a break."

"We are alone and as deep behind enemy lines as you can get, Karpov. This is not the time to get complacent."

"That's right," Karpov said. "Enemy lines."

"I'm so very glad you agree." McFarran turned to get his armor.

Karpov reached behind his own station. "They are the enemy. Glad to see you getting on board."

McFarran said nothing and averted his eyes until his helmet was latched in place. He fought to keep his voice steady as the duty stations reported in. He didn't record the drill completion time. It didn't matter. This drill was for him—and anyone else on watch about to lose it.

With a final check of *Roland*'s systems, McFarran muted his mic and allowed himself to weep for his sons. A full wailing break-down was unacceptable. It would be improper for the second-in-command to carry on so. But he couldn't forestall the sobs that came—he hoped the armor would hide them. Tears pooled in his eyes and snot drifted from his nostrils.

His screams rang in his ears. He fought the urge to pound the console with his armored fists, to slam Karpov's head. Everyone on the suicide squad with him—Kirsk, Trese, Stungart, and Devlin—needed a good drubbing too. A final urge to kick Karpov filled him, and he let it pass.

General Anahita Khadem hadn't bothered to include any warming details about Clement or Robert in her farewells. No pictures of their families, no touching photos of the men they grew into after their papa was declared perpetually MIA. How arrogant did Oswald have to be to use the loss of his own family as a rallying point when the entire crew had suffered the same? And without the benefit he had of knowing what became of their loved ones.

General Khadem and Oswald had a child together. He couldn't blame her for keeping him particularly in mind. She had no expectation that *Roland* would return one day.

He knew that if Oswald had turned down this mission, they'd all be dead already. Or maybe not. Maybe Nunez would have failed and the wormhole would never have been created. But *Roland* would probably still have been destroyed.

The true problem was virtual Anahita. Oswald claimed he was just trying to trick it into giving up information, some hidden Proximan secret. That secret would be over four hundred years out of date. Useless. But it was pretense, anyway. McFarran could see the lover's look in Oswald's eyes when the FC went to "review the logs." He passed up no excuse to talk to Anahita's ghost. Instead of feeding Oswald secrets, that ghost seemed to be feeding his desire for vengeance. But McFarran didn't think it was some maniacal plot of the ancient Ay-Yon. Oswald was more than capable of talking himself into pursuing the war he claimed so much to hate.

Oswald had agreed to come to Earth. But McFarran knew the colonel was still of the blood-for-blood mindset. He could see it in the man's eyes. But there might be hope, if Karpov could be silenced somehow or shown for the fool he really was.

"Are you going to make me wear this to my bunk, Aux?" Karpov asked. "Or are we pulling a double?"

McFarran checked the mission clock. He'd let the rest of the shift pass in reverie. That wasn't like him and fear crept up from his belly. This is what happened when one indulged in self-pity. He had been completely unaware of the tactical situation during that time.

He slid open his visor and saw Oswald floating nearby, concern in his eyes.

"Everything OK, Aux?"

McFarran rubbed his eyes and nose on the helmet's face sponge, hoping to clean away any trace of his breakdown. Oswald reached forward to help remove the helmet, and McFarran batted the colonel's hands away.

"Hey!" Oswald rubbed his left wrist, but looked more surprised than hurt.

McFarran finished rubbing his face on the sponge and unlatched his helmet. He could feel his lips twist in rage, ready to stare down the colonel, to glare at him in hate, and scream at him about Clement and Robert.

But he lived by his duty. It was what he was most proud of. He'd never shirked it before, never stepped down from a difficult task or delegated something that was his to do. Major Hashi McFarran had stood in the face of enemy fire, radiation storms, catastrophic mission failures. He'd served with and commanded astronauts both fair and foolish. And he'd always done his duty. He would do his duty unto his death, if called to do so.

At least, he hoped he would.

McFarran squeezed his eyes shut and took a final breath, before removing his helmet and facing his flight commander with a professional smile. "Yes, Colonel. Everything is fine. Just fine."

# Chapter 33

*ROLAND* jumped to the far side of Earth during one of the re-occuring high-traffic windows Trese had discovered. There were no complications, no cardiac arrests, and the ship arrived only a few kilometers from the edge of Earth's jump threshold. Oswald couldn't have asked for a better jump. It gave him a ray of hope for the rest of the upcoming missions.

"Command, Tactical," Karpov said. "T-REX away."

McFarran spoke over the commander channel. "This might make our investigation a bit more... complicated, Colonel."

"And how easy would it be to investigate with an enemy station overhead? I doubt they'll have a tour of historical preservation markers waiting for us." Oswald shook his head and muted the channel.

It was a small station, one *Roland*'s remaining laser array could destroy. But Oswald needed to take it out without warning, before they could send a distress call. They only had a few T-REX warheads left. If they were going to investigate, *Roland* would need time. An over-the-horizon attack might give him the surprise he needed.

The T-REX sped towards Earth and into a retrograde orbit to intercept the station. It skimmed the planet's atmosphere to keep out of the target's line-of-sight. The engine flared as its fuel burned out, relying on momentum and orbital mechanics to get on target.

Twenty minutes after launch, the warhead became a tiny star just above the curve of Earth's frozen husk. The T-REX's thermonuclear payload generated multiple deadly x-ray beams, all aimed at the station. Oswald hoped it would be cut to pieces before anyone on board knew what had hit them.

"T-REX detonation," Karpov said. "Estimated eleven minutes before enemy station clears the horizon. Then we'll see if it worked."

"Might not mean much if they are using a tight beam, or some quantum entanglement shit," Trese said, "but I didn't detect a transmission, no RF, no jump comms."

Oswald watched the big-eye display. If the station had sent off an RF signal, it would take hours to get anywhere he knew of. If a quick-response force showed up, his plan was to evade until the jump gate generators were ready, and then start the attack run. In that case, he hoped some of the planetary defenses might be out here looking for *Roland*.

A sparkling red streak came into view around the edge of the Earth, followed by another. Dimmer flickers danced in the upper atmosphere. Then three brilliant fiery tails burned across Earth's face, accompanied by a swarm of smaller sparks that spread out around them like a burning shroud. A cloud of whirling debris hung above the lights, too high to hit the atmosphere yet.

"Showing debris along the target's orbital track, FC," Karpov said, a pleased lilt in his voice. "I think we got 'em."

Oswald grinned. It felt good to be back to what he knew. Pick a target, make a plan, kill some Proxies. It was much more satisfying than guessing in the dark, scrambling from one mystery to the next, each answer leaving him more frustrated and confused than the last.

He could raze this sleepy system to ashes and scrap with a wing of starships. "Good job, *Roland*. Not only have we led the first attack in the Proximan home system, we've just taken out a base. Another kill for this old girl." Oswald patted his station console fondly.

"Norris," he said, "light the LANTRn and burn for orbital insertion. Gresh, let's get the full sensor sweep, and drop nav and sensor sats. And get atmospheric conditions into the flight computer. Trese, keep scanning and jamming."

His crew answered sharply, their voices lacking the hint of dread he'd heard so much of lately. Except for McFarran. The aux put a good face on, had always been professional and always backed the FC in front of the crew. They were traits that made McFarran an excellent auxiliary flight commander. But his old friend had changed, and Oswald wondered if McFarran could even see it.

The aux's tone was defeated, resigned. As if he was following orders because he didn't know what else to do. And that might be the case. But Oswald couldn't afford to have the crew hear their aux's voice like that, any more than he could allow Karpov to bully them. Karpov was at least cheering for the right side.

Each pass painted a darker picture of what had happened to their home. The oceans had gathered at the poles, exposing the sea beds to the stars above. Everything was encased in ice. Even the atmosphere had frozen, growing thick as it contracted. The distant foster star of Beta Hydri offered Earth no warmth.

"I still don't know what could cause this," Oswald said.

"It's almost like they sent it through a jump gate, Colonel." McFarran's voice was distant and full of wonder. "Imagine that frozen second of a jump transition and what it might do on a planetary scale."

Oswald drummed his fingers on the station. "It would lose its momentum. Spin, ocean currents..."

"Magma circulation," Gresh said.

"That too," Oswald continued. "Hmm. With no spin, the oceans might recede from the elongated equator, making the water seek its own level."

Norris sobbed. "Can you imagine what it was like when the jump was over? Everything would be washed away by the oceans escaping. That's why we're not seeing any ruins and why the landmarks look so different."

"It almost makes me glad everyone was already dead," Breen said. "And the Lord promised he'd never destroy the world with water again."

"Technically, all life was destroyed by an alien plague," Karpov said. "If that makes you feel any better."

Breen sniffled. "Not really."

It was one thing to accept a tragedy. It was quite another to be confronted with a corpse in grim detail. Earth's new face was revealed to them, degree by degree, minute by minute, second by second. It was an ugly face, beaten and bruised by her attackers. Oswald rubbed his eyes on the helmet's face sponge.

The Proximans made no response while *Roland* completed the preliminary mapping orbits. Oswald ordered a change in inclination to increase coverage. Nothing stood on Earth, except a large dome in the center of Africa's frosty plains and a rail system over one thousand kilometers long, crossing the ice over what was once Siberia.

"Command, Gresh. We have thermal and EM signatures from the dome. Looks like maybe twenty human-sized heat signatures. The rails have a power signature, but no bodies I can see. Might be underground though."

Stungart zoomed the big-eye on a landing platform near the dome. "That looks like our best bet. I don't see anything like it by the rail."

"We can land there easily, Colonel," McFarran said. "If they don't shoot us down."

"Norris, plot our landing and make sure we land with our working laser array oriented towards the dome."

"Will do, FC."

Oswald ran his own landing simulations and verified them against Norris's. The computer would be doing the flying, but it needed good instructions. Everything checked. Oswald ran them again. Then one more time.

"Plot once, crash once," Will Zaphrim used to say. It always pays to run the numbers again.

Oswald selected a series of points in *Roland*'s path. "Karpov, I want ORBAM deployed in these orbits. Need any help?"

"Negative, FC," Karpov said. "Relor and I got it."

"Roger that, Tac. Norris, ready for landing?"

"Uh, yes, sir."

"Do you have this, Pilot?" Oswald asked. His voice was soft but firm. If she wasn't able, he'd have to do it.

"I've got this, FC." Her voice was more confident this time. "Thirty minutes until landing burn."

"That's better, Pilot."

There was no chatter on the duty net as they rounded the Earth for the final time. Oswald felt the push and spin as *Roland* pivoted her thruster towards Earth.

Oswald clenched his teeth against the shaking as the ship hit atmosphere. The skies were clear in the landing camera and Earth rose up impossibly fast. Though no sound penetrated his helmet, Oswald imagined he could hear the screaming of reentry.

The external temperature alarms flashed red, filling him with the memories of their fiery jump into Sol that had killed so many of his crew. The landing boosters fired at their full and Oswald's back tightened painfully. A strangled cry escaped as he watched the surface race up to meet him. Everything in the camera's view became obscured with fire and smoke.

He barely felt the touchdown.

Oswald's breath came in gasps. All indicators were green and the stabilizing feet extended from the fins. *Roland* rocked slightly for a second and settled back in place.

"Touchdown successful," Norris said breathlessly. "Landing locks engaged and stable, surface stable."

"That was an amazing job, Norris," McFarran said.

"Hell, yeah," Karpov said. "I thought you were going to bury our asses two stories down."

Breen gave a nervous laugh. "That was something new. Hell of a ride."

"Secure that chatter," Oswald said. "We have a welcoming party."

# Chapter 34

THROUGH THE HEAT AND steam of *Roland*'s landing, the camera showed ten Proximan troopers in sealed combat suits taking shape. They surrounded two armored vehicles, each aiming a stubby turret up at *Roland*. The soldiers were carrying some manner of rifle, though it was impossible to tell what kind. They stared up at the ship, some pointing with their fingers. Only a couple had their weapons at the ready.

"Oh, shit," Breen said, almost whining. "They got us already."

Oswald connected to Rocketman's interface and selected online. The display of the cargo bay showed the robot unfold from behind a stack of crates from Luna. It stepped into the center of the compartment and halted. From this viewing angle, it reminded Oswald of a praying mantis. He hoped it was ready to bite some heads off.

"Rocketman, lock and load," Oswald said.

The robot grabbed two of the remaining laser cannons from the Ranger gear. It stood on one leg, while the other fitted the lasers to its arms and secured the power packs to its thin midsection.

The robot's video feed was shown in a wide angle to give operators a decent, if distorted, peripheral view. Oswald set Rocketman to semi-autonomous assault mode and hoped he'd properly designated the troops outside as enemies.

"Karpov, Trese, Stungart. Get to the airlock with sidearms. Make ready to secure the cargo hatch if any Proximans decide to board." Oswald knew if *Roland* was boarded, the fight would be lost. He'd just have to toss McFarran out there to beg for leniency if that happened. He grinned at the image. It was all about contingencies.

"Arggh, mateys!" Karpov growled. "I've always been wantin' to repel boarders, Skipper. Even when I were a wee lad."

Oswald watched the three men struggle down the handholds in the main shaft. The suits' bulk would be hard to deal with; they'd never worn them in anything like a full gravity. Even without the armor, they weren't acclimated to Earth's heavy pull. If they'd spent much more time in zero-g, everyone would be as helpless as overturned turtles.

A scream came over the net, and Oswald glanced at the monitor just in time to see Trese plummet past Karpov and slam into the deck.

Trese staggered to his feet. "I'm OK." His voice was strained.

"You sure, Trese?" Oswald asked.

"Sure, FC. I guess I'll get the weapons since I'm down here already."

"You cheated," Karpov said with labored breath.

Oswald waited for the three to attach laser pistols to their suits, calibrate the reflex sights to their visors, and take position behind Rocketman. "Relor, sweep the laser from one tank to the other. We need to get rid of those first. Then targets of opportunity. Open fire as soon as I open the cargo hatch."

The Proximan troops didn't spread out or take any aggressive action. Oswald knew little of small unit infantry tactics. But he knew enough that if they viewed *Roland* as a threat, they should be taking cover—or blowing holes in her. It bolstered the idea that the Proximans weren't on a war footing. Why would they be after slaughtering every Earther in existence?

If their home planet defenses were as soft as this platoon, maybe *Roland* could succeed.

As soft as the enemy might be, Oswald commanded astronauts, not infantry. He wasn't that familiar with Rocketman's capabilities, but Oswald was counting on that robot. They all were.

"Relor, get ready to bring the hate." Oswald cycled the cargo hatch. The soldiers on the screen looked down. A few levelled their weapons and one took partial cover behind a tank.

A plume of blinding plasma erupted from the top of the first tank as *Roland*'s laser array fired. The tank burst into flames. The laser cut through three Proximan troops on its way to the second tank.

The second tank sparked and flared as the laser worked its way across its hull. The vehicle's turret twitched and an internal damage indicator flashed on *Roland*'s status screen. Then the tank's turret melted in on itself and it, too, burst into flame.

Oswald felt a spike of panic. The tank's weapon had pierced *Roland*. Nothing happened. No systems reported damaged, only hull breaches. Whatever it was had punched clear through the ship, without hitting any crew or vital systems.

He tried watching Rocketman's video feed, but it was too jerky as the robot raced around. The ground cameras gave Oswald a better overall view of the action, though they lacked detail.

Rocketman sprinted along the barren ground, jumping and rolling while firing its laser cannons simultaneously at different targets. Three more Proximans were burned down while they stood staring at the wreckage of their tanks.

Oswald sincerely hoped the Proximans didn't have their own warbots.

Two turned and stared dumbly at the robot. Sparks erupted from their faceplates as Rocketman continued its hunt. They fell lifeless as the lasers burned through their heads. One trooper's right leg continued to twitch on the ground.

The final two Proximan soldiers raised their rifles and fired at Rocketman as they ran for cover.

Shrapnel erupted from one of the robot's lasers and it immediately detached the wreckage from the arm. Rocketman swung its remaining laser and fired, catching one of the evading Proximans in the side as he leaped for cover. The soldier went limp in midair and landed in a sprawl on the ground.

The final enemy soldier was behind a stout rock and spraying projectiles in Rocketman's direction. The robot scrabbled in the dirt and took cover behind a smoldering tank. Sparks danced over the tank's ruined hull as enemy rounds struck. Oswald thought he saw a couple of hits on Rocketman too.

The robot's sensor cluster extended around the side of the tank and scanned the area. Rocketman crouched, as if making ready to leap. Then a geyser of superheated plasma erupted beneath the final Proximan. The trooper's twisted suit crashed to the ground and bounced. Smoke drifted from the gaping hole where the soldier's head and shoulders used to be. Like a lobster whose insides had been scooped out by *Roland*'s laser.

The scene in the display grew still. All the Proximan troops lay motionless, except for that one twitching leg. Oswald panned the camera all the way around to make sure no enemy had flanked them. It was clear.

When he focused the view on the dome, Oswald could make out several human shapes inside. Hands and faces pressed against the transparent shell. After a moment of calm, several people ran towards the inner area of the dome.

"Rocketman, patrol," Oswald said. "Don't engage unless engaged." He unbuckled from his couch and clambered down the ship to the weapons locker. With a few sweeps of his arm, the reflex sight on the laser was calibrated to his helmet display.

The gravity brought aches to his back and hips. It was almost impossible to remain standing. Oswald glanced at Karpov, Trese, and Stungart and saw they were kneeling. He staggered to the cargo hatch and took a knee with them. The armored plates covering their visors were raised so they could see out of the helmets.

Karpov saluted. "All boarders repelled, Cap'n!"

"Knock it off," Oswald said. "Aux, get those breaches sealed. If we have to stay in *Roland*, I want to be able to take this damned suit off."

"At once, Colonel."

Oswald leaned in close to the three crew with him. It seemed the thing to do, though they were using their radios. "We're here for some answers, so let's not kill anyone else if we can help it. Do not fire unless fired on. Understand? Karpov?"

"I'll be as peaceful as a lamb, FC," Karpov said.

"Aux," Oswald said. "We're heading out."

"Shouldn't you send someone else, Colonel? The FC's place is in flight control."

McFarran was right; SDF procedure would have a mid-grade officer in charge of such an action. Not that *Roland* had ever participated in any boarding actions. They were exceedingly rare. By the time a hostile ship was damaged enough to safely approach, there was little reason to. Not to mention the delta-v expended to match vector. And trying to dock with a friendly vessel traveling at many kilometers per second was difficult enough. Impossible if they weren't being cooperative.

McFarran was really asking if he should be the one to go. And he should—normally. But Oswald didn't trust him. The thought put a heaviness in his chest. They'd fought together for years. McFarran was looking to undermine the mission. Even Anahita saw it. She'd used the word seditious. Oswald wondered if McFarran realized what he was doing. Fear could twist up even the stoutest veteran. He could forgive the aux for that, but now McFarran had to be watched like Karpov.

"As the senior surviving officer of the SDF, I'll be acting representative," Oswald said. "We're going in. Don't fire unless they attack."

Oswald gave a thumbs-up to each of the three men with him. They returned the gesture. "Go!"

A bolt of pain shot through Oswald's back and legs as he landed hard. Trese fell into a heap of splayed limbs. Karpov and Stungart pulled him to his feet.

"Fuck me," Karpov gasped.

Oswald braced against one of *Roland*'s fins. "Rocketman, protect us."

The robot galloped towards Oswald on three limbs. It took position fifty meters to the group's right flank, its sensor cluster whirling in silence. Oswald watched the cargo hatch slide back into place.

A thick layer of mist rose to Oswald's waist, a result of *Roland*'s landing booster and laser array thawing the frozen earth around the landing pad. The ground was slippery with a thin layer of mud that was quickly freezing again. Oswald trudged towards the dome, sweeping the area with his laser.

He was panting by the time he stopped at the dome's airlock. Three dark-skinned Proximans glared out at him. The most common theory held that whatever had transplanted the Proximans to their new home world, had taken the original stock from the Mediterranean or what had once been called the Middle East. Seeing these men, Oswald could see why.

Oswald pointed to the outer door and made an opening motion with his hands. One Proximan gesticulated and mouthed unknown words back at him.

Oswald looked over his shoulder to verify he was still in line-of-sight of *Roland*'s laser array. "Relor, when I point to my left, I want a nice short blast over that way. Something to impress the natives but not melt my face."

"Definitely don't melt my face," Karpov said. "I'm too pretty to die in a suit like this."

Oswald motioned again for them to open the airlock. The Proximan flipped Oswald the finger.

"Well, shit," Karpov said. "It really is the universal signal to fu—"

"Shut up," Oswald snapped. He raised his fingers and curled them one by one. When his index finger was the only one remaining, he pointed it to his left.

The ground nearby exploded as the laser flashed the permafrost into superheated steam. The Proximan flinched, but kept his defiant gaze.

Oswald waved his crew away from the dome. Making sure the man inside was watching, Oswald pointed at the airlock and raised his fingers.

The Proximan glowered, but reached out to a nearby control panel when Oswald had only two fingers left in his count. The outer door opened. The airlock was large enough for all four crewmen with Rocketman squeezed between them.

The inner door cycled open and Oswald spread his team out, not wanting to remain clustered together as the smoking Proximans outside had done. They were met by a crowd of around twenty civilians, dressed in a mix of loose robes and heavy utility suits. They stared at the intruders with fear and anger. Aliens, but still human.

Oswald had seen Proximans before, but only in news feeds and SDF media releases. He knew these people mostly as blips on his tactical screen. Had fought a war without ever meeting one in the field. High-velocity starship engagements didn't leave many oppor-tunities to take prisoners.

He wondered if any of them liked Delamain. It didn't matter now if they did or not.

Oswald motioned for them to move against the wall. He held up his laser pistol and burned a small hole in the floor to make sure they realized he and the crew were armed. None of them moved.

Oswald was about to call McFarran to get the Proximan trans-lation program running, when two Proximans ran from a darkened room. Each held something slung over their shoulders that looked like a jackhammer. The weapons, or tools—there was little differ-ence at this point—hung at their hips. Oswald couldn't hear their screams, but he saw it on their faces as they pulled the triggers.

The Proximans struggled forward against the recoil of each shot. Thick black spikes flew at Oswald's team. They missed Rock-etman's skinny frame, but Stungart crashed back against the inner airlock hatch, impaled by two spikes that went through him and jutted out the back of his armor.

Rocketman returned fire before Oswald could call a warning. Both Proximans fell, smoldering holes where their faces used to be. The heavy tools pulled the limp bodies to the floor as if they were rag dolls.

"Look out!" Karpov yelled too late, jumping behind a row of low desks.

If the Proximans had fired at Oswald before Rocketman re-turned fire, he knew he'd be as dead as Stungart. He turned to dive behind what looked like a large material printer.

He growled as his back clenched and his legs splayed. The im-pact on the floor sent another jolt of fire up his spine. Oswald grit-ted his teeth against the pain, but didn't trust his trembling legs enough to try standing.

He pointed his arm towards the Proximans, using the sight on the laser pistol to see what was happening. It was easier than trying to roll over like a wounded beetle. The Proximans charged. Some wielded wicked-looking pickaxes.

He fired into the crowd. They were packed close enough together he didn't need to aim. Two men and a women fell, clutching their wounds, before the crowd was on him. Somewhere, McFarran and Dr. Hines were screaming about status reports.

His helmet rang as someone brought a pickaxe down on him. People piled on. His weapon arm was pinned and he had no strength to break free. The leering face of a middle-aged woman filled his visor. She sat on his chest and aimed a pistol at his face.

Oswald went rigid. The visor would stop a bullet; they were designed to protect against high-power shrapnel. But if it was a laser weapon, it might pass through the visor straight to his face. "Button up!" he shrieked.

The metal faceplate slid into place just as three high-pitched *plinks* rang in Oswald's helmet. He struggled to bring his weapon arm to bear, but there was too much weight. Something was covering the laser's sight. He couldn't tell if it was an attacker in front of the weapon or part of his armor.

Oswald yelled as an unfamiliar claustrophobia enveloped him. He couldn't breathe. They had him pinned, trapped, getting ready to jam spikes through his heart. He had to get up. He couldn't.

Then the weight was gone. The laser's reflex site was clear and he couldn't see anyone nearby. He swept the laser all the way around, before struggling to his feet.

Proximans were strewn over the floor, writhing and bleeding from wounds to their heads and faces. Arms and legs twisted at impossible angles. Oswald lifted his metal faceplate to get a better view.

Rocketman had two men cornered, its arms spread wide and pistoning as it moved in like a murderous, mechanical boxer.

"Rocketman, capture!" Oswald scanned for threats as he stumbled forward. A feeble thud rang against his right leg. He twisted to see a man glaring up at him. The man was lying in a pool of blood, a hammer barely clutched in his fist. He raised the hammer again and Oswald burned a hole in the man's chest.

Something slammed into Oswald from behind, almost knocking him over. He didn't know if he'd be able to get up again.

"You OK, FC?" Karpov staggered into view. The two men leaned against each other for support. "Stungart got pinned like a schoolkid's bug collection."

Oswald nodded and turned towards the body. Stungart was curled into a fetal position, unmoving. The armor's auto-sealing function had kept blood from pouring out of the punctures. But the man's face was twisted into a grimace, visible through the visor. Stungart's eyes were rolled up into his head.

Oswald surveyed the scene. Trese had two women cowering against a wall, his laser covering them. Rocketman held the men it had been preparing to kill moments earlier in headlocks. Karpov was motioning with his laser for the survivors to get back against the wall.

"Colonel? Colonel?" McFarran's voice trembled. "This is *Roland*. Please give your status."

"*Roland*, this is Oswald. I think we have the dome secured. For now."

"Vitals show Stungart is red, Colonel. Is he hurt?"

"He's dead, Hashi." Oswald staggered to a blood-spattered desk and sat on it. He leveled his laser at the prisoners, not wanting them to think he was as weak as he really was.

"*Mon dieu*," McFarran whispered.

"Get Hines over here with an air sampler. And two more crew. We need to sweep this place. And we need cable ties or something for the surviving prisoners."

"Surviving, Colonel?"

Oswald felt his eye twitch. "It got messy over here." He feared how much messier it would get.

# Chapter 35

OSWALD COULDN'T REALLY tell it was Earth's air. But it seemed he should be able to taste its sweetness. Even though it was frozen, pushed through alien filters, and under a distant and uncaring alien sun, part of him was convinced he could smell the atmosphere of his home world by a simple primordial connection. He was a child of Earth.

It was romanticism at its worst. The last whiff of air he'd taken on Earth was tainted by the pollution of Xichang. And the air here smelled of the blood coagulating on the floor.

Their vacc-armor was stacked by the airlock. Oswald had ordered the new arrivals to use the much lighter EVA suits now that the prisoners were secured. Everyone had stripped down to their uniforms to start interrogations.

He'd ordered McFarran to stay on *Roland*, working the repairs. This was not the time for the man's whining.

It was difficult not to grimace each time his back spasmed. Oswald was still trying to hide his injury from the captives. If they got out of hand, his crew would be hard-pressed to control them with anything short of a robotic bloodbath. He didn't want to encourage them to try.

Oswald had chosen an office around the corner from the prisoners in which to hold the interrogations. They were not going well. He was experiencing how much a language can change in four hundred years. Cultural references are forgotten while new ones take their places. The meanings of words shift like sand, and writings once commonly read become understandable only to dedicated academics trying to keep history alive.

Those references were important to the translation program, and *Roland* was having a hard time of it. The Q-puter, along with a bulky super-cooling system, had been moved inside the dome, but Breen's efforts hadn't helped much. Two of the crew had known a smattering of Proximan. Usher was dead and Richter was a lunar mutineer.

Oswald managed to get the names of a few irresolute prisoners. Some shrugged or shook their heads quizzically when Oswald's tablet tried to translate his questions. Others glared at him in silent rage until taken back with the others.

The few snippets of conversation he could make out consisted of them demanding to know what he wanted or who he was. They seemed to believe the Earthmen to be strange Proximan criminals. Some asked why they would kill their own people. Oswald didn't try to explain the truth, he just pressed on with the questions. They needed to get their answers and get *Roland* back into battle. Oswald's back twitched again—he wasn't looking forward to liftoff.

Whatever the Proximans may have done to Earth before moving it, it was now sterilized, bereft of its life and history. The land around the dome was rock and dirt. No landmarks, no vegetation, no dead stumps. Earth was forever a frozen wasteland. It could never be more than a domed theme-park mockery of the blue jewel it once had been. There wasn't even a day or night, only a black sky with alien stars overhead.

Oswald was satisfied the investigation was a failure and their efforts had been wasted. They'd found nothing useful, which is what he'd expected. But he'd done his best. Hopefully, McFarran would get back in line now. It was time to load everyone up for launch.

Karpov pushed an old man into the office. "Rocketman found this guy hiding in a cubby upstairs. The place was full of things like this." He tossed a small pink disk to Oswald.

Oswald caught the item and examined it. It was a yo-yo, missing its string. It bore a faded red star and the outline of some indistinguishable letters. He raised a brow at Karpov.

"Oh, yeah," Karpov said. "Apparently, he's some sort of curator. I saw old calculators, Barbies, a bunch of plastic bottles, and a can of Spam. I was almost tempted to open it up and test how long it really lasts."

Oswald looked at the old man. This was a waste of time. He was ready to go and Karpov brings him some pawnshop clerk. "What is your name?" The tablet translated the question a second later into archaic Proximan.

The old man crossed his arms and leaned back in the chair. He looked Oswald up and down. His gaze paused on Oswald's ribbons and SDF patches. When he looked back up into Oswald's face, the old man's expression was one of skepticism. He was staring so intently, Oswald put his hand on the butt of his laser pistol.

"I am called Tok-Een-Glet."

Oswald glanced down at the screen, waiting for the translation. But the translator program gave him no output, audio or visual. It hadn't been the tablet's voice he'd heard. "What did you just say?"

"I am called Tok-Een-Glet in the Ay-Yon language." The old man was speaking in broken English. The syllabication was terrible, but Oswald could understand the man better than some officers he'd worked with.

"I wasn't expecting any of you to speak an Earth language," Oswald said.

Tok-Een-Glet smirked. "Where did you learn Earth English? I know all the professors. Tell me."

"Ms. Brandson is the first grammar teacher I remember. But I learned it from my parents."

"There are no teachers of Earth languages who are bound in coupling. And I know of no Mis-Brand-Son. That's a nonsense name. Whoever it was didn't teach you proper inflection." Tok-Een-Glet shook his finger at Oswald. "You are lying to me. Certainly the least of your crimes this day."

"We're sitting on the scene of the greatest crime in human history," Oswald said. "What's happened here today is nothing compared to what happened here centuries ago or what I still plan on doing."

Tok-Een-Glet glanced nervously at Karpov, then back at Oswald. "Are you some kind of protestors or activists? Or are you squatters? That is a strange ship you have."

"Protestors?" Oswald raised a brow as Karpov. "Do people protest the genocide of Earth? After all these years?"

"Who are you to ask such questions?"

"Answer me."

Tok-Een-Glet leaned forward, putting his hands on the table. "Once some people felt bad at what we did to Earth. As with other horrors of our past, most have forgotten. Shamefully soon, I must admit. I hope that by studying the people of this place, it will help us remember. Help us make better decisions." The old Proximan shook his head. "To that end, I am not hopeful."

"What is this facility?"

"How can you be here and not know what this place is?"

Oswald stared at the man in silence.

Tok-Een-Glet shrugged. "This dome was built to protect the jump machinery and is now used as a headquarters and sleeping place. The dome is made of some type of liquid diamond stuff. But I'm no engineer and I lack the words in this language. Why do you insist on using it?"

"We'll stick to English," Oswald said. "What do you do here?"

"I get a small payment to run the historical enclave you pulled me from. Unfortunately, so little is accessible. I've nothing worth stealing."

"We're here for information."

Tok-Een-Glet motioned towards the lobby with a nod. "It looks like you are here for blood. What do you want? The Protectorate is going to deal harshly with you."

Oswald snorted. "They already did when they killed Earth. Do you know the Earth measurement kilometers?"

"Somewhat."

"I was born about fifteen thousand kilometers that way." Oswald pointed to what he thought would be west.

"You are a squatter. This place is under the Resource Protectorate. Your fight is with them, not us. You've murdered no one but workers here."

"And soldiers," Oswald said. "Resource Protectorate? Doesn't Ay-Yon have enough water? You killed Earth for water?"

"No, no. There is enough water with recycling advancements. They moved Earth so long ago as a..." The old Proximan made a juggling motion as he sought the right words. "A pride project. To show we could. It was later decided to use Earth's water for terraforming Ay-Rik and Ay-Fan.

"It was very controversial at the time. And there were concerns the bioweapon might still be active."

"Yeah, it'd be a damn shame if your whole planet died choking on their own poison," Karpov said.

"Yes," Tok-Een-Glet said earnestly. "And some were afraid of what Earth might do to other orbits. So they put it well away, and someday the motion of the other planets is supposed to pull it into a stable orbit. Are you from one of the colonies?"

Karpov chuckled. "He's not too bright, is he?"

Oswald tilted his head. "What if I told you we were all born over four hundred Earth years ago?"

"I would say you still lie."

Oswald pointed at his ribbons. "You seemed to recognize these."

"Costumes."

"Is our starship a costume? Our robot?"

"Maybe." Tok-Een-Glet narrowed his eyes at Oswald. "I don't know your game. But I'm not believing you are ancient men from Earth. All that matters to me is that your hands are covered in blood. In fact, there's no reason to suffer your English anymore."

Tok-Een-Glet began speaking Ay-Yon. Karpov backhanded the old man. "English."

Tok-Een-Glet glared up at Karpov and fired off in the alien language again. The translator was having trouble keeping up. Oswald didn't know Ay-Yon, but he knew when someone was cursing.

Karpov backhanded the old man again, this time knocking him out of the chair. "English, please." Karpov then helped Tok-Een-Glet back to his seat.

Tok-Een-Glet held a hand to his face where he'd been struck. "Well, as the ancients say, you're the ones with the lasers."

Karpov smiled. "See? I knew we could be friends."

Oswald stood. "I guess it doesn't matter what you believe. Take us to the machinery that moved this planet."

The old Proximan stood and looked cautiously at Karpov. His hand was still on his cheek.

Karpov swept his arm towards the door. "Lead on, friend."

Tok-Een-Glet flinched as he walked by Karpov. Karpov hadn't moved, but he nodded and followed the old Proximan out. Tok-Een-Glet led them to a two-meter dome in the center of the complex. He slid a hand along the dome's surface to reveal a small, featureless panel. "You'll need a pass crystal. This is a restricted area. I've never been inside."

"Where can we get one of these crystals, friend?" Karpov asked.

Tok-Een-Glet glared. "Do not call me friend. I suppose the prime administrator has one."

"Take us to him," Oswald said.

"To her. I'll have to point her out."

Karpov swept his arm back towards the lobby where the prisoners were being held. Tok-Een-Glet led the way. Three of the other prisoners started shouting at the old man as he looked them over. He glanced at Karpov and stepped out of arm's reach. "I don't see her."

Oswald pointed to the row of dead bodies. "Look there."

Tok-Een-Glet stared at the bodies and then back at Oswald, his face twisted in horror. He screamed something in Ay-Yon. Karpov stepped forward. Tok-Een-Glet cringed away and returned to speaking his broken English. "You are murderers! Monsters!"

"See if she's there and get this crystal," Oswald said. He crossed his arms and stared at the old man.

Tok-Een-Glet covered his mouth with his robes, exposing his hairy, saggy legs. He stumbled forward along the line of bodies. Stopping in front of a woman, he pointed and slipped in her blood. Tok-Een-Glet flailed his arms to keep his balance. Sobbing into his robe, he pointed at the woman again and tottered away to collapse on a nearby bench.

Oswald recognized the woman as the one with the pistol. The top of her head was caved in, freezing her dying rage forever on her face. He nodded at the woman. "Karpov."

"Sure thing, boss." Karpov stepped forward and rummaged through all the woman's pockets. He returned with a small wallet, a worn book, a handful of bullets, and a small sparkling disk. He handed the disk to Oswald, and began rifling through the book and wallet. After a moment, he tossed them on the woman's chest.

Oswald took the crystalline disk and tapped Tok-Een-Glet with it. "This?"

Tok-Een-Glet nodded. Oswald motioned towards the central dome. When the old Proximan shook his head, Oswald pulled his laser pistol. He would have pulled Tok-Een-Glet up, but felt it as likely that he'd be pulled down instead. The old man glared, struggled to his unsteady feet, and led the way back to the inner dome.

Once there, Oswald swiped the disk over the flat panel. A hidden door slid open to reveal a small platform. Karpov raised a questioning brow at Oswald. Oswald shrugged and stepped onto it. Karpov gently pushed Tok-Een-Glet ahead of him. Oswald found a single button and pressed it. The platform descended nearly ten meters.

A door at the bottom opened to a short hallway of a solid black material. At the end of the hall was another door, this one with yellow and green diagonal stripes. Stern-looking Proximan glyphs were stenciled across the door.

There was no access panel in sight. Oswald rubbed the crystal over the surface of the door and nearby walls. Nothing. He turned to Tok-Een-Glet. "What does that say?"

Tok-Een-Glet seemed too nervous to approach the door as he read, "'This room is off-limits by order of the High Security Protectorate. Violators will be subject to execution according to the Seventh Protocol.' I'm not sure anyone on this planet has access to this room."

"Now why would that be?" Karpov asked.

"It is dangerous. And top secret."

Karpov pounded on the door. Oswald and Tok-Een-Glet both flinched. "Open up in there! I get it. You don't want just anyone stealing your planet, right?"

The door looked solid, but there were visible seams where it had been bonded to the hinges. Oswald drew his laser and started cutting. It took him and Karpov nearly an hour and four battery pack replacements before the door finally fell in. Tok-Een-Glet jerked awake at the loud crash.

The compartment beyond was packed with screens, instrument panels, and thick bundles of cable. In the center of the equipment stood a metallic box the height of a man. One screen displayed a star map and the other was flashing red. It smelled of burning plastic.

"That's probably an alarm," the Proximan offered.

Oswald nodded and continued exploring the room. A series of touch screens illuminated with countless icons as he ran his hand along a nearby frame. "Get Breen down here."

Another display came to life, showing a spiderweb overlaying a topographical map of the Earth. Some of the glowing tendrils extended thousands of kilometers into the dead seabeds of the Pacific and Atlantic oceans. The center of the web looked to be the dome.

Tok-Een-Glet peered over Oswald's shoulder. "I think they call that the jump grid. I don't know much about it, only what we learned as children. It took nearly one hundred years to lay out, plus the time to clean out all the junk the Earthers left in orbit."

A voice speaking Ay-Yon came from the flashing red screen.

"What's it saying?" Karpov asked, picking his nose in front of the monitor.

"It says that it is forbidden to interfere with this machinery and to leave this room at once. Security Protectorate forces have been dispatched." Tok-Een-Glet listened a moment longer. "It says it again. But that is the seal of the Security Protectorate. They will send someone right away."

Oswald ran his hand across the large central box. He felt a smooth patch in the center. As soon as his fingers left it, a round portal opened at head height. He stared inside.

The strength drained from his legs. His knees buckled, pitching him forward against the box. If not for the box, he'd have fallen. But there was nothing to grab, so he slid face-first towards the floor, weakly hitting it with his fists. "No. No. Oh, no..."

Karpov rushed to the portal and looked in. He stared open-mouthed while Oswald continued his weak protests from the deck. "Fucking Karma, man."

Tok-Een-Glet stepped cautiously towards the portal as Karpov found a piece of equipment to sit on. Oswald stared up at the old Proximan as he peered inside. Tok-Een-Glet cocked his head one way, then the other.

"What is that?" he asked, glancing at Oswald, then looking back through the portal. "It's like I can't see it. Like my eyes know it's there, but won't look at it. How strange. What a day."

The UXA inside emitted a familiar thrum but, to Oswald, it sounded like cruel laughter.

# Chapter 36

MCFARRAN STARED IN horror at the corpses on Rocketman's video feed. He knew why Oswald had left him on *Roland*, and it wasn't because McFarran was the best remaining engineer. The colonel apparently had no real interest in investigating Earth, despite his supposed commitment to the vote he'd called for.

There was no escaping the conclusion that his old friend's depression had become bloodlust, pushing reason aside. That bloodlust, combined with his tactical genius, could kill untold Ay-Yon. If that happened, they'd find no peace here or anywhere. From the look of the line of bodies and Rocketman's blood-splattered limbs, they had already started down that path. He hoped it wasn't too late for them all.

"Norris, I'm going to take a look at the primary breach site."

"Roger that, Aux. I'll go help Trese at the other end. We can meet in the middle."

That would leave Relor and Gresh at their stations, monitoring weapons and sensors. They'd have to be on the ready when the Ay-Yon decided to respond. Perhaps they'd be more reasonable than Oswald.

McFarran went to the tool room and pulled a damage control kit from the locker. He made the arduous climb to the impact point. Sweat tickled his brow by the time he hefted the tool kit over the edge of the deck. Repairs were much easier in zero-g.

He set the kit down and found the outer breach, and where it continued on deeper inside. The holes were about five centimeters across, and the edges were cratered in the direction the round had travelled. The impact had peppered the inner bulkhead with a spray of shrapnel and spall. The tank had hit *Roland* with a high-speed, armor-piercing round. McFarran carefully ran his thumb around the inner puncture. That had been close.

He peeked up and down the main shaft, and around the corners nearby. His chest grew tight and his heart pounded. After a couple of minutes, McFarran had heard no one approaching. After a final look around, he climbed to the next level and stopped in front of munitions bay two.

The hatch came open with a tug. He walked to the munitions locker and keyed in the commander's code. McFarran glanced over his shoulder, even though he'd heard nothing. Being as quiet as possible, he opened the locker. There, strapped securely on a shelf, were the disassembled bombs Danner had planted around *Roland*.

They'd been hidden well, requiring two full shifts of centimeter-by-centimeter searching. If one had gone off, it would have crippled *Roland*. Or worse.

Danner's bombs were quite clever. He'd created hand-sized canisters with two bags inside filled with explosively reactive chemicals: jump gate generator coolant and the bonding agent for high-density molding resin. At the top of each he'd attached a funeral rocket. If one fired off, the flame would be enough to burn the bags open, mix the agents, and then ignite the compound.

Karpov had suggested keeping the bomb components ready but separated for some foolish imagined contingency. But McFarran was now thankful as he slipped two bags into a canister and sealed it. If the tactical psychopath had ever built the new and better triggers he'd promised, McFarran didn't know where they were.

The funeral rockets were on the next shelf down. He'd studied them enough to know they could be ignited with a simple short circuit. It had been a while since McFarran worked on electrical systems, but he could still rig a length of conductor to a battery.

He listened again for a few seconds, before picking up one of the rockets. As he was going to shut the locker, he noticed two were now missing. McFarran had inventoried them at least three times and they'd all been there. Someone had already taken one. Only three people had access to this locker.

"How's it coming over there, Aux?" Norris asked over the duty net.

McFarran started and juggled the rocket. He tried to catch it, but it was too fast for him in the high gravity. He squeezed his eyes shut when it clattered on the deck. When it didn't go off, McFarran let out a slow breath and picked it up. "Fine here. Looks like a high-velocity penetrator. Hole's not too big. We got lucky."

"Looks like it split apart and started tumbling after it went through Chun's suit." Norris paused for a second. "Good thing he doesn't need it, I guess. Anyway, the holes on this side are a bit messier."

"Need help?" Gresh asked. "Relor can watch the sensors."

"No, no," McFarran blurted. "Keep to your station. I'll go help when I'm finished here."

He slammed the locker shut and strode quietly back to the damaged hull section, keeping the canister and the rocket far apart. The repairs were easy. The small holes allowed him to apply the repair gel and curing agent without further shoring. When it hardened, it would be strong enough to withstand liftoff and atmospheric burn and re-entry. At least a couple of times.

Not that it mattered. *Roland* wasn't leaving Earth if this worked.

*Mon dieu*! What was he thinking? How had it come to this? Sabotage. Oswald would think him a coward, but what was more brave, fighting to an inescapable demise or risking your final victory for the chance at peace? They were the last eleven—no, ten now—people from Earth.

Unless there was a surviving colony world out there, one that Oswald couldn't be bothered to find. The Ay-Yon might know if there were any survivors. Would Oswald even ask?

That damned box Oswald called Anahita wasn't helping. Virtual Reality Withdrawal Syndrome was a real, and sometimes dangerous, condition. Users subjected to extended or emotionally powerful VR experiences sometimes had trouble differentiating the real and virtual worlds afterwards. McFarran needed to destroy Oswald's Anahita to snap him out of his VR psychosis.

But not now. Under the pretense of searching for stray damage, McFarran wandered the deck looking for a place to plant the bomb. Handling it terrified him. He wasn't a demolitions expert and didn't know how big the explosion would be. Hopefully, Danner had designed them to cripple *Roland* without destroying her. McFarran didn't want to kill anyone, he merely wanted to ground Oswald before he rekindled a pointless, ancient war.

If it were Karpov alone on *Roland*, then maybe the whole ship going up in flames would be acceptable. They'd just have to survive the prisoners' wrath until the Ay-Yon authorities showed up.

*Roland* still smelled charred in some of her recesses. McFarran ran his fingers along the inside surfaces. If he could do enough damage, blow a big enough hole in the hull, they wouldn't be able to lift off. The repair resin could fill nearly any-sized hole in space, and *Roland* could operate with most of the inside exposed to vacuum. But a larger exposed patch of resin probably wouldn't survive the atmosphere and transition to orbit. Surely even Oswald would be able to figure that out. If McFarran could mount the canister behind that valve cluster, then run his conductor around the corner and up the—

"What's up, Aux?"

McFarran's heart leaped when Norris walked around the corner. "What the hell are you doing here?"

The smile slid from Norris's face. "Hadn't heard from you in a while. Just making sure you didn't need any help, sir."

McFarran tried to look nonchalant. He felt like a child trying to hide a cookie as he slipped the bomb parts behind his back. How many times had he seen his trouble-making son Clement do the same thing? "Yes. I mean, no. I am fine. I was looking for stray damage. If we're to lift off again... well, better safe than sorry, *oui*?"

Norris frowned. She glanced at the framework behind him, then down at his feet, likely at the coil of conductor he hadn't had time to hide. He stared placidly back at her.

"Something, Flight Sergeant?"

"I was thinking," Norris said, "how glad I was Danner didn't put a bomb there. If it went off, the explosion would probably cascade into the booster just outside that section of the hull. We'd all go nova.

"Since he said he didn't want us to die, I think he might have put one two levels down on the inside housing of the booster interface-controller subsystem. Yeah... nothing volatile nearby and we don't have any spares for that." She let out a long sigh as she shook her head. "Number two booster would never ignite without it. But I don't know if he did or not, I didn't search that section. We probably got them all."

McFarran swallowed hard. He had the urge to kick the coiled conductor away, even though it was far too late for that. "That is very interesting information, Norris. I'm quite capable of finishing the repairs in this section. Please return to your work with Trese."

She looked at him with sad eyes. With a final, uncertain nod, she turned and climbed up the main shaft.

McFarran's throat was suddenly parched. "*Merde*," he whispered. He'd almost blown them all up. But now he had a tacit ally, or at least an accomplice.

Taking a moment to catch his breath, he climbed two levels down and found the booster control housing. It had remained unused during his entire time on *Roland* before the DPV mission. It was in a small, armored compartment usually used for extra cargo and occasionally excess personal belongings when Oswald was being generous.

McFarran secured the hatch tightly behind him, and hurriedly attached the canister and rocket to the housing with large gobs of repair resin. Connecting the wires to the rocket's ignition terminals was easy using small drops of resin to hold them in place.

The next step was to run the conductor to the electrical patch panel near the exit. He considered the connections inside, trying to decide if there was a circuit he could wire the bomb to that would allow him to detonate it remotely, without someone else setting it off inadvertently.

McFarran snapped his fingers. He pulled up the compartment's schematics and wired the conductor to the circuit that sent the ignition command. No one was likely to fire that before it was time to launch. The other booster might fire, but *Roland* had a dual booster activation interlock. If they didn't fire simultaneously, both boosters would automatically abort.

He winced as he clipped the conductors down, imagining setting the bomb off early as so many amateur mad-bombers before him had done. When he again wasn't blown to bits, McFarran gave a final tug on the connections and peeked out of the hatch. There was no one in sight. He slipped out and locked the compartment with commander-only clearance. Not even Karpov could get in there now.

He raced back up the ladder. His exhausted fingers slipped and he dashed his brow against a protruding handhold. Blood rolled down his cheek and neck, staining his flight suit. He pressed his hand to the cut and it came away crimson, covered in blood.

# Chapter 37

OSWALD STARED INTO the darkness beyond the dome. It wasn't really Earth anymore, no more so than Stungart's corpse was Stungart. This was an alien world under alien stars. The heavens and Earth bore witness that it wasn't their home anymore.

The astronomical map highlighted Delta Pavonis as Oswald panned his tablet above him like a window to the stars. They were all so uncaring, so long-lived. Yet, many that still twinkled for him now were long dead. He'd been thinking about death a lot lately. Death for the Proximans. Death for his crew, for him.

His entire life of trouble was nothing now. The whole of humanity was nothing more than an unseen dust mote blown away on a solar wind. Every human could die and not one celestial eye would blink. Stars only blinked when meeting their own death.

"I am become the destroyer of worlds," Oswald muttered.

He laughed at himself. Getting sappy wasn't going to help.

But he wished on those uncaring stars that *Roland* had been destroyed trying to jump from Sol to Delta Pavonis. Or that the alien defenses had killed the Rangers before they landed. Or that an alien interceptor had disintegrated *Roland* before they inadvertently opened the wormhole and been frozen in time for four centuries.

Then he wouldn't have doomed them all by leaving the alien artifact behind. The Proximans had used his failure to deliver Earth to her frozen grave. Seeing the artifact stare back at him like a malignant eye from the planetary jump machinery had sent him into catatonia. He didn't remember leaving the jump room.

If *Roland* had been destroyed, Anahita would have come up with something. She could have saved the Earth.

"Back with us, FC?"

Oswald turned to see Karpov had sidled up next to him. "Yeah, sorry. I just..."

Karpov gave a lopsided grin and held up his hands. "I get it, FC. That thing down there? Shit. Threw me for a loop, too. I wonder if it's the one you left on the planet or if they got it from the Ranger wreckage."

"Doesn't matter. I left them both behind." Oswald nodded. "Did I miss anything while I was off in Wonderland?"

"Well, McFarran's been keeping watch."

"He's here?"

"Yeah. He called you a few times and, when you didn't reply, he hopped on over." Karpov leaned in close. "I'd keep an eye on him, FC. I'm afraid maybe he's gone native. He's been chatting with the old guy since he got here. More like whispering, really, if you know what I mean."

Oswald pulled his bleary eyes from stargazing. Karpov was right; McFarran was leaning in close to Tok-Een-Glet. He didn't think the aux was simply trying to build repertoire with a captive. Or was Oswald being paranoid? It would be easy to get that way with someone like Karpov doing his own whispering. But as the old saying goes, just because you're paranoid doesn't mean they aren't out to get you.

"That's a hefty charge to make against your aux officer."

"Look, Pierce," Karpov said. "The fleet is gone. We've transcended it, or at least outlived it. The last set of orders we have are four hundred years old. We're just men and women fighting for what we've lost. Don't get me wrong, because I mean no disrespect to you. But McFarran isn't standing with us. I don't consider him in charge of anything."

Oswald had been a commander long enough to see a set-up coming. Karpov was relatively new to *Roland*, having joined the crew in Barnard's Star. Oswald had come to dislike the man. But in the middle of his sarcasm and bullying, Karpov spoke truth.

Oswald locked eyes with him. "I'd like to keep at least a semblance of military bearing, Lt. Major Karpov. And for the very reason you want to dismiss it. With the SDF gone and a big job still ahead of us, this crew needs structure. We need to stick to our routines and our training. We need something to hold us together besides my good looks and your personal charm."

Karpov rubbed his scalp. "Alright, Colonel. That makes sense. So let me make an official, bona fide observation as *Roland*'s tactical officer. You need to get your head back in the game, FC. Our mission window is shrinking"—he gave McFarran a sidelong glance— "and I don't think everyone is on the same page."

Oswald gazed back up at the stars. They were so quiet, had no expectations or demands. Those distant lights didn't care, nor did they judge. "Noted. Since my head has been out of the game, catch me up. Breen making any progress?"

"He managed to get the Q-puter to interface with their system. Apparently, Proximan numbers haven't changed as much as their language. This so-called Security Protectorate was counting on their soldiers, locks, and mankind's sanity to keep people out." Karpov crossed his eyes and twirled a finger at his temple. "They obviously weren't counting on us.

"Anyway, he thinks he's figured out how to program it. He's been staring at his Q-puter screen as long as you've been staring out into space. Bawk-Bawk-Bawk, or whatever the old timer's name is, helped out. I made sure he was feeling helpful. Not that putting Earth back where it belongs will help."

Oswald lifted his chin. "There's a part of me that thinks that would be the right thing to do."

"We do that, we'll never pull off our attack run. And Earth would just fall into the sun anyway."

Was the mission even possible now? Was it worth it? Could it end in anything except *Roland* burning up in Ay-Yon's atmosphere? He could feel Karpov staring at him.

"I'd like to share something with you, FC." Karpov tapped his Lucky Star patch. "Only one other person ever earned three of these, though 'earn' might be the wrong word. The other didn't get a fourth, but I hear her monument on Luna is—was—very nice."

"You don't need to tell me—"

"No, FC. I want you to hear this. No one has ever heard what actually happened on *Starlancer*. Not even the flight psychologist who cleared me for return to duty."

"They cleared you without hearing what happened?"

"They heard a version of what happened. I'm going to tell you the truth. Our flight commander was Lt. Colonel Maricopa. She'd just taken us through a knife fight in Alpha Centauri. This was about the time you were first deployed in Barnard's Star. Her shit was wired tight; she ran things kind of like you.

"We jumped in on what was supposed to be a transport convoy. And it was, but three of the so-called transports were actually disguised warships. We hit them hard and managed to survive the counterattack.

"Something hit us though. When the squadron jumped, everyone got away. Except us. Our jump generator blew out the whole deck and *Starlancer* split coneward of the reactor."

Karpov turned to stare off into the stars. "It was probably a good thing. If the reactor hadn't fallen off and drifted away, we'd have all been slow-cooked. The fuel core had sort of lost containment.

"*Starlancer* was done. The Proximans knew it. And so did the rest of the squadron. One of our ships detected the radiation spike and watched us split apart, before jumping away. The fleet decided not to mount a rescue. We were deaf, dumb, and blind. Fortunately, the forward compartments maintained integrity.

"Ol' Maricopa tried everything, though. We manually ignited rockets for the munitions, tried every transmitter we had left, and even got out in EVA suits, waving flashlights. But between us and the Proximan we'd fragged, there was too much debris and radiation for any patrols to see our signs of life. Know how long before they schedule a salvage sortie?"

Oswald nodded. "Six months is standard fleet protocol."

Karpov tapped the tip of his nose. "Exactly. Six months minimum. Well, fortunately, I'd already been stashing things away. *Starlancer* wasn't my first disaster."

"And to think you once claimed to be a good luck charm. Am I going to have to shoot you at the end of this story?"

"I guess you'll have to decide that, FC. I won't stop you if you do." Karpov paused for a long moment and turned to face Oswald. "Maricopa discovered I was hoarding and confronted me after the explosion. It was in private to try to keep things calm. She wanted to make me see reason. I offered to share with her, but she said everyone needed it. I already knew there wasn't enough to go around. I had to kill her.

"Then the games started. People began to realize what they'd need to do to survive. A few killed themselves, others formed into small teams. But it was already too late for most of them. It's amazing what you can turn into weapons on a starship. Especially if you're in the tactical department. You can make plenty of things that go boom. Some things will make toxins; people don't even know they've been poisoned. That time, I didn't wait for a lottery."

Oswald put a hand to the butt of his laser pistol. "You killed all the survivors?"

"No. A lot of them killed each other. I just started early. No point wasting good O2 on people who weren't going to be needing it in the end. Including Maricopa, I only killed six.

"The last guy besides me, the penultimate survivor, if you will, found himself on an unscheduled EVA. He'd booby-trapped the main shaft and hid in the cone. I had to go and depressurize his compartment from the outside. Should have seen the look on his face as he went tumbling away."

"And they let you on my ship?" Oswald whispered.

"Don't blame the shrinks, FC. I lied my ass off. I sure as fuck wasn't going to Luna Correctional. As cozy as it might be, all I did was survive. I killed some people who were already dead."

"It would have kept you out of the war."

"I don't want out of the war. I want to kill Proximans. I want to kill them as much as you do, and as well as you do."

The earnestness in Karpov's voice was disturbing. Oswald was used to accolades from his commanders and juniors for his fighting prowess. Pride of the fleet. Proximan-killer. Karpov's praise sounded almost cultish.

Oswald cleared his throat. "Why tell me all this now?"

Karpov adopted a beatific smile and crossed himself. "To confess my sins, Father." The smile slipped from his face. "To make sure you know what I'm willing to do to win this fight."

"What if I decide McFarran's right? Then what will you do to me to make sure you win?"

"Maybe I've got you figured wrong, FC. But you don't really seem the sort who could enjoy sitting back, sipping tea and eating alien petites in the velour parlor of those who committed genocide on your people. McFarran I can see asking for his slippers and seconds. But not you."

Oswald slid his finger across the dome. It was smooth and cool to the touch. He watched as the streak from his finger faded.

"Something I don't get, Tac. You keep telling us these grim stories of the lengths you'll go to to survive. Yet you know our attack is probably going to get us killed. Maybe you and the aux should get together. He seems more intent on living than you do."

"McDipshit... apologies, Colonel. Major McDipshit thinks the Proximans are going to find it in their piss-filled hearts to let bygones be bygones. Which I guess is easier to agree to and forget the past if you're the genocidal maniacs. And maybe he's right. But I'm not willing to walk into the monster's den with my hands up. They annihilated and stole Earth.

"Showing up like that seems the sure way to get killed, to me. I think maybe he's forgetting how they give honor to their admired enemies. Like Anahita. I say we go out fighting. Maybe we die, maybe become POWs. But we don't fucking surrender. And I think you already know that, so I'm not worried what you'll choose. Even if you think I'm an asshole.

"So the point of my little stories—did I ever tell you I was in talks with a 3-D studio for my last book? Damn the timing. Anyway, it isn't just about survival. There comes a point where you have to choose how to live. I choose to live in a way that means justice for the fuckers that killed our home planet and everyone we gave a shit about."

Oswald considered the words for a moment. "Even if we kill every man, woman, and child, it won't bring Earth back."

"Neither will surrendering." Karpov punched the palm of his hand and rubbed his fist there. "But this isn't about bringing people back. It's not even about surviving. We're already dead. This is about blood-for-blood. Avenging our fallen. Making sure the Proximans don't get away with it. I meant it when I said no one kills them like you do, FC. And no one can help you fight like I can, Colonel." Karpov popped a sharp salute, turned on his heel, and strode away.

Oswald stared after his clearly insane tactical officer. The commander in him was screaming that he should pull his pistol and burn Karpov to the ground, regardless of anything else.

Karpov had now confessed to murdering seven crewmates, including a flight commander. But if Oswald wanted the attack to work, Karpov was right. And he was right about the Proxies not getting away with killing Misty, Mara, and Mary. And Anahita. And Ululani. Karpov ran the tactical station like a well-tuned symphony, and he was committed to the fight, to Oswald. Did it matter if Karpov died in front of an ad hoc firing squad of one, or if he burned up on *Roland* with the rest of them?

It would matter, if Oswald sided with McFarran. That would be an interesting conversation.

Bile rose in Oswald's mouth. He remembered the image of the commanders of Saturn Station. The laser holes burned into the backs of their grinning, desiccated skulls were clear in his mind. He didn't want to die like that. Karpov wouldn't be the first mad prophet to utter truth and wisdom, then destroy his followers. Oswald wondered if considering those truths made him a madman too.

He'd have to ask Anahita.

# Chapter 38

OSWALD HAD LIMITED the reports submitted to him to ship status, tactical updates, and prisoner condition. There weren't enough crew left to compile or read extraneous reports.

But he had to chuckle at Dr. Hine's report on Proximan rations. The food was composed of compatible proteins, carbohydrates, sugars, and a litany of other nutritional compounds. The doctor's final note was, "Tastes like shit without heavy doses of condiments. And my personal field experiments show it can result in explosive diarrhea."

Breen's report wasn't as humorous as the doctor's, but it was far more useful. Interface between the Q-puter and the planetary jump machinery was verified, and Breen believed he could program jump coordinates and initiate the jump. He couldn't verify much about the security systems or what that jump would exactly do. It would, as he'd explained to Karpov, take years to understand every-thing.

Karpov's tactical report was brief. Weapons ready. He'd found the controls for the accelerator that launched the blocks of ice for terraforming. With Breen and Bawk-Bawk-Bawk helping, it might be possible to drop some high-speed ice on the Proximans.

If they could program the launcher, Oswald had a few ideas for targets. Nothing that would help them in the short term, but if he could keep them alive for a few months, large chunks of ice moving at several kilometers per second would make for a good distraction. He'd have to come up with that plan soon.

An incoming connect request from Relor chimed on his tablet.

"FC, *Roland*."

"Oswald here."

"Colonel, I detected a lone jump signature and one of the sensor sats is tracking a heat source heading for Earth orbit." Relor gave a nervous chuckle. "I think the Proximans have sent the calvary."

"Probably just a scout at this point," Oswald said. He used his tablet to access *Roland*'s tactical display, but the target profile had no useful information yet. The chances the Proximans would send anything *Roland* would recognize was nil. "You know what to do. T-REX if they come in firing, KKC if they make orbit."

"Roger that, Colonel."

Oswald dropped the connection and saw McFarran approaching. The aux cast a disapproving glance at Rocketman as he passed. It was now armed with two Proximan rifles, and festooned with spare magazines and grenades. It loomed over the prisoners like a steel gargoyle.

"They've come at last, Colonel."

"Looks like it."

"May we talk, Colonel?"

"This isn't really the time, Aux."

McFarran offered an apologetic smile. "With all due respect, Colonel, I think it is. You are about to engage one of their spacecraft. Why not try contacting them?"

"Look, I agreed to come and investigate Earth. We've learned about all we can. They killed it. They took it. To be honest, I've not seen anything here that has swayed my mind about carrying out the attack. And I doubt they'll appreciate what we've done here."

McFarran looked from the bodies to the prisoners. "Yes, Colonel. It would have been better if we hadn't attacked first."

Oswald snorted and cocked his head. "In case you forgot, *they* attacked *us* first. In Proxima Centauri. Remember? Started the whole war thing? Broke two peace accords? Any of this ringing a bell?"

"These people weren't part of that."

"This isn't the time. There's nothing for us here, we need to go. Get everyone back on *Roland* and suited up." Oswald glanced at the tactical display on the tablet. "Hopefully, we can finish this guy off before he gets a good look at us."

"Colonel..."

"Are you my auxiliary flight commander or not, Major?"

"Yes, Colonel. I'll get everyone aboard. What of the prisoners?"

"We'll leave them tied up for now. They'll send a rescue team soon."

McFarran popped a sharp salute and spun on his heel without awaiting a reply. Oswald shook his head and returned to watching the unfolding tactical situation. As he thought, *Roland* didn't recognize the incoming ship's profile. It was approaching in a highly eccentric orbit that would bring it fast and low over the base.

Just what Oswald would do... for a low-threat recon pass. Relor detonated the KKC warhead right on time. The Proximans may have registered the explosion and incoming shrapnel field, but not quickly enough to avoid it. At least now he knew that class of ship wasn't heavily armored.

The crew paused from donning their vacc-armor and EVA suits to watch the remains of the Proximan craft streak across the heavens through the dome. The crew finished dressing and took turns holding guns on the prisoners as Rocketman lugged the Q-puter back onto *Roland*. Oswald didn't think they'd really need it, but it was impossible to know. And he didn't want it to fall into the hands of the enemy, even if it was four centuries out of date.

It took much longer to get the crew ready than Oswald thought it would. Everyone was already exhausted, and climbing in the full gravity and bulky suits was strenuous. More than one person fell. Oswald ordered them to transfer all controls to the lowest stations available to reduce their climb distance.

By the time Oswald strapped in, he was panting and feeling light-headed. "How's the launch profile, Norris?"

Norris said something over the duty net, but her voice wavered and broke so that Oswald couldn't understand. "You good to go, Norris? Are we set for launch?"

Her loud gulp was audible over the net. "Y-yes, FC. We're, we're ready to launch."

"You OK?"

"Yes, Colonel. Just nervous. Just another never-done-before... thing."

Oswald pulled up Norris's vitals. Her heart rate and blood pressure were flagged red. Under normal circumstances, he'd have the doctor dose her and get someone else to fly. But that wasn't an option. He hoped she calmed down before the launch; that kind of stress made it even harder on the body.

With a final check that all hatches were sealed, and all crew suited up and strapped in, Oswald approved the countdown to launch. Due to the process needed for the boosters to warm up and fire properly, five hundred seconds was the shortest countdown allowed. It seemed an eternity.

"T-minus fifty seconds," Norris announced. Her voice was growing more tense as she counted. Nothing Oswald could do about it now.

"T-minus thirty seconds."

"T-minus twenty seconds." Norris was almost shrieking.

"Calm down, Flight Sergeant," Oswald commanded.

"Y-yes, Colonel," she said. "T-minus—"

An explosion rocked *Roland*.

Red status flags appeared on Oswald's screen and a flashing warning sign filled his visor.

*Booster 1 Failure. Launch Abort Initiated.*

Oswald gritted his teeth, wondering if he'd see the explosion before it killed him. Booster failures were fiery ordeals. *Roland* had several tons of munitions, rocket fuel, and reaction mass, in addition to the pressurized coolant systems and liquid oxygen.

He hoped it would be quick.

"Boosters successfully shut down, FC." Norris was almost laughing. "Shit, that was close."

"What the fuck happened?" Oswald asked. "You cleared the boosters, Aux."

"I did, Colonel. And I stand by that. All booster integrity tests passed."

"Well, the whole booster obviously didn't go, or we wouldn't be here. What was that explosion?"

"It looks like it was the number one booster control compartment, Colonel," McFarran said.

Oswald considered the deck plans. "There's nothing in there that should explode."

"Maybe we missed one of Danner's bombs," Norris said. "I know I didn't look in the booster rooms."

"I looked there at least three times," Karpov said. "There were no fucking bombs in there. Or in number two booster control. No way."

"Maybe you missed something, Karpov," the aux said.

"No fucking way."

"Alright. All crew check in." Oswald waited and got positive acknowledgements from everyone left. "No one's hurt, at least. What are our options? We need to get off this rock."

"Colonel," McFarran said, "we don't have spare controllers. We never use them."

"Norris, can we get to orbit on a single booster?" Oswald asked. "We'll have to dump mass, but I'm looking for options here."

"I don't think so—"

Oswald squeezed the arms of his station. "Don't think it. Run the fucking numbers."

"Yes, sir."

"Colonel," McFarran said. "Even if we could dump the requisite mass on *Roland*, we don't have the ability to remove booster one on the ground, or dump the fuel. It would take a full launch tower and technical crew."

"We can jettison it."

"It would explode when it struck the ground, Colonel."

"Godammit, Hashi."

"And even if jettisoning it didn't detonate it, Colonel, it would explode in the flames from the other booster when we launched."

"Give me some options, Aux. Not excuses!"

"If the controller cannot be repaired or replaced, I cannot think of one, Colonel."

Oswald clenched his teeth. "Or you don't want to think of one."

"I'd have to take a look, FC," Gresh said, "but we might be able to slave the output of controller two to booster one. That might trick booster one to fire. But I'd have to study the output logic. And check to see if there still is any output connection at all."

Oswald was breathing fast. "Good, Gresh. Take, uh, Karpov with you and check out the damage."

After several minutes, Karpov reported in. "It looks like a bomb went off in here, FC. Outer hull is good, so no blowback from the booster or other damage I can see. But the controller housing is fucked."

"Did we miss a bomb?" Oswald asked.

"I didn't, FC. And if one was missed, by some strange chance, they were all wired to go off with the remote. Something else would have had to set this one off. If it was one of Danner's."

"Perhaps stray damage from the tank hit, Colonel?" McFarran said. "A stray voltage that set off Danner's bomb?"

"Danner didn't set that bomb," Karpov said. "But it will take a while to get this figured out. We might want to send some folks back in to make sure the prisoners don't make any mischief. And they might have a better tool room than we do."

Oswald groaned at the thought of climbing back down and trudging to the dome. "They might. Karpov, I want you and Relor switching shifts on tactical. Everyone else will cycle through guard duty and think about how to get the hell off this planet."

Three hours later, another Proximan craft jumped in, this time on the dome side of Earth. Oswald was sure it managed a good sweep of the area and *Roland*, before the T-REX detonated and cut it open with concentrated x-ray beams. There was no way to know if they managed to transmit the data before dying. But it would still take several hours before RF or laser comms reached any of the Proximan bases.

Gresh was struggling to make the repairs work. She was an expert with circuits, but no one had ever worked on the booster controllers before. The damage to the housing was extensive, requiring time to detangle the mess to determine where the output to the booster was.

Oswald frowned, despite his feeling of grim satisfaction at watching the Proximan ship go dead. They were grounded with only a handful of warheads left in position to defend themselves. Time was running short. And his second-in-command wasn't helping.

The prisoners began crying out, drawing Oswald's attention. Rocketman held a man in the air by his throat and was sweeping a rifle over the crowd. Another man glared at Oswald and screamed at him in Proximan. Karpov came trotting around the corner with his laser pistol in hand.

Oswald found Tok-Een-Glet among the prisoners. "What's he on about?"

The old man held up his chin. "I've been telling them what you people have been saying. This man is angry that you have destroyed our ships. His son might be serving on one of them."

Karpov glanced at Oswald. "Oh, Lord! Save us from the fury of the Earthmen."

Oswald grinned at the play on an ancient refrain about the Vikings attacking English churches. Was it from Shakespeare? Some claimed the Norsemen were actually noble people, but Oswald figured that depended on which side of the axe one stood. How would he and *Roland* be remembered?

Oswald looked to the screaming Proximan, then back to Tok-Een-Glet. "Tell him it might be his son that drops the bomb on all of us, then."

He led Karpov out of earshot of the old man. "It's a pain in the ass, but get Rocketman to haul that Q-puter back over here, and get Breen to help you start launching those ice chunks. It might not help much, but it's something."

An hour later, three more Proximan starships jumped in, far within Earth's usual jump threshold. It was proof they'd improved on their jump tech since Oswald's time. The ships accelerated forward in a tight echelon formation at over twice the acceleration *Roland*'s LANTRn could manage.

Relor detonated a kinetic kill warhead prematurely. The Proximans reacted quickly and spread their formation. Their high thrust allowed them to avoid most of the shrapnel. If they were hit, it didn't change their thermal profile.

"Sorry, FC," Relor said. "I wasn't counting on that thrust. I should have seen it."

"These commanders know what they're doing," Oswald said. "And they have ships more capable than what we're used to. They're probing what we've set up in orbit."

Relor detonated a T-REX as the Proximan squadron came around Earth's horizon and into line of sight of the base. *Roland*'s telemetry indicated hits on each of the enemy starships, but only one shed debris and changed its thermal emission pattern. Minutes later, it began tumbling towards Earth.

Oswald frowned as the feeds from both the nav-sat and the sensor drone were replaced with a yellow *Signal Lost* warning.

"It seems they've poked our eyes out, Colonel," McFarran said. "We're grounded and we're blind. Continuing this fight is pointless. The longer we keep killing Proximans, the harsher they're going to deal with us. It is a foregone conclusion at this point, Colonel."

Karpov rounded on McFarran. "You shut your fucking mouth. You want to have your friends 'give you honor', then just walk out that airlock. Vacc-suit is optional."

"Enough!" Oswald glared at McFarran, then at Karpov, shoving him back towards the rail launcher controls. "Relor, set all remaining orbitals to proximity detonation. If we can punch them in the nose hard enough, we might get the time needed to fix the booster."

"Roger that, FC," Relor said. "Sorry."

"My fault, not yours," Oswald said. "It was going to happen sooner or later. I was just hoping for later. Keep the laser array ready in case they start dropping troops."

McFarran threw his arms in the air and stormed off.

Oswald connected to Gresh. "How's my booster controller coming?"

"I think it's doable, FC." Her voice was harried. "Ignition is a standard go, no-go logic pulse. But the jettison subsystem is completely different. It has mechanical and logical safety interlocks. We can get up, I think, but we'll have to figure out how to dump the boosters later."

Oswald grinned. "Good job. Excellent. How long?"

"At least an hour I'd say, FC. But still, there's not going to be any of the other safety or control functions. We'll have to let them both burn dry."

"Takeoff would use most of what's left anyway. Get to it."

"Yes, sir."

Oswald strode over to where Karpov, Breen, and Tok-Een-Glet were huddled over the rail launcher controls. "How's my ice cannon coming, Mr. Karpov?"

Karpov looked up and smiled. "Ready when you are, FC. Ol' Breen really knows his stuff. We can get planets two and three within a few months. The home world's launch window for an impact this year ended two months ago. But I've got one plotted for two and a half years out. I've got another station around a gas giant we can hit in three years."

Breen frowned. "They'll figure out what happened after the first station goes down. They'll just move the others."

Karpov slapped Breen on his shoulder. "Never underestimate the foolishness of large governmental organizations. And even if we only get one, that's still a pretty big win.

"Just think of the poor, poor Proximans on that station months from now, regardless of what happens to us. They've probably thanked whatever gods they thank for deliverance from the evil Earthers. They'll be rudely awoken one day by the proximity klaxon. Death from beyond!"

Karpov affected warbling, high-pitched tones as he acted out a conversation between a man and woman. "Why, whatever is that alarm, dear?"

"I just can't imagine, honey-britches, what with those darned Earth people dead and gone. It must be a sensor malfunction. Go back to sleep."

"Oh, dear. You always know best-AAAAHHH!"

Karpov mimicked the impact by punching a fist into the opposite palm, then spread his wriggling fingers apart as he mouthed "BOOM."

Breen grimaced as if he tasted something rancid.

How long had Karpov been working on that little skit? "I'm sure Xorblox would approve."

Karpov and Breen both asked, "Who?"

Oswald shook his head. "Never mind. Tactical, throw me some snowballs. As many as you can."

"Yes, sir, FC sir." Karpov saluted. "We'll show them what a good old-fashioned Earth ice ball to the kisser feels like."

# Chapter 39

OSWALD WATCHED ROCKETMAN haul the bodies from the dome to a shallow gully fifty meters away. It wasn't something he'd planned on being around to deal with, but the stench had grown overpowering in their short absence. It still lingered.

He'd ordered Stungart's corpse left in its vacc-armor with arms crossed beneath *Roland*'s booster. It might just blow away, but Oswald was hoping liftoff would incinerate the body. As far as fitting astronaut funerals went, it sounded appropriate.

McFarran, Hines, Norris, and Trese stood watch over the wailing prisoners while the robot did its work. Trese gave an apologetic shrug. Norris and McFarran looked on with tear-filled eyes. Hines stared into the distance as if he was thinking about his next golf game. Oswald was glad when Rocketman resumed its watch; he wasn't sure his crew had the stomach to shoot the prisoners if needed.

With the robot back in place, Oswald made his way down into the jump machinery controls where Breen and Karpov were working.

"Think you've got it, Mr. Breen?"

"Yes, FC."

Oswald leaned over the Q-puter display. "If we can't get *Roland* off the ground, we'll escape and take our planet with us. Won't that be a sight."

"They'll just track us down," Karpov said.

"Maybe," Oswald said. "That's why we're going back to Sol. If they can follow us, we might as well put Earth back where it belongs. Maybe we could get Danner and his people to help with repairs."

Karpov chuckled. "I know they're not going to help."

Breen looked up from his screen. "Never know until you ask."

"Exactly," Oswald said. "You find a good place to drop us in Sol?"

"It's a no-win scenario, FC," Breen said. "I mean, without an orbit, Earth will fall into the sun. Too far out and she'll stay frozen like she is now."

Oswald touched the screen interface and selected different destinations. Several star systems were available on the command menu. "This is a nice interface you've set up, Breen. We can't bring Earth back no matter where we drop her. So put us about one AU outward from Luna. That's close enough to maybe work with Danner and gets us closer to Saturn Station in case we decide to strip it. Or move there."

Oswald walked to the canister with the red and orange trefoil symbol. A series of conductors were wired from the nuclear warhead to a small contraption of Karpov's making. "And this will make sure they can't steal it back."

"Do we really need a nuke, sir?" Breen asked.

"Only way to make sure the UXA gets destroyed," Oswald said. "And even with a nuke, who knows?"

"Just seems creepy to have a nuke in our basement if we're going to have to live here."

Oswald grinned. "True. But we don't plan on living here. We'll leave it disarmed until either we've jumped or *Roland* is ready for takeoff. Just in case. Keep at it, I'm heading back up."

The prisoners' wailing had petered out to soft weeping. Rocketman hadn't killed anyone else that Oswald could see.

Norris stood staring through the dome. He admired her curves with furtive glances, thinking back to their lovemaking. Being the last Earth people to make love on Earth seemed a noteworthy achievement. He considered asking if she wanted to slip off to one of the empty offices upstairs, but the thought of it felt awkward. Especially since she had something to do with the booster failure. The hot memory of *Roland*'s conference room would have to suffice.

She caught him staring and smiled coyly. Maybe the proposition wouldn't be so awkward. Oswald returned the smile and took a single step forward before his comm chimed.

"Incoming ordnance!"

All thoughts of Norris disappeared as Oswald whipped out his tablet. His practiced fingers brought up the tactical display. A cluster of missiles was streaking in towards *Roland* from over the horizon. There was a lot of ground noise on the radar and the missiles were using the dome as cover.

Oswald enabled the gyroscopic synchronization on his tablet, tying in directly with *Roland*'s sensors. He held up the screen in the direction of the incoming missiles and saw what Relor was seeing on her targeting display.

Five burning contrails glowed in the IR scope. Flashes of superheated air appeared on the tablet where *Roland*'s laser array was firing. It was strange seeing them in the display—the lasers weren't visible to the naked eye and there were no flashes above the dome.

One of the missiles flared and burst into pieces as *Roland* scored a direct hit. Oswald considered ordering everyone into their suits, but this fight would be over in mere seconds.

Another missile exploded, this time visible through the dome. Oswald lowered his tablet and could see the faint glow of the missiles' exhaust plumes. One of the Proximans saw where Oswald was staring and pointed. He shouted something and the rest of the prisoners looked up.

Everyone except Rocketman watched the flames race across the night sky.

Another missile expanded into a cloud of icy vapor and falling metal, the destruction visible momentarily in the flash of the explosion. Oswald pumped his fist as two more missiles fell from the sky.

The final attacker streaked through the dissipating clouds of the destroyed missiles. It jinked and dove as it approached. Sparks flew from the missile's fuselage as *Roland*'s laser found its mark again. The missile dipped out of sight.

Oswald turned to Norris and smiled just as the missile streaked meters above them, trailing sparks that struck and slid down the dome.

Oswald dropped his tablet and ran to the edge of the dome. His forehead pressed against the glass as he tried to get a glimpse of *Roland*. Norris stood next to him, her hands splayed on the dome as if she was trying to push the missile away.

The missile flew by in slow motion. More sparks erupted along the side from *Roland*'s laser. It fish-tailed and went tumbling. But it was too close, moving too fast.

It struck the landing pad and exploded in gouts of fire and debris. *Roland* tilted away from the blast. The nearest landing stabilizer was shredded by shrapnel and flames, like flesh stripped from bone and sinew.

When *Roland* swayed back upright, the damaged stabilizer groaned as it tried to hold the ship's weight. The groan turned into a mechanical scream as the stabilizer failed catastrophically. The watching crew screamed along as they understood what must now happen.

*Roland* continued to topple over. For an instant, it seemed to freeze in mid-air, as if the ship may never fall and all would be well. It crashed to the ground and split into pieces. Relor's screams of terror registered somewhere in the back of Oswald's mind.

Pipes cracked and tanks exploded. Fire engulfed *Roland*'s corpse and ember-filled smoke billowed into the dark sky in a swirling column. Shattered sections of her hull crashed to the ground outside the dome. There would be no survivors in that hellish firestorm.

*Roland,* one of the most decorated, not to mention the last surviving, warhorse of Earth's final conflict, was down in flames. At least she'd gone down fighting. After twenty years of war, it was time for her to rest in peace.

Oswald's knees trembled so that he had to press his hands against the dome to keep from falling. He'd already done that lately and didn't care to again. Numbness came over him, as if a heavy, damp blanket was wrapping around his mind.

"I don't know if I have the words to express just how fucked we are," Karpov said. "I mean, we're really, *really* fucked here."

Oswald felt oddly comforted by the genuine resignation and fear in Karpov's tone, behind the facade of sarcasm.

"Ask not for whom the bell tolls," Oswald whispered. "It tolls for thee."

"Oss-balt!" a voice screamed.

Oswald turned to see one of the prisoners staggering to his feet, his hands still tied behind his back. Rocketman's rifle was inches from his head.

"Oss-balt!" he screamed again. "Die-Die!" He flashed a victorious smile and laughed maniacally.

Oswald's vision shrank into a pulsing tunnel, with the laughing Proximan prisoner at the center. Heat burned Oswald's face and the room's noise faded beneath the throbbing in his ears. He couldn't hear the man's laughter anymore, but Oswald could still see him leering at the end of his tunnel vision. The prisoner started thrusting his crotch back and forth at Oswald.

A small flame erupted from the prisoner's chest. The smile twisted into a surprised grimace, before he fell to his knees, then onto his face.

Sounds came crashing back, a cacophony of shrieks and screams. The room brightened as his tunnel vision faded. Oswald felt his rage flare at whoever of his crew had murdered the man. He turned to find Karpov.

Karpov stood watching the prisoners, but his weapon wasn't drawn. Norris was turned away, sobbing. Trese was staring at Oswald. McFarran's hands were pressed to his forehead as he gaped at the dead man. Rocketman was still holding the Proximan projectile rifles. Oswald looked and saw no one with a laser weapon drawn.

Until he looked down at his own hand.

There was no memory of drawing the weapon or aiming it. He didn't remember a conscious thought of gunning the man down. But the laser's battery charge indicator showed it had been fired. Oswald put the laser on safe and slid it back into his belt. He turned his head to face Karpov.

Karpov shrugged and nodded towards the approaching Mc-Farran. "Here comes Captain Capitulation. Just remember what I said."

Things were still slow and dreamlike as Oswald turned to meet his second-in-command. He knew what Major Hashi McFarran was going to say. Time to surrender, Colonel. With *Roland* gone, the mission was a failure. There would be no attack on the Prox-iman home world. His options now were to surrender or jump Earth from system to system. He didn't even know for sure they could jump Earth, and Karpov was right: the Proximans would simply follow them. It wouldn't be safe to let the Earthers have a planet they could drop wherever they wanted.

Not safe at all.

"Was that necessary, Colonel?" McFarran demanded.

A thick calm descended on Oswald. It reminded him of the time Anahita's brother passed them his hookah on leave after grad-uating the academy. It was the only time he'd tried that. Booze was good enough for him. "How many Proximans have I killed already, Hashi?"

"Unarmed Proximan prisoners? None that I remember."

"I'm sorry. If you've come over to berate me about prisoner treatment..."

"I've come over to see if you will speak with me, Pierce." McFarran stared at Karpov and spoke loud enough to make sure the tactical officer could hear. "Alone, Colonel. Please."

Oswald nodded and led the aux around a nearby corner.

"Farther away if you please, Colonel." McFarran motioned up the stairs. "To your new office, perhaps?"

Oswald scanned the dome. His crew looked on in various states of shock. The prisoners were grim-faced and silent, refusing to meet his eyes. But he could read it in their expressions. They understood that *Roland*'s destruction changed things. Their captors could no longer escape. He could read the terror in the faces of those who understood what it might mean.

Rocketman stood motionless, rifles leveled.

Oswald swept his hands towards the stairs. "After you."

# Chapter 40

MCFARRAN FOUGHT THE urge to insist Oswald go first. Oswald's blank expression as he burned down the prisoner wouldn't leave McFarran's mind. What he'd seen on Oswald's face wasn't the stoic consideration of deciding who needed to die in battle. Those eyes had been empty, as if he hadn't even been there. McFarran feared he'd lost his friend and comrade. And he feared getting shot in the back.

He marched in front of Oswald's desk and snapped to attention. Oswald followed with infuriating casualness, as if they were not all about to die for the most foolish reasons in the universe. Though Oswald's pace was slothful, his steely gray eyes held their hard edge once again. Those were his dangerous eyes. The eyes reserved for his enemies.

Oswald closed the door and fell into his chair. He motioned to the seat on McFarran's side of the desk. "Please, Hashi. Take a load off."

"I'll stand, thank you, Colonel."

"I suppose you're here to make a final plea for surrender."

McFarran rolled his neck to push down the rising anger. Oswald added a derisive stress when saying "surrender," as if he thought McFarran a coward. "That or know what better plan you have. This fight is over."

Oswald pulled the holo-cube from his flight suit and set it on the desk. With a swipe of his finger, Anahita's image appeared in the air. "What do you think, Ana? Is this fight over?"

"He certainly seems to have run out of fight," the projection said. The digital face was younger than when Oswald had first started toying with the damned thing. It turned to McFarran and offered a grim frown.

"Pierce, can we turn that off, please? It serves no purpose."

"Anahita is full of good advice."

McFarran could hear his accent growing thicker. The melody of his mother tongue always came out when he grew stressed. The beauty of it compared to English or Chinese was calming. Usually. "That thing is a Proximan program, Colonel. A hostile one, I'd venture."

"I think Anahita here hates the Proximans a mite more than you do." Oswald looked into the projection of Anahita's eyes. It returned his gaze. McFarran had never seen General Khadem fawn like that. Not even over Oswald.

"That is an adaptive program that analyzes you and tells you what it thinks you want to hear, Colonel. It's nothing more than a carnival game. It can probably guess your weight too."

"You're wrong there, Hashi. This is Anahita. It's her essence, her personality." Oswald leaned back in his chair. "It is a perfect computer matrix of the Anahita I knew. I might have to reconsider the digital translationists."

McFarran scoffed. "Crackpots. That's nothing more than very expensive euthanasia. All proceeds going to their church, naturally. Besides, they're all dead."

Oswald waved his hand as if fanning away smoke. "Enough about her. We're here to talk about you."

"With all due respect, Colonel, we're here to talk about you."

Oswald raised a brow. "Oh?"

"It would be redundant to make my case again. We fought, we lost. The war is over. The only thing you can achieve with this obstinate behavior is all of our deaths." McFarran held out his hands. "There will be no glory in it."

Oswald stood and opened the door several centimeters and motioned McFarran over. "There doesn't have to be glory in an action to make it right, Hashi. Take a look out there. What do you see?"

"Norris?"

"Look farther."

"Surely you're not pointing at Karpov."

"Farther."

McFarran peered through the opening. There was the crew, some bloodstains, the dome, and furniture. Nothing that was the obvious prop for whatever point Oswald was driving at. He sighed. "I don't understand, Colonel."

Oswald scowled and stabbed his finger at the scene below. "Look past the dome, man. See that frozen, lifeless wasteland that used to be Africa? That used to teem with life? Where blessed rains fell? That was our home. The Proximans wiped it out. Not just humanity. Everything. No possibility of recovery.

"Hashi, I look at you and hear your words and realize that I'm the one who doesn't understand. My family. Your family. Every family of our entire crew. All dead. And all you can talk about is surrendering."

"Now we are speaking in circles, Colonel. Tell me plainly. What do you plan to do?"

"To be honest, I'm not sure. Now that *Roland*'s gone, we don't have many options. But I have a hunch that someone stabbed *Roland* in the back. Someone blew that control housing so we couldn't complete our mission." Oswald set his laser pistol on the table. "I have a good idea who that was, Aux. How do you think I should handle that?"

Every hair on McFarran's body stood on end. Every muscle clenched. He could feel a trickle of sweat rolling down the small of his back. It took every ounce of will to keep his expression calm. The laser aperture was still closed, but it radiated death.

"Colonel?"

"How should we handle a traitor like that, Aux? I know it's hard to believe, but it was Norris."

McFarran almost sighed with relief. "Norris, Colonel? Are you so convinced it was sabotage? And why her?"

Oswald shook his head. "I never would have thought it, Hashi. Not on *Roland*. But I checked the locker where we put Danner's bombs. Two were missing.

"You heard her during launch. She knew what was going to happen. I could hear it in her voice." Oswald nodded at the pistol. "Treason during war, Hashi. On *Roland*."

McFarran cleared his throat. "We're not at war, Colonel."

Oswald glared at him. "Not at war? So you think we should let her get away with it? Fuck, Hashi. I fart sideways and you file a report. Norris cripples the last SDF starship in existence and you want to ignore it?" Oswald glanced at Anahita's hologram.

The hologram shook its head.

Oswald stood and holstered the laser. "Fine, Aux. You carry on doing whatever it is you were doing. Karpov and I will take care of Norris. It's not like we need a pilot now anyway."

"Colonel, don't..."

"I get it, Hashi. You're a good officer. But you've gotten too close. I mean, really I get it. I'll take care of her." Oswald turned and reached for the door.

"Wait..."

"This has to be done. She's an honest woman, I'm sure she'll tell the truth." Oswald glanced back over his shoulder at McFarran. "Then we'll discuss what to do."

"Colonel..."

Oswald held a hand up towards McFarran and pulled the door open.

Fear shot through McFarran like lightning. He clenched his hands into fists to stop their trembling. "It was me," he blurted. It was out. He couldn't let Oswald's madness loose on Norris. Right or not, McFarran had sabotaged his own starship. It was time to face up to that decision.

Oswald turned slowly, his eyes wide. "What?" he whispered.

McFarran thrust his chin high and straightened his back. He had to swallow before he could speak. The *gulp* thundered in his own ears. "I placed the explosive."

"What?"

"I took one of Danner's explosives and attached it to the number one booster control housing, Colonel. It was wired to go off when launch was initiated to force an abort condition."

Oswald stumbled back into the room. He grabbed the desk to steady himself and turned to the hologram. "Did he just say he did it?"

Anahita's image glowered at McFarran. "Like I said, seditious."

McFarran grabbed the holo-box and slammed it on the desk until Anahita's face started flickering. The image's expression didn't change as it began to fail. Then he threw it onto the floor and jumped on it. The box collapsed with a satisfying crunch beneath McFarran's feet. Anahita's blurred image blinked away, to be replaced by a coiling puff of smoke.

McFarran brushed off his uniform. "Shut up, bitch!" He turned to face Oswald.

Oswald stared at him, eyes red, a single tear rolling down his cheek. "How could you, Hashi?"

McFarran didn't know if Oswald was asking about the bomb, smashing the box, or both. He should have smashed that box long ago, and possibly disabled *Roland* back then while he was at it. He'd clung too long to the hope that Oswald would see reason and it had cost everyone. It was time to free them from this madman.

"Colonel Pierce Oswald, I am hereby relieving..." The rest of the words stuck in his clenched throat.

Oswald's laser pistol was leveled at McFarran's chest. The aperture cover slid open like the eye of a waking predator.

Oswald's look was more terrifying than when he'd shot the prisoner. It was not vacant, but filled with black despair. McFarran had isolated Oswald with his betrayal. He'd left Oswald alone with Karpov. He'd left Oswald alone with a monster.

"Stop!" McFarran screamed. "Don't! Don't! Don't you do it!" But he saw in Oswald's eyes what must happen next.

Oswald's face softened for an instant. "*Je suis désolé, mon ami.*"

McFarran tried to jump over the desk, but found he couldn't breathe. All his limbs trembled and lost their strength. He collapsed backwards into the chair. Something was burning. It was his flight suit. Embers danced around the rim of a blackened circle in his chest. It was perfectly centered between his name tape and ribbons.

He clutched at the gaping wound. It was unclear to him why. Then came pain so intense it barely registered. Tears tickled his cheeks. His throat was suddenly parched, causing McFarran to cough. A thick dollop of blood spurted from his ruined chest, leaving a crimson Rorschach blot on the belly of his flight suit. In it, Major Hashi McFarran saw the faces of his sons, before he died with a final, wheezing aspiration.

# Chapter 41

THE ACRID SMELL OF McFarran's charred uniform filled the office. Oswald stared at his dead friend's body. At least, McFarran had been a friend. Once. Before becoming a traitor. Or had he been a traitor all along? He sure loved to write reports against his FC.

McFarran hadn't died as well as Anahita, but he'd died well enough. No begging for his life, no whimpering. But hadn't he been begging for his life for weeks with his constant pleas to surrender? Whatever hope McFarran had found in the Proximans, Oswald couldn't see it.

He stared at his laser for a moment, then slipped it into his holster. Anahita lay in a pile of smashed components at the foot of his desk. He'd lost her again, this time with no chance for a goodbye. Damned Hashi. Why'd he have to do that? It didn't matter. He didn't need her. He didn't need anyone now.

The door to the room burst open. Oswald drew his pistol as he spun. Karpov stood in the doorway with his own pistol trained on Oswald. With a quick glance at McFarran, Karpov holstered his laser.

"Hold on now, FC." Karpov held his hands up. "You hurt?"

Oswald shook his head. "What're you doing up here?"

Karpov inclined his head towards the body. "I saw him staring at me through the door a few minutes ago. I got suspicious and moved to the stairs. Then I heard some commotion and the aux yell. When things went quiet, I thought you might need some help."

"Anyone else hear?"

Karpov shook his head. "I don't think so, FC. What the fuck happened?"

Oswald believed McFarran's confession. The truth of it made him light-headed. Oswald stared at the gaping hole in the body's chest, as if focusing on its gory depths would keep him steady. "He did it."

"Did what, FC?"

"Planted the bomb in booster control."

"What?"

Oswald nodded and holstered his laser. "Yeah. He confessed. I was asking him what to do with Norris. I thought it was her, but then he told me what he did. Said it was to stop our war."

Karpov's face twisted in rage for an instant, before he nodded. "That motherfucker. I knew it. I knew it. All that shit about peace and fluffy clouds and sparkly unicorns. Fucking coward." Karpov walked over to McFarran's body and spat in its face.

"Stop that," Oswald snapped.

Karpov looked at Oswald, confused. He shrugged. "If you say so. You did what needed doing. Now what?"

Oswald stared at Karpov, considering what to say. Karpov's brow furrowed and his hand slid towards his pistol.

"You're freaking me out, FC."

"What you said before..."

"Yeah?"

"You with me? I mean, really with me, Tac?"

"Fucking-a straight, sir. What's the plan?"

"We kill them all. We kill every single Proximan."

Karpov smiled and started to speak.

Oswald cut him off. "We won't survive."

The smile never left Karpov's face. "I've been ready for that for a long time, FC. I'm a bit sick of this universe, anyway. If it kills those sons-of-bitches, I'm in."

Oswald silently appraised Karpov's expression. He'd been too trusting and been burned too often. Anahita and Ululani. McFarran. Norris—she knew about the bomb even if she hadn't done the dirty work. What he saw in Karpov's eyes wasn't the look of a loyal friend, but a zealot. And a zealot was what he needed now. He was done with friends.

"Get Breen and meet me in the jump room."

Karpov popped a quick salute and left. Oswald watched the door close, before turning back to Hashi and Anahita. They were gone and he had nothing else to say to them.

"Go on, Pierce. What's left to live for?"

Oswald left the room and looked around. No one in sight. He cut the outer handle from the door with his laser and tossed it into the room. The sound of the latch engaging seemed to echo in his ears. Oswald placed his hand and forehead on the door of the ad hoc tomb. Everything was rushing at him now. They were both gone, and soon he would be too. He took a final deep breath and followed Karpov.

"Everything plotted, Mr. Breen?" Oswald asked.

"Yes, Colonel." Breen smiled and stroked the Q-puter. "Couldn't have done it without her. I set the drop point like you said. Since the Proximans haven't shut this down, I guess I managed to shut off all the remote access ports."

"Great job," Oswald said.

Breen blushed. "It will take years to decipher all the security via software. It was the only thing I could think of."

"And this is the jump initiate button?" Oswald asked, pointing to the Q-puter interface.

"Yes, sir. If the system isn't lying to me, the jump should be ready. It's a big process, but the activation script the Proximans designed is straightforward." Breen waved his tablet. "I've also got the Q-puter interface linked here."

"Very well, Astrogator. Please go assemble the crew. Hand me your tablet and tell everyone who has vacc-armor to suit up just in case. But I'm hoping this dome was designed to protect against the jump." Oswald patted Breen on the shoulder and eased him to the exit. "Karpov and I will secure the warhead."

Breen frowned as he stepped onto the small lift. "Do we really need a nuke, Colonel?"

"Like I said, it's the only way to make sure the UXA gets destroyed." Oswald reached forward and pressed the lift's button. "But don't worry. If it does go off, it means we're already dead."

Oswald led Karpov back into the control room and stepped in front of the Q-puter. The navigation menu appeared under his fingers. The interface was almost childish in its simplicity. Karpov gasped when Oswald confirmed Earth's new jump coordinates.

"Holy fuck..."

Oswald looked over his shoulder at Karpov. "That going to be a problem, Tac?"

Karpov stared at the screen for several seconds, before letting out a low whistle. He smiled and shook his head. "Nope."

"Good. Let's rig this warhead. Anyone comes down, the lift goes boom."

"Everyone goes boom, FC."

When Oswald and Karpov returned to the lobby near the dome's airlock, the remaining crew were gathered in a circle. Everyone except Oswald, Breen, and Karpov had opted to come over in the lighter, more comfortable EVA suits. Since the EVA suits had no defibrillators, there was no point in wearing them for a jump. The rest of the armor suits had been lost in *Roland*'s fiery death. If the dome didn't protect from the usual jump-induced myocardial infarction, anyone without a suit would need manual CPR to survive.

Not that it would ultimately save them.

"Where's McFarran?" Norris asked.

The lie came easily to Oswald's lips. "He's monitoring upstairs as a contingency. He'll be down after the jump."

Norris pursed her lips, then nodded. "What about defibrillators?"

"This dome was built to withstand the jump," Oswald said. "It should protect us."

"And if it doesn't?" Dr. Hines asked.

"Then the three of us in suits will do CPR. But we probably won't need it. Cardiac failure is rare as it is, and they have improved the technology."

Norris inclined her head towards the prisoners and whispered, "What about them?"

Oswald glanced over his shoulder and shrugged. "Everyone ready? It's been a hell of a ride. And I don't know what will happen. But Earth will be back where she belongs if all goes well. After that..." He shrugged again. "It's been an honor serving with you. No crew could have pulled through better."

Breen stepped forward and reached for his tablet. "I'd like the honor of jumping Earth, Colonel."

Oswald withdrew the tablet out of Breen's reach. He couldn't think of a reasonable objection that wouldn't sound suspicious. Breen was conscientious and might see the coordinates had changed. Oswald glanced at Karpov.

"Hey, Breen," Karpov said. He smiled and put an arm around the astrogator. "I think the FC should do it. There's no doubt you did all the heavy lifting getting the jump program working but, you know. This is big. Really big. It should be the flight commander." Karpov laughed and slapped Breen on the shoulder. "And if it goes wrong, it'll be his fault. Not yours."

The look of disappointment on Breen's face almost made Oswald give him the tablet. But he couldn't risk Breen interfering.

"You've worked miracles here, Mr. Breen," Oswald said. That was no lie. "If we decide to jump around the universe on the good ship Earth, you can hit the button every time."

Breen chuckled. "We don't even know it'll work yet, FC."

Oswald latched his helmet in place and spoke over the duty net connection to the crews' tablets. "We find that out right... now."

Oswald tapped an armored finger on the large red button that filled the tablet's screen.

The air started to sparkle.

# Chapter 42

THE AIR IN THE DOME came alive with the alien tune Oswald recognized from the UXA in *Roland*'s cargo area. The sound rang in his helmet until his ears buzzed with it. He should have listened to Hashi instead of killing him. Or even killed him for the traitor he was and then surrendered. As a shimmering purple cloud writhed in beautiful loops outside the dome, Oswald was consumed with a single thought.

The dome wasn't going to protect them.

Nightmare landscapes rose and collapsed before him. Impossible colors, shapes, and smells tore at his mind. A haunting cacophony wound through the inside of his helmet, trying to rob him of his sanity. He laughed out loud when he realized he hadn't any to steal.

The last Delamain in the universe had burned on *Roland*, and that made him sad. But it was OK because Hashi McFarran, fresh blood oozing from the hole in his chest, was walking through the dome with a bottle of chicken-flavored schnapps! Now Oswald was happy.

Hashi gave him a friendly wink. *"Oans, zwoa, drei, g'suffa!"* He took a long pull on the bottle and looked down to watch the schnapps spill from his chest. The visage should have bothered Oswald, but it didn't. There was nothing better than chicken schnapps—except drinking in German.

Oswald took the bottle and chugged. It burned his throat on the way down, as smooth as a carbonaceous chondrite flying at 100 kilometers per second. He laughed and handed the bottle back. A skeletal hand snatched it away. A rotting corpse in a tattered SDF flight suit saluted and blew away in an electric wind.

"Now that was just stupid," Oswald tried to say. But he was not breathing. The pain in his chest that had always been there drove deeper and sharper, until it was an overwhelming burning ache right in the center of his being. Where he'd shot Hashi. A bolt of lightning made his body convulse and threw him to the ground. The echo of the impact rang in his ears.

He awoke to a throbbing pain in his chest. A red light shone through his eyelids, then changed to green. His mind and body were equally unresponsive. There was no inkling of where he was or what was going on.

There was a knocking nearby. Oswald struggled to open his eyes. When he managed to, he saw Karpov's familiar face above him, faceplate-to-faceplate. A bright green indicator on Oswald's visor blocked part of Karpov's face.

"Holy shit, FC," Karpov said. "I think I could go another lifetime without jumping again. Fuck the wonders of the universe."

"I don't think you'll have to worry about that," Oswald croaked. He squinted at the green information window and had to cock his head to bring it into focus. It read:

*Was defibrillation successful?*

Oswald coughed. "Yes." The green window registered his response and the message changed.

*Report of defibrillator activation in queue due to network error. Please report to Life Support department for immediate treatment.*

He deleted the helpful instructions. Oswald couldn't remember most of what he'd seen. It was like waking from a nightmare and only remembering how terrifying it was. Oswald reached out, and he and Karpov helped each other up. A moment later, he stood alone on trembling legs.

Oswald stumbled over something as he tried to take his first step. It was Norris's hand. She and Hines were curled in fetal positions, back-to-back, mouths gaping. Her arm lay towards him, like one of the rapturous women in Renaissance artwork, reaching for the mercy of heaven's light. He had neither mercy nor light for her. She was a betrayer too.

The rest of the crew lay dead around him. Oswald turned slowly to look at the prisoners. They, too, were in lifeless clutches, their faces twisted in terror and pain. Rocketman stood over the bodies, waiting for someone to move so it could kill them.

They were all better off dead this way than to witness what was to come.

Breen came stumbling out of Oswald's peripheral vision and crashed into him. If Oswald hadn't grabbed Karpov, all three of them would have been sprawled on the floor.

"We've got to give them CPR, Colonel. Hurry!" Breen pulled off his helmet and tossed it away.

Oswald removed his own helmet and grabbed Breen's shoulder. "Leave them be, son."

Confusion washed over Breen's face. He looked at Karpov, then back at Oswald. "But, Colonel, you said when we get to Sol—"

"We're not in Sol," Oswald said. "If we revive them now, they'll just die again in a few hours. Like the rest of us."

Breen reached down and grabbed his tablet from the floor. He swiped through the screens. "Not in Sol? Did the jump go wrong? This is all wrong. Not even close to where I plotted. How'd we get here, Colonel? Someone must have changed this." Breen looked up at Oswald as he pointed to the screen. His mouth dropped open as understanding came over his face. "But why, sir?"

Oswald wondered if that was what his face had looked like before murdering Hashi. "Think through the problem, Breen. If we went to Sol, then what? We starve. We would have been the only three survivors anyway.

"Then the Proximans come and take Earth back. Then they win. This way, they don't win and they don't get away with what they've done."

"But this? No, I can't let you, Colonel!" Breen started flipping through screens on his tablet.

Oswald reached out to take the tablet, but Breen turned away. When Oswald tried to step forward, he tripped on Norris's body and fell to his knees. The weight of his suit forced the air noisily from Norris' s lungs. "Stop that now, Breen."

The tablet burst into flames.

Karpov stepped closer, laser pistol attached to his suit's arm. "Sorry, man. Too late for that now. And if you're thinking you can go change it from your Q-puter, you'll set off the bomb we set for the Proximans."

"You always were a dick, Karpov," Breen said. "But, Colonel? I don't get it."

Oswald motioned to the outside landscape. "Look out the dome long enough and you will, Mr. Breen. Maybe you won't agree, but you'll understand. You've followed me into death many times. You're an excellent officer."

Breen stormed into a nearby office.

"Should we see to him?" Oswald asked.

Karpov shook his head. "Does it matter now? Let him spend his time sulking if he wants."

Oswald struggled to his feet. He stood there swaying for a moment, trying to clear his head. A crash came from the office Breen had fled into. Oswald rushed in. "Breen! Breen, you OK?"

Karpov rushed behind. "I guess not."

Breen was lying spread-eagled on the ground next to a toppled pile of chairs. He'd removed his gloves, and a laser pistol lay on the floor near one outstretched hand. The top half of Breen's face was a charred wreck.

*It wasn't me!!!* was scrawled across the dome in indelible ink from a maintenance marker.

After a quick check of his O2 levels, Oswald said, "I'm going for a walk. I'm about sick of this dome."

He put on his helmet and made his way to the airlock. His chest was growing tighter as his death neared. It didn't matter to him what Karpov did at this point, but he was glad to see the only other Earthman alive following him.

Rocketman was still standing over his dead wards.

"Rocketman, post at the lift to the jump equipment room. Prevent unauthorized entry."

"Who is authorized, Colonel Oswald?"

"No one."

"Roger, Colonel Oswald." At that, the robot strode to the lift. The mechanical murderer would end its existence as a humble doorman. Oswald waited for Karpov to join him in the airlock.

Oswald's dosimeter alarmed as soon as they exited the dome. "Must be from *Roland*."

His ship was an unrecognizable pile of slag on the landing pad. The jump freeze had extinguished some of the fires, but red flames still flickered from deep within and black smoke rose into the sky.

"Burn, baby, burn."

Beta Hydri peeked over Earth's horizon. The edges of the landscape and the tendrils of rising mist from the ground shone in brilliant orange. Oswald wondered what the Proximan world looked like.

"Earth's long night has finally ended," Karpov intoned, "though the respite be short and the finale dire."

"I know you were famous and all that," Oswald said, "but I never realized you were such a thespian."

"It comes with having these Bollywood good looks."

Oswald grunted and continued trudging up the nearest hill. He wanted a good vantage point to see the end, preferably a view without that alien-infested postule they'd just left.

It was tough going, but Oswald was in no rush. His labors were ended. His body was still alive with fear, but his mind calmed at the thought. The war was over. There had always been a hope of making it through the war alive, but that was gone now. Who was he to survive when good people like Gryphon, Sherman, and Chen hadn't? Good people like Hashi McFarran. It was all out of his hands. Events were now as set as the orbits of the planets.

As Oswald crested the hill, a familiar hum filled the air. The scream of the UXA seemed to come over his headset and through his helmet. An electrical tingle numbed his fingers and toes.

"The Proximans must be in the system," Karpov screamed into the mic.

Oswald was amazed at his own calm. It was still out of his hands. Even if the Proximans won. "Breen probably opened access before you shot his tablet."

Arcs of electricity raced through the air towards the dome. Long glowing spokes appeared along the ground around them, radiating out from the dome to the horizon. The rising mists writhed down the hill like frosty serpents. Frozen wind moaned across Oswald's armor, threatening to carry him along back to the dome. Beautiful embers danced into the sky.

"Do something!" Karpov cried. "We can't lose now."

They could lose now, actually. It would be his last chance to give Hashi's plan a go. To give up and let the Proximans kill him. Or maybe pardon him. There wasn't anything he could do about it from here. If the Proximans had regained control of their planetary jump gizmo, so be it. And maybe it would be for the best.

There was something he could do. And now was not the time to turn back. He hoped it wasn't too late. Oswald closed his visor plate.

"Rocketman, descend on the lift."

The dome lit up with blinding light. For an instant, Oswald thought it might hold, but the pent-up fury of the warhead could not be contained. The structure split open like a flower in bloom, releasing a finger of nuclear fire into the sky. The gathering energy of the jump effect dissipated as if the Earth had blown out a candle.

The explosion illuminated the strange, dark wasteland, and the shockwave buffeted Oswald to his knees. His dosimeter alarm chimed again.

"Now that," Karpov said, "was quick thinking, FC. And that's one hell of a funeral pyre."

Now, for certain this time, everything was done. Even if the UXA had survived, the machinery was gone. There was no way the Proximans could save their home world. Now he'd finally won. Oswald watched the growing mushroom cloud with a dread satisfaction. "We will burn with them."

Oswald continued over the ridge and Karpov followed. He stopped at a pleasant rock outcropping that afforded a good view out to the horizon. Oswald imagined the pictures of the savannah he'd seen as a child. It was hard to match them to the landscape below. Soon the mist obscured the flat land and caressed Earth's last sons.

Karpov pointed into the distance. "Will we be able to see the planet before we crash?"

"I'm not sure. Maybe part of it. There wasn't an option about changing orientation. Even if we don't see the impact, we'll get a hell of a light show."

Two hours later, a spread of a dozen contrails raced through the shifting curtain of the aurora borealis covering the sky.

"It's beautiful," Oswald said.

"I never got to see the lights planetside. Saw them from space a couple of times, but never from below. Now I wish I had."

"I saw them once in arctic survival training, way back when they thought crews might survive crash landings on distant moons." Oswald chuckled. It seemed ironic to him now that "Star-Captain Yasmina and the Ice Pirates of Dronthul VII" was one of Anahita's favorite episodes. A tremor rumbled deep beneath them.

"Shouldn't be too long now," Oswald said.

Karpov opened the tool compartment on his vacc-armor and pulled out a small flask. He extended a thin hose from the flask's lid and handed it to Oswald. "Want some?"

"What is it?"

"Does it matter?"

"As long as it isn't schnapps, I guess not. You first."

"Naw," Karpov drawled. "I brought it to take the edge off, but now I want to be sober when I go. Though you..." Karpov shook his finger at Oswald. "You might need a strong drink."

Oswald hooked the tube to his vacc-armor's hydration supply connection. "What do you mean by that?"

"Pierce, if there is a God, a creator that cares about his creation, and, mind you, I'm not claiming there is, but if there is, you'd better hope he's as merciful as they say. Or that he doesn't care what we little ants do in his sandbox.

"But if he does care, you're destroying about ten billion deity-hours of work. Planets, especially life-bearing ones, take a long time to make, you know."

Heat rose on Oswald's face. "And how will he judge you?"

"People are easy come, easy go. I doubt God even notices when people die. Look how many he's killed." Karpov took a deep breath that roared in the mic. "I am more worried about how those people I murdered will judge me. If there is an afterlife, I expect they'll be there waiting. And I hope to God that they are more merciful than I was. But you…? God'll take notice of this."

"You're a real son of a bitch, Karpov. I think I hate you."

"Me too."

Oswald sipped from the hydration tube in his helmet. The liquid burned his throat and warmed his belly. He didn't care if it was drive coolant. Divine judgment didn't scare him, though he did occasionally wonder if there was something out there calling the shots. If so, Oswald was doing what was ordained.

A deeper, more powerful rumble shook them.

"You know," Karpov said, "I joined the fleet because I hated Earth. Well, I hated people. Hated that I had to be around them. But seeing the Earth like this, barren, abandoned, well, it just isn't the same."

A distant flash in the sky caught Oswald's attention. A dozen bright lights traversed the atmosphere at high altitude. One exploded into a tiny cloud, its debris spreading into short-lived fingers of fire.

"I think those are Proxie escape ships," Oswald said. Two more burned up as Earth's atmosphere grabbed them and shook them apart. Then another was ripped to pieces as it tried to flee. But two made it, skimming the atmosphere and disappearing into space.

Karpov saluted the sky. "I hope they make it."

So did Oswald.

The ground was now constantly trembling. A slim crescent of Ay-Yon peeked over the horizon. The aurora covered the entire sky. It looked angry. A distant wall of fire rose to obscure the other planet. Purple mountains began shattering.

Karpov struggled to pull a tiny black transmitter from his tool compartment. He showed it to Oswald.

"What's that?"

Karpov laughed. "My self-honoring device. The other bomb. I was going to set it off if we got captured; you know, a booby trap. I hadn't really thought it out."

It was growing harder to hear the radio over the screams of Earth. "I thought McFarran stole them both."

"I stole mine first. Glad I did." Karpov's voice was in a near panic. "How can you stand this? You're made of steel or some shit! I can't watch. I can't watch. I-can't-watch!"

Karpov was shaking so hard from the quakes he almost couldn't bring his hands together. Almost. His suit went rigid for a second when the bomb inside detonated, then it collapsed limp on the rock. Red paste covered the inside of Karpov's visor.

Oswald was alone. What the hell had he done?

His head swam as he sucked down the remainder of the flask. He was slammed into the ground. Something in his ribs shifted. Anahita's face floated in his vision.

The rock outcropping snapped in half with a thunderous crack, sending him flying down a newly formed slope.

"Stop it!" he screamed. Over and over he screamed. It didn't stop.

The sky above grew angrier as the atmospheres of Earth and Ay-Yon wrestled to claw each other to shreds. Lightning poured from the sky, silhouetting roiling clouds and sending great gouts of earth spewing into the air. Oswald's visor automatically filtered the blinding flashes to a comfortable level.

He grabbed an upturned shard of rock and clung with his failing strength. His bones jarred in their joints and his teeth cracked together. Karpov's limp body bounced into the air and disappeared into a deep rent in the earth.

The ground rose beneath Oswald and launched him high in the air. Fire blossomed in his knees as they shattered. A sharp, unbearable pain bore deep into his ears and suddenly stopped with a loud pop. Then he heard nothing. The new silence was a welcome dis-ability. Warmth flowed from his ears, nose, and mouth.

Earth and sky tumbled by. For a second, he was reminded of his free-fall training. The vomit-comet was a cadet's first experience with zero-g or, more accurately, extended free fall. The plane went up as high as it could and then fell back to Earth, while the cadets moved around the cabin, trying to keep their lunches inside and perform simple tasks of dexterity. Was this his life flashing before his eyes?

Oswald's skull bounced against the inside of his helmet. His left eye went dark. A blinding flash, that lit the entire atmosphere, strained the suit's light dampener and left a glowing residual image of the smoldering land now several kilometers beneath Oswald.

Mountain-sized rocks flew around him, like titanic hunks of flesh carved from Earth's body, dripping lava as blood. They exploded an instant before the final shockwave stripped Oswald's armor from his flesh, and his flesh from his bones, and blasted his bones to dust.

Earth's last son screamed with his dying breath, knowing, in that final instant before oblivion, that he had settled the score and avenged his family and the Earth. Eye-for-eye, tooth-for-tooth, world-for-world.

# Epilogue

HIS SHRIVELED LIMBS bobbed in the gentle waves as the life-support tank trundled along its track. The preservative fluid was growing cold again. Or was it just him? It was getting harder to determine, but it wouldn't matter much longer. The last of the Ay-Yon would die today.

His arms had atrophied beyond use over one hundred years ago. Their waving was relaxing to watch, but they didn't feel anything except the cold. So cold. He'd increased the fluid temperature as much as possible, without damaging the restorative polylipoid michostructures that kept him alive. If the safety interlocks allowed it, he'd bring it to a boil.

So cold. He couldn't even wrap his arms around himself.

He stopped the tank in front of a picture of people long dead, celebrating some occasion lost to history. Behind them, towering buildings cast shadows on the bustling, dancing streets. He once knew the name of the Ay-Yon city, as well as the names of the man and woman carrying smiling children on their shoulders.

They were his direct ancestors. Was it three or four generations ago? Hard to say. His life spanned several generations by the reckoning of the people in that picture. Being the last of the last generation of humanity made the notion of generations obsolete. There would be no more.

He could look up their names if he wanted to. But, like the name he'd once used, it was useless data. He'd placed that picture there because he knew their story and it was important to him. Or had been important to him centuries ago.

They had carried those children to safety, escaping the destruction of his world. Those children had grown and fought to keep their own children alive in deep space. They survived to give birth to his parents. Or was it his grandparents? But the enemy had destroyed his world fifty years before his birth. Fifty years was considered a generation in those times.

The tank sloshed as he moved on. The lapping of the fluid against the glass and the rustle of tiny bubbles were the only things his waterlogged ears had heard in a long time. He stopped the tank in front of shelves of shriveled homunculi.

They were his children from long ago, beloved more for the hope they offered than for any parental bond. Yet, he still loved these dead ends as much as he could love anything. One experiment in a long string of failures to save humanity. Now they were curled and shriveled in their own tiny, liquid-filled jars. Miniatures of their father.

Some belonged to her. A few belonged to him and her, from a time when their bodies could still couple. Hope had died bit by bit with the failure of each little one. His own shriveled body now lacked not only the ability to procreate, but the desire.

He longed to reach out and touch his children one last time, maybe put their tiny bodies in his own tank. The desire for at least a semblance of human touch still moved his heart, even on this last day. It was a fool's thought, a macabre vision. Anything that touched his long abstinent nerves would either go unfelt or feel like erupting flames.

He'd leave them to their eternal nap time in the mortuary jars.

The compartment held other mementos of their five-century quest to save humanity. But he didn't love them. They weren't alive. Merely tricks and gimmicks thrown together out of desperation. The whole starship was a museum to those doomed efforts, but this was the showcase. She never entered this room. He continued along the track.

The hatch opened as his tank approached her compartment. He'd come to see what she was doing on her last day, but he knew already. She'd be staring at the stars.

Her spirit had died long ago. The hope she'd cast into the universe had not been returned, and now she was like the universe. Dark. Cold. Hollow. Dying. It had taken her longer than him to get that way because she'd had farther to fall.

Her tank was on the outer hull, as he expected. The thought of it made the cold dive deeper into his bones. He wheeled his tank to a nearby portal. She was stargazing in her usual spot.

He cast his optical replacements to the whirling ruins of the two planets below. Their smashed wreckage had merged into a dancing morass of dark shards of rock. Somewhere in that mess were the remains of the Destroyer. The man from Earth who had smashed two planets together in his grief and rage, dooming humanity from the galaxy. The Destroyer was who they'd striven against these many centuries, fighting the extinction he'd wrought. Today the Destroyer would claim his final victory.

The ancestors in the picture had escaped Ay-Yon at the last moment. The woman had been sufficiently ranked to earn a slot on an escaping ship. Her diaries told of seeing Earth appear in the sky in a blinding flash and how some of the ships burned up in Earth's encroaching atmosphere.

All of the ancestors' tales were of narrow escapes and luck attributed to a beneficent creator. They had reached the third planet's orbiting station. Though terraforming had begun, the facilities couldn't handle the sudden refugee crisis. It started small but, as panicked colonists tried returning home, they had little choice except to turn them away. Violence followed.

Months later, the orbital station and the crammed colony below were pulverized by ice blocks from Earth, using the very launch rail used to provide water for the terraforming project. It was later determined the Destroyer had launched them before Ay-Yon's destruction. The incoming projectiles escaped notice in the chaos of a dying people.

At first, he hated the Destroyer and believed the people of Earth had deserved their fate at the end of the war. As the ages passed, he accepted that thinking as childish. The Destroyer had simply done to Ay-Yon what Ay-Yon had done to Earth. He would have done the same if the Destroyer struck first. Everyone would still be dead.

In the years when he and she were still flying from system to system, looking for survivors from Earth or Ay-Yon, they'd learned the Destroyer's name on Luna. There were pictures of the Destroyer, and of Earth in its azure splendor.

The colonies of Earth didn't survive the war. Those of his own people hadn't survived Ay-Yon's destruction. Even after four hundred years of peace, advances in colonial sciences could only delay starvation and collapse. The home world was still the heart of the colonies, despite cries of sovereignty and science. Alien worlds could be lived on, but not lived with. Biology was too different, and even the most self-sufficient colonies relied on Ay-Yon in ways not considered until the planet was gone.

It wasn't long before the colonists were reduced to subsistence living, scraping by on the meager produce of their growth domes and algae farms. He and she had been born on such a colony, where the struggle to survive was the only concern.

Even molecular printers fail and controlled ecologies collapse. The biology of the alien worlds provided no safety net for failures. So the colony wars began. First, as interstellar trade at gunpoint, then as raids, then as complete destruction of competitors. They saw it in system after system. Their own home colony died the same way.

They soon stopped their exploration after constantly being set upon by desperate wolves, who had once been their brothers and sisters. The survivors they sought to rescue sought to kill them in return. The superior Ay-Yon culture hadn't survived the death of the home world either.

She was refusing his calls, but he knew she was still alive. The distant stars had her full attention again. He felt an urge to scan the darkness a final time for lost survivors, but he'd done so for hundreds of years already. The recorders would only have star songs and static. No people.

Leaving her to her wanderings, he steered the tank to the track into what the Earth people called Saturn Station. He'd integrated it into their starship over her objections long ago. At the time, he'd felt it important to preserve the knowledge of Earthers, as well. Another futile effort.

The remains of three humans floated in a large preservative tank. They had been given honor as worthy enemies in the ancient Ay-Yon way. If he'd puzzled out the timeline clues correctly, it had happened hundreds of years before the Destroyer smashed the two planets together.

The station's design was one of function over form, all sharp corners and exposed equipment modules. Nearly one thousand years old, Saturn Station stood in contrast to the vessel it was now attached to, an ugly dinosaur fossil in an elegant museum. Yet, both would suffer the same fate. Oh, insurmountable entropy.

The repository was on the other side of the Earth station. In it was his one spark of hope, though spark might be too strong a word. He and she gathered every record, every piece of data, every hint and idea, they had found in their five hundred years of searching. The information was compiled in every Ay-Yon and Earth language available to them, along with binary, hexadecimal, and Yog-Sho-Got translations for any far-future visitors to this haunted library of the dead.

If humanity couldn't be saved, at least it may someday be remembered. Maybe even mourned. Unlike the alien ruins of Delta Pavonis. There was proof of their existence, but they'd left no accessible knowledge of who they were or where they went. He and she had never found another trace of them, either. He'd never know if those aliens had been the ones to seed humanity among the stars.

What would those aliens think if they could see humanity now? Maybe their civilization had fallen into a similar trap.

"I'm ready," she said. The medical computers had long ago perfected translating the noises that gurgled from their ancient throats.

"I'm coming." The fluid in his tank swirled and splashed as he raced back to her observatory. Her tank was now just outside the portal, facing him. Her shrunken, wrinkled visage held nothing of its bygone beauty. "Don't leave me."

"It is our agreed time. We've spoken little this last decade, but know I love you still. I wanted to see you before I go, beloved."

"Don't."

"You needn't watch," she said. "I believe we shall meet in the next universe. We will be together soon." Her shrunken hand wriggled in an approximation of the Ay-Yon love wave. Then her pod detached in a breath of frost and dipped out of sight. Disconnected from the ship's medical computer, she'd die before freezing. She was probably already dead. After all those centuries, he was finally alone. It was that realization he needed for the strength to join her. They had been together longer than most nations on Ay-Yon or Earth had survived.

He took the long way round their—now his alone—starship. The sights didn't comfort him or change his mind. He drove back to the repository, and lifted his tank up and out of the way of any beings who might visit.

The solar panels and gravity potentiometers were at one hundred percent, and could keep things running on minimum for as long as the star lived. He'd done what he could, but not even his years of expertise could halt the rigors of time, freezing space, or cosmic radiation. Nothing was immune to entropy. But he'd done his best.

An ancient bottle of wine hung before his tank. It had come from the vineyards of his great sire in the picture of his ancestors. He had sampled the vintage from another bottle ages ago, when his tongue still worked. It was a sweet, fruity taste he remembered well. Far better than the preservative fluid that kept him alive, which was slimy and contaminated with sloughed-off bits of his decaying flesh. That his tongue no longer worked was a blessing.

"Are you there?"

It was foolish. Her umbilicals were severed; she couldn't answer even if she was alive. He knew she was dead. Worse than his fear of death, though, was that of leaving this world with her still in it.

The flesh around his optical implants began to sting and a pain came from deep in his throat. He made sure the wine had not yet been poured into his tank. The medical readings were normal, except for an expected warning concerning his plummeting emotional state. All tank diagnostics passed.

He realized his body was trying to cry.

He let it. His atrophied limbs jerked and his wrinkled body twitched. A strange squeal came from his throat and echoed in waves around the fluid. He sobbed for almost an hour. It was a catharsis born of generations of heartbreaking struggle, side-by-side with the woman who now drifted dead somewhere outside their home. He couldn't remember having such a cry in well over two hundred years, and it felt wonderful.

She had found comfort in the belief they'd meet in the after. He shared no such belief. She was gone and he was utterly, hopelessly alone with his fading memories. He replayed her last words a dozen times.

*I wanted to see you before I go, beloved.*

She'd still loved him.

The label on the bottle had partially peeled away and folded over, hiding part of the ancient Ay-Yon script and the once-vibrant picture of the long-dead flowers fermented inside. The medical alarm flashed a warning; his heart was racing at a dangerous twelve beats per minute. At his command, the robot arm shook the bottle vigorously and emptied it into his nutrition tube.

His limbs jolted as fire shot through them. The colors his optical implants presented to his brain wavered and melted together, as if water had been poured on a painter's pallet. The tank spun and his stomach screamed. He could feel the stream of bubbles escaping his mouth roll up his face. He could feel the burning.

Then comforting numbness washed over him as he took his dying breath. He wished he could see his parents again. Maybe he would.

The last human left the universe, not far from the resting place of the man who'd sealed the fate of two worlds, and wiped out an entire species, centuries before.

The Destroyer had won.

# THE END

# Thanks!

I HOPE YOU ENJOYED reading "With Our Dying Breath" as much as I enjoyed writing it.

Please sign up for my newsletter[1] to keep up to date on my work, releases, deals, and other news. You will also get a FREE prologue to this book in ebook and audio .mp3 formats. Find out what happened at the Battle at Barnard's Star... and to Oswald's daughter.

You can also visit my webpage at www.arkavli.com[2] to sign up and for more information.

Please let me and other know what you thought of this book by leaving a review for this book on whichever platform you purchased it. It not only helps me with feedback on my stories, but helps the book's visibility in the stores and search algorithms. This is important for every indie author, so help us to continue providing excellent content.

---

1.    https://www.subscribepage.com/Book_Reader

2.    http://www.arkavli.com/

# Cast and Crew

EVERY NOVEL IS A COLLABORATION in one form or another. I'd like to give special thanks to the following people. Any fault you find with this story should be placed firmly at my feet, not theirs.

Front Cover art: www.selfpubbookcovers.com/Saphira[1]

Developmental Editor: Chersti Nieveen

Proofreader: Sam Kates

And special thanks to my beta reading team:

Diane White, Chrissie Kavli, Shane Taylor, Yvette Bostic, and Don Koehler

---

1. http://www.selfpubbookcovers.com/Saphira

# About the Author

A. R. Kavli is a starship captain, seeking fame and fortune among the stars by way of crafting fiction books since orbital mechanics are far too complicated for him. Seeking that same adventure in the real world, Aaron joined the U.S. Navy for six years, only to learn that F-14 Tomcat avionics technicians don't get cool theme music like the pilots. He is still glad he joined—and left. When not leading a squadron of raiders against the oppressive EarthGov, Aaron is moving miniatures he's painted around a table and rolling dice, crossing swords with fellow historical fencing students, and traipsing around Middle Tennessee with his beautiful, former F-14 Tomcat avionics technician, wife and four vundabar children.

Read more at https://www.arkavli.com.